THE LOCK

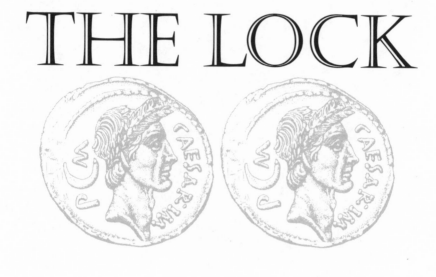

THE LOCK

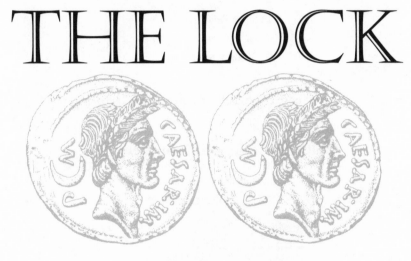

By
BENITA KANE JARO

BOLCHAZY-CARDUCCI PUBLISHERS, INC.
Wauconda, Illinois

General Editor:
Marie Bolchazy

Production Editor:
Laurie Haight Keenan

Page/Cover Design and Typesetting:
Cameron Marshall

Contributing Editor:
Jeff Schmitz

Cover Illustration:
"The Lock" by Thom Kapheim

Maps:
Kurt Reichenbach

Portrait of the Author:
Benita Kane Jaro

© copyright 2002 Benita Kane Jaro

Bolchazy-Carducci Publishers, Inc.
1000 Brown Street, Unit 101
Wauconda, IL 60084 USA

www.bolchazy.com

Printed in the United States of America
2002
by United Graphics

ISBN: 0-86516-535-1

Library of Congress Cataloging-in-Publication Data

Jaro, Benita Kane.
 The lock / by Benita Kane Jaro.
   p. cm.
  ISBN 0-86516-535-1 (pbk.)
  1. Rome--History--Republic, 265-30 B. C.--Fiction. 2. Pompey, the
Great, 106-48 B.C.--Fiction. 3. Cicero, Marcus Tullius--Fiction. 4.
Caesar, Julius--Fiction. I. Title.
  PS3560.A5368 L63 2002
  813'.54--dc21

                                          2002071687

To The Scholars

. . . let us confess that Cicero saw what was good and what was evil, though he was mistaken in believing that the good was still within reach.

—**Anthony Trollope**

Motum ex Metello consule civicum
Bellique causas et vitia et modos
Ludumque Fortunae gravesque
Principum amicitias, et arma

Nondum expiatis uncta cruoribus,
Periculosae plenum opus alea,
Tractas et incedis per ignes
Suppositos cineri doloso...

—Horace, Odes II.I

Your theme is upheaval and civil war
from the time Metellus was consul—
   its causes, evils, measures, means,
   the sport of Fortune and
    ill-omened
      alliance of great men:

you must take up
weapons still smeared with the unpurged
   blood of slaughter—
    risky work, full of danger;

you must set your foot upon fire
     still buried under treacherous ash...

**—Translated by William Stahr
and Benita Kane Jaro**

PREFACE

Set in Rome during the turbulent and passionate times of the dying Republic, Benita Kane Jaro's three-volume cycle — *The Lock, The Key,* and *The Door in the Wall* — spring from the ideal marriage between the historian and the novelist. Many historical novels are good novels but bad history, full of inaccurate details and anachronistic confusion between the attitudes and values of the past and those of the present. Others get so bogged down in historical minutiae that they never emotionally engage the reader, as any good novel must. These three volumes are both historically accurate and emotionally engage the reader in the lives of some of the most fascinating characters from the best documented period in the history of the Roman Republic: Catullus, Cicero, Caesar, Pompey, Publius Clodius, and Clodia Metelli.

Benita Kane Jaro deftly brings these characters to life through the eyes of Marcus Caelius Rufus, who knew them all and has left us a number of witty and insightful comments on people and events in letters to Cicero. Indeed, she has carefully researched not only the letters and speeches of Cicero but also the other relevant ancient authors and many works of modern scholarship in order to be as accurate as possible. On those rare occasions when she has had to exercise literary license in regard to known facts, she alerts the reader in the appended notes to each volume.

Reading historical novels, particularly good ones like these, is something of an illicit pleasure for the academic historian trained according to the standards of rigorous scholarship. Such an historian must be wary of making broad generalizations or speculative inferences without thorough documentation and careful consideration of reasonable counter arguments and qualifications, all duly footnoted. The scholar has to be on constant guard lest, beguiled by an unwarrented hypothesis or personal bias, she or he should soar untethered into the realms of unreality. The good historical novelist, not bound by the cumbersome conventions of scholarship but using a lively imagination disciplined by sound research, can go beyond the facts to a degree that the academic historian might secretly wish but cannot do with a good conscience in scholarly publication. Some scholars have recently experimented with combining conventional scholarship and the historical novel's imaginative reconstruction of undocumented gaps in the historical record in order to make their work more lively and interesting to a wider audience. Such a practice is dangerous, however, because the unwary reader attracted by such an approach to history can easily become confused about what historians know and what they do not know. It would be far better for such historians to write good historical novels separate from their scholarship.

Good historical novels like the ones presented in these three volumes are an excellent, painless way to enhance historical inquiry. They present the basic characters, events, and social context of a particular historical time and place in a lively, memorable, and concrete way. They provide a welcome change of pace and make the material in traditional history books and documents seem more interesting, relevant, and real. They can also stimulate questions about what really happened, what a character was really like, or what happened beyond the confines of the novel. That will stimulate greater interest in the "hard" history gleaned from textbooks, documents, and the works of scholars. We need to learn how to do "hard" history, or we shall end up in an Orwellian world in which history will be whatever anyone wants it to be. Nevertheless, good historical novels can soften the task.

—Allen Ward
University of Connecticut

PRINCIPAL CHARACTERS

THE NAMES BY WHICH PEOPLE ARE MOST COMMONLY
IDENTIFIED IN THE TEXT ARE HERE PRINTED IN **BOLDFACE.**

Marcus Tullius **Cicero:** a lawyer and senator, former consul of Rome

Marcus **Caelius** Rufus: a young politician, pupil of Cicero

Tiro, later Marcus Tullius Tiro: a slave, later freedman, secretary to Cicero

Terentia: Cicero's wife

Quintus Tullius Cicero: a Roman politician, the younger brother of Cicero

Quintus Caecilius **Metellus** Celer: a Roman political leader, senator and consul

Clodia: wife of Metellus, sister of Clodius

Publius **Clodius** Pulcher: a politician, brother of Clodia

Gaius Causinus **Schola:** a farmer, friend of the Clodians

Gnaeus Pompeius Magnus **(Pompey the Great):** a Roman general, conqueror of the East

Gaius Julius **Caesar:** a rising politician. Pontifex Maximus and City Praetor

Gaius Scribonius **Curio:** a young politician, friend of Caelius

Marcus Licinius **Crassus** Dives: a consul. One of the richest men in Rome

Gaius Valerius **Catullus:** a young poet, friend of Caelius

Marcus Porcius **Cato:** descendant of a great family, a senator

Marcus Calpurnius **Bibulus:** a Roman politician, a consul

Titus Annius **Milo:** a Tribune of the People

Quintus Tullius **Teucer:** freedman of Quintus Tullius Cicero

Philo: a freedman, servant of Caelius

Birria: a former gladiator

Hortensius, Gabinius, Flavius, Piso, Lentulus Spinther, Lentulus Crus, Lucullus, Catulus, Sestius, Hybrida, Flaccus, Plancius, Serranus, Metellus Nepos, Appius Claudius, et al: Roman politicians and military men

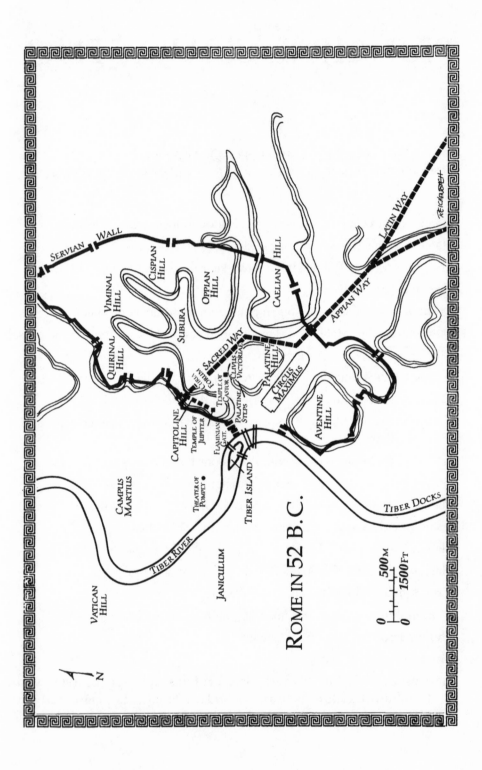

ROME IN 52 B.C.

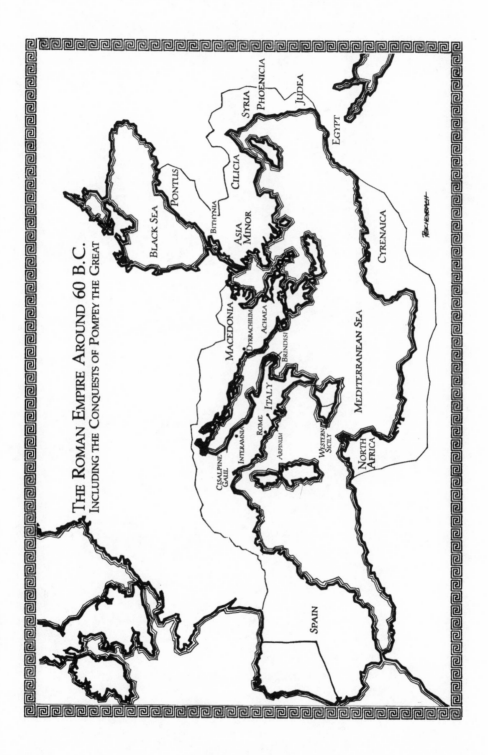

The Roman Empire Around 60 B.C.
Including the Conquests of Pompey the Great

SPAIN

CISALPINE GAUL
INTERAMNA
ROME ITALY
ARPINUM
BRINDISI
WESTERN SICILY
NORTH AFRICA

MACEDONIA
DYRRACHIUM
ACHAEA

BLACK SEA
PONTUS
BITHYNIA
ASIA MINOR
CILICIA
SYRIA
PHOENICIA
JUDEA
EGYPT
CYRENAICA

MEDITERRANEAN SEA

PROLOGUE

PROLOGUE

All day the rumor hung over the city like the uncertain mass of the gray December clouds; it whispered and fretted among the temples and porticoes, and in the jumble of shops near the old Basilica, where the jewelers congregated, the price of gold rose, then fell, then rose again.

After four years the greatest general Rome had ever seen was returning in victory from the East. Pompey was coming home.

Towards evening the clouds departed and the Forum was bathed in a golden haze. The Senate, finishing its meeting, trailed through the door of the Curia, faces drawn and uneasy. The crowd surged forward. "Cicero?" they murmured, but he was not among them. The senators drifted away to their mansions at the top of the hills, talking in uneasy voices among themselves.

For a time silence fell on the city. In the west the storm had left traces: a mass of purple, still fringed and gilded around the edges, sat like a hand over the burning horizon; the last sunlight, passing between the fingers, cut slanting shadows across the sky so that the huge shape seemed to reach out over Rome. The buildings around the Forum blazed with crimson fire; the paving stones were splashed with pools as red as blood.

The last of the crowd scuttled away. Out of the Curia a man appeared. Looking up at the sky, he settled his toga on his shoulders and blinked at the sudden evening dazzle.

He walked steadily through the gathering darkness, his eyes turned inward to his thoughts. Seen in the shadows near the Curia he looked solid and heavy, though slightly blurred in outline, like a bear in a twilit wood; out under the transparent glow of the open sky there was still something ursine about him—a suggestion, perhaps in the set of his shoulders or the ease of his stride.

Though the Forum was nearly empty now, he had not gone a dozen steps before several people came up to him to look anxiously into his face and ask him about the news. "Did you see the omen? Did you see the hand in the sky?" He smiled and spoke to each of them.

Just past the Rostra he paused, for someone was calling his name. The voice rang out, shockingly loud in the hush. "Marcus Tullius Cicero. Wait a moment." The speaker ducked his height under an arch and ran toward the older man, who peered at him nearsightedly through the darkness. "Why, it's Marcus Caelius," he said, and his flexible mouth twitched into a smile.

A tall boy with a typical Roman face, square-jawed under level brows, came to a stop in a flurry of long arms and legs; behind him his shorter, stockier friend ran up. He was out of breath. "Have you heard the news? Pompey is coming home."

"Yes, so I understand. I've just had the pleasure of reading the Senate a letter I received today from him telling us all about it."

Behind him the other boy remarked in a hoarse, pleasant voice, "What Caelius means to say is that Pompey is bringing his army with him."

Cicero rubbed the bridge of his eyes with his thumb and forefinger. Deep lines had cut themselves there, and he looked worried and upset. "Oh, no. He can't be. It's illegal—"

"It's all over town. Everyone knows, everyone's talking about it."

"What Caelius means," his friend said hoarsely, "is that he heard it in a bar."

"Oh, I see."

"That doesn't mean it's false," Caelius cried hotly.

"We heard it from a fellow just off a ship from Rhodes. He said he'd seen the legions being marched aboard the ships with his own eyes. The soldiers said they were coming home, but they were polishing their armor and sharpening their weapons and generally behaving like an army going out instead of one coming back. They told this man that they had no orders for dismissal either."

"Oh, no. Not Pompey." But he wasn't sure. "If he brings them and refuses to dismiss them, the Senate will have to act. We gave him his commission—we can't just sit back while he breaks the law. If he still refuses, it might lead to..." He glanced behind him at the Curia, now fallen under the advancing shadows. "We might have to..." he began again. Then, heaving up a sigh from deep in his heavy body, he finished his thought. "The Senate might, in the end, decide that it means a civil war."

These words silenced the little group. Their faces gleamed anxiously in the dusk as they stared at one another. Overhead the last pale violet faded in the sky; it arched over the Forum now like a deep purple bowl as dark as wine. A breeze had come up, and there were a few stars.

"He's been away a long time and won enormous victories," Caelius said softly. "He's rich, respected, and popular. He's Pompey the Great—as great as King Alexander of Macedon, in ancient times, they say. If he wants..." His voice trailed away, a wisp on the night air.

"What Caelius means to say," his friend whispered, "is that if Pompey wants to bring his army into Rome, what is there to stop him?"

There were lights in the temples and some of the shops now, points of warmth, gold or crimson, in the darkness. Overhead, stars bloomed in the windy sky; Cicero could smell the silty damp of the river. Rome. Pompey had won his wars first in Africa, then in Europe, and now in Asia. "Why," he exclaimed aloud, "Pompey has conquered the whole world."

"That's right," a woman called. An iron shutter rattled as she pulled it closed over the door of a shop. "The whole world," she repeated anxiously. Then, recognizing his voice, she cried, "Marcus Tullius Cicero." The shutter made its hideous clatter again. She was shouting for her husband. "It's Cicero, the consul," he heard her say as the man came out, wiping his hands on his apron.

There were people all around him now, like the chorus at a play. Torchlight fell irregularly on their faces: an eye, which had filled up with light like a bowl of milk, the shine of a cheekbone, a nostril glowing with fire, as red as a tiny oven. He walked a little way with them, offering what reassurance he could. On the porch of the Temple of Castor a priest called down, "Did you see the hand in the sky, Marcus Cicero?" and a perfumed senator, jolting on his litter down the Palatine Steps, leaned over and whispered, "Do you know how many men Pompey has?"

In the courtyard of a mansion at the top of the Palatine Hill a well-known financier was packing his family and his treasure into wagons to hurry them out of town. He lifted his melancholy features from a chest of antique pottery and urged his servants to hurry. His eyes followed Cicero, passing in the street outside. "Marcus Tullius," he called in his cold, dull voice.

"Licinius Crassus. Are you going away?"

In the courtyard a mule flicked its ears and stamped, Crassus' wife called out to her maid. "Just till this blows over," Crassus said. "You know, Pompey is coming home."

"So he is. But you have nothing to fear, surely? You were his co-consul—surely your prestige is nearly as great as his."

"He's bringing his army with him."

"I don't know that I believe that."

"It's true. Do you know how many men Pompey has?"

It was a good question. He had to think. "It was a long war; we sent out more men to him. About fifty thousand men—say, ten legions? A good-sized army anyway."

"Fifteen." He made the number fall between them like a dead bird, brought down by the chill in his voice.

"Oh, no. That's impossible."

Crassus had gone back to the wagons; he did not seem to hear. But as Cicero turned to go he lifted his head and stared at him. His black eyes looked dull and lifeless. "Did you see the sky tonight? The omen?"

A crowd had gathered down the way at his house. He could see a man, hardly more than a white glimmer under the lamp, passing something through the grille in the door; he turned to walk away and the light fell on his oval face, his fine toga. A patrician. "I'm needed at my house," Cicero said. "I see I have a visitor." From the entrance to his courtyard Crassus called after him, "Pompey has fifteen legions.

If he wants to bring his army into Rome, what is there to stop him?"

It was the third hour of the night; in his atrium lamps were lit and glowing on their pedestals. A hum of voices greeted him. "Tiro," he called. As the secretary approached he lowered his voice. "What are they doing here at this time of night?"

"They heard the rumors, Marcus Cicero." Tiro handed him a stack of messages. "Many others have called as well."

Through the brilliance of the lamplight Cicero could make out familiar faces: old clients, friends, colleagues.

"Quintus Metellus," he said, recognizing a senator as he floated through the light.

Metellus was just leaving. He was a military man with an immobile look, polished and glossy, like an iron statue of a soldier. For a long moment he looked silently and contemptuously at Cicero; it was a surprise when he spoke, as if his mouth had not been designed to move. "Have to do something about this. Pompey has seventeen legions. If he wants to bring them into the city..."

Who must do something? Metellus? He? Seventeen legions. "No," Cicero said to someone else—the City Praetor. "I don't believe Pompey would bring his army into the city." But the voices were all around him, clamorous and pressing. Old Lutatius Catulus, the famous general and his neighbor from down the street, was whispering, "See that you do something, Cicero." He was short and dignified, with small, busy eyes and lips like pilot boats guiding his noble, prow-like nose across his face. "You are Pompey's friend."

He seemed to wait for a comment, but someone was pulling at the hem of Cicero's toga, and his attention wandered. I'm tired, he thought and rubbed his stinging eyes. Before him Lutatius Catulus' lips gathered and his nose proceeded on its journey. "When you were consul last year you managed to do us some good." His voice creaked like a rope, grudging the praise. A shopkeeper who rented his store from Cicero muttered in his ear, "Marcus Tullius Cicero, when you were consul you saved the city." A voice nearby whispered, "Help us again," but he could not tell whose it was.

He was rubbing his eyes, trying to read the messages. Seventeen legions. "Tiro," he whispered. "Tell them to go home."

"They're very anxious," Tiro muttered. "I'm not sure they will."

It was not seventeen legions, it was twenty-four. And six thousand cavalry, as well. Or about that. It was here in his hand, cut hastily in the wax boards of a note. He held it at arm's length to see it better. A man named Publius Clodius Pulcher— did he know him? He thought perhaps he might—Publius Clodius Pulcher had called to tell him the news: he wished to remind Cicero that he had served with the army in the East himself. Twenty-four legions. "Tiro," Cicero whispered. "Tell them I'll take care of it. Tell them anything. I need to be alone." Twenty-four legions. That was...a hundred and twenty thousand men. And six thousand cavalry as well.

He was pushing through the crowd, smiling, bowing to the aristocrats, rumbling his reassurances to the rest; behind him he could hear Tiro, barking like a sheep dog, herding them all toward the door. Before him was the cool and welcoming darkness of the back of the house, like the entrance to a cave, unpeopled and unlit, grateful to his strained and anxious eyes. He had thought he knew Pompey, but now he was not sure. A hundred and twenty thousand men. If Pompey wanted to bring his army into Rome, what on earth was there to stop him?

By midnight the rumors had spread everywhere, and the city was on edge. In the bars men drank silently and quickly, and did not go home. The brothels were full, as were the temples, and near the Basilica a man addressed a small mob that had collected, reporting an omen on a farm nearby: a horse had been foaled with toes on its feet instead of hooves. At the City Praetor's house, where the Festival of the Good Goddess was being held, a man broke in. The women, half-naked and screaming, drove him out, but the rite had been profaned and the city put at risk.

Cicero in his study felt the anxiety of the city as if it were his own. The lamplight trembled across his walls of neatly rolled and pigeon-holed books, making them look insubstantial and meaningless. He could not sit easily in his chair. Every time he tried to think he was disturbed by noise from the street: footsteps, voices, an occasional barking dog. Once, from the direction of the Forum, came the crash of something breaking and a rumble of shouted oaths. "Drunks," he muttered, but he knew the night sounds of the city, and these were different.

When he was consul the year before a man named Catiline had tried to start a revolution. The city had that feel again. Rome was wakeful, and worried. A hundred and twenty thousand men. Well, he thought, rubbing his fingers across his eyes, he wasn't getting any sleep himself, and he was anxious, too.

He picked up his stylus and drew a waxed board to him over the polished pearwood surface of his desk. Slowly he engraved a few words.

MARCUS TULLIUS CICERO, SON OF MARCUS, TO GNAEUS POMPEIUS MAGNUS, SON OF GNAEUS, GENERAL WITH THE ARMY

Rome. The third of December in the 692nd year from the founding of the city.
GREETINGS

If you and the army are well, then everything is well with me, too. Your official letter to the Senate gave everyone, including me, the most incredible pleasure. You disclose in it so much hope of peace—just as I have always promised everybody, for I relied on you...

By morning he had finished this and written twenty letters more, to friends of his in the country—important men in the provincial towns who had supported him when he was consul. He had, in addition, made an outline of a short book on his consulship for Tiro and his clerks to write out. He would send it to Pompey, and to his friends in the Senate and the municipalities of Italy. It wouldn't hurt them to remember that he had saved them from a revolution before.

For a long time he sat at his desk, staring in disgust at the futile stack of documents. Finally he drew another board to him, and began to set out a speech to the Senate.

All day the city was silent. In the Forum citizens hovered near the Curia, but no one came out to speak to them. In the baths voices were hushed among the splashes and the steam; the markets transacted their business sullenly under the deferred threat of rain. Only the little wind of late December fretted and grated on the stones, wearing itself out in noisy distress. Cicero sat in his garden, as he had for days, with his toga pulled over his head. He had a book on his lap, but he had not unrolled it. Over his head clouds gathered and dispersed, but no rain fell.

It was nightfall before the news came, a long swell of sound like the wind rising in a forest, shaking leaves, bringing down branches with a crash. "Pompey," he heard in the noise, and the light of torches bobbed and ran over the roof of his house, making it seem to bow to the name.

"Pompey has landed in Italy," Tiro said, coming out into the darkness. The fountain rang with ice, the iron tracery of the trees sliced the wind to shards. "Has he?" Cicero said. Beside him the young man Caelius cursed under his breath and whispered, "His army? What about his army?"

Tiro shrugged. Far away, in the Forum, the noise was rising, a storm travelling fast.

A servant had come out to hand across a black wax tablet, unreadable in the dark. "Publius Clodius Pulcher left it for you, Marcus Cicero. He said to tell you that Pompey—"

"Yes, come on, man, what did he say?" Caelius cried. The boy was vibrating like a taut rope in the wind. "The army? What did he do with the army?"

"He dismissed it."

He could hear Caelius' yell of joy as the wind whipped it out of his mouth. At the same instant, all over the city the clouds opened and the rain fell with a crash.

BOOK ONE

I

It was April; fleecy clouds trailed across the sky, and blue shadows flocked docilely after them over the buildings of the Forum. The spring by the prison clattered into its basin; the river sent out a mysterious scent of green and growth. Cicero, coming out of the Curia with a crowd of senators, passed through the flickering light and shade. To the boy Caelius he looked discouraged. "Gentlemen," he was saying, "about Pompey. He needs that grant of land for his veterans—"

The little group passed through the open space of the Comitium and out between the railings into the Forum itself. Under the cool blue arc of the Rostra's shadow a cluster of benches had been set out on three sides of a square. Men in togas sat on them, facing a woman in a low-backed chair. A typical morning crowd of shoppers and idlers was accumulating around the edges.

"It's a trial," one of the senators said.

Cicero lifted his head. "A trial?"

"No," the boy Caelius cried. "You wouldn't be interested in that."

"Why not?" The large head had come up and seemed to scent the air in the Forum, and the smile twitched. "I like trials."

"What about Pompey?"

"I suppose so." He sighed. "Gentlemen, now that Pompey is back—"

But the senators around him were interested in trials too. Half of them had sat down on the spectators' benches already and the rest were following.

"Gentlemen—"

The woman in the witnesses' chair was saying, "I didn't let him in. I knew nothing about it."

The lawyer looked disgusted. He had a face made for the expression, long and aristocratic, like an offended goat.

"Of course you didn't let him in. But didn't you give orders to your maids to do it?"

"Ah," Cicero said, settling himself happily and tucking his toga around him. He had heard the hostility in the lawyer's question. "What is this? The trial for the break-in to the Women's Festival? I see. Curio's the counsel for the defense, is he? Where's the defendant?"

The secretary, Tiro, was tapping Cicero on the shoulder. He looked up and saw that he was pointing toward the buildings that surrounded the Forum.

From the shadows at the corner of the Basilica Porcia a small figure had appeared, achingly white in the sunshine. Behind him came a group of young men, patricians, lounging and chatting like people at a theater, looking over the crowd. They had women with them, brightly clothed and even more brightly coiffed, as drunk as they were, laughing and pulling at their dresses to show their bodies and stumbling to keep up. "In the Forum, in broad daylight," Cicero said, disgusted. After them came a mass of dun, brown, and straw-colored plebeians in their ordinary working clothes, equally intoxicated.

"There's Publius Clodius Pulcher," Caelius said.

The small figure swaggered into the Forum through the dust and sunshine, his head lifted and his fists on his belt. Pigeons flew up at his feet, voices rose. From the market stalls, where they congregated, idlers called to him. "So that's what he looks like. Hercules, he's handsome," Cicero said.

Clodius came forward. His slight body was elegantly balanced on his fine, strong legs. He squinted against the sunshine in the Forum, but even this did not mar his looks: it only gave him the air of a sultry god. As he approached the court he seemed to hear something—a familiar voice, a call—and he threw back his head. His black hair flew up like the wing of a raven.

"Even his name means 'beautiful'," Caelius observed.

"Yes," a senator said. "All that family have looks."

"Great Gods, if only Phidias had seen him." Cicero took a deep breath, moved by genuine, and purely aesthetic, appreciation. "What a Mercury he would have carved. What a Dionysus."

"Narcissus, more likely," said another senator, and they all laughed.

Publius Clodius had taken his place on a bench surrounded by his aristocratic companions; the workmen lined themselves up behind. Out in the open space Curio the counsel drawled, "If you didn't give the order, how did he get in?"

"He was dressed as a woman," the Pontifex Maximus' ex-wife said from the witnesses' chair.

"Publius Clodius was disguised as a woman?"

"Yes. As a musician, coming to play for the ceremony."

"Really," Curio said. It was not a question. "Do you expect us to believe that you couldn't tell that he was a man? Publius Clodius Pulcher?"

"It's possible," Cicero said. "He's not too tall, and his features are very fine. In a wig and a long dress, why not?" A senator snickered, and Caelius' bright hazel eyes shone with a blissful light.

"I didn't know," the unfortunate witness was insisting. "Not until he was already inside and had seen...what it is forbidden for men to see."

"Well, how did you discover Clodius' amazing secret, then?" Curio demanded. His face looked mild and sheep-like, but his teeth were showing—huge, square, yellowish blocks that seemed to glitter at her.

"He spoke," she said simply. The jurymen, until then silent on their benches, gave a shout of laughter. Cicero looked over and nodded to one or two he recognized. "Well, he was drunk," the woman said, but the jury and audience only laughed louder. On his bench, Clodius flushed a bright, angry scarlet as if he had been slapped.

"Get her out of there," Cicero muttered to Curio. "Enough is enough. Even a moment more and she'll hurt your case."

Curio, who could not have heard, must have had the same idea, for he bowed once to the woman with an air of considerable contempt—"Nice touch," Cicero murmured—and turned away. Down on the prosecution bench a man with gray-white hair like a cloud around his shining bald head bounced up with ferocious energy and boomed out, "I call Gaius Julius Caesar, the Pontifex Maximus, and City Praetor for last year."

"That's Hortensius Hortalus," Cicero said to Caelius. "A most distinguished lawyer." He was once the most distinguished of all, until he, Cicero, had taken that honor away from him, when he had been young and first made a success himself. He had thought then that he was catching up to Pompey, but of course that was foolishness. The witness, a tall, slender, fashionable man of about forty, was already coming to take the woman's place. The breeze lifted his light-colored hair and ruffled his long, embroidered sleeves. Hortensius waited until he was settled in the witnesses' chair before he looked up.

"You are Gaius Julius Caesar?"

"Yes," the man said, as if he weren't but it was too much trouble to deny it.

"And your wife was in charge of the festival of the Good Goddess last year?"

"Yes."

"You were not present yourself?"

"No. It's forbidden for men to be present, or even in the house, even slaves. I took my male servants and went to stay at another of my houses."

"When did you learn of the appearance of a man at the festival?"

Caesar leaned back and looked easily at the crowd that had collected. His eye travelled to Clodius, who leaned back on his bench with a similar arrogance, watching Caesar.

"The next morning," Caesar said, running his hand over the sparse yellow strands of his hair. He had combed them forward over the bald place in his scalp, but now they stood up straight as soldiers. His extreme elegance made a strange impression, as if the court were really another kind of function altogether—a dinner party or a picnic in the country—and they were all friends together. "Well, they are," Cicero rumbled, amused. "They're all patricians. They're probably cousins, too, or some such thing."

"What did you do when you discovered that a man had gotten into your house?" Hortensius was asking.

The blond man said crisply, "I divorced my wife."

The crowd gave a gasp and stood up straighter, the jury stared at Clodius, who glared at them in return. "Very proper," one of Cicero friends commented from the bench behind them. "If she was entertaining a lover, he had no other choice."

Hortensius had sat down and was talking to a colleague with obvious satisfaction. The jury eyed him, plainly wondering if that were all, but from the defense bench, without even troubling to stand up, the sheep-like Curio said casually, "Would you care to tell us why you did that, Pontifex? Did you think she was guilty of adultery, as my distinguished colleague plainly implies?"

Caesar looked around at the crowd, which had grown larger and more interested. His eye seemed to fall on the workmen behind Clodius—there must have been a hundred of them now—and he smiled at them, a faint lifting of the corners of his mouth. "I divorced her," he said slowly, "not because I believed she was guilty, but because Caesar's wife must be above suspicion."

There was a shout of approval from the spectators, and laughter on Clodius' bench.

"A very proper answer," a senator said.

"A very political one," Cicero muttered. He had seen the glance at the workmen. "Virtually the only answer that won't offend anyone. He's a very clever man, this Pontifex Maximus."

Someone else had taken Caesar's place. In the low-backed chair a little man in a farmer's homespun clothes but wearing a knight's gold ring was saying, "Yes, my name is Gaius Causinius Schola." He was one of the least appealing men Cicero had ever seen: his features were jammed together with brutal carelessness around his pointed nose; his eyes swiveled nervously.

"Looks like a rat," Caelius said, loudly enough to be heard on the jury benches.

Schola spoke in a high, anxious squeak, too, as he took the oath, and he passed his tongue nervously over his grayish lips. Curio, smiling, asked him where he lived. "Interamna. I farm there."

"Ah. And where is that exactly?"

"In Interamna," the man repeated, obviously failing to understand the question. He jumped in panic when the Forum laughed; he seemed not to have noticed the spectators before.

Schola grinned back at them, revealing a few very sharp, pointed teeth. "It's about ninety miles from Rome."

"Good. That's very clear. Do you remember the night of December the third last year?"

"Of course," said Schola, looking around for someone to share his indignation. "That's why I'm here." Everyone was laughing now, even the man behind Cicero who had thought Caesar's answer very appropriate; Clodius was wiping tears from his eyes, while his friends held their sides and roared.

"That's right," Curio said with impressive self-restraint. He was gathering the eyes of the jury to make sure that once they had enjoyed the joke they were ready to listen. "Tell us what happened that night."

"You already know. I told you, when you—"

"Tell the jury, then," Curio cut in hastily.

"Hercules," Cicero said, drawn in at last. "What a witness. This is murder." He was choking into his fist with laughter. One of the senators behind him leaned forward and tapped him on the shoulder. "All right, are you?" the man whispered. "Yes, thank you," Cicero said, turning to face him. "I was just thinking—thank the gods it's Curio and not me up there. I've had some bad ones in my time, but never anything like this."

"What happened on the night of December third?" Curio demanded once again. He had a sheep's humble patience too.

"Publius Clodius Pulcher came to visit me. That's what happened," the little man said triumphantly.

"When was this?"

"When?" His little eyes swiveled desperately. "But I told you—"

"Tell the jury."

Schola stared at him. "About ninety miles from Rome."

It took some time for the noise to subside. Curio waited until it was over, then asked easily, "When did Clodius arrive there, then?"

"Not long after dinner time?"

"Yes. Good. And what time is that?"

"When I eat."

"Yes, but when do you do that? The tenth hour of the day? The twelfth? The first hour of the night? Earlier? Later?"

"Oh," Schola cried, turning like a cornered rat on a ferret. "I'm a plain man. I can't go bothering with dancing girls and garlands and what all, like you people here in Rome. I eat just after sunset, as the gods intended men to do. As soon as the cook has had time to wash. He's my shepherd, too."

It was too much, even for Curio; his suppressed amusement burst from his now scarlet face in spite of everything he could do. "At least he washes first," he muttered, and had to turn aside, shoulders shaking, until it had passed.

"I see," he managed at last, when the Forum was quiet again. "And Publius Clodius Pulcher came to see you shortly after the first hour of the night on the third of December of last year."

"Yes," said Schola.

"How long after?"

"How long after what?"

"Really," Caelius said. "No one could believe this."

"Look at the jury," Cicero said. The jurymen were squirming on their benches;

even from where Cicero and his friends sat they looked angry and disquieted. "They have a lot of sympathy for this witness, in spite of everything. They don't like to see a plain man mocked by someone like Curio—and they think a court should be a more solemn and decorous place."

"So it should be," Cicero's friends agreed, sobered.

"Then they should be angry at Clodius for bringing in this greasy little liar."

"They don't know quite whom they're angry at," Cicero said. He was smiling, but his clear, deep eyes were grave.

Curio had recovered himself now and had taken up his questions again. "How long after dinner did Publius Clodius Pulcher arrive at your farm—in Interamna, of course? At what hour?"

"The third hour of the night."

"The third hour of the night," Curio repeated, staring at the jury to be sure they understood. "You are sure?"

"Yes."

"How long did he stay?"

Schola was consulting the heavens again—it occurred to Caelius that it was a way of not looking at Clodius, who was watching him intently from his bench. "He stayed till almost daylight. Almost daylight."

"Be careful of what you're saying," Curio warned him in a soft voice. All his rank and authority were in his tone, and the Forum fell silent to listen. Clodius leaned forward on his bench. "Be sure of your testimony. You are in a court of law. If Clodius was with you from the third hour of the night until almost morning, there is no way he could have broken into the Festival of the Women's Goddess. That appears to have happened sometime just before sunrise. How long does it take to travel from Rome to Interamna?"

Schola was ready for this question. "A day. At least a day."

"So he could not have come to Rome in time if he was with you."

"Yes. I swear he was with me. I swear by Orcus and Mania, by Dis Pater and Libitia, by..."

"Yes, yes," Curio said, cutting off this list of obscure and vaguely threatening underworld witnesses. The jury looked impressed, but from his bench Clodius laughed.

"He was there until morning," Schola protested. "He never left my sight until then."

Down on the prosecutor's bench men were muttering angrily. "Now I've heard everything," someone said. Cicero had gone very still and alert; to Caelius he looked like an animal scenting the wind. He made a gesture that he did not finish, he closed his eyes, pressing the space between them with his fingers. "The night of December the third," he said to himself.

"What is it?" Caelius whispered.

Cicero looked over at the defendant's bench. "It's just that Publius Clodius

Pulcher came to bring me the news about Pompey that night. I recognize him now. I saw him in the street outside my door."

There was a little silence while the others on the bench worked this out. The boy Caelius shuffled his feet uneasily and turned away. "Then Clodius doesn't have an alibi after all?"

"No." Cicero had raised his hand to catch the attention of the prosecutor.

Immediately there was a chorus of alarm from his supporters.

"Think who he is," Caelius cried in anguish.

"I know who he is. But think who I am too. I have a duty to testify—I know that lies have been told to this court. I have been an advocate in this city for more than twenty years; I have served as a magistrate; I have been consul. I can't just let it pass."

His colleagues were all around him, lined up facing him as if to block his way, their voices making a wall between him and the court.

"Clodius is connected by birth or marriage to most of the aristocratic families in Rome."

"The Claudian family goes back five hundred years, to the founding of the city—"

"Then their descendant ought to be above committing perjury."

"But should you be the one to say so?"

Cicero nodded over toward the jury. "They'll believe me, you know. I'm one of them."

"But Clodius has friends—"

"So do I." Cicero looked pointedly around him, but the eyes of his supporters did not meet his.

"One of Clodius' friends is Pompey."

"Cicero," Caelius whispered.

"Well, of course Pompey is Clodius' friend," Cicero rumbled, amused. His large nose twitched, and he smiled. "But he's my friend too. We've known each other for thirty years."

"Clodius helped him get the command in the East," a senator warned in an undertone.

Cicero had lost his patience; he turned away and signaled the prosecutor. "So did I. So did I."

"That's true, that's true." And the ex-consul added, "Cicero made speeches for Pompey—"

"Cicero," Caelius whispered. "Marcus Cicero."

The senators had united. "Don't do it. Don't take the risk."

But Cicero's massive head had come up, his solid body straightened. "I don't see why I shouldn't."

Several of them looked anxiously at the crowd behind Clodius; it had grown in the last half hour and was finding it difficult to fit into the space behind the benches. Some of the men in it looked very hard indeed.

"If you don't see that then you are blind."

They called after him, but he had escaped them, strolling through the forest of spectators to the prosecutor's bench.

Caelius had run up behind Cicero. "Marcus Cicero, please—"

"What is it, Caelius?" Cicero growled, annoyed. He was trying to catch the prosecutor Hortensius' eyes.

"Cicero. Please. They're right, you know. Your friends. It's too dangerous." He waved his hand—it was as oversized for his young body as a puppy's foot—at the glum and anxious group he had just left. Cicero smiled and turned away.

"Please," said Caelius, holding onto Cicero toga. "Let me testify instead."

"What do you mean?"

"I was there," Caelius said.

The buildings around the Forum seemed to retreat around them; they stood in an open space with nothing in it but themselves and the soft, timeless light of the sun.

"You broke into the Festival of the Good Goddess?" Cicero said quietly, so as not to disturb the sudden silence in his ears.

"Not into it. I mean, I stayed outside, with a friend of mine. We'd been drinking—Clodius and this friend and I. Clodius got the idea to visit the City Praetor's wife..." He looked like a schoolboy owning up to a misdemeanor and expecting to be beaten for it. Cicero lips curled, but he spoke gravely.

"I see. And you decided it would be an amusing way of passing an evening? Committing a sacrilege, putting the city at risk with its gods, frightening the women...?"

"It wasn't like that."

"No doubt you told yourself it wasn't. And what prevented you from carrying out this most entertaining program?"

"There weren't enough dresses go around. We could only borrow one."

Cicero put back his head and gave a roar of laughter. "Well, how did you decide who got it? Draw lots?"

"Clodius was the one that was sleeping with her."

"Oh, I see. He had a right to the dress." This time he laughed longer, but Caelius, anxious and upset, pulled on his toga. "Please. You don't see. It's dangerous. Even the City Praetor, her own husband, doesn't want trouble with the Claudians."

"I didn't say it wasn't dangerous All I have said is that I have a duty to testify. And, as far as the danger goes, my friends—" He glanced over at them, a large crowd, white and shining in their fine clothes under the winking shadows of the trees. "My friends will look after me. So will Pompey, if necessary."

"You don't understand," Caelius cried, making one last effort. "I've got friends, too."

"No," said Cicero, looking at him gently. "It's you who don't understand. In this context, you have only one." He shook himself free and walked toward the benches.

If Pompey had not quite managed to come home to the city, at least Cicero had. He was in the Forum of Rome, and it was set out for a trial. For twenty years he had lived in this place: his promising youth and young manhood, his successful middle age, had all been spent here. He smiled to himself, for he was happy here as he had never been anywhere else, not even in the village where he was born. The huge buildings seemed to reach out to embrace him, the shops, the crowds, even the gray paving stones, growing hot in the sunshine now, welcomed him as if after an absence. They were part of him, they were his natural habitat. He was as safe among them as bear in his woods.

He took another few steps forward, the soles of his shoes scraping on the pavement. The Forum had grown so quiet he could hear the little sounds above the whispering of the leaves and the splash of the fountain. "Hortensius," he said clearly, in his best and most melodious voice. "A word with you, if I may? I'd like to testify."

Across the way Clodius sat up. His dark eyes glittered. Around him the air seemed to crackle with tension. The young patricians crowded nearer to him, the workmen behind them stood very close together, their lips drawn back over their teeth. Their hackles had risen like dogs', stiff on their thick necks.

Cicero stared back, smiling lightly, confident in front of a crowd.

In the silence someone's feet clattered on the stones, a woman cried out. Clodius sat in perfect stillness, watching him.

All at once there were a dozen men around Cicero, standing with their backs to him and their eyes outward. There were more, until Cicero was standing behind a wall of bodies. It was the jury: the entire mass of them had risen from their seats to escort him to the witnesses' chair. He smiled at them in gratification. No, he thought, I have never had any reason to fear a mob.

"We'd be honored," Hortensius was saying. "Take the oath, consul." The presiding officer of the court was pounding on the table with his hand. The jury sat down, and visibly cloaking themselves with their function, turned their faces to him. He bowed in return. "Marcus Tullius Cicero," he said, giving his name in his loud, clear, beautiful growl. "Son of Marcus, grandson of Marcus, from the village of Arpinum. I was one of the two consuls of this city two years ago."

"The whole city remembers that," Hortensius said with composure. He might never have noticed Clodius and his men. "You were awarded the title of "Father of Your Country" by the Senate at that time, were you not? And a public service of thanksgiving was held in your honor at the Temple of Jupiter?"

"Yes."

"You are the only civilian ever to have received this honor?"

"I am."

Hortensius nodded. "I believe you have something to tell us about this business we are engaged on today?"

"Yes," said Cicero, looking over at Clodius' men. "I do."

"Then, if you please, will you go ahead and tell it in your own words?" Hortensius cried, contriving to convey the impression that he knew what his new witness was going to say.

"Very well." Cicero looked over at Publius Clodius, who glared back at him, then at the jury, making sure that they could all see him and that they would not miss what he had to say. They were silent, waiting; the tension in the Forum had reached such a pitch he thought he could hear them breathe. "All I want to say is that Publius Clodius Pulcher cannot have been in Interamna on the evening of the Festival of the Good Goddess. Not at the third hour. He was calling on me at my house on the Palatine Hill here in Rome that night. I saw him myself, and though I did not speak to him, my doorman did, and my secretary. Publius Clodius had come, very kindly, to tell me that Pompey had won the war in Asia and was coming home to Rome. Perhaps you remember that night?"

"I'm sure we all do," Hortensius said with warm appreciation. "Such good news."

"So it was," Cicero said, glaring at Hortensius, who was one of the senators least likely to vote for Pompey's requests. When Hortensius moved aside he turned to the jury and said, "You know my secretary, Tiro, don't you?" He could see several of the jurymen who went to the debates in the Senate nodding their heads. "Tiro made a note of the meeting, and the time," he said. "So did my doorman. They will certainly remember. If you think it necessary, I give you permission to question them." On his bench Tiro went pale—he knew how they questioned a slave.

"Not at all," Hortensius said suavely, and Tiro slumped against his assistant in relief. "Your word is enough for us, Marcus Tullius. And I won't insult you by reminding you of the importance of this, but just for the sake of clarity: are you sure of the time?"

"Absolutely. I had been talking to Licinius Crassus; I'm sure he too will be glad to corroborate what I say."

The crowd hummed at this prestigious name.

"So you see," Cicero said, "It's not possible that Publius Clodius was in Interamna at dinner time—whatever time that is, first hour, third hour. He was here, in the city. He could not have reached Interamna in much under a day—as we know, it's all of ninety miles from Rome."

The jury laughed. Clodius, face flushed angrily, was standing up; his men stepped forward as if at a command.

"Thank you, Marcus Cicero," Hortensius said hastily.

There was movement in the Forum; it was hard to see exactly where, but feet were shuffling forward; there were cries and an ominous ringing clang, as if someone had a sword and was taking it out of its sheath. Surely not; Cicero thought, surely Clodius had not brought armed men into the Forum.

The jury had risen as one man to its feet, all its members staring in fear or horror or dismay at the men behind Clodius' bench. Someone was shouting—the praetor in charge of the court, was banging on his table. "Adjourned until tomorrow. Adjourned until tomorrow," he shouted, but the noise was growing all the same, hammering off the buildings around them, mixing with the dust and the heat, growing louder and louder.

"We want a bodyguard," a juryman bellowed. "Give us a bodyguard." The others took it up; the crowd joined in. "Bodyguard. Bodyguard." Clodius, standing on a bench, raised his voice and called incomprehensibly.

"Certainly," the praetor cried and one of the consuls of the year, appearing beside him suddenly on the tribunal, added, "The Senate will provide one in the morning. Go to your homes now. Keep quietly there tonight. Everything will be all right, and we will see that you have your bodyguard in the morning. Go to your homes. Go to your homes."

They did not obey him, at least not at first. Again they had formed a wall around Cicero; they were leading him from the Forum, through the roaring crowd, calling his name and his title in a thunder of approval.

The jury led him toward the Palatine Steps, their shoulders set massively together, the backs of their necks red with anger; he could not see Clodius over their heads, but he heard his voice floating on the noise in a long, bitter laugh, like the cry of a furious bird. Then his feet were on the stairs; he glanced back, but the Forum was boiling with movement; it was impossible to make out any individual. They went a few paces further, they were outside the ring of benches, they were crossing the open space—

"That was wonderful," said Caelius, appearing at his side as he climbed the Palatine Steps; the jurymen eyed him but they let him through. His eyes were shining, his handsome mouth was curved in a grin of joy. "Clodius will lose his case, won't he?"

"I imagine he won't even defend it." They had come to Cicero's door now; he turned and made a little speech to the crowd, thanking them and reminding them to appear in the Forum in the morning to record their vote. They roared at him in approval, promising to share their bodyguard.

"What will Clodius do?" Caelius asked as they passed inside and the doorman, looking out anxiously, bolted the door after them.

"Disappear, I suppose. He's probably down at the docks now, getting on a ship."

"Good."

But Cicero shook his head again. "He's a ruined man. It's sad to see a member of a noble clan like that destroyed in a moment of foolishness."

"You hadn't any choice."

"No," said Cicero, looking at him peculiarly. "After you...after a certain point, I hadn't any choice at all."

II

Caelius was worried. This man, Quintus Metellus, whose house they were to visit that evening, was related to Clodius, married to one of his sisters. Yet Cicero did not seem disturbed.

"Well, no one invites you to a discussion just to tell you they're not going to invite you to any more," Cicero said, rumbling out his laugh.

"But he's one of those old senatorial aristocrats. His family must be the most important thing in the world to him. You know how they are."

"That's true," he said, taking his cloak from the servant and swinging around his shoulders. He was smiling to himself. "His family is very important to him, all right, but I don't know if it's the most important."

"What could be more? You know those patricians, and their pride."

"His advancement."

"Oh."

"Metellus is an old friend of Pompey's. He and his brother served with him out East, as his legates. I think you'll find that they are prepared to back him here. They know where their best chance lies. The Metelli are generally very shrewd."

He was in a good humor; he set his cloak on his shoulder with a jaunty motion, and grinned broadly at Caelius. "I anticipate a profitable evening," he said. His wife was at the door; he bowed to her absently as he went out. Caelius, who knew her as well as her children did, saw the anger and disappointment on her face. "Cicero," he called, meaning to mention it to him, but his friend was already disappearing up the street. So Caelius, too, bowed and hurried after him.

"Pompey needs three things," Cicero explained to Caelius as they walked up the now deserted street under the flickering torchlight. "Ratification of his acts while conducting the war, a grant of land for his soldiers, and a triumph for himself. I don't know if you've ever seen a triumph?"

"No," said Caelius, looking into each shadow they passed. He had insisted on accompanying Cicero to Metellus' house; he had even pressed the gardener and the kitchen boys into coming with them in case there was any trouble. Of course there was none, the fashionable street, the Clivus Victoriae, was empty and quiet in the chilly spring night.

"The triumph is a beautiful ceremony. I can see why it's worth it to Pompey to wait for the honor," Cicero said. "The opportunity for enhancing his popularity, the recognition before the city and its the gods— But it is making this land bill business very difficult. He can't come inside the walls, you see. That means the burden is all on me."

Caelius had heard about Pompey's style of waiting, out there in his magnificent villa in the hills. Every day crowds poured through the gate, journeying out along the road to it; no one knew what they expected from this pilgrimage, since Pompey, it seemed, showed himself only very rarely. If their hero did not appear they trekked back to the city; no one among them seemed disappointed.

Beside him Cicero sighed. He was thinking that there were dozens of things he had to do: ever since he had come home Pompey had kept himself busy bombarding his old friend with urgings, suggestions, demands, until Cicero felt like a city under siege, pounded to pieces by the letters, which arrived sometimes two or three times a day, crashing heavily on his desk. Now he intended to drop some of these boulders at the feet of Metellus' aristocratic and powerful cronies.

Metellus' atrium was crowded with distinguished men, all sitting in a circle, with their secretaries and assistants in a ring outside them. In the dim light of the antique oil-lamps he recognized their faces. Very few of them were sympathetic to Pompey at all.

"Amazing scene this afternoon," Metellus said, by way of opening the meeting. His drawl exaggerated his contempt—he might have been saying that it was disgusting.

"I do not see that I had any choice," Cicero said, lifting his head and looking Metellus in the eye. "I am a former consul. I have an obligation to the state."

Caelius, on his seat, shifted uncomfortably. Why does he care what they think? he cried in his mind. He's greater than any of them, more intelligent, braver, harder working. He's done more for his country than any two of them. He glared out from behind Cicero's back at the patricians in front of them.

Metellus was a man with a high military polish and a trim and shiny look. He raised his glossy, gray head and stared down his nose at Cicero. "That boy is related to me."

There was a silence and a clerk, caught in the tension, coughed noisily.

"Distantly."

Metellus' narrow nostrils flared with rage.

"No, Celer. He's right. He had no choice." A figure bent forward into the circle of lamplight: Cato, thought Caelius, recognizing him. He was young, under thirty—too young to contradict someone like Metellus—but Cato's family was very great. "He had the same obligation we have," he rasped. "The same as any Roman citizen. He must speak out. Right is right."

"It certainly is," a retired general named Lucullus called lazily from the back of the room.

"Amazing scene." Hortensius, the prosecutor, rolled out the words ponderously. "I don't remember the like in thirty years. Good thing you stood up to him."

Aware that he had captured their approval, and with it their attention, Cicero came to the point. "Gentlemen, I think we ought to be considering the future now. I have received a number of letters from Pompey. He is waiting to come inside the walls and talk to you, but he asks me to make a few proposals on his behalf before he does. He says he holds the Senate in the greatest esteem."

That was met by a murmur of doubt.

"While he was out there," he said hastily, "Pompey made a number of arrangements, as any general has to. Treaties and so on. Gifts to subject rulers. A promise of land for his veterans. He needs the ratification of the Senate for these now, of course. That's perfectly normal, too—"

They were shouting long before he had finished. "Arrogant creature," Lucullus the general cried. "He wants us to approve these? We need to consider each one..." and Hortensius, back stiff with rage, let loose his powerful voice. "Who does he think he is, to make his own arrangements without consulting us?" All around him their voices rose in outraged vanity.

"There was really nothing else he could have done, was there?" Cicero said soothingly. "He was out there, on his own: he had to make decisions quickly. Metellus, who has served in the area under Pompey will tell you what conditions were like..."

But Metellus had turned away and was talking over his shoulder to his brother.

"Let Pompey give them the land," Bibulus, a former praetor, was telling the company. "He's rich enough now."

"Money. It doesn't make him any better, though he thinks it does," Cato sneered.

"A grant of land," Lutatius Catulus sighed windily, as if he thought it might be located in his own garden.

Cicero, smiling grimly to himself, tried to reassure them. "Pompey suggests a tract the city already owns. Several thousand acres."

Outside the night had been only a little chilly, but Metellus' house was old and damp. Some of them had put on two or three tunics under their woolen togas. Only Cato did not wear even one. He never did: he said the tunic was un-Roman. Their ancestors hadn't worn it, and neither would he. His fingertips were purple with chill, the skin of his arms raised in spots like a plucked chicken's. It was carrying conservatism a bit too far, Cicero thought, concealing a bark of laughter under a cough. He wondered if Cato had given up wheat flour for ground acorns, and if he ever bathed.

"These men do deserve a reward."

"No doubt," Metellus said, joining the argument for the first time. Cicero sighed in relief. Metellus had made up his mind a long time ago.

"It's customary," Cicero said, giving them a list of precedents to which they all listened with care. They loved the past, all of them, conservative and popular equally, for to them it was simply the arrangements their ancestors had made. Hah, thought Cicero. Got them. Now for a quick vote.

"Pompey's not thinking of the good of his veterans," a voice cut in, so peculiarly dull and cold they all turned to look. It was Crassus. His long, hollow face looked back at them, his black eyes shone, unwinking, like the eyes of a corpse. He had not moved, but somehow the circle had widened, and he was now the center of it. "He's not thinking of his soldiers. He's thinking of what they'll owe him if he gets them free land. He's thinking of power, and how to hold onto it."

Under his breath, Cicero swore.

The trouble was Crassus was right, or right enough. Certainly Pompey wanted popular support; he had no other kind. These men had thousands of dependents, tenants of their farms, shopkeepers in their villages, artisans who worked their wool and iron and wheat or bought them for the products of their own handicraft. They could count on these people to vote as they wished them to. But Pompey was not born an aristocrat, he was a knight's son from Picenum, and he had to find votes where he could.

"I doubt that Pompey—" Cicero began, but Crassus—Crassus who was richer than any of them, who hardly bothered to control the votes of tenants and shopkeepers but owned the votes of those who did—Crassus was saying, "The good of the city cannot be purchased with free land," and the others, the conservatives, were nodding their agreement.

It was like pushing against a mountain to make it move. They were stubborn, strong-willed, deaf to everything but their own claims and the claims of their class. His patience began to wear thin; he was afraid the bright metal of his anger might show through. And Metellus, Metellus who should have been his ally, was as remote and chilly as a mountaintop. He sat and stared down his nose, and could not be induced to add another word.

"It needs study," Cicero said quickly, hoping to cut off argument before their opposition hardened. It seemed to work; they were all nodding and murmuring in their irritating way, but now they were agreeing with him. Seizing the opportunity, he mentioned the triumph.

Only Crassus was really opposed to the triumph, but so great was his influence, it took Cato's sincere if unenthusiastic argument that the city's gods might be offended if they were denied the rituals and sacrifices of victory to make them agree to sponsor the event. The date they set was September the twenty-ninth.

"September?" Caelius murmured as the meeting broke up. "That's six months away."

"The twenty-ninth is Pompey's birthday," Cicero said absently. He was trying to catch Metellus' eye, but the patrician was avoiding him. Or perhaps it was merely his impression. "Perhaps they hope Pompey will take it as a compliment."

"Well, but making him wait half a year..."

"I know," said Cicero, baring his teeth in a grin. "They know what they're doing. Good night, good night, gentlemen." He was hoping for a word with Metellus, but the dim gray figure had disappeared... "Good night, Marcus Cato." A draft of cold air bustled through the door as Crassus departed.

"What do you mean, they know what they're doing?" Caelius had wrapped his cloak around himself; all that showed were his handsome eyes. The others were filing out around them; a servant—not one of his own—came up and pressed a note into Cicero hand.

"Go home, Caelius," Cicero said, holding the note close to read it near-sightedly. "Take the gardener and the kitchen boys with you and drop them at my house, will you? If Terentia is still up, tell her I've been delayed but I'll be home soon."

"Yes, certainly." Caelius nodded to the doorman, who pulled back the black and silver leaf. The night poured in around their feet.

"What did you mean?" the boy asked, hesitating on the doorstep. "Why do they know what they're doing?"

"Oh," said Cicero. He was laughing. "How else can they be sure of keeping the most popular hero in history out of the city for six whole months?"

Metellus' house was huge, full of dark rooms and glimpses of unexpected glories: a tiny garden in a corner off the dining room, an alcove with a lighted statue at the end, a fountain in the shape of a shell with a rattle of cold water falling into it. Cicero was glad of his guide, a young man in a white tunic banded in black, who hurried down what must have been the length of the building. The servant stood aside and pulled open a door as a draft of cool air full of the smells of the spring night swirled around them.

He stood alone under a colonnade in a garden—at the back of the house, he supposed. It was an odd place for Metellus to ask for a talk. Walls closed off two sides, a row of cypresses reached black fingers into the luminous blue of the sky, a pool glimmered. Over it bent a white shape that separated into two as Cicero moved forward. One shape was a statue of Venus, marble, and cold to look at in the dark; the other... It strode toward him, lifting its head as it came.

"Good evening," Cicero said.

"Is it?" Publius Clodius Pulcher answered. He had come to a stop a few feet away and was looking at Cicero with challenge and hostility in every beautiful line of his body.

"For some of us it's better than for others, I suppose," Cicero said, smiling.

Instantly the young man was in a rage. "Don't joke. You turn everything into a joke." His hand travelled along his belt.

It came over Cicero that the day had been very long. He sank onto a stone bench, his eyes on the angry man in front of him. "What do you want, Pulcher? I'm very tired."

It was like dealing with a wasp. The small man hovered over him, never still long enough for the eye to rest on him, buzzing dangerously all the time; he had a sting too, in his belt. Something caught the moonlight and winked colorlessly—the grip of a knife? In the dark it was hard to be sure.

"What are you saying, Pulcher?" Probably he really didn't want to know.

"I said, take it back."

"Take what back?" His eyes ached; he put his fingers to the bridge of his nose to rub, feeling the day on his back like a weight.

"Take back what you said about me." Now that Cicero's eyes were closed Clodius' voice sounded different. The aggressive hum in it was gone, it sounded young somehow, and sad, or frightened. He might have been a child, afraid of the dark. It was so strange that Cicero spoke very gently to him. "My testimony, do you mean?"

"Yes," said Clodius in a small, still voice.

He was standing just in front of Cicero, his dark eyes wide, his delicate mouth curved in a hopeful smile. It was like looking at a statue or a painting; the same shock of perpetual astonishment at its beauty went through Cicero, the same involuntary lift of delight. There cannot be another human being like him, he thought. He's as different from the merely handsome as wine is from water.

"Will you?" Clodius whispered.

"I can't, Pulcher. You know I can't."

"Why not?"

Cicero sighed. "Because it wouldn't be the truth."

Clodius snapped his tongue against the roof of his mouth. "The truth," he repeated with contempt. "Look." He was kneeling at Cicero feet, his face turned up. One beautifully shaped hand rested in appeal on Cicero's knee, a signet ring flashing with the small man's breath. "Look. I helped you once."

"Yes, you did," Cicero said, remembering. "When I was consul. You volunteered to be in my bodyguard." It was not a knife, then, it was only the ring. Or at least he thought that was all...

"It was dangerous," Clodius bragged. "I risked my life."

"So did I, or I wouldn't have needed a bodyguard."

"Don't joke," Clodius cried; his hands went to his belt again. "I'm warning you. Other people can joke too."

This time he was not afraid. "Hush, Pulcher," he said, as if he were talking to a child. "Just tell me what you want."

Oddly, the small man obeyed this instruction. He leaned forward on his hams, studying Cicero's face. "I've got friends. You know what I mean."

"No, I'm not sure I do."

"Votes," Clodius said impatiently. "People who'll do what I ask."

"I don't need the votes of your bankrupt and degenerate companions," Cicero said. "I saw them in the Forum—believe me, supporters like that do more harm than good in a campaign. They give the whole patrician class a bad name."

Clodius was on his feet again, weaving a complex pattern back and forth in the dark, his arms thrown out as if he were going to fly. "You saw the others too? Poor men, in working clothes?" Cicero nodded. "The city is full of them, wearing out their souls laboring here," Clodius muttered. He sounded very drunk. "Once they had farms, out in the country, small places you know, nothing important. But still, they managed. Too bad—Sulla's armies marched right over them. Or else they went to war—to fight for him, or in Asia or Spain, with the expeditions there. There were a lot of them in those armies, you know. Wherever. So they had to mortgage their little farms. Then the big landowners came in with hundreds of slaves. Prices went down in the market, and bam! the little farmer is out. Or else their banker wants to send his money overseas, now that Pompey has made it safe. Calls in his debts. Raises the interest. Bam! Ruined again. Finished."

"They mismanaged their holdings, you mean," Cicero said with distaste. "That doesn't happen if farms are well managed, even small ones."

Clodius did not appear to hear him. "They come to the city," he went on. "You know. In Rome they don't starve, even if they can't find work. They get the cheap wheat, and the oil..."

"Which the Treasury subsidizes."

"They're Romans. As much as...anyone." It seemed to Cicero that he could hear the unspoken "you." "They're citizens," Clodius was saying. "They paid taxes once, when they could. They have a right..." He was in full flight now, moving quickly in the dark as if motion underlined his argument. "But there's no work for them in the city—there are too many people out of work here already. Bam. See? Do you know what it costs to rent a workshop or a store in the Subura nowadays? Or a room—even one little room—for a family?"

"Of course I do. I have tenants, like everyone else."

Clodius clicked his tongue. "And how much have you raised the rent in the last five years?"

"That's unjust, Pulcher. I'm not a rich man, and you have no idea how much a political campaign costs, especially if you're running for consul. I had to borrow, and interest rates have gone up for me, just as for everyone else. Of course I raised my rents."

Clodius ignored him. "So what do they do, with no work and no money?"

"Why should they have no work? I know ex-slaves who have flourishing businesses, who have even married and supported a family. Surely a freeborn Roman can do as well."

"Slaves have trades. Bakers, millers, potters, architects, doctors, schoolmasters. A lot of them can read. Greek and Latin. They were taught all that. What can a farmer do? Carry a hod? Unload a ship at the docks? When he can get the work. Or when slaves don't do it cheaper."

"Nonsense. You're exaggerating. Most of your poor men from the country settle down here very well. Your friends don't, of course. They don't want to work. They waste their time in the bars and the baths. They must have money, because they go to the games, and they make bets on the outcome. They form clubs, which they call religious sodalities or workmen's guilds, but which are really excuses for idleness and disorder. They drink, they sell their votes, they commit crimes. It's shameful."

"They'll do anything. They're desperate. They'll listen to anyone who cares about them."

"We all care about them. You mean they'll listen to anyone who makes them promises."

"Of course I've made promises." Clodius had achieved a kind of honesty, it was as if he had stripped himself of his class, his name, his anger, his pride. He was as beautiful without them as he would have been without his clothes. "They have to trust me, and they do." He came closer. "They know I can do something for them," he said. He smelled strongly of wine. "That's the thing, see? That's what I want to tell you. You said you care about them—well, they know that. You're popular. You're a hero. I could tell them that you're willing to help them—"

"Of course I'm willing to help them. Everyone is. It's a bad situation. No one wants to see people suffer if something can be done."

"That's right. Well, that's good. I'll tell them that."

Cicero sighed. "It's not so simple, Pulcher."

"Why not?"

"Oh, you know, I think," Cicero said, feeling his weariness again. He sat down; the bench had turned cold and slippery with dew. "In the first place, no jury asks for a bodyguard to protect itself from ordinary working men, even if they're unemployed. No, they saw what those ruffians were really like. We all did."

"Prejudiced," Clodius cried. "The jury was prejudiced from the beginning."

"I doubt it, Pulcher. Oh, I admit it might have started that way, but in the end it's been even-handed enough, hasn't it? It was chosen by lot, in the usual way, and your lawyer challenged the people he thought might not give a fair verdict. They were all dismissed." He smiled to himself. "I've asked," he said, "and Curio turned away everyone from the jury with a shred of respectability to his name, like a kind-hearted trainer of criminals for the gladiatorial combats. And Hortensius, the prosecutor, was equally summary with the rogues, like a good censor keeping the voting rolls pure." He laughed a little to himself.

"Don't joke," Clodius protested vehemently from the darkness by a topiary hedge.

"No," Cicero said, considering Clodius' claim with all the dispassionate honesty at his command. "I don't think you can complain about unfair treatment from that jury. But there is one thing you haven't noticed about it."

"What?" Clodius demanded suspiciously.

"They asked for a bodyguard for tomorrow, when they present their verdict.

Why was that, do you think?"

"Because they were trying to turn people against me. Make my friends look bad..."

"No. Because they intend to convict, and they don't want any trouble from your gang. They wouldn't ask for protection from you if they were going to acquit. Do you understand now Pulcher? You won't be in any position to tell anyone anything tomorrow. Or not in Rome, anyway. You'll be on your way into exile."

"Not if you take back your testimony."

Cicero said softly, "You know I won't do that."

The small man glimmered indistinctly in the dark a few feet away. Cicero could just make out his hands at his belt. He wondered if Clodius really had a knife, and if he intended to use it. He was alone here. He didn't think Metellus would condone a murder. Still, he might; they were very close, these aristocratic clans. He was sorry he had sent Caelius home. No, he wasn't, it was better to keep the boy out of it. Of course it was. Of course.

He opened his mouth to speak. He had always been able to save himself with his voice.

But it wasn't necessary. Astonishingly, the white figure seemed to flash brighter, then go out like a flame. The path where he had stood was empty, the bushes behind it dark and still.

Cicero got cautiously to his feet. The night was very quiet; only a few leaves whispered, the water in the pool hardly slapped against the sides. He could not make out anyone; he was alone with the little statue which bent, quizzical and graceful, over the water. "Pulcher?" he said. There must have been a door in one of the garden walls, for the only answer to his question was its slam.

Metellus had a statue to match the one by the pool—over by the door the servant had shown him through. He could see it as he turned, gleaming white in the deeper darkness under the colonnade; it was odd that he hadn't noticed it when he came out. The statue seemed to follow him with its eyes. As he approached it said, "I'd like a word with you, Marcus Tullius." It turned and flowed into the blackness, fortunately so quickly it did not see his flesh leap on his bones in surprise. His heart kicked in his chest like a mule. It hadn't been a statue, of course; it had been a woman in a white dress. He was following her, back through the maze of corridors in the chilly house. They passed an alcove; the light of a bronze lamp fell on her face, and his heart gave a jolt worse than when he had thought she was a statue. He had just been looking at that face: the wide, dark eyes, the arched nose, the sulky and elegant mouth. Some god must have taken the form of the young man outside, but for some reason disguised himself as a woman. The hair rose on the back of his neck. In spite of himself, he had an impulse to extend his fingers in the sign against evil.

"I'm sorry to receive you in here, Marcus Tullius," the woman, or the goddess, said, pulling open a curtain. "But my husband has gone to bed and I don't like to disturb him."

Metellus' wife then: Clodia. No wonder she looked like Clodius Pulcher—she was his sister. Metellus had married very well. He was smiling at himself for his superstitious fear when he came into the lamplit room, but his smile faded as he looked around. It was a bedroom, lavishly decorated, and uncomfortably feminine. A tapestry with Cupids on the wall, a vast black and silver bed. It smelled deliciously of beeswax candles and essence of roses. A woman might receive a lover here, but that she had invited him was an insult. She wouldn't have done it to one of Metellus' friends. And if Metellus, who was, mysteriously, already angry, should find out—

Metellus' wife did not seem to have intended an injury to him; she smiled gently in the middle of the pink and gold space, indicating a chair. "We won't disturb anyone here. We're too far from the rest of the house."

He wondered if her voice really had a promise in it, or if the warmth and the light were disorienting him. Certainly he felt confused and a little feverish. The room seemed to waver in front of him, and he thought, for one light-headed instant, that there was something wrong with his eyes. No, it was the heat that was causing the tapestry to sway gently on its pins. He loosened the fold of his toga around his neck.

On a cluttered dressing table her maid had left a tray with a silver pitcher of wine and a pair of cups; Clodia poured them each a drink with grave attention, and he studied her face. She was far more beautiful than her brother, though he would not have believed until he saw her that such a thing were possible. He tried to see why, for they were so alike in feature, but something was dazzling him, and he gave it up. All he could decide was that the vein in the hollow of her temple, faint as a brushstroke and blue as distance, tugged him uncomfortably under his ribs each time his eye fell on it.

She turned to him and smiled. "I heard you talking to my brother." Homer reported that Juno, the wife of Jupiter, had "ox-like" eyes; he had never seen, until this moment, how that could be lovely. They must have been like Clodia's, huge, black, the whites so clear that where they were shaded by long lashes they were violet.

"It was...educational," he said. He could not keep a certain effect of a growl from his voice.

She was far more intelligent, and more self-possessed, than her brother, too. She laughed. "He's rather clumsy, isn't he? You must understand, he means well."

He thought she must be around his own age, though there was little enough to go on for this estimate. Her skin was unmarked, her hair entirely black. She had the figure of a young girl, her slender flanks and small breasts reminded him poignantly of his daughter's...

"He was trying to suggest that we have something in common, Marcus Cicero."

"We do?"

She smiled again, amused at his doubt. It was all very odd and uncomfortable. "Of course, we do. We have a vision of what life could be like in Rome. For everyone. We're interested, you and I, in more than just the perpetuation in power of a few old families."

"It's certainly true that I am," he said. "I hope to see someday a true concord of all the classes... Well, never mind that; it's boring to you, I'm sure. But surely your family is one of..."

She threw up her head. "My family," she said distinctly, "has dedicated itself for five hundred years to the good of Rome. Ever since our ancestor, Attius Clausus, led his tribal warriors out of the Sabine Hills to ally himself with Romulus, we Claudians have looked after the poor and humble, as well as the rich. We gave this city its first code of laws, to protect all the classes; we built the roads and the aqueducts so everyone can live well; we provided the consuls and the censors, the generals and the priests. And priestesses. We have not done that by narrowing ourselves to the interests of just one class. No, Marcus Tullius, others of less nobility may not be, but we are above all that. Why, my brother, to show his sympathy with the plebeians, has adopted their way of saying his name. My sisters and I have followed him—we are Clodians, not Claudians now."

There was snobbery and snobbery, he saw. She looked down on the ordinary patrician class from a height as great as that from which they looked down on him.

"Nor have we accomplished this by blinding ourselves to the merits of men from other backgrounds than our own," she added. She gave him her smile again; this time he was more certain of the promise in it. She had seated herself on the edge of the bed—a cover woven with scenes from the life of Ariadne billowed behind her, stretching away with tragic beauty to the black and silver headboard. She leaned forward. "Another cup of wine, Marcus? I may call you Marcus, mayn't I? It's just that I feel we could be...such good friends." Her eyelashes cast a shadow over her grave and thoughtful eyes. It lay on her cheekbones, mysterious as a line of chant, an oracle's muttered phrase. He could feel the warmth of her body; he almost touched her. The cool surface of the wine cup she pressed into his hand brought him back to himself.

"What did you have in mind?" He forced himself to lean back in the rather fragile chair. At least from there he could take a deep breath...

"An alliance, Marcus."

The scent of roses that pervaded the room was coming from her, from her smooth, pale skin that seemed to take the light along its surfaces so that it shimmered like the air above a flame. He blinked and shook his head. "What sort of alliance did you have in mind?" he managed to say.

She smiled and took a sip of her wine, her eyes on his. "I am a useful friend. For instance, now that Pompey has divorced my sister-in-law, I can..."

"Pompey has what?"

"Oh, yes. Didn't you know? It's all over town tonight."

"He's divorced Mucia?" No wonder Metellus had been so hostile. How could Pompey have done such a thing? To alienate the Metelli, his most consistent supporters... "Why?" he said, puzzled, not realizing he had spoken aloud. "Why would he do such a thing?"

Her smile of approval dazzled him. "That's right, Marcus. It just shows how right I was about you. You are a man who has risen above the narrow prejudices of those around him—unlike Pompey, who divorced that poor girl with only the vulgarest, most tasteless of excuses. She had children by him, too."

She was waiting for his response. but after all her flattery he did not want to reveal that he had no idea what she was talking about. "Tasteless, you think?" he said judiciously.

"Well, what would you call it?"

"Oh, tasteless. Certainly, tasteless."

She was smiling again, leaning forward on her chair.

"That's right," she said. "I knew you were a gentleman at heart. I mean what did he expect her to do, all that time that he was away in the East? What if she did have a lover or two? Is that any reason to divorce her?" She leaned forward and gave him a dark, liquid glance, full of meaning, like a cup full of wine.

All at once his vision cleared and he saw what she was offering. And what she wanted in exchange. He could have laughed at himself. She had not moved, but somehow he could see her differently now; a woman, nearly middle-aged... Beautiful, certainly—his bewildered eyesight could not deny that—but pathetic in her anxiety for her worthless brother. And as clumsy as that young man had been in her effort to align his support.

"Clodia, I—ah—"

She was intelligent; she must have seen the change in his expression. Lightly she turned away from it, unwilling to push him to refusal. Instead she gave him a soft smile, as if he had agreed, and stood up, clapping her hands for the servant.

"I'm—ah—I'm very flattered," he said, easing himself out of his chair. He did not want to give the impression of haste: it was undignified, and it might offend her. And, in spite of her foolishness, he did not want to do that—she was a Claudian, after all. He could not risk offending Metellus; things were bad enough already. Imagine divorcing Mucia...

"Then you will consider what I said?" she asked.

"My dear, of course. I'm very flattered. But I'm afraid it's impossible. My wife would object, for one thing." He laughed softly.

"Oh, I'm sure there won't be any problem," she said. She was perfectly sincere. Why not? he wondered. Did she think he would silence Terentia? Get rid of her? Did she think it didn't matter? She was a Claudian, but for him a scandal meant... He knew he was clumsy now, he didn't understand the situation, and it struck him as dangerous. He had to get out of that place. If Metellus found out...

"It's certainly something to think about," he said hastily, backing away toward the servant, now waiting with perfectly trained unobtrusiveness by the door.

His wife had waited up for him. Her pale face gleamed at him in the dark as he came into the house. "What happened? Why didn't you come home hours ago?"

"Didn't Caelius tell you I'd be late?" he asked wearily. "I got involved in a discussion—a political discussion." He had to repress a smile, for he thought of Clodia, perfumed and yielding, elegant, graceful, beautiful; his unease about her husband walked in the back of his mind like a ghost.

"You had a talk with Metellus?" she said eagerly. "Then he's not angry? He's pleased with you?"

He had to tell her that Metellus had not given anything that could be interpreted as a sign of pleasure. He sighed. It was chilly in the hallway. He was tired. He did not want to talk about his evening, or his worries for the future. "It's late, Terentia," he said gently. "Let's go to bed."

"Is Metellus pleased with you or not?" she cried. Her mouth made an "o" of worry and concern in her pale face.

"I don't think so."

"Then we must do something about that."

All at once the fatigues and disappointments of the day grew too strong for him. "Let us go to bed," he said through his teeth. "I do not wish to discuss this any more."

"He divorced Mucia," she said, ignoring this. "What do you think of that?"

"I don't think anything of it, my dear. It's too late to think, and I'm too tired."

"He wants to marry Porcia, Cato's daughter," Terentia said.

Really, these women. How did they know these things? They must have lines of communication, like spies behind an enemy's position. The thought made him uncomfortable, and he snapped, "Cato will see him dead on his bier first."

"I don't know," she said judiciously. "Pompey has gotten to be a very great man. Perhaps he can hope for a marriage to a Cato after all."

He thought she was making a comparison between Pompey and him. His temper, which he had swallowed all day, burst from him. "Go to bed, Terentia," he roared. Startled, she opened her mouth, but thinking better of it, turned on her heel and disappeared into the shadows.

Later, as he was getting into bed he thought of it again. Pompey married to Cato's daughter. It was almost like something in a dream. It was almost as if he had accomplished it himself.

III

By morning he still did not know what to do about Metellus. If Pompey really was going to marry Cato's daughter there would be no problem, of course. But in the cool light of dawn, he doubted Terentia's information. Women's gossip. There had been no word from Pompey.

When he came into the Forum the crowd there took him by surprise. Ah, he thought, recalling his mind to this with difficulty: Clodius' trial. The verdict—the condemnation—is this morning. It seemed a very trivial matter now.

The crowd was even larger than the previous day's, and its composition had altered considerably. Most of the shoppers and strollers were gone, the booths themselves were noticeably fewer, and some of the permanent shops were still shuttered from the night. There were more of the rough-looking plebeians from the previous day too—they stood in solid blocks, almost like military phalanxes, eyeing the crowd with an air of hostile expectation.

"Who are they, Tiro?" Cicero asked, as he and his entourage of secretaries and clients took their seats.

Tiro considered the question. "Poor men, and freedmen, I think. Some of them are discharged criminals who have served their time in the arena, though. I recognize one or two of them." He went to all the games on his holidays, sitting up in the highest seats with the other slaves; the walls of his room were painted with the portraits of his favorites.

"They look like the crew of a pirate ship, don't they?" Cicero said. "You almost expect to see the beards and gold earrings." He laughed, and so did Tiro, but presently the secretary whispered, "Some of those men might have knives or clubs. I can't be sure, but—"

"Well, it's a good thing the jury asked for a bodyguard," Cicero said.

The fifty-six jurymen, already seated, were surrounded by lictors in bronze helmets and short red cloaks, holding the bundles of sticks which were the symbols of their authority. They were watching the men behind the defendant's bench with steady eyes. "Nasty looking crowd, isn't it?" someone whispered in his ear. He looked up to see Caelius grinning at him. "Mind if I take a seat?" He winked and pulled back his toga to show the dagger he had thrust into his belt.

"Caelius, I don't want you here."

"It's just a precaution. I won't start anything. I just want to sit here quietly, minding my own business. May I?"

"If you behave yourself, you may sit with Tiro," Cicero said repressively. Caelius' grin widened and he raised his arm in mock salute. Cicero heard him a moment later, talking with Tiro on the bench behind him.

Across the way Clodius had come in and taken his place in a roar of cheering from his supporters. He bowed to them, and held up his fists like the victor in a boxing match, turning so everyone in the Forum could see the triumphant blaze of his handsome face.

"Look at him smirking over there," Hortensius said, and on his other side, Metellus bent forward stiffly from the waist and remarked, "Looks like a man who thinks he's going to win."

"It's astonishing that he's appeared today. You have to give him credit for courage."

"Insolence, more likely," Hortensius said sourly.

"It's a disgrace to the family, to have an exile in it," Metellus muttered. In spite of his granite quality, he looked shaken and upset; he really feels this personally, Cicero thought. He'll never forgive anyone for this.

"My dear Quintus Caecilius Metellus Celer," he said. "No one could blame a family as distinguished as yours for this. It might happen to anyone. Why even the Olympian gods have Mercury, who is nothing but a thief."

Metellus opened his hard, dark eyes; he might have been surprised to be addressed so familiarly. "That is so," he said stiffly. He seemed to be trying to smile. "But this is not the sort of experience I'm used to—to hear my wife's brother condemned to exile. I find it has actually upset my digestion." Perhaps it really had; Metellus' gray face was pale around the jawbone, and his eyes glittered.

The praetor was hammering on the table, calling the jury to order; over the unabated noise of the crowd, Curio stood up from the defense bench and shouted.

"What?" Metellus cried. "What's he say?"

Caelius leaned forward and said in Cicero ear, "He's announcing that the defense will call no further witnesses. Does that mean that he's giving up the case?"

"I see no point in further witnesses," Metellus agreed. "It would only prolong this disgraceful affair."

"No," said Cicero, laughing. "And anyway, the last one didn't do them much good."

Curio was still on his feet; the Forum was falling quiet to hear him. "That concludes the case for the defense, then."

The praetor glanced over at the prosecution bench; Hortensius, following his bald spot and his cloud of white hair upright, bowed and said loudly, "The prosecution is content with the case as it is. Anything to put it to a vote and get this farce over with as quickly as possible."

"Well, how's that for taking the opportunity to make an extra speech?" Cicero said, and Caelius laughed.

It was plain that Hortensius had not intended anything dishonest; he was simply angry. They could hear him as he sat down, speaking to a colleague. "How can any jury be expected to deliberate in an atmosphere like this?"

"Might as well be in the arena," Metellus agreed, nodding once, as if that were the ration of agreement the army allowed him.

The ballots were being handed out. It was so quiet now that Cicero could hear the spring breeze among the thin new leaves of the fig trees, and the creak of a windlass at some distant construction site. He smiled and stretched himself in the sun with a soft growl of pleasure, thinking that he was going to enjoy this moment. It was rare that justice could be so satisfyingly served. One of the jurymen was nodding to him, too. Someone who recognized him, who had voted for him, perhaps. He didn't know everyone who knew him. The Father of His Country.

The ballots had been collected; aediles, earnest young men for the most part, were counting them, their heads together as they whispered.

"What's the matter?" Metellus demanded loudly. "What's holding them up?"

"Some of the jury must have marked theirs illegibly or something like that," Cicero said. "There are always one or two."

Around them a murmur began, full of restless energy. He could hear men filling their lungs, shifting nervously on their feet. The aediles stood up and presented their tally to the praetor. Now the noise had grown; the praetor had to pound on the table. "Silence. Silence there."

Slowly the great open space grew quiet. The praetor picked up the tally. "Twenty-five votes for guilty, thirty-one, not guilty. The defendant, Publius Clodius Pulcher, is cleared of all charges. The jury is dismissed."

There was a moment of shocked silence, then a great roar of noise. Cicero, still bewildered, thought for a moment that a building had fallen down, an earthquake had opened the ground. There was even dust in the air, and pigeons were circling overhead.

Presently he saw that the noise came from the crowd. Men were stamping their feet, mouths open to shout, hands struck together. Louder and more violent the sound came, thrown back by the buildings like waves from a breakwater, crashing together over their heads. His ears began to ring.

Across the way Clodius had leaped to his feet, laughing into the commotion. His head was thrown back, his hair flew up from his forehead. He had raised his hand; on his finger his ring winked like an angry scarlet eye. His friends were drawing their swords; in their midst Clodius stood, ablaze with aggression. He caught sight of Cicero, still confused, standing among the senators; the small man glared into his eyes over the empty court; then, opening his carved lips, Clodius spat, very deliberately, on the ground in front of him. His friends moved, there was a swirl of motion, and he was gone.

The praetor had disappeared; so had the jury. Hortensius had climbed on his bench and was shaking his fist into the storm of sound. "What happened?" Metellus cried, stupefied, like Cicero, by the noise. "What happened?"

"Oh, Gods, can't you see?" Cicero cried, finding his voice at last. "We've lost the republic, that's what happened."

Caelius was worried. He kept his head down, but he was watching Cicero all the time through the gloom and dimness the lamps in the Curia did nothing to dispel. He was sitting in the first row of benches behind the special chairs set aside for dignitaries, the former consuls like Cicero, the priests, and—even more exalted— the censors. From time to time he glanced across the open space in the middle to the benches on the other two walls; once in a while he chewed nervously on his thumb. He did not like the way Cicero slumped in his chair.

The Curia was filling up. Metellus had come in and was standing very quietly in the aisle; Hortensius, the prosecutor, was marching quickly down the aisle to the empty seat on Cicero's other side. Caelius caught a glimpse of his friend's face; it was stormy with anger. "The jury was bribed," Hortensius said, without troubling to lower his voice. His white hair seemed to have detached itself entirely from his head in his indignation, and was drifting around it like a cloud around a mountaintop.

"Really?" Cicero glanced at Metellus' face, but the patrician was giving away no secrets. "It can't be. Clodius hasn't got money. His father made some unlucky investments; he left the children very badly off." He spoke with his usual cold contempt for the world, and Caelius, remembering how he must know, wondered suddenly if he had been deceived over his marriage settlement.

"It wasn't Clodius' money," Hortensius said. "He went to someone, I don't know who..."

Cicero had turned to Caelius, beckoning him forward. "See if you can find out."

"Yes, Marcus Cicero," Caelius said. leaping to his feet, relieved to be away. As he went, he heard Lutatius Catulus raising his voice to shout to a juryman, "What did you need a bodyguard for? Were you afraid of having your nice fat purses stolen?"

It took Caelius a long time to discharge his errand. He had wandered around, visiting the baths, which were nearly empty, and the bars, which were full, but unhelpful. He had tramped out to the Subura, a poor and lively district where the red-haired poet Valerius Catullus lived: he had great faith in Catullus, who knew everything that went on in the city, but this fountain of information had dried up— his friend was not at home. Finally he thought of another source—a man named Calvus, whom he had met while listening to some lectures at Crassus' house some years before, when they had both been students. Calvus had told him the answer, but it had all taken a couple of hours, and now in the Curia, Cicero was on his feet, addressing the Senate. Caelius sank onto a bench, frantic with impatience, hardly able to listen to the speech.

It was probably a good one, too—full of eloquent phrases and strong argument.

Anyway the senators were nodding in agreement. "But let me tell you," he was saying, and his voice rose; the rafters, dimly painted and hung with useless little lamps,
gave it back—"unless some god remembers us, our republic has been seized from our
hands by this trial. If you can call it a trial when thirty-one of the most worthless
villains in Rome have torn down all of the law and of justice for money, and a
handful of criminals has sworn that a thing did not happen which every man, every
beast in the fields, knows for a fact is true."

Not bad considering how few of the facts he actually had. The Senate was leaning forward now, the whole hall was open like an ear to hear him.

"Yet we must not let ourselves be ruined by a single blow, though the wound
cannot be disguised," he cried, and in the back someone groaned as though he felt
the sword in his own body. The senators swayed, and one or two looked ill. "Still,
this wound must not be feared, for fear may lead us into cowardice. Nor should we
ignore it, for that may lead us to act in blind folly..."

There was a disturbance at the back. Publius Clodius and four of his friends
were pushing their way in from among the spectators in the lobby, shoving aside
the aediles at the door. Nothing could make him ungraceful. Even with his arm outstretched to shove the confused young magistrate away, even with his face distorted by his anger, he was as beautiful as an arrow in flight. "Just a moment there, just
a moment," one of the consuls was shouting. He had stood up so suddenly that his
chair had fallen over and was knocking against the benches. "Throw him out,"
Metellus shouted. Someone was calling for the lictors.

"No," said Cicero from down in front where he had come out to peer into the
gloom by the door. He seemed not to have raised his voice, but the hall fell silent
immediately. Even Clodius paused where he stood, poised on one foot, the arrow
arrested in midair. "Let him come forward," Cicero said, smiling. "I have something
to say to him."

Very deliberately Clodius set down his foot; his hands were on his hips and his
head was back. "I'll stay here." His carved mouth was curled in contempt, his body
seemed to crackle with it. He was not afraid; his scorn travelled the distance
between them that he would not go, but Cicero did not seem to see it.

"You are mistaken if you think your acquittal means anything, Clodius," Cicero
said. He had lifted his own head, and his wedge of a nose seemed to sniff the air.
"The jury saved you all right, but not for the public career you hoped for—they
saved you for an even more public disgrace." His voice lowered to a growl on the
last word. "Your turn will come."

"A public disgrace?" Color had come into Clodius' face, making scarlet patches on his white skin, as if he had been slapped. "Are you joking? Who are you to
talk? Call yourself Father of the Country? You spend all your time at the resorts,
pretending to be a patrician..."

"One would think," Cicero said, and in the gloom his eyes twinkled, "that you
were accusing me of spending my time in the bars, pretending to be a plebeian."

A snicker passed through the rows of senators, and Clodius' men moved closer to their leader.

"You bought an expensive house," Clodius cried. "Where did a man like you get the money? Make a joke of that if you can."

"Ah, Clodius," Cicero said, laughing. He was timing his pause. "You seem to think buying a house is like buying a jury."

This time the Senate's reaction was open and prolonged. Some of the senators clapped, all of them laughed. Clodius had gone pale again, and he took a step forward, thrusting back his toga. His hand had begun to move toward the knife. Caelius found himself on his feet, starting down the aisle. "No," Hortensius said, shooting out his arm and pulling him back. "He'll take care of it. See?"

And indeed, Cicero was leaning forward, his heavy shoulders in an easy slouch, his eyes on the angry figure of Clodius, whose friends were trying to lead him away. But Clodius was shrugging them off. "The jury? You'd better not mention them. They gave no credit whatever to your testimony, even under oath."

"Twenty-five of them did. And thirty-one of them gave you so little credit they demanded their money in advance."

A thunderclap of laughter shook the building. Even the crowd in the lobby was roaring with it. The aisles were jammed with senators, all shouting and shoving, but Caelius could see, over their heads, Clodius being led away, his white face still turned toward Cicero, his mouth still working, though no sound came out of it. What he could hear instead, very distantly under the noise in the hall, was Cicero, down in front, chuckling to himself.

"It was Crassus," Caelius said when he could get near Cicero. That was not until quite a long time later. The Senate had been furious with indignation—there had been proposals and a vote. There was nothing they could do to Clodius, but his most active supporter Piso, one of the consuls, had been deprived of the governorship of the rich province of Syria. That was some help, at least.

So he has roused the Senate, Caelius thought, proud of his old teacher. He can make people do anything; he has only to open his mouth.

After the meeting the senators had all crowded around Cicero, repeating his jokes to him as if they thought he might not have heard them, and laughing at them again. Cicero had been in no hurry to shake them off, either. Caelius, looking at him with worry and with love, thought that he understood why not. They were the old families, the descendants of heroes and demigods; he had worshiped them as a boy. Caelius knew how he felt: before he had come to Rome he had made his offerings at that shrine himself.

The trouble was, Cicero still did. He had never seen that they were not much, these men. Lazy, self-centered, pompous, proud... But to Cicero they were still the founders of the Republic, the great men of Rome. They were what he had come to Rome to be, why he had entered first the law-courts, then politics. He lived for their praise and affection, their support was what he had risked his life to keep. Now he was one of them. No wonder Clodius' sting had not gone home: Cicero did not care about the mansion, the money, even the titles, or not for themselves, anyway. What he loved was this, the affection of these very ordinary men. He could not live without it. He was bowing and turning, grinning at his friends like a dancing bear at a street festival. His fine, deep, thoughtful eyes were warm with pleasure; his laugh rumbled out as innocent and happy as a boy's.

So Caelius had not liked to disturb him, though he himself was suffering from a series of complicated emotions that made him twitch with impatience. He hung back on the outside of the crowd, confident that his height announced him. But it was not until they were strolling through the long afternoon shadows in the Forum that he was able to tell Cicero what he had found out.

"It was Crassus. I found the man he used to help him—his name is Licinius Calvus. They did it last night, Calvus says, together with one slave and an ex-gladiator who has served his term in the arena and been discharged. I could find out his name if you want me to."

Cicero waved this away. "What exactly did they do?"

"Calvus says he and the gladiator went around to the jurors and got most of them to go to Crassus' house. There was a sort of party there, with tables of food and drink, and trays of money. He had hired most of the women in the city, at least the best-looking and most expensive ones. Calvus says he was sorry he wasn't at the party himself, but he was out rounding up the stragglers."

"I see. I'm sorry I wasn't invited myself."

"No, you're not," Caelius said, wondering why even at this point Cicero was making jokes. "You don't go to parties like that."

"No, I don't."

"There were even promises of introductions to boys of good family, too, and the gods know what else besides. Crassus pointed out to the waverers that even being at the party was proof of dishonor, so they might as well take what was offered. It went on all night."

"Infamous. And Crassus was once a consul himself."

There did not seem to be anything Caelius could do to help him with that, so they walked on in silence for a while. Presently Cicero lifted his head like an old animal hearing a challenge to his territory. "Well, at least I've repaired some of the damage. After that scene in the Senate I don't think we'll hear much from Clodius for a long time."

"No," said Caelius because Cicero seemed so sad. But he could not prevent a shudder from passing over him as he walked, which he hoped Cicero did not notice. He did not want to tell him that the danger was greater than ever, now that Clodius had acquired such a powerful friend. Nor did he want to mention that as the small man had been led out of the Senate, he, Caelius, had seen what Cicero had not. The press of bodies in the aisle had parted for a moment, and over the heads of the crowd he had caught a glimpse of the look in Clodius' eyes.

BOOK TWO

IV

Over the next few days it became clear to Caelius that it was his duty to tell Cicero about that look. There were peculiar disturbances in the city, moments at parties, or in the bars he and his friends went to afterwards, when silences fell, and people looked at each other while the whole city seemed to catch its breath around them. Often, at such times, one or two men would come in—certain aristocrats of bad reputation to the parties, certain freedmen or plebeians to the bars. Everyone would look away, and the talk would resume. It was possible to imagine that nothing much had happened. Indeed, for some time Caelius told himself that nothing had.

But there were other indications. Someone was chalking slogans on the walls. No one saw them appear, but every morning the new sun would pick them out, washing their obscenities in clear, strong light that made them look even worse than the words intended. Many of them were just vague spewings of rage, directed at the city or the Senate, but a large number of them mentioned Cicero by name. Some of them claimed that Clodius was the only hope of the plebeians against these enemies. "Nonsense," Cicero said when Caelius finally grew uneasy enough to tell him. "I'm not the enemy of the plebeians, and they know it. You saw how they behaved at the trial, how they supported me. Why they rushed to join the knights and the patricians when they came to my defense. It's always been like that. This is the work of a few—a very few—malcontents. Don't let it bother you."

Caelius tried, but he could not help it. Groups of men began to appear in the public squares, hard little knots that did not dissolve in the stream of the city's life. Ten or twenty of them would spend all afternoon leaning against walls at busy street corners, forcing pedestrians to eddy around them, a dozen or more together circulated in the Forum, watching the crowds; more clustered by the temple of Castor where they jeered and called to the rich men going up and down the Palatine Steps to their mansions at the top. Hortensius Hortalus, the prosecutor of Clodius, added five sturdy-looking slaves armed with clubs to the retinue that followed him every morning into the Forum; Lutatius Catulus, the leader of the Senate's conservatives and the man who had made the joke about stolen purses, never went out now with fewer than twelve.

"You ought to have some too," Caelius said, mentioning this with considerable urgency to Cicero in his study one afternoon. They had just come up from a meeting in the Curia, and had passed the mob around the Temple of Castor.

"Don't be silly. Tiro, have you seen the letter to Pompey I was writing? I've mislaid it somewhere."

"Really. Couldn't you at least bring some men down from one of your farms?"

"A good idea," Tiro muttered, holding up the letter. "It would make life much easier around here."

"Thank you. What do you mean, easier?"

Tiro turned his rough head away. His hair caught a shaft of sunlight slanting through the shutter of the study and glowed like straw.

"I didn't want to bother you. It's just that it's hard to get anyone to do errands. There are always men waiting around the door."

"There are things written on your walls, too," Caelius said. "Tiro has men out there cleaning them off practically every morning before you get up."

"I see," Cicero said. Still, a bodyguard seemed to him a silly and over-dramatic reaction, the kind of thing that people would talk about in the city, too. "You don't want them to think I'm afraid."

"Probably you ought to be," Caelius said, but Cicero laughed and shrugged his heavy shoulders. "Really? Afraid of Clodius? I?"

All the same he yielded to their pressure to the extent of making sure that he had more than the usual number of friends with him when he went down to the Forum, and to guard the house he bought a dog. It was a Molossian, bandy-legged and strong-jawed, and it was, like all the best guard-dogs, entirely black. It was kept chained beside the doorkeeper, to the uneasiness of that poor old man, and it growled alarmingly through the bars of the gate if anyone went by on the street.

"There," said Cicero. "That ought to be sufficient. If it's all right with you gentlemen, could we please stop worrying about nothing and get back to work?"

It was Pompey he was thinking of, and he was still thinking about him two nights later as he padded through his sleeping house. He supposed he ought to mend whatever fences the trial had blown down between them. He did not know what Pompey had promised Clodius, if anything, nor could he guess how much Pompey might mind the ruin of a man to whom, after all, he owed a debt. It might not matter that it was very slight compared to what Cicero himself had done for him. Clodius had made speeches to the army on Pompey's behalf. That was still a favor owed, and Pompey was too intelligent to neglect what was after all the currency of Roman politics. He supposed that he ought to make some sort of gesture to Pompey to show that they were still friends.

His house distracted him, his beautiful house. He had built it with the help of loans and gifts from his friends after his consulship, for though some of them had offered, he would not have dreamed of taking money while he was in office. The house was the sign and symbol of his success; it might have belonged to a family ennobled, not as he was by his own efforts, but by centuries of dignities, and of taste. The passion for building had come on him late in his life, but it was all the stronger for that. He had houses now in Rome, at Formiae, in Arpinum, at Tusculum—eight in all. None was as beautiful as this. In the atrium marble nymphs watched him from the shadows, their stone eyes alive in the dark; the mosaic floor of the colonnade around the garden whispered to his feet; the fountain arched its neck and tossed the white plumes of water toward the dusty raveling of stars above. He stood under the crisp fluting of a column and looked out over the garden toward the back of the house; for a moment he thought the walls had dissolved and he could see his wife asleep in her bedroom, his five-year-old son turning over and opening his lips. A pearly bubble of froth broke on them, and the little boy sighed. His daughter... But Tullia was gone now, had been gone a year, had never lived in this house. She was grown up, fourteen years old, and married. If he had known how much he would miss her he would never have arranged the match. In her room his wife Terentia clenched her fists and struggled with a dream.

He called his mind back to his work. To Pompey. Even now he could not plan what to do about Pompey. It was the past and not the future that held him. The tossing plumes of the fountain, like fine horses... He remembered the day he met Pompey.

He was sixteen, fresh from the little mountain town of Arpinum where he had been born, a solitary boy with a thin voice and a nervous stomach; he was sitting in a wagon, rumbling over the hillsides of Northern Italy, looking for a war. Behind him in the carts were all his past, and what he thought would be his future: chests stuffed with books, and a small cedarwood casket with a hundred lines of an epic poem he was working on all about wars and heroes.

On his marble bench now, he bent to smile at his sixteen-year-old self. A poet. He had never been anywhere but the schoolroom in Arpinum and the olive groves below the small hill-town; he had never known anyone but his parents and his teachers and his younger brother Quintus, but he was going to be a poet.

The cart trundled along the tracks of the northern countryside; at the top of the hill he reined in the mules and searched the valley for a camp. There was nothing below but farmsteads and cypresses and the gentle amble of the road up and down, across country to the blue-white smudge of the Alps on the edge of the sky. Behind his wagon, his horse—the town council of Arpinum had provided one in accordance with the law, since the Ciceros were knights—threw up his head and called. The mules flicked their tall ears. Over the amber hillside a boy was riding, barebacked and barefooted, in a scarlet tunic that blew like a trumpet call against the sky. His bronze hair floated over his head, his blue eyes raked Cicero like a handful of pebbles. The horses called again, and the blue-eyed boy kicked his own mount into a canter. From behind the hilltop a dozen more riders appeared, shouting in answer.

The cavalcade swept down the hill, the boy in the lead. The mules, uneasy, backed and tossed; Cicero had to hold them, so that when the boy arrived in a drumbeat of hooves he was sweating like a farmer and muttering in dialect to his beasts.

"Are you Marcus Tullius Cicero?" the boy asked.

"Yes."

The boy turned and said something to his troop. They were all grown men, bearded and heavily muscled, but they listened to him.

"You're from Arpinum, aren't you? I was born in Picenum." There was reserve in the boy's voice and the heavy-lidded eyes looked oddly blank. —

Cicero said nothing, but he was glad this boy was a provincial like himself. Picenum was bad enough—a big district, and rather important, while Arpinum was only a village. But if it had been Rome…

"They told me you were coming," the boy said. "You're very brilliant, aren't you? Marius, here, says that in your town the fathers of the other boys come down to the school to hear you recite your lessons. Is that true?"

A dark soldier said, "They say they do it so they can tell their grandchildren that they heard Marcus Cicero when he was still a boy."

He knew the man: it was indeed Marius, who was a distant cousin of his, so there was no use denying it. He hated it, though—the other boys had not liked to hear their fathers compare them to him. He had hoped that when he left Arpinum he might leave this all behind. "Yes," he said, and his voice squeaked embarrassingly.

The boy was walking his horse around the wagon, looking at it with what seemed to Cicero to be the blankest contempt. When he came to the town council's horse he shook his head and said something under his breath to one of his men. Cicero sat on the bench of the wagon, staring between the ears of the mules. "I'm Gnaeus Pompey," the boy said suddenly behind him, so that he jumped. "My father is the general Gnaeus Pompeius Strabo; he's in charge of this sector. I lead a century of cavalry myself, and you're in it."

"Oh," said Cicero. "How could…?" He meant to ask how a boy of sixteen or so, for that was what he plainly was, could command a hundred men, but he could see that the question would not be welcome. Besides, he thought doubtfully, perhaps this boy could.

He could hear noises from the back of the wagon: Pompey was directing a servant to pull back the canvas. "What's in these boxes?"

"Books."

"What do you want books on campaign for? Don't you know we're at war?"

Cicero looped the reins around the whip handle and stood up in the wagon to look at Pompey. It was the first close look he had had at him.

The boy was beautiful, and angry, like an autumn morning with the frost on it. He was everything a Roman ought to be—tall, upright, strong. There was no need to ask why he commanded a century of cavalry; his genius sat on his shoulder like a god's familiar, and they both stared back at Cicero with all the glory of their future in their eyes. "I'm going to be a poet. I need the books."

"Well, what do you want to come here for then? We're fighting men."

A sea-wave of anger broke over him, nearly knocking him off his feet. He was a Roman citizen, wasn't he? He had a duty—and a right—to defend his country. Did they think that because he was a scholar he was a coward? Or that because he came from Arpinum he was not a real Roman? But he was very conscious that beside this boy he made a poor showing: he was thin and stoop-chested, and his voice was liable to crack.

There was hostility in the faces of the boy's troop, too. He could see them waiting for him to say something foolish. Perhaps they hoped he would turn tail and run. He saw himself for a moment doing exactly that. Well, he would show them that he was as Roman as they were. He said steadily, "I am the son of a Roman knight. I have an obligation to be here." He saw them nod, understanding this, and perhaps accepting the dignity of his rebuke, but he was not finished with them yet. "You know, poets have to know about war, as much as soldiers do. It's their job, too."

"Why?" Pompey asked.

"They write about fighting men, after all." He let his eyes move noticeably over the handsome boy. "That's why I'm here. And perhaps you won't always think it's such a bad thing." He smiled at the soldiers. "Perhaps Achilles here has met his Homer."

All his life he had been unable to resist a joke; this one wasn't much, but it worked. The men laughed, again, this time with a good-natured sound, and the boy Pompey laughed with them. He reined his horse around and cantered out in front of his men, lifting his arm for Cicero to follow. "When we get back to the camp," he called back, but in a friendly way, "see to it that you get a better horse."

That was Pompey. Of course, Cicero did not serve under him, that was just youthful boasting. He had his appointment on the staff of Pompey's father, like three or four other well connected young knights and aristocrats. All the same he saw a lot of Pompey. He liked him—he supposed now that it was truer to say that he had come to love him.

They were often together on the various duties around the camp, running errands for Pompey's father, in the mess, on patrol. Once, at night, they lay in a bed of reeds at the edge of a river waiting for a troop of enemy soldiers to appear on the road over their heads: they passed the time whispering to one another the secrets boys long to tell someone—he couldn't remember now just what those had been. Boasts about women, he supposed, or even confessions of inexperience. He remembered Pompey saying, "I mean, they seem so different from us, don't they? I... I'm afraid I won't be able to..." "To what?" he had said in a voice that was hoarse only partly because of the river damp, and Pompey had answered shyly, "To talk to them." "Oh, yes, I know," he had breathed, relieved beyond measure not to have to think further than that. What was even better was that he had known that Pompey felt the same.

Several times they had been in scrapes together, going away from the camp when they were not supposed to and wandering in the hills, or the pacified towns—earning incidentally the waspish condemnation of Pompey's harsh-tempered father. Still, in spite of the humiliation of these remarks, and more strongly, in spite of his constant desire to be well thought of, Cicero had never wanted to give up those in truth very innocent excursions. Pompey too had loved them: the blazing boy seemed to seek out Cicero; he was always in his company that year. He asked Cicero about his reading, he argued with him about philosophy—the boy was well educated in the usual curriculum and had a surprising taste for intellectual pleasures. He talked of politics: it was a bond between them that they were not patricians and not born in Rome; Pompey's father was a New Man as they were called in the city, and it was not a compliment. "We'll make them swallow that," Pompey had sworn more than once, and he had answered, "Yes, the two of us," for it was his ambition to be a New Man himself. Pompey had smiled his incandescent grin.

Oh, they were good friends. Pompey even asked to hear a little of the epic poem, but this was not such a success. Pompey listened without comment; his eyes had gone a peculiar flat blue, as if they had no shine or reflection. "Oh, that's very good, Marcus, as good as Homer," he had said when Cicero had finished, and Cicero had always been grateful to him for that—though of course he had not quite believed him. For several days whenever they met, Pompey praised the poem and asked after its progress; Cicero, for his part, was glad his friend admired it, but all the same, very soon he ceased to work on it, putting it away in its cedarwood casket for what turned out to be a permanent rest. Years later it occurred to him that the poem might already have served the purpose he had designed it for.

So he came to love the bronze-haired boy. There was no question that he was lovable, and he was admirable as well—particularly his very Roman austerity and simplicity, which were famous. Pompey—unlike most men of his class—cared nothing for luxuries; he was known to be able to go all day on nothing but a bowl of gruel in the morning and a cup of wine and some bread at night; he slept on the ground like his men, and absented himself from his father's elaborate feasts and lavishly furnished tent; he gave away his share of the loot to his soldiers.

His success was as well deserved as it was rapid. At eighteen Pompey won a battle for his father, while Cicero, military service finished, was in Rome, sitting at the feet of the two famous jurists, the Scaevolas, father and son, learning civil law. At twenty-three, Pompey had defeated the rebellious general Carbo in Spain, and King Iarbas in North Africa. He celebrated a triumph for that, though it was illegal, for Pompey was only a knight. Besides, he was under age. Still, the Senate had given in to pressure, and recognized the young general's brilliance.

That was the year Cicero had his first case, and it caused him some burning in his heart to reflect on their differences at that stage of their lives: Pompey, famous and admired, riding through Rome in a gilded chariot with his army singing at his back and a slave to remind him that he would not live forever; Cicero defending a nobody in an anonymous dispute about a will—to an empty Forum, too. No one had to remind Cicero that day that he was mortal. He slept badly, wrestling with his envy and humiliation; he had always considered it one of the victories of his life that he was great-souled enough to win that battle.

And in time he had his own successes. Finally. In the days when Sulla the dictator had smothered Rome under a blanket of terror, Cicero's moment arrived. No one had stood up to Sulla, no one had dared; if they thought to do it, there were two thousand heads of his opponents on poles in the Forum to remind them that prudence was a virtue. Even Pompey, magnificent Pompey, had led his legions into war in support of the new order; Sulla gave him the name "The Great" for that. Pompey the Great. But one night, late, there had been a knock at Cicero's door...

He stretched himself on the bench, feeling old. His joints seemed to have frozen to the marble, too. The fountain glittered now; the water had turned into sparkling foam, blown over the long black shadows that washed the lawn. The moon was up, gliding past the cobbled roofs on the opposite side of the house. From somewhere notes of music dripped, plangent and serene, into the quiet. Stiffly he got to his feet and went in search of it.

Under the white cloud of an almond tree in flower he found it. Old Diodotus, his teacher, with a cithera in his lap, was touching a spray of sound from the instrument. Cicero stood under the colonnade, listening, the sweet almond blossom in his nostrils. Presently the old man lifted his head and stared blindly in his direction.

"Who's there?"

"Cicero. What are you doing up so late? Are you all right?"

"Yes, fine."

"Do you want anything? Some wine, a little food?"

"No, thank you. Everything's fine. You are kind to think of it." The notes again. A few petals had fallen on the old Greek's head. "What time is it?"

"The sixth hour, something like that." He sat down on the bench opposite Diodotus.

"Did the noise wake you?" Diodotus touched the lyre-like instrument and it gave its note again, but he did not mean the music.

Another voice, sleepy and querulous, said, "Crassus' party, across the street, do you mean? It certainly did."

It was Tiro, his secretary, yawning under the doorway, rough and twisted as a young apple tree, with a thatch of dark hair and furrowed skin, like bark. "Another one. How can he hope to get any business done in the morning if he's up to all hours with parties the night before?"

Now that they mentioned it he could hear something; it didn't sound like a party, though—more like people gathering in the street. "He does business at those parties."

"So he does. What are you doing up? It's late for you." Tiro had been born in Cicero's household; he treated his master like an old friend, easily, and with a kind of loving contempt, as a wife might a husband whose life she shared, but whose weaknesses were apparent to her.

Diodotus smiled and played a little more. The quiet lapped at their feet, the moon sailed above on the currents of the cool night sky.

"I've been thinking about the Roscius case," Cicero said.

Diodotus smiled at his sightless memories and touched a chord. "I was proud of you. Not everyone would have taken it on."

"Well," Cicero said, genuinely entertained. "I didn't have much choice. My waiting room wasn't exactly full, you know."

"It was empty," Diodotus told Tiro, who was too young to remember. "He was just starting out, a new lawyer, like hundreds of others." He rippled the notes out again. "But all the others refused."

Roscius was a victim of Sulla's persecution, a man robbed and humiliated by the dictator's henchmen and brought to trial on a trumped up charge when his protests became embarrassing. Cicero had had to make his first important speech under all those putrefying heads. He had the impression that those dead, abused, insulted eyes were watching him, those mouths, caked with black blood and flies, open to urge him on. Among them was Scaevola, his own teacher, one of the first to go, though he could not tell which head had been his—

He had been so sick the Forum had turned around him, the ground heaved and buckled under his trembling legs. "Well," he said, "at least I won."

"You won brilliantly."

"I scraped by. I didn't get much for poor old Roscius, but I did manage to save his life; I suppose anyone could have done it."

"It made him famous," Diodotus informed Tiro. "He became, in people's minds, a kind of unelected tribune—a spokesman for the rights of the dispossessed and unrepresented citizens. You should have seen it. He was mobbed everywhere he went, his house was jammed with well-wishers. There were dozens, perhaps hundreds, of men who asked him to take cases for them. He could have had his pick."

"It was terrible," Cicero said, laughing. "I had to leave town."

"I thought you wanted to be famous," Tiro said.

"It wasn't that," Diodotus explained. "He had to get out of the way of Sulla's anger."

"Yes," said Cicero. "I told people I was travelling for my health."

Tiro was laughing like a drainpipe, but all the same there had been a germ of truth in it. Cicero had gone to Greece, to the rhetoricians and the gymnastic trainers. He knew by then what his destiny demanded of him. He was not, after all, to sing of other men's triumphs, but to have victories of his own. He needed to be prepared. There, in the dusty agoras and palaestras, he let them make him what he had to be. They taught him philosophy, argument, technique; they put him on special diets for his stomach, and regimes of exercise for the weakness of his chest. He had gone so far as to hire actors to train his voice. The life had pleased him so much he had thought of staying. But there were letters from home, people who begged for him, needed him. His brother, his now elderly father, his friends and their clients. Even Pompey, who had changed sides and turned against his old protector Sulla. He had written too. A very civil letter.

"Because Sulla's power was on the wane," Diodotus said.

"Oh, no," Cicero said. "Pompey isn't like that. He just came to understand what harm Sulla was doing to the republic, and naturally he couldn't support him any longer. He's a little slow perhaps—and don't forget, he had been away from Rome with the army, so he may not have realized—"

Diodotus gave a small snort.

"No," said Cicero, answering what it implied. "Pompey's a good man at heart."

He knew he was right. Look what Pompey had done for the city since. Pompey the Great. It may have been a political title, but he had lived up to it since. He had fought the city's wars, settled colonies, made treaties, collected tribute. Rome would not be what it was today without him. They said that his conquests in the East had added twelve million people to the empire, and doubled the size of the Treasury.

"It wouldn't be the same without you, either," Tiro said, twisting out his arms like branches and yawning.

It was true that he had done something for his country. Perhaps in its way, it had been nearly as much. He had been able to because of the Roscius case. Impoverished, ruined as he was, poor old Roscius had given him a great gift.

He had come back to a city completely transformed. Sulla was gone, dead of a disease so horrible it was like the vengeance of a god, with maggots in his bowels and the stink of his own rotting flesh in his nose. The Forum was clean again, the poles taken down, the lists of the proscribed burned in a cleansing fire. And Cicero had found himself a hero. Nothing was too good for him: when he ran for office— which he did as soon as he was eligible—he was elected overwhelmingly, even against men with money and famous names to help them. When he pleaded a case, he was listened to with rapt attention, and his causes won. When he was ready to marry he was able to ask for the daughter of an outstandingly patrician house, a half-sister of the Fabians, with a fortune of her own. His reputation grew. He was no longer troubled by illness; he had become confident, and his work was a joy to him. He did not envy Pompey now, though he still admired him. He supposed that after he was elected consul he did not envy any man in the world.

The noise from the front of the house was louder; it could not be ignored. Thumps, crashes, running feet, the dog, barking loudly enough to wake the whole street. Tiro had leaped up; Diodotus was holding the cithera to his chest as if he thought he might have to protect it. Cicero lumbered to his feet and started after Tiro.

Going through the house was like plunging into cold water; the darkness was absolute after the silvery wash of light outside, and the air was frigid and still. There was silence now, the commotion from outside had either abated or was too weak to penetrate here. In the atrium a ghost of light fell on the pool; the eyes of statues looked out of the gloom, glittering. Someone was shouting out by the street.

It was the doorkeeper, his mouth open, a clamor coming from him louder than anyone would suppose such an elderly creature could make.

"What is it?" Tiro demanded, shaking the frail old man to make sense of his noise. Cicero gave them a glance and lumbered past them to the gate. There on the ground the black shape of the dog lay stretched out on the stones, twitching and straining on the end of its chain, as if it were asleep.

"Agh," Tiro cried, coming up beside him and looking down. He clapped his hand over his mouth and bent away into the shadows, while the old doorkeeper wrung his hands and sobbed.

Cicero knelt down and touched the matted fur. It was warm, and his hand came away from it wet and sticky; his fingers looked black in the moonlight. "Hercules."

The dog seemed to hear him. Giving a convulsive start, it slid forward. The head remained where it had been, the teeth still bared in a grin of rage, the eyes still rimmed with white, but the neck was no longer joined to the body. It slid away separately over the stones, the nails making a little clicking noise, leaving a trail of darkness after it.

"Tiro." Cicero rubbed his hand on his toga. "Get someone to clear this up. I don't want my little boy to see it. Or my wife."

"Yes, sir." Tiro's lips were as pale as his skin, and he sweated in the cold moonlight. The doorkeeper blubbered in the corner, unintelligible except for his fear.

"Poor dog," Cicero said.

"Thank the gods it wasn't one of us." Tiro shot a glance at the doorkeeper.

"It won't be," Cicero said angrily. "I'll see to that."

V

The road was crowded. Wagons rumbled over the stones, pedestrians jammed the verges. It looked like a market day, or a festival, except that everyone was going out of the city instead of into it; perhaps the rumors were right and the whole of Rome was migrating to Pompey. Pompey the Great. Cicero supposed that he had seen such things, during a war, when people left their homes to walk along the highway with their possessions on their backs. A depressing thought; perhaps the dog was still bothering him. And these people were enjoying themselves, they were all dressed in their best clothes. Well, he thought, twitching his large nose appreciatively, I am overdressed too.

They had left the highway and were travelling among the hills. And here were the gates to Pompey's estate. People were camped in front of them; it looked like an army, with tents and cooking fires, though it was not laid out like an army camp in regular streets and squares, but in a ragged huddle of canvas and mud and crowds. The mob was thicker at the gates, jammed against the wrought-iron grilles. His servants gave his name, and he was through, the horse trotting briskly up the road to the house. For the first time he noticed that there were birds in the sky, long strings and clouds of them, migrating north. A line of cypresses stretched out on either side of the road, and tiny yellow flowers powdered the grass. It was not spring yet, but it would be; it was a promise in the birdsong and the softness of the air.

He could see the mansion ahead, a long, wide-winged villa, two stories high; a double row of columns, one above the other, grinned across the first tender green of the hill. It was painted a rich, earthy yellow, except for the white columns and a line of statues along the roof. "Why, Pompey lives in a golden house," he said aloud, and the branches of the cypresses clucked at him in the breeze.

The entry was empty, except for the servant who showed him in. Black and white marble squares, a single statue—an athlete, very fine, tying his sandal. A Polyclitus, a genuine Polyclitus, he thought, glancing quickly to see if a copyist had left a signature. There was none. An original, then—well, the quality of the work alone had told him that. Pompey had bought only the best, out there in the East.

The servant was saying, "Right this way, Marcus Tullius Cicero. He's expecting you," and hurrying him through the beautiful space. He could see, quickly, out of the corner of his eye, room after empty room, as lovely and spare as the entry. The servant stopped before double doors, citron-wood and carved with acanthus leaves in recessed panels. They must have come from a temple somewhere. Loot, he supposed. Could a city have given them to Pompey as a gift? "Marcus Tullius Cicero, my lord," the servant cried as he heaved them open. My lord? Well, no matter, the doors were beautiful. He ran his hand along the smoothness of the wood as he went in.

His first thought was that he was in a cave; then that it must be a tent. The light was dim, fretted through silver and gold, swallowed by deep carpets of maroon and cream worked in designs that seemed to move underfoot; folds of cloth hung from a point high overhead, breathing softly in the gloom as the door closed behind him. The smell of incense floated cloyingly, everywhere, like the smell in a temple. There wasn't a good right angle anywhere in the room; everything was sinuous, draped, hidden. It was hot, too. For a moment he was visited by the impression that the curtains and the soft rugs exhaled the scent and the heat.

It was so dark he could not see anyone, and there was no furniture to guide him, only heaps and stacks of cushions in a gleaming fabric that he did not recognize. There was gold woven into it.

"Marcus," a deep voice said out of the shadows near the back. "Come closer. I want to take a look at you."

He knew the voice, lazy, resonant, careless. It belonged to the bronze-haired boy with the broad forehead and the bold blue eyes that had reminded people of Alexander the Great; he had heard it call confidently over a hilltop when they had both been sixteen; he had heard it whisper among the sighing reeds and the secret chuckle of a river; later it had risen, a little thick with wine, over dinner tables, or in cheerful harangue in the Forum. He knew it as well as his own.

"Gnaeus," he cried, happy to be in his company again. Suddenly he felt young again himself.

"Come closer. It's been a long time."

Down at the end of the room a figure lay stretched on its side on the cushions; he thought it was a statue, a colossus, in the dim light of the pierced lanterns. It lifted its huge bronze head.

"Hello, Marcus," Pompey said.

The blue eyes looked out of folded eyelids, the cheeks were fat, the lips thick. The vast body—surely larger than any purely human shape—heaved and lumped its way into the aromatic shadows. Gnaeus Pompeius Magnus. Pompey the Great. Pompey the Huge was more like it. Appalled, Cicero stared at the shining face, round and red and sweating, like the sun. "Gnaeus?"

"Take a seat," Pompey said. "They're more comfortable than they look. I got them out in Asia."

Comfortable. Well, they were, surprisingly so, but was that any way for a Roman general to talk? Comfortable. Pompey, who had once been famous for his austerity. He couldn't believe it. The bright, shallow eyes blinked at him through the yellow light, and the meaty red hand reached out and took a handful of stuffed figs from a tray in front of him. He gazed at his visitor expectantly.

"Gnaeus, I... I wanted to see you. It's been such a long time."

"That's true We have a lot of business to discuss."

"Business?" He had thought they might talk about the old days, the night in the mud by the riverbank, the afternoon on the thyme-scented hillside when Pompey had brought down a blackbird with a single stone, the days in the camp, his father's rages... But it was plain that Pompey had no time for these memories. He was looking at Cicero expressionlessly from under his thick eyelashes, and his huge fingers were drumming on the table in front of him.

"You wanted...?"

Shocked by this brusqueness, Cicero hunted in his mind for something to say.

"Congratulations on your victory," he said, arriving at sincerity. "It's a wonderful thing. All Rome is in your debt."

"It was nothing." Pompey spoke modestly enough, but his lazy voice tasted the words, and Cicero could see they were as sweet in his mouth as the figs.

"No, that's not true. It was splendid. And I believe the Senate will vote you a triumph for it—which you deserve, my friend. Which you deserve."

"You believe?"

"Well, you know what the Senate is."

"Yes, I suppose so." Pompey seemed to have lost interest in the triumph. "Well. Tell me the news from the city. What's been happening since I've been gone?"

"Don't you know? I mean, didn't people write? I sent you a description of my consulship."

"Oh. Oh, yes. So you did." Pompey took another fig and chewed it thoroughly. It made a lump in his cheek which he had to talk around. "Quite an honor for you, Marcus. Voted a service of thanksgiving, and the Father of Your Country, too. That's almost as good as a triumph. Almost." Was he jealous? Cicero wondered. No. It was impossible. He smiled at Pompey. "And now there's a problem. This business with Publius Clodius Pulcher..."

Pompey was searching the bowl, probing it with a finger as thick around as a child's wrist. There was only one more fig. "I need land for my men."

"Yes, I know. I've been trying—" Perhaps in Asia Pompey had gotten into the habit of talking with a soldier's bluntness. But this was Rome, not the plains of Bithynia. Perhaps he didn't quite realize that yet.

"I promised my men a bonus. Out there in Asia. I said I'd give them a share of the loot. You always do that. Your men expect it. It's one of the things they enlist for."

"Yes. I suppose it must be."

"Morale was so bad when I went out there, I had to promise them more. I said I'd see to it that when the war was over they'd each get a little plot of land to farm."

"That was a long time ago, when you went out there. Perhaps with the loot they have now, they don't expect more?"

"They expect it. I had to promise them again when I got them to go home."

Somehow Cicero doubted this. Surely all he had to do was tell them they were discharged? Pompey was their general, after all. But he knew nothing about armies himself, and Pompey knew all there was to know. No doubt it was just as he said. He pressed his fingers against his closed eyelids, and the lights behind his eyes made patterns like the rugs.

"Come on, Marcus," Pompey said impatiently. "The Senate's rewarded successful armies with grants of land before."

Not a hundred and twenty thousand men, Cicero thought, but aloud all he said was, "I understand. And I've been doing my best for you with that. Again, however, it's very difficult. I do have some influence—considerable influence—since my consulship, but it would help if you took a more active part—made some speeches, for instance. We could arrange for meetings to be held outside the walls."

"You take care of it." Pompey took another handful of sweets—apricots in honey this time—and chewed hastily. His flat, pale tongue came out and licked the honey from his lips.

"All the same I wish you would help. Your prestige..."

"You take care of it. You're my friend, aren't you?"

"Of course I am." He smiled at Pompey, suddenly happy. "We have always been friends, haven't we, Gnaeus? Do you remember that night out on patrol, when we were hiding near that bridge—?"

"Bridge? Oh. Oh, of course, of course I do."

Well, Cicero thought sadly, there must have been a lot of patrols since then. "Staying out here—some people might think it's a sign of weakness, Gnaeus.

"Look, Gnaeus. Let me help you—I know what I'm talking about. A long time ago, when I was a very young man, and just starting out, I got a position as quaestor to the governor of Lilybaeum, in the province of Western Sicily, just across the island from the other one—the province of Syracuse. I was one of the governor's assistants, and if I say so myself, I did a wonderful job. I had youth, and enthusiasm, and I liked the natives. I managed to send a huge shipment of grain to Rome, to relieve the shortages here. I know it's not like winning a war," he said, holding up his hand, for Pompey seemed about to interrupt. "But let me go on—to compare a small thing with a big, as they say in the schools. You're my oldest friend, and I want to help."

"Your oldest friend?"

"Of course." Cicero smiled. "Well, I was very pleased with what I had been able to accomplish, and I thought everyone in the city must realize what a fine job I had done. On the way home I stopped in Puteoli. It was the height of the season, everyone was there to take the waters, and the social life was very brilliant. I thought they would take me up, make a fuss about me. Well, the first person I met asked me what the latest news from Rome was. I couldn't answer, but fortunately some better informed citizen told him I had been in my province and hadn't come from the city at all. Except that he told him that my province had been in Africa. Another, a friend of mine, corrected him, saying, 'Don't you know? This is our quaestor in Syracuse—which is in the wrong part of Sicily.' " He waited a moment for Pompey to laugh—he had always considered it a very funny story himself. But Pompey said nothing.

"Well," Cicero said lamely, "I gave up. I saw that Rome does not have ears, but it does have eyes. Since that day I have made it a point to appear in the Forum every day, just so they will know."

Pompey lowered one eyelid as thick as a fold of parchment. "The Senate will give me what I want. I've conquered all of Asia."

"Perhaps it isn't that simple?"

"Of course it is."

He was ready to warn Pompey about Crassus, that he was preparing to use Clodius. He explained about the trial, and the attack on his house.

But Pompey had had enough. A servant had come in, a dark-skinned, black-bearded creature with some sort of cloth wrapped around his head. He was bobbing up and down like a bird on a branch. "More of these," Pompey muttered. The man took the empty dish and to Cicero's astonishment lay down with it on the floor. Then he scrambled to his feet and backed away. Pompey looked up. "What were you saying?"

Cicero gaped at him, unable to utter a word. He had never seen anyone do this, though he had read that oriental kings required their subjects to prostrate themselves before them. But in Rome even a god would not expect it.

"Nice custom," Pompey said. "I have all my people do it. It shows respect."

"I daresay it does."

The tartness of his voice was lost on Pompey, who was looking among the cushions for something. "Here." He had dragged out a chased silver box. "I'd like you to have this. A small token of my affection."

"Thank you."

"My servant will show you out. It was delightful to see you. After so long. It makes it all worthwhile, to come back and see old friends. You philosophers are right." The great man smiled sentimentally. "That's where the real pleasure in life is, in friendship. It's better than riches, or glory."

"Yes, I suppose that's very true." He struggled out of the embrace of the cushions. "Well, goodbye," he said, feeling awkward and depressed. "We must get together again—when you're in Rome, after your triumph, perhaps you can come to dinner? Terentia would be delighted."

"Yes, of course." His voice was muffled by another mouthful of fruit. "There's nothing like old friends."

"I was dismissed," Cicero said to Caelius, who had come out to meet him at the city gate. "Like an ambassador from a petty state to a great court. He even gave me a present. Look."

"Are you angry?"

"Yes. No. I don't know. Surprised. Disappointed. It's almost as if... as if he were someone else, and the real Pompey were still out there in the East. He's—he's living in some sort of tent."

"Tent?"

"It's true. By Hercules, he's forgotten Rome, the past, everything. In his mind he's still out there in Bithynia, where he can be treated like an oriental prince. He hasn't really come home at all."

They walked on toward the gate, Cicero's wagon rumbling after them.

"What about Clodius?" Caelius asked. "Did you tell him about the dog?"

"The dog?"

"Yes, of course. It was a treat, wasn't it? Well, what does he plan to do about it? What does he have in mind?"

"All he has in mind is a plate of figs," Cicero said. Caelius looked at him blankly.

"It's all right. Don't worry about the dog—Pompey will take care of it, I'm sure. He told me several times he was still my friend. What could that mean except that he intends to defend me? Of course he is on my side, as I am on his. Always. He's been my friend for thirty years. All the same—"

"Yes?"

"I wondered..."

He was gazing at the city walls, their thickness, their great height, the vast doors, propped open now. He seemed to doubt that they were strong enough. "No," he muttered. "That's it. In his mind he's never really come home."

"You wondered?" Caelius prompted.

He gave the boy a smile, but his large, fine eyes were hurt. "I wondered if I were supposed to go out backwards, too."

Caelius wanted him to take a bodyguard—a ridiculous notion. He was only going down the street, to a party at Metellus'. No one would dare. He had been a consul. Besides, Clodius had left town. "A little later than we thought he would," Caelius said to Cicero.

"Too late for the republic," Cicero snapped back.

Clodius had gotten himself elected as a quaestor and was serving in the provinces. "It's all those workingmen's clubs. He has managed to organize plenty of support in them." Perhaps Cicero was envious—though it had been nearly as easy for him to get elected in his day, for after the Roscius case he had been famous— "and for me it was much cheaper," Cicero rumbled, wrinkling his nose with amusement. "I didn't have to bribe anyone."

Clodius was going, by some strange coincidence, to Cicero's old province in Western Sicily. "Is he getting out of town to let the scandal die down?" Caelius asked. He was helping Cicero with his cloak, for the May night was cool.

"Very likely." But that could not be the whole story. The quaestorship was the first step in a political career: did Clodius intend, then, to start one? All over the city there had been posters painted on the walls. In the poorer districts, there was hardly a pocked and peeling surface that had not been improved by these announcements of the young man's candidacy and the endorsements of the various guilds. If he were really planning a career, this was surely how he would start.

Cicero mentioned this worry to Metellus some time later when his host was showing him to his place in the dining room. "How could he be thinking of it?" Metellus asked, indicating the couch next to the head as if he were ordering Cicero to take the position. "The scandal would put a stop, surely—"

"Oh, yes, the scandal." Cicero was smiling. "It doesn't seem to have bothered the Plebeian Assembly." He could not make out Metellus' attitude: was he angry that Cicero had been so instrumental in getting Clodius disgraced? Was he, even, pleased? Did he care at all?

"It bothered the Senate, though. Glad you could join us tonight," Metellus remarked, looking down his nose.

"Delighted," Cicero said warmly, and with sincerity. "Really delighted. So kind of you. Do you think, perhaps we'll get a chance to talk later?"

Metellus put back his head and stared down at Cicero.

It was a curious kind of party. Most of the guests were very young—not at all the sort of company he expected at a distinguished man like Metellus' house. He recognized one or two—Crassus' former pupil, and his accomplice in jury-tampering, Licinius Calvus, short and squat as a garden bench and as lumpy as if he had been left out in the rain; Valerius Catullus, Caelius' friend, fiery-haired and a little too loud. He knew a couple of the others, too. He nodded to Metellus, who was talking to his brother Nepos on the head couch, then to Clodia, seated at the end of the table in her ivory chair and looking like an image of night in her black dress sown with pearls her brother must have brought back from the East. They looked like tiny full moons in the dark sky. She bowed to Cicero and gave him a smile, rather warmer than he expected. "Marcus Cicero," she called, sending her low voice like a flute under the talk of the party. "I'm so glad you could come."

A curious party. Well, his wife had warned him. "I won't go to that woman's house."

"I'm sure it's Metellus who's giving this party. And in that case I really ought to be there."

"Then go alone." And Terentia had given a small, ladylike snort of contempt for his innocence.

Normally he loved dinner parties, but now, uncomfortable, he saw that Terentia had been right. Clodia appeared to preside over the evening; she ordered the courses of the dinner, and the entertainments between them. When at last the wine was brought in, it was she who decided the proportion of the water—not very much—and the games that accompanied it. The games were wonderful; contests to improvise little poems, very witty, and sometimes startlingly lyrical as well. The boy Catullus seemed to excel at this, and Calvus gave him a good second. In spite of his unease, Cicero began to enjoy himself.

The drinking continued. Presently there was music, and a line formed to dance. Cicero could see that Clodia, getting up from her chair, was coming over to him, her hands outstretched in invitation. Hastily he turned away as if he had not seen her, and caught her husband's eye.

"A word with you?" he mouthed over the flutes and lyres.

Metellus rose to his feet. It took some time, and Cicero was annoyed to discover that the delay increased his nervousness. Across the room Clodia was leading the file of dancers, her thick hair coming down from its pins, her face flushed. Her hand lay on the shoulder of the young Catullus, who was scowling as Calvus came forward to take his place.

"Your wife dances very well," Cicero said for the sake of something pleasant to say. Better than a respectable Roman woman should, he added in his mind.

Metellus paused. His always immobile face tightened further, and his small, dark gray eyes glittered like points of frost.

"Glad you think so," Metellus said, and Cicero understood that he had passed a test. Metellus would have resented any hint of criticism, especially from someone like him; the aristocrat was actually relieved now that he did not have to. He curved his stiff mouth, and Cicero saw that he was smiling.

Out on the floor Clodia had put both her hands on the young red-headed poet's shoulders. Hercules, she was kissing him. Shocked, Cicero glanced at Metellus, but he had looked away. He was suddenly very glad that Terentia had not come.

"It's very gracious of her to invite me, especially after what happened to her brother," he said. She was not the only one who could be gracious. And something had to be done to thaw Metellus, who was marching at his side down the hall as rigidly as if he were on parade.

"I invited you myself," Metellus said stiffly. "My wife knows her duty to her husband, I hope."

"No doubt she does," Cicero said, suppressing a glance back over his shoulder.

"You wanted a word?" Metellus sat in his study with his eyes fixed on the door, as if he could see something through it. He seemed to be listening to the sounds from the dining room.

"I went to see Pompey a few days ago. I felt it would be useful to talk over the situation here with him."

"Situation?"

"The land he wants for his veterans," Cicero said, restraining his desire to shout as if Metellus were deaf. He bent forward with his elbows on his knees and looked at Metellus. "I was very worried by Crassus' support for your brother-in-law," he said. He was trying to get Metellus to look at him, and not succeeding. In the other room the music rose, then dropped into silence. "Why do you think Crassus bought off that jury?"

Metellus was surprised by the question. A slight stiffening of the flesh around his iron-gray eyes betrayed it. "That is obvious, I should have thought. He saw some advantage in it."

"Advantage to himself?"

"Yes, of course." The music had started again. Metellus' attention turned toward it.

"That's the point," Cicero said hurriedly. "What sort of advantage? Why does he want a man like Clodius in his debt?"

"You tell me."

He smiled. "All right, I will. What I imagine—guess—is that Crassus wants Clodius' popular backing. He must feel confident enough of support in the Senate—or feel he knows how to get it."

"He owns half the men in the place," Metellus said with surprising pertinence. "Some of my own family, I'm sorry to say..." He would have liked to do something about it; his gray cheeks flushed and his eyes shone with anger. "I dislike indiscipline."

"No doubt."

"Our family," Metellus began, but thinking better of it contented himself with another freezing stare down his nose.

Cicero concealed a smile. He was beginning to understand his man—the stare was for the absent renegades, not for him. "Crassus hasn't much backing among the people. He's never been admired or loved the way Pompey has. So by helping Clodius he gets a genuinely popular agitator, with access to Hercules knows how many plebeians. For him, Clodius is a political prize of the first importance."

"Why should he want such a thing? He has everything he could want. It's not money—he made enough money to satisfy anyone—after Pompey he's the richest man in the city. He was a consul, years ago—" From the dining room a crash echoed through the house—overturning furniture or some such thing. Metellus' eye swiveled toward it, then quickly back to Cicero.

"That's the question," Cicero said, fixing his gaze on Metellus urgently to indicate that he had heard nothing unusual. "As you say, Crassus has already been consul, so he isn't aiming at that."

"Higher?"

"I think so."

"He wants to be censor, does he? I wouldn't have thought it was difficult for him. He's got money, a good reputation, he comes from a good enough family. The censorship's a great honor, of course. Still, I wouldn't have said it was out of reach for Crassus."

"I think there's a sense in which he's looking for something better than that."

Metellus raised his eyebrows in astonishment. "The censorship is the highest office in the city."

Cicero shook his head. Metellus was positively gaping at him now. "You mean he wants to be dictator, a king, something like that? It's impossible. We got rid of the kings five hundred years ago. And why would we need a dictator? We're not at war, the city hasn't been attacked."

He was so shocked he simply sat and stared.

Cicero let the silence prolong itself more than was entirely polite. "He's afraid Pompey will get there first."

"I'm only giving you what must be Crassus' view," Cicero said after a pause to let Metellus take this in. "I don't believe he's thinking of it now. Pompey's not that kind of man, you know. He had a chance to try something like what I'm talking about, when he came back with his army. He didn't take it. That's to his credit, of course. Pompey is an honorable man."

"I have always thought he was," Metellus said with a return to his old stiffness. "But it cannot be good for the city if Crassus tries to take over some sort of dictatorial power. And I do not know what Pompey will do if he feels threatened by some move of Crassus'."

It came to Cicero that Metellus was very shrewd; he had never appreciated the fact enough before. He thought he might risk going a little further. "And the root of the problem is Clodius," he said, conscious of a drop in the temperature in the room. Metellus' family pride again, he supposed. Well, he would have to hear some time, there was no point in softening the blow. "Without Clodius, Pompey and Crassus balance each other very nicely: Crassus with his senatorial support, Pompey with his popularity among the other classes." And he himself, with some of both and his old friends the knights, to keep them in check. Without him, there was no telling what would happen. Pompey and Crassus might fall to fighting over the city like two dogs with a bone...

"Clodius tips the scale, eh? Is that your view?"

"Yes."

Metellus' eyes had gone to the door again, but this time absently. He was thinking of what Cicero had said, and the noise from the dining room made no impression on him.

"What do you think I can I do?"

"I think you should run for consul."

The music from the dining room was louder and faster; there were voices in it, laughing and singing. What are they doing in there? Cicero wondered. They must be getting very drunk.

"Why don't you run yourself?" Metellus asked, a gleam of suspicion in his cold gray eye.

"It's only a year since I was consul; I haven't the right—the law says you have to wait ten years to run again."

Metellus nodded. There was a long silence, during which Cicero heard the sound of the flutes and the cithera again.

"Pompey wants this?" Metellus asked finally.

It was a discerning question. "Yes. I've talked to him. He does." He had been back twice to the house in the hills, explaining to Pompey the difficulties of his position, the need for support in the Senate, the monolithic opposition of the old conservatives. At last, reluctantly, Pompey had agreed to help. They had, between them, made up a list...

"You'll back me, too?"

"Of course. That's why I suggested it." He spoke for a moment or two about what he had in mind in the way of organizing support for Metellus' candidacy.

"I have resources of my own."

"Yes, certainly. No doubt very excellent ones."

Metellus face smoothed out again in gratification. "As good as anyone's in the city."

"Just so. I was sure of it."

"I've thought of running for consul."

Yes, thought Cicero, but you wouldn't know how to lower yourself to ask a man like me for support, though you need it. I am better known, and more popular than you, for all your money and your rank. "Well," he said aloud, smiling warmly at Metellus, "what did you think your chances were?"

That was too much for Metellus: he was offended at such a direct question. "I'll take it under advisement," he said, dismissively, rising to his feet. "I'll let you know when I decide."

"Yes, indeed. That's an excellent plan. Do think it over. Discuss it with your brother, perhaps. If you decide you can't do it, perhaps your brother would be willing? Or one of your distinguished friends?"

He was on his feet and looking around for his cloak and his outdoor shoes. Part of the art of politics, he had always told Caelius, was knowing when to go home.

Metellus' rigid face looked shocked. "Oh, no need to ask them," he said quickly. "I'll do it."

"Good," Cicero said, sitting down again; he was trying to conceal his amusement. "Well, we've got a lot of work to do, then, don't we?"

It was late when he got home, and he was tired. His eyes stung.

"Well," said Terentia, who had waited up. "Was I right? Was that woman there?"

He was in no mood to narrate the events of the evening. "I spent most of my time talking to Metellus. Privately. I think it went very well."

"Privately? About what?" She was pleased, and naturally she wanted to know more, but he had a letter to Pompey he wanted to get off in the morning and several things he needed to think through. "My dear," he said kindly, for he had no wish to hurt her feelings, "you attend to the household, and let me mind the politics, will you? You must be tired. Why don't you go up to bed? I'll be along in a little while."

"Yes, but Marcus..."

"My dear, it went very well. We are on the way to getting Pompey everything he needs."

"Yes, but what about Clodius? Didn't Metellus mind?"

"Really," he said, losing his patience slightly. "Isn't it time you were in bed? I have a lot to do."

She waited a moment, but he did not change his mind. Her lips compressed and she lowered her eyes , then turning on her heel she walked quickly toward the back of the house. He did not watch her go, but stood rubbing his aching eyes. What he had told her was the truth. They were well on the way to getting everything they wanted. Pompey was going to be very pleased.

VI

At the end of June the Senate formally voted Pompey his triumph. Cicero, not very happy with this delay, came upon old Lutatius Catulus and the white-haired prosecutor of the Clodius case, Hortensius Hortalus, in the lobby of the Curia just after the voting, when they did not know that he was there.

"An upstart," old Catulus wheezed.

"You're right. He thinks he's as good as anyone else now."

They had drifted away and he had not heard any more. All the same, though he could not have said why, he was sure they had been talking about Pompey.

The same prejudice could be seen operating in more substantial ways. The grant of land—Pompey was still showering Cicero's desk with requests about it—had to be passed by the Senate; to this end a tribune who was Pompey's friend introduced a perfectly unexceptionable bill. At least Cicero would have said it was; to him its virtues were obvious and its defects negligible.

Not to the Senate. They argued and amended, postponed and tabled, formed committees and rewrote drafts until it was plain that they had no intention of passing the land bill in any form whatsoever. Frustrated and furious, Cicero threw himself into the campaign for Metellus' election, but he could not help thinking, in the few quiet moments he found during the day, just how angry Pompey must be over the whole business. Of course, it would have helped if Pompey had campaigned for his bill more actively, but from the great golden house in the hills there came only a leaden silence. No doubt his friend had his reasons, but the senators were plainly offended, feeling that Pompey took their compliance for granted—"A thing no politician can ever afford to do," Cicero told Caelius. "And certainly not Pompey, who must avoid looking arrogant."

"Then why is Pompey doing it? He's not stupid, or inexperienced."

Caelius was right: he was neither. "I don't know." But in his mind's eye he saw Pompey again, lying on those cushions. "Perhaps he thinks he should get everything without lifting his finger for it."

"He's been in the East too long if that's what he thinks," Caelius said.

In July Metellus won the consulship, sharing it with another friend of Pompey's called Lucius Afranius. Cicero smiled and rumbled in his chest with satisfaction when the news was brought to him. "That ought to block Crassus for a while at least," he told Tiro, who looked at him out of the corner of his eye and busied himself with a stack of letters a messenger was waiting for. "Everything is going very well, Tiro," Cicero snapped, annoyed by this subtle form of criticism. "Tell the servants to pack, will you? We're going to the country."

"Yes, Marcus Tullius," Tiro said, his long, craggy face falling even further. "Do you think we ought to?" he burst out. "Now?"

"Of course," Cicero said, feeling better now that he had made Tiro lose his self-control. "We need a holiday."

"Yes, Marcus Tullius," Tiro muttered.

VII

They were back in September for the triumph. The first person Cicero saw was Caelius, sitting with his long legs stretched out in a shaft of sunlight in Cicero's atrium. He leaped to his feet to embrace Cicero and wring Tiro's hand. "Have you heard? Pompey has given a gift of six thousand sesterces to every soldier in his army. It works out to twelve and a half years' pay per man. Everyone says it's true. And his triumph is going to take two days. Imagine. He won't even appear before the second. When he does he's going to have elephants to pull his chariot."

"It's a wonder he's not going to get the God Mars to ride with him."

"The city has been quiet—all anyone's talking about is Pompey."

It was true. The city had filled up; every house had guests, the inns were putting up people ten to a room, the poor were camping in the streets along the route of the procession. Prices had gone sky-high, and it was difficult to get around— "For everything but rumors, that is," Cicero said. "They go everywhere."

"Everyone has certainly turned out for it," he commented to Metellus a few days later as they walked up the slope of the Capitoline Hill to the Temple of Jupiter. As consul elect and former consul they had their places in the ceremony, just behind the two consuls for the current year, and just before the rest of the Senate. After them the wagons were already rumbling through the Forum, loaded with treasure and tribute from the captive cities. They could have traced their passage, even without the rumble and screech of their wheels, by the roar of the crowd that greeted each one.

"I have heard a dreadful thing," Metellus confided to him when they had taken their places under the awning provided for dignitaries. In front of them the priests were busy with the sacrifices: a dozen white oxen with gilded horns and flowered garlands, fifty sheep, equally decorated, a hundred hens in a cage so large it had to be transported on a cart.

"Yes?" Cicero's eyes were on the floats—models of captured towns—as they jolted past: a placard announced that Pompey had taken a thousand forts, nine hundred cities, nearly eight hundred pirate ships based in the Eastern Mediterranean. In addition Pompey had founded forty new cities of his own. "The same number as his age," Lutatius Catulus said sentimentally, but Cicero smiled. Whoever was responsible for that rumor was flattering Pompey—who, like him, was forty-five.

"I heard that Pompey purchased the election of Afranius," Metellus said coldly.

Obviously he did not care if anyone heard, and, in fact, someone did. Hortensius pushed his way forward and thrust his white head between them. "They say he passed the money out in his own garden."

"That makes it so much more illegal, of course," Cicero muttered.

On the other side, Cato grated, "If the Senate had made an alliance with Pompey, we would have been party to this dishonor."

Fortunately the wagons with the loot and tribute had begun to arrive, so heavily laden that further speech was impossible. They made a noise so vast it must have gone straight up into the sky—where, no doubt it was pleasing enough to whatever god might be listening. His own garden, indeed. What could it possibly matter where Pompey had bribed the voters? If he had bribed them at all, of course. These old conservatives would believe anything of Pompey, if it were bad enough.

There were so many wagons, and they took so long to pass, that the crowd began to grow bored. All that gold and silver, flashing in the bright autumn sun, all those heaps of jewelry and coins, the statues, the crowns presented to the conqueror. It bewildered the eye and fatigued the mind. "Look," Cicero said, pointing Metellus toward the crowd. Crassus stood alone in it, surrounded by the open space, as if the chill of his presence were keeping people away. He alone of all the spectators was neither tired nor pleased—his dark eyes burned in his cavernous face as they followed every wagon, every display, all the way to the temple courtyard, where they drew up and halted.

"I see what you mean," Metellus shouted in a parade ground voice that rang out over the crowd, for the last cart had passed and a silence had fallen as thick as the dust settling back on the stones. Crassus looked over and gave them both an ironic bow. "He's jealous, isn't he?"

Cicero smiled and looked pointedly at the crowd.

"Yes, Pompey's popular."

Metellus snorted. He made it sound angry.

A ragged group of people had appeared, struggling painfully up the hill from the Forum. Cicero heard the clink of chains. The crowd heard it too, and began to cry again. "The captives," Hortensius said.

"The sacrifices, you mean," Cato corrected him.

"Sacrifices?" cried Caelius from the back of the group. "You mean they're going to kill them?"

"Yes." Cicero was staring with pity at them—princes, kings, queens, all walking steadily in their garish foreign clothes toward the temple precincts. There was a little girl among them, no more than five years old. She looked out under her dark curls with wide, shy, solemn eyes. Some little Asiatic princess, Cicero supposed. His own daughter, his beautiful Tullia, used to look at him with the same level look from under her eyebrows when she was that age. The women under the awning across the way, seeing the small captive, broke into moans of grief.

"Of course they're sacrifices," Cato said. "It's the tradition."

The hostages were passing into the temple now; the little girl among them, clinging to her mother's hand.

"It's too bad King Mithridates isn't here," Hortensius said. "I'd like to have seen him in this procession. He started this miserable war—I'd like to have seen the priest's knife at his throat. But he's dead." He had taken poison, knowing his fate if he were captured, but had survived. All his life he had feared assassination so much he had taken small doses in his food every day. In the end, when his wives and children already lay dead at his feet and Pompey was at his gates, he had stood in his hall, filled with what furious pride and grief Cicero could not guess. Tears, they said, ran down his cheeks, but he was unable to die. A friend had taken pity on him and run him through with a spear.

"It shows he was afraid of us, at least," Metellus said, and Hortensius nodded with satisfaction. "His cowardice was as good an advertisement of Roman power as this." He waved his hand at the last of the hostages, trailing sadly into the temple. "As this is going to be. Let our enemies be warned." Around him, the senators agreed solemnly.

"I think I'll go home now, if you gentlemen will excuse me," Cicero said, feeling that if he didn't he might be sick on the spot. Catching Caelius' eye at the edge of the crowd of dignitaries, he turned his back on the temple and hurried off down the hill.

The second day of the triumph the army marched behind their bronze eagles on the tall poles. The banners snapped over their heads, their voices swelled in song, and the whole city seemed to echo to their tramping feet. Pompey appeared toward the end, dressed in a purple toga and riding in a chariot drawn by white horses hung with garlands of flowers, crimson ribbons, and small gold balls. He was accompanied by his sons. His face was painted scarlet like an ancient king's; a slave held a gold crown over his head, but he whispered constantly in the great man's ear. You could see by the movement of his lips that that he was saying the traditional words: "Look behind you and remember that you are only a man." Pompey did not seem to hear. Nor did he notice the crowds that lined his route, cheering and shouting as he approached, or the women throwing flowers, the boys who broke out and ran along side his horses, calling his name. He rode forward, impassive and immobile as an image.

At the entrance to the temple Pompey stepped down and turned to face the crowd. His eyes were very blue in his painted face, his bronze hair looked almost gold. Like a statue he raised his right hand: the palm was crimson, too. "I make a gift to the city. The captives will not be sacrificed," he boomed. He could have been heard far away, in the leafy gardens of the Palatine Hill, out among the building of the Campus Martius, down in the rabbit warrens of the slums. The roar that greeted his words could have been heard farther than that. Pompey did not wait to listen to it; he turned and went quickly into the temple. The purple toga billowed out behind him in the wind of his passage.

"How could anyone not love him?" cried Cicero, grinning happily. Pompey was a great man, a truly magnanimous soul; he was proud to be his friend. He had refused to sacrifice his captives, though it was his right. A great man. In the cheering Cicero embraced young Caelius, as others were throwing their arms around the people nearest them. No one had liked the idea of the little girl... Even Cato was grinning, an expression so unfamiliar that it nearly made him a different man. "How can they refuse Pompey anything after this?" he said to Metellus, who smiled rigidly back at him.

"What happened to the elephants?" Cicero asked as, cheerful and satisfied, he and Caelius walked home that evening.

"They wouldn't fit through the Triumphal Gate. He had to have horses, like everyone else."

Cicero laughed.

Caelius was gone, to North Africa, to learn to administer his father's large estates there. Cicero missed him, hearing his footsteps or his voice in the house twenty times a day. It was like the absence of his daughter Tullia; it was worse, for he missed his help as well. He was occupied with bills in the Senate, trying—in vain, as usual—to persuade the conservatives to pass some version of the grant of land for Pompey's veterans. He could not give as much time to this as he hoped, for a delegation of knights had come to him asking for his help. It was the knights who had the traditional right to collect taxes in the provinces, but this time they had bid too high for the privilege and were losing money. "So now they're asking for a renegotiation of the contracts," Cicero wrote to Caelius, dictating it to Tiro, who grinned. "Nice for them if they can get it," the secretary murmured.

"Oh, I'll get it for them. I owe it to them; they were my earliest supporters, when I first came to Rome." He did, but it took time away from Pompey's business, and the holidays were rapidly approaching.

In a short while he had a distraction from these worries. His younger brother Quintus came home from the province he was governing in Asia. He had brought his wife and young son with him to stay while their house was being readied for them. For a time Cicero's mansion was full of the joyous squeals of small boys and the bustle of women. He and Quintus spent hours in the garden under the grape arbor, talking. It was like being young again, like their days together in the schoolroom in Arpinum. Sometimes it seemed to Cicero that he had never been able to talk to anyone else. He unburdened himself of his anxieties, and his brother, over the pieces of the board games on the stone table, smiled and argued and advised.

"Marcus," Quintus said, one steely day in November when the asters by the by the pool were prostrating themselves defensively against an imminent rain. "You have helped me over and over, you know. I wouldn't have gotten my province without your intervention."

"It was nothing. The one advantage of being elected consul is that you can do things like that."

"I haven't ever asked you for much, have I?"

"No, not very much. But I have a feeling you're going to now."

His brother laughed. "Not very much this time either." He looked like their mother, shorter and darker that Cicero was himself, and far more aristocratic; he had never had Cicero's brilliance, though he was a solid and capable man. He had been a good propraetor out in Asia. "I need something to do," Quintus said, moving his piece on the board. "I can't sit here idly, playing games with you all day long—pleasant as it is. That's no life for a Roman."

"You do a lot," Cicero said warmly. "You help me..."

The little boys were tumbling on the grass. "Quintus, will you look at them?"

Without raising his eyes, Quintus said, "We were like that once." He moved a piece on the board.

So they had been, once, when they were the age of their sons; they had been like two puppies out of the same litter, Quintus and he. When he had come to Rome, Quintus had followed, to study with the same teachers; when he had gone to Greece, his brother had been with him; when he had returned to the city to take up his destiny, Quintus had followed again, acting as his campaign manager. Quintus had been tireless in canvassing votes, talking to people, getting out the crowds, all the thousands of chores a successful election campaign demanded. In his turn, he had done the same for his brother when Quintus, having reached legal age, began his own career, though since he had been busy he had not been able to do much personally. But he had lent his brother his very experienced freedmen and his assistants, and all the money he needed. He was sure that Quintus had understood. Yes, of course he had. The proof was that they were here together so pleasantly today... He pushed his own counter forward on the table. Quintus was blocked in the back row: if he didn't watch out he was going to lose the game.

"What kind of work did you have in mind?" he asked.

"Anything." Quintus stared at the game on the wooden board. "I'm going to lose, aren't I?" he said moodily.

"It's only a game."

"Well, I usually do lose when I play with you."

The voices of the little boys rose. They were tossing a leather ball back and forth; it was charming to see how the older, Quintus' boy, was taking such trouble to throw gently to his smaller cousin. And there was Quintus himself, smiling in the sunshine with all the strength and warmth of his character showing on his face as he watched the children.

"Of course I'll help you find something," Cicero murmured. He was studying the board very carefully; when he made his move, he smiled secretly to himself.

Quintus turned back to the board. "Well, look at that. I must have been in a stronger position than I thought." He pushed his own piece forward. "You've lost the game, Marcus."

"So I have," said Cicero. Laughing, the two of them went to join the children on the lawn.

Pompey came to dinner as he had promised, bringing Terentia a necklace of garnet beads from Asia like clusters of pomegranate seeds, and a length of the strange, thin cloth that covered the cushions in his own house. She smiled and seemed pleased, but left him alone with her husband when the talk turned to politics—a thing she had never done before. Cicero watched her go. "She's angry with you about something," Pompey said.

"Yes, I know." He sighed.

Pompey, too, seemed much affected. "It will be nice to be married again," he said, looking after Terentia's retreating figure.

Cicero sighed again, but for a different reason. "Gnaeus, about this marriage. Are you sure it's going to happen?"

"Of course," Pompey said. He beamed in satisfaction. "Cato's daughter, eh, Marcus? Better than a half-sister of the Metelli any day."

"Well, that's what I wanted to talk to you about. Metellus is still very angry, you know. I saw it at the triumph."

"Don't be silly, Marcus. Why should he care? With the Catos backing me, his position is just that much stronger."

"Will the Catos back you?"

"Of course. When I'm married to Porcia."

"Well, yes, but just to be sure, in the meantime, don't you think you'd better make certain of Metellus? Invite him out to your place, and explain that you didn't mean to insult him—"

"No," said Pompey stiffly. "I don't think so. He can see it as an insult if he likes. What do I care? He has to support me anyway. He wouldn't have been elected without my help. And he knows who really holds power in Rome nowadays. It's not those old women in the Senate, let me tell you..."

"It's possible that he doesn't see the situation in just that way."

"Nonsense. He'll see it the way he's ordered to. He was my legate in Asia, he served under me. He knows what he must do."

"This isn't Asia now, Gnaeus."

The great brow furrowed and the blue eyes iced over with anger. "Excellent food Terentia's given us, isn't it?" Pompey said. Try as he might, Cicero could not get him to return to the subject.

VIII

I n January, Metellus became consul and immediately announced his opposition to Pompey and all his proposals. In the first place, he would not allow the land bill to be brought to a vote, and all the efforts of Cicero and his friends could not force him to. Afranius, the other consul, promised several times to intervene, but Cicero could not get a commitment from him about any specific measure. In addition, Metellus had suddenly become very friendly with the retired general Lucullus; when the question of the ratification of Pompey's acts in the East came up and Lucullus insisted that every measure in them had to be considered separately, Metellus agreed. So, unfortunately, did Cato and all his crowd.

"What's that about?" Tiro whispered to Cicero under cover of the debate the afternoon the ratification came up.

"I had better go see Pompey," Cicero said, and sighed.

Pompey was not as indifferent as he had seemed. He had left his huge golden house, and was living in his villa in the city—an imposing enough place, with a beautifully carved door and a small wooden balcony above fronting directly on the street. There were many houses in Rome like it, though most were not so grand. The servant who let him in, however, was foreign—turbaned like the one in the country; to Cicero's relief he merely bowed and led him into the great man's presence.

"Gnaeus," Cicero said when they had greeted each other. "I'm very worried. What is going on?"

"Everything's under control, Marcus."

"Is it? Metellus is opposing your wishes, and lending support to the opposition, Cato is just as adamantly against you as ever..."

"Don't worry. I'll take care of it."

"But how? Afranius is useless. He's a lightweight—more interested in dancing at parties than doing any solid work as consul. I assure you that none of the conservatives has the least respect for him. This marriage..."

Pompey turned away.

"Look, Gnaeus. It's important to plan our strategy. There are people we have to talk to, bargains we'll have to make, feelings that are going to need soothing, all that sort of thing, if we're going to rescue this situation That's politics. Perhaps you don't think much of it, but it has to be done."

For the first time in many years, he saw Pompey angry. His red face flashed with it; his eyes appeared a startling blue against his rage. "No, it does not have to be done. I will not stoop to that sort of thing. There are other ways. Good night, Marcus."

"Other ways? What do you have in mind?"

"Good night," Pompey cried again. Cicero bowed and silently took his leave.

What Pompey had meant quickly became apparent. A tribune, Lucius Flavius, asked permission to speak in the Senate. When it was granted—not without some discussion, for it was well known that he was a friend of Pompey's—he proposed not only a grant of land for Pompey's veterans but for any citizen who wanted it as well. The uproar in the Senate was immediate and prolonged, and its leader was Metellus, shouting into the noise, his gray head raised and his arm outstretched as if he were directing an army to throw itself against the walls of a recalcitrant town.

"What on earth did you add that for?" Cicero demanded of Flavius. Down in front Metellus was condemning Flavius' bill in a cold, angry voice.

"I thought they'd like it—it would be more popular—if it wasn't just Pompey's veterans who benefited."

"You thought?"

"Well, we both did, really."

"I see." And he did—Flavius meant Pompey, obviously. A flame of anger burned in him, scorching his gut. He almost put his hand to his stomach to touch it. All his work, thrown away because Pompey thought he knew better. The arrogance of it. The blind, unthinking, wrong-headed...

Flavius had gone down to the front and was shouting something at Metellus now; he could not hear what it was over the noise of the rest. Suddenly the tribune threw down the paper he held, leaped forward and grabbed Metellus. There was a gasp, and Cato shouted, "No."

Flavius ignored it. Roaring like a bull, he twisted Metellus' arm behind his back and marched him down the aisle to the door. Metellus held his head up and did not struggle, but his face had gone dead white and his eyes were murderous. The Senate was wailing and crying, shouting like a congregation of women at a funeral; several men darted forward to rescue Metellus, but Cato, mounting the podium, called to them to leave off: the tribune's person was sacred, they must not offer him any violence. At that they all shouted together and in a mass followed Flavius and Metellus out the door. Cicero let himself be caught up with them.

Outside the sunlight glared in his eyes, and it took him a little time to see where Flavius was taking Metellus, but presently that became clear. They marched across the end of the Forum to a small jaundiced stucco building, gleaming unhealthily in the sun. "Oh, gods," Cicero muttered. Beside him, Tiro, suddenly materialized, said, "Where are they going?"

"The prison."

"The prison? He's going to put a consul in prison?"

"So it appears."

And he did. Over the protests of the Senate, Flavius ordered the door opened and thrust Metellus inside. Immediately Metellus' head appeared in the doorway again, glaring out at the tribune. "I convene the Senate here, in this building."

The mob that had gathered shouted with laughter, but several senators prepared to comply and more showed signs of joining them. "Bring me a bench," Flavius shouted, barring the way. The senators backed off, trembling with anger, like dogs called back from a hunt by their masters.

There was a delay while a bench was brought and Flavius installed himself on it, spreading out his cloak with ostentatious care and calling for a jug of wine and something to eat. "He's prepared to spend a long time there, isn't he?" Tiro asked.

From inside the prison Metellus shouted that he had ordered a hole to be cut in the wall to let the senators in.

"Oh, gods," Cicero sighed. "I think we had better be prepared for a long wait, too. I wonder if we could arrange for another bench?"

"Aren't you going to do anything?" Tiro cried.

"I've been told to mind my own business."

"But this is a crisis."

Cicero nodded calmly. "If this is an example of Pompey's new method, it won't be the last."

"But you can't just leave it at that."

He did leave it; nothing anyone could say would persuade him to budge. As he had threatened, he sent for a bench from the Records Office and sat down with his clerks and secretaries around him, watching the doorway of the prison as he dictated his letters and notes for legal cases, just as if he were at home. The shadows in the Forum grew long, the crowd began to mutter angrily. Flavius sat on his bench, his arms folded, indifferent to the noise; Metellus remained invisible in the prison. After a while a gang of workmen appeared, but Flavius, standing up, ordered his friends to chase them off. For a moment the two groups of men stared at each other; then the workmen marched out of the Forum, swearing to return with reinforcements. The stand-off continued.

Towards evening, Metellus appeared in the doorway behind Flavius' head. Flavius gave no sign, but Cicero had an idea that he knew perfectly well that the consul was there. Certainly the crowd, which had been growing bored, came to attention. Metellus said nothing, but stared out into the gathering darkness. "He's looking for something," Tiro whispered.

"Not something, someone." Cicero, keeping his eyes on Metellus, rose to his feet. He had been sitting all afternoon; his knees were stiff and his back ached.

The man in the doorway stared across the empty space at him. For a long time their gazes seemed to stay suspended in the cold blue air of the approaching evening. At last Cicero bowed; the man in the doorway gave him a brief nod and disappeared. The crowd let out a sigh, and prepared to wait again.

He was not stiff now; climbing the slope of the hill in the winter cold with his toga snapping around his knees, he felt warm and vigorous, young and full of strength. His anger was like a potion, spreading through his trunk and legs, restoring him. He kept it inside him, warm as a small furnace, while he demanded entry, and was shown into Pompey's presence; he continued to husband it while Pompey set out the chairs and sat himself down. "What can I do for you, Marcus?" he asked genially.

"How could you be so stupid?" Cicero said. "Really, Gnaeus, how could you be such a fool?"

"What are you talking about?"

"Is this your idea of a better way to accomplish your ends? Violence to a consul? To Metellus Celer, who is so proud that you have to plot for days to get him to change his mind about an invitation to a party, let alone about a grant of land from the public Treasury? Are you out of your mind?"

"Let me remind you who I am," Pompey said.

"Oh, you don't have to do that."

"Well, then, let me handle this."

"You can't. You're making a mess of it."

Pompey flushed scarlet with anger. How thin his skin is, Cicero thought, watching the blood flood to his face. He's as fair—and as sensitive—as a girl. And as unaware of what Roman politics is really like. Yet he was Pompey the Great, who had risen from provincial knighthood to be one of the most important men in the country. How could he have accomplished such a thing if he would try this?

"The people will support me." Pompey preened himself, letting a beam of satisfaction shine out from his face like a ray of sunlight shooting between the clouds.

"Will they? Then where are they?" This was foolishness. Pompey must have known—why, the very street outside his house was deserted, the crowds that usually loitered anywhere that Pompey was had gone. "In the Forum they're laughing."

"Laughing?" Pompey sat down. "Is that true, Marcus?"

"Yes, I'm afraid it is. This is like a holiday for them, something novel and amusing happening in the Forum. And it's by no means certain that they'd be on your side if it came to a confrontation. Or rather, if you pursue the one you've already provoked. Metellus has powerful friends and plenty of money; it's only this year that he was elected consul. He has votes committed to him."

Pompey stared at him blankly, his blue eyes as vacant as the lapis gaze of a statue.

"All right, I'll take care of it."

"Gnaeus—"

When he left, Pompey was still sitting on his chair staring into space. He had the impression that he was leaving the sickroom of a friend.

There was no end to Pompey's ineptness over this. He sent word to the tribune Flavius to release Metellus from the prison. "So far so good," Cicero said, but his satisfaction did not last long: Pompey tried to claim that Metellus had asked him for this favor. At this there was laughter in the Forum, for everyone knew that Metellus would have starved to death in the prison before he asked Pompey for a crust of bread. The Senate, spitefully, voted down every provision of the bills Pompey had requested; Cato announced that he had married his daughter Porcia to Bibulus, one of the praetors, and a man of most distinguished ancestry. Pompey said nothing, but he retreated to his house in the country, from which no sound emerged for the next several months.

IX

This seemed to satisfy the city, which was very quiet and went about its business without disruption, until, in the early spring, Clodius returned to Rome. He arrived in secret, and at night, and the first Cicero knew of it was the following morning, when, going down the Palatine Steps to the Forum with his entourage, he passed the porch of the Temple of Castor. The door was open, a sharp geometric cut of light and dark, and in the doorway Publius Clodius stood, looking as if he had never been away.

"Surprised to see me?" Clodius asked. "I hurried back."

Tiro was pulling on Cicero's arm, and Quintus was frowning, but he could not resist the moment. "Did you, Pulcher? Why was that?"

"I thought you might have missed me," Clodius said, raising one perfect eyebrow. "I thought a lot about you while I was gone."

It was plain that Clodius had been travelling; he still wore his cloak and sword, and there was dust on his legs. On his hand his scarlet signet ring winked like an eye. "It took me only seven days from Sicily to Rome, travelling day and night. I came quietly, by night, because I didn't want the city to have the expense of sending a delegation to meet me."

"Seven days from Sicily to Rome." Cicero seemed to be admiring the accomplishment. "And the other time it was three hours from Rome to Interamna. You travelled by night then, too, and no one met you—though it would have been better for you if they had."

They had attracted a crowd from the idlers in the Forum; now it laughed. Clodius went white. More urgently than before, Tiro yanked at Cicero's elbow, and Quintus was positively glaring, but it was too late. Clodius ran down the stairs and planted himself in front of Cicero. "I told you before not to joke," he said in an undertone, so that no one but Cicero and the few people around him heard. "I'll get you. I'll see your head on a pole in the Forum."

"You're raving, Pulcher," Cicero said, wrinkling up his powerful nose. "Stand aside, please, you're blocking my way."

Clodius cursed, hardly above a whisper. There was a kind of intimacy in it, he might have been leaning forward to offer a caress. "I'll kill you," Clodius breathed. "If I have to do it myself."

An undertow of threats began to lap at Cicero's feet as he went around the city:

words scrawled on the walls of his house, jeers and calls when he walked through the Forum, heckling when he spoke at public meetings or trials. "It's dangerous," Tiro said. "You've made an enemy."

"Don't be an old woman," Cicero snapped. He had heard a lot of this sort of thing lately, and it annoyed him. He thought of Caelius and his reckless enthusiasms, missing him. He was surrounded by timidity and old age now that the boy was gone. "What can Clodius do? In spite of his name, he's nobody, just a rather drunken and aggressive young man with nothing better to do."

"He has Crassus behind him."

"Oh, Hercules, how long can that go on? Clodius isn't getting anywhere, and Crassus has never kept an unprofitable investment yet."

"Clodius is doing something about that," Metellus said, coming in and sitting down. He had never mentioned the day Pompey had had him put in prison, but from that time he had treated Cicero differently. The change was subtle, but it was there. Before he would not have stopped in when he was passing, as he had this morning; before he would never have smiled stiffly as he held his hands over the brazier. It had been raining outside; his clothes steamed gently in the heat as he sat, impassive and stiff but somehow at home in Cicero's study. "Clodius is trying to marry the daughter of old Fulvius Bambola. She's the old man's only heir, and has a fortune. He's going to need it—he wants to run for tribune." A servant had brought wine but Metellus waved it away. "A touch of indigestion. I couldn't get away to take the waters at Baiae this year."

"You mean that Clodius wants to be elected tribune? That's absurd. He's a patrician, and the office is only open to plebeians. That's the whole point of the tribuneship, as I understand it: to protect the classes that don't have regular representatives in the Senate."

"I put a stop to it. I said I'd speak to the girl's guardian. They listened to that." He looked a little white around the jowls. Perhaps it was only indigestion.

"I'm sure they did."

"Is he supporting you, or opposing his wife?" His brother Quintus asked. "I heard, someone told me, that she has a lover—some young fellow she invites to her parties." But he waited to say it until Metellus was gone.

"Possibly. But she's the source of this story, I'll bet you anything you like."

It was some days after that Cicero found out the answer to his unspoken question. Clodia had indeed given Metellus his information—she had been the one to suggest the tribuneship to Clodius in the first place. It was she who had talked to the girl, Fulvia, as well, sounding her on the notion of marriage to Clodius, and persuading her of the delights of involving herself and her money in his political career. Clodia had told Metellus herself, apparently without any shame whatsoever, in the course of one of their periodic and violent quarrels. It was a good thing,

Cicero reflected, that Metellus had restrained her. Really he could not imagine a woman more unsuited to be the wife of a consul. And if she had a lover as well it didn't bear thinking about. No wonder Metellus was touchier than ever and walked around looking as if he had eaten sour fruit.

FROM MARCUS TULLIUS CICERO, IN ROME, TO HIS BROTHER QUINTUS, IN ARPINUM.

July, just before the elections

...The news here is that Publius Clodius Pulcher has gotten himself adopted by a plebeian family. They chose the day of old Lutatius Catulus' funeral, when everyone would presumably be out at the tomb on the Appian Way for the rites. I was myself—a very sad occasion: the city has lost a good man, though a very conservative one, and I have lost a good neighbor, though a bad opponent.

Anyway, about Clodius: no one was supposed to know about the adoption, but when he went with his new father to the Temple of Jupiter to have himself inscribed in the censors' rolls under his new name and status, there was Metellus, talking to the priest. He pretended that he just happened to be there, but he had all twelve of his lictors, and his colleague in the consulship, Afranius, with him, and he was angry. He stood on the steps of the temple shaking his fist and shouting. (I had this from Tiro, by the way, who was looking something up for me in the temple archives.) Metellus, Tiro says, shouted, "It's illegal. All adoptions must be ratified by thirty lictors representing the Curate Assembly, and supervised by the College of Augurs." No one had ever heard of this before—and indeed, it must mean that half the adoptions in the city have been done improperly and a lot of rich men are enjoying fortunes they had no right to inherit—but it turned out that Metellus was right. So Clodius and his new father had to go down the hill again, with nothing to show for their effort. This handsome little Priest of the Women's Goddess had been working very hard to get elected to the tribuneship—using the method that Philip of Macedon said would successfully besiege any city, however well defended, to which a donkey laden with gold could climb. Now all that money is wasted.

Just to make sure, Metellus pushed his bill outlawing the workingmen's clubs through the Senate. Everyone was glad to vote for it; those organizations, which are supposed to be devoted to the worship of the patron god or goddess of the various trades, are really nothing more than excuses for a lot of underemployed and discontented elements to air their grievances. Even a not very clever politician—and Clodius is certainly not clever—can use them to stir up a lot of trouble. Well, he's blocked from doing that now, and very ably, by Metellus' quickness and foresight, which everyone is talking about.

To be sure that there would be no problem, Metellus put on the public games these clubs are usually responsible for, by himself. Can you imagine the expense? Crassus used to say that no man was really rich who could not sup-

*port a legion out of his own income. Well, I think Metellus must qualify.
Imagine putting on games, all by himself. I thought I was doing pretty well, but
I assure you, I couldn't even dream of doing that. Anyway, though it is unnec-
essary just now, since everything is fine, it's still a good thing to have friends.
The conservative pack—Hortensius, Cato, Lucullus and the others—may be
reluctant, but guided by Metellus' willingness to take my part even against his
own class and family, they are doing what they can. I don't see how I can be in
any danger while he is so busy on my behalf...*

In December Caelius came back from Africa, but Cicero did not see much of
him. He was preoccupied with the veterans' land bill and the knights' tax-collect-
ing problems, both of which the Senate preferred to ignore. There were one or two
important cases to defend in the law courts, and increasingly it was becoming difficult to go out. Clodius and his men were everywhere; they progressed from calling names and making loud remarks to shoving, and once to throwing stones.
Cicero brought down some very large and sturdy slaves from a farm of his in the
upper Tiber Valley, and they went with him most places.

He had hoped that once the elections were held and the new consuls chosen
there might be a chance to reintroduce the land bill, and this time to get some version of it passed, but it was clear that this was not going to happen. The election
went to a man as rigidly conservative as Cato himself, Bibulus, now Cato's son-in-
law, and to Gaius Julius Caesar, whose connections with the aristocracy were as
impeccable as anyone's in Rome.

In the drawing for provinces, Metellus had gotten Gaul, the richest and most
important of all the governorships. He was going to be out of the city for a year,
administering it. From Cicero's point of view this appointment was a good thing—
even from Gaul Metellus would easily keep his volatile brother-in-law bottled up,
and as the former governor of such a prize his word would have more weight when
he returned, but in a larger sense, he had to admit, it was too bad. Without
Metellus, the conservatives' hold on the Senate was going to be firmer than ever.
Not that he wanted to see radicals like Clodius get in, but they were putting so
much pressure on the Senate that even moderate voices like his own were growing
fainter in the din. He wrote to his brother that the conservative aristocrats were as
blind to the good of the city as always. "As long as they can keep their mullets in
their garden pools they think everything is all right," he said, "and these Tritons of
the Fishponds think that they don't need to concede so much as a sardine to the
other classes, who, after all, have rights too." It did not promise to be a very good
year.

On the first of January it suddenly became much worse. It was the day of the installation of new consuls, and a holiday in the city. Remembering this, Cicero got up early and went to the Temple of Jupiter Best and Greatest. The stars had gone from the sky, and it was very dark; only the bobbing lantern in the slave's hand showed him the way. It was like a moment from his childhood, walking to school with his guardian before the town was awake, the smell of cold stone in his nose, the weight of books on his arm. Rome asleep was still the little country town it had once been; in the darkness the massive buildings were like the ramparts of the mountains near his village, and the air was full of the scent of earth and the cold invisible river.

As he climbed the Sacred Way toward the Capitoline Hill the sun came up; first a band of scarlet like the hem of a robe, then the slow, spreading clarity in what was still darkness and night, then the burst of color and the first birdsong.

Up on the hill the sun struck the pillars of the temple; as old as the hill it stood on, as old as Rome, it glowed like a hearthfire against the chalky blue sky. A young priest was sweeping the forecourt, singing under his breath. For a moment they were alone together, suspended in the quiet like a drop of air in a piece of Egyptian glass; Rome, faceted like a crystal, lay below them, tiny, remote, and still.

Then the noises from down below rose around them, and the city began its day. A thread of music came up the hill, followed by a veil of violet-colored smoke from the altars and cooking fires; in the streets minute figures had appeared, busy with the preparations for the holiday. There were crowds in the squares now, clustered around booths and altars and small, brightly-colored awnings; on the balconies of the tenements, green garlands had been hung out. A distant rumble of footsteps floated up on the breeze to the temple. "It's a lucky day," he said to the priest. "A good day for beginnings."

In the Forum a trumpet was blowing, its notes came on the wind, a thin, mellow sound. The procession of officials was forming. Presently it came in sight: first the priests brilliant in white, the Pontifex Maximus in purple, the College of Augurs in a splendor of gold, the various flamens in their colored robes. The knights followed them in their traditional short capes and bronze helmets. Behind them came the twenty-four lictors of the consuls, marching up the hill, solemnly shepherding the two new consuls, white-togaed and crimson-banded, their faces polished by the morning wind. Next strode the old consuls, then the praetors and all the lesser magistrates, and the ponderous and dignified senators. Lowing like the trumpets, the white bulls and heifers for the sacrifice trod heavily up the way, tossing their horns. A crowd dressed in holiday clothes pressed on them, and the whole colorful mass moved slowly up the hill.

Halfway up it staggered; a shudder seemed to run through it. All the colors changed: white became gray, red turned black, the gold of the augurs dulled to clay, as if a shadow had passed over it. The shape of the huge mass broke into pieces and trembled at the edges. "Something's happened," Cicero cried, and ran down the hill.

The mass of priests and lictors had compacted; though he shouted and pushed, he could not get through it. Then, suddenly, there was an opening, a saffron back shouldered in front, holding it for him. It was the young priest; he had not heard him following. "Thanks," Cicero flung at him and plunged into the space, hearing nothing but the roar of the voices, the confused bellow of the animals, the scrape of feet on the pavement. All at once he was in the middle of the crowd. There, on a patch of gray stones, like a bundle of laundry thrown down, was Metellus, in all his finery.

It was very bad, he could see that at a glance. The patrician face was the color of the stones, the lips and eyelids blue and drawn back in a grimace. Under his cheek there were traces of vomit and froth; his eyes turned whitely to the sky.

"What happened?"

Bibulus had come to a halt beside him. "He collapsed; we were talking and all of a sudden he just—" and two or three voices began to tell him about it in low tones. He paid no attention: he had seen Metellus' chest flutter. "He's alive." They said nothing, and, angry, he shouted at them, "Get him home. Can't you see he needs a doctor?"

He could not bear to see Metellus lying on the ground: he looked dirty and dishonored there, as if he had been caught in some sordid bed in a brothel; he looked diminished, exposed to the hardness of the stone, the stares of the crowd. He was an aristocrat, he would have resented it; it was worse that now he could not.

They obeyed him, lifting Metellus up as his toga flapped like a banner and his voice creaked out a moan. From his mouth spittle flew, catching the light in a fine, silvery spray. "This way." Cicero's anger had given way to distaste; he despised the crowd for its vulgar, gaping mouths and its hard, unblinking eyes. He felt sick himself. He stared back at them, letting them see his displeasure; they fell away and he led the sick man's porters out into the open space of the Forum. There the air felt cleaner, and he took a deep breath of it. "This way," he said. "He lives up on the Palatine Hill." The loathsome men had the temerity to groan at the news.

It was a day full of strange portents. When the little party arrived at Metellus' house there was no one there to let them in. They pounded on the door—it was a vast affair of black and silver worked all over with a pattern of acanthus leaves; it shuddered when they hammered on it with their fists, but no one came. Finally a panel opened. Metellus' wife looked out at them from the doorway. When she saw what the men were carrying her eyes widened and her mouth fell open like a child's. Then she was all right, every thing was as it should be: she drew herself up and became calm and competent. "This way. I'll get the maids—it won't be a moment before they can have his bed ready."

She managed the servants, and sent for the doctors; Cicero, waiting in the small bedroom at the back of the house, was not sure how, since when they had arrived he could have sworn the house was empty. But there everyone was, four doctors with their silver spatulas pressing down the sick man's tongue while their fussy eyes went from one to the other of their colleagues; the maids came in and out with stacks of clean linen and bowls of hot water; the men who had come from the Forum—he saw Hortensius, worried and pale, Metellus' brother Nepos, biting his thumb in anxiety, several others—all huddled together, looking down. Metellus lay on the bed, a fine gray blanket drawn up to his chin, his white hands busy as spiders scratching at it. His arrogant nose rode over his sunken eyes and half-open mouth and his breath came clogged from his throat. For a long time it was the only sound in the room.

It was a day of horror, in which people came and went without Cicero's knowing how, and with no interval between them or reason for their appearance. Sometimes Clodia, for instance, sat in her chair, her hair now impeccably smooth and polished, her dress fresh and white under a long black cloak; sometimes the chair was empty, gaping significantly with its arms held out to embrace the air. Once Caelius appeared, smiling crisply in a kind of contrast with the long tedium of the day; he sat on a stool at Cicero's feet with his legs drawn up under his chin and studied Metellus' face, but he said nothing. Most of the Claudians came: the senior, Appius, dignified and correct, bowing over his sister's hand; Clodius Pulcher, talking to a man in the corner with a pallid, pasty face and thick curling hair, whom Cicero did not recognize, all the time watching Metellus like a ferret waiting at a rat hole; Clodia's sisters, as heavily veiled as if they were widows themselves.

Metellus' neighbors appeared: Hortensius with his white hair floating so far above his head that it seemed ready to leave it altogether; thin Cato, bitter and distressed, biting his narrow lips; Crassus, sad and, oddly, rather surprised, as if he had not known that it ever came to this; even Pompey, bulky and somehow pinched with chill in his white toga. Cicero had no sense of how long they stayed or what they said; the hideous day wore on, measured only by the tidal scrape and rattle of Metellus' breathing, and the futile gestures of the doctors.

It was all inexpressibly dreary and wearing, like certain endless days in childhood; he felt like a man trapped in a memory, compelled to repeat the same sequence of thought in boredom and disgust for the rest of his life.

In the afternoon the new consuls came, trailing an atmosphere of incense and bustle from the ceremonies; tall, blond Julius Caesar bowed his slender elegance over the bluish figure in the bed, spoke a word to Clodia and another to the doctors, then stood by the window, his elbow on the sill, chatting in a low voice to the men of the family. Bibulus, the other consul, bent his freckled baldness to Metellus' brother for a moment, smiled frostily at Clodia, and left.

Still Cicero did not get up. The chair pressed against his back, his legs tingled, he longed for something to eat, to read, to say, then forgot what he wanted. He shifted his weight and the hardness of the chair caught him in a new place; he looked around the room, but the featureless gray daylight gave no indication of the time. On the bed Metellus sat up and cried aloud.

"Catulus. Catulus." His voice was unrecognizable, the cry of fear or pain might have come from anyone in the room, or from anywhere. He raised his hand and hammered on the wall next to the bed.

It was impossible that he knew what he was doing: he looked much worse than he had even an hour before. His eyes had fallen into his head, foam spewed from his bloodless lips. Against the wall his nose made a curve as sharp and white as a bone; it was sinking back even as Cicero watched, his flesh was deserting it, leaving only his bluish skin to cover the skeleton of his face. His mouth opened and shut like an inanimate thing, worked by the strings of his neck; he called again. "Catulus. Catulus."

The doctors fluttered around the bed, Metellus' wife had risen from her chair and was holding a cup to her husband's lips. There was a clatter as it fell from her hands, rolling across the floor. Cicero saw it gape like Metellus' open mouth, the liquid splashed from it in a long gout across the floor. He watched as it rolled toward him; bending down from his chair he picked it up. It was a beautiful object of heavy silver, with a raised design of satyrs and nymphs under a band of ivy. A little liquid still puddled in the bottom, but the depth of the cup made it hard to see: he could not tell what color it was, or if it was thick or thin. Curious, he sniffed it: it had a pungent, sickly odor of garlic and medicinal herbs that offended the nose. Then Clodia was bending over him, smiling, taking it from his hand.

Metellus was pounding on the wall again, crying out. His voice had lost all human character; it made no more sense than the neighing of a horse or the creak of a rope in the wind. His wife bent over him. "Here. Drink this. See?" She took a swallow from the cup.

Metellus stared at her with his sunken, meaningless eyes and drank. The doctors pressed him back; he lay on the bed, quietly, almost like a man asleep. Then his body gave a great convulsive jerk as if he were trying one last time to sit up, his mouth opened and closed, his eyes went around the room. For a long moment he stayed like that, arms outstretched, then he gave a long hoarse cough, and fell back. There was no sound in the room.

It took a moment for Cicero to understand. The breath that had rasped back and forth through the room all afternoon, so constantly that he had ceased to hear it, had finally stopped. The figure on the bed, drowned in the blue light of evening, was no longer a man. Metellus was dead.

He had not expected this conclusion; he felt shocked, as if he had received a painful blow. He could not say why, for surely everything in the long and weary day had been leading up to it, yet it came as a surprise, and it hurt him. He drew his toga over his head and under its cover he wiped his eyes, unwilling for anyone to see his tears. He could not explain them; they made him feel false, for he thought he had never really liked Metellus, who had treated him with arrogance and disdain. The sordid afternoon was over, the body lay, neatly folded and rather beautiful with its white pallor and its meaningless dignity, its hollow eyes and bony fingers, its thin sharp nose. It did not look especially like Metellus, it might have been any man, it might not have been a man at all.

Figures were moving in the cool light now, voices hummed in quiet conversation. On the floor a maid was kneeling, scrubbing at the place where during the long afternoon Metellus must have vomited, perhaps more than once. Cicero could not remember it at all. But the woman's haunches were working as heavily as a mule's pulling a load up a hill; he could hear the swish of the cloth, like the dead man's dying gasps. Suddenly he could bear the room no more; he rose and bowed to Clodia, looked once more at the thin face, now receding as if it were being carried away on the gray tide of the blanket, and left.

Outside the last of the afternoon sun was silver on the roofs, the sky was blue, hazed by the violet tracery of the branches. Already there were long shadows, the beginning of night, gathered like pools among the paving stones. He took a deep breath; he could feel the air in his lungs as sharp as little knives, but it was clean.

The evening was clearing his head; warmth was beginning to move in his muscles and thoughts stirred in his mind. Scenes from the day came back to him, moments he had not thought of or noticed at the time; a servant bringing in a tray, a man with tightly curling hair turning from the window to reveal a pockmarked and pallid face with a shine as unhealthy as Metellus' own, a sharp smell of garlic and herbs, a dead man saying "Catulus" over and over as he pounded on the wall.

"Catulus lived next door to him," he said aloud, glad to hear his own voice after the long silence of the day. Metellus might have been trying to summon his neighbor; he must have thought he needed the support.

"Lutatius Catulus has been dead for six months," Caelius said, coming up from the wall where he had been leaning. Cicero gave a start—he had not seen the boy waiting there in the shadows.

"I know."

They walked on in silence. Caelius, tactful as ever, did not try to speak.

"She murdered him," Cicero said.

Caelius paused, looking at him open-mouthed, but resumed his stride without saying anything.

"She did, you know," Cicero insisted, as if the young man had disagreed. "It was as plain as the paint on the walls, it was everywhere in that room."

He was remembering a bedroom, the rose and gold of the walls, the stifling sense of being enclosed with a frantic and dangerous woman. Poor Metellus. He wasn't much of a man, but he deserved a better end than that.

XI

Metellus' death changed something; it was hard to see what, exactly, just as it had been hard to see his influence during his life. But it was there, a subtle shift in the city, as if there had been an earthquake in the night that no one had felt, but in the morning tiles were down from the roofs, and doors hung askew that had always been straight.

There was violence in the city now, a note like the rumble of distant thunder over every conversation. There were ugly threats in the Senate, disturbances from the crowds around the speakers at the Plebeian Assemblies, and more than one public meeting ended in a brawl. Those who could afford them began to go around with bodyguards: Hortensius had a dozen strong-armed men to walk behind him; Crassus, always anxious, had fifty. But the center of the trouble was Cicero. He could not go out of his house without finding messages scrawled on his walls and crowds of rough-looking men, gathered as if by accident, on the street. He liked the look of them so little he increased his own bodyguard—and when the men took to following his wife, Terentia, he provided twenty slaves to accompany her too.

It troubled him enough to mention it to Pompey, who was frequently in the city now, trying to get his land bill passed. They had repaired their friendship—Pompey had sent him a note, saying that he understood that Cicero had been concerned for him—he did not take amiss his opposition to Flavius' bill. He was sure that Cicero knew that sometimes one's supporters went too far. They meant well, but they did not always have the mature judgement of one's oldest friends. Cicero, smiling to himself, wrote back that he understood perfectly. Well, he did, better than Pompey would really like, he supposed. Still, he was glad to be back on good terms with the great man—and now that this problem with Clodius had come up, he was doubly so.

"Don't worry," Pompey told him when they spoke of it one afternoon in the lobby of the Curia. "I'll see to it that no harm comes to you, my friend. You're helping me, I'll help you. If anyone should raise his sword to strike you, he'll find my shield over you." He must have liked this phrase, for he repeated it at a public meeting when he was asked about the violence in the city. This time he seemed to mean that his shield would cover all of Rome. Cicero, reassured, went back to getting him his long-overdue legislation.

He made some progress. The new consul, Julius Caesar, agreed to help him. "Well, he knows I'm not a person to trifle with," Cicero said with a complacent smile. "I have influence, and backing, of my own." But he could not disguise his unease at Caesar's methods. There were shouts during the debates now, interruptions, a violence of speech and gesture that had never been there before, and that the new consul did nothing to discourage. The conservatives responded by obstruction and delay; a kind of sullen bitterness came into their remarks. In the Forum and at dinner parties in the city, men looked at one another uneasily and muttered about the danger to the republic. "You were right," Hortensius said to Cicero at one point. "You said Clodius' acquittal would be the end of law in Rome. No one believed you, you know."

"Oh yes. I'm as good as Cassandra," Cicero said. It was a joke, but his voice was grave.

Poems began to appear in the city, recited at parties, scribbled on walls, repeated in bars—where they inevitably provoked fights between Clodius' supporters and what Cicero called, "Good, law-abiding men, the salt of Italy." Caelius brought one to Cicero.

> Prettily they agree, these two prancing boys
> Mamurra the effeminate, and Caesar.
> No wonder, either—they're filthy, both.
> One is Roman filth, one filth from stinking Formiae;
> rubbed into the grain of one another,
> they can never be washed out.
> Both sick with the same sickness
> in one bed, spouting pompous poetry.
> One is no less voracious in adultery
> than the other—rivals, and companions,
> in the girls.
> Prettily they agree, these two prancing boys.

"Who wrote it?" Cicero asked.

"My friend, Valerius Catullus. You remember him, don't you? You met him the night Pompey was coming home."

"Oh, yes, of course." He studied the paper. "You say this is written on the wall of the Temple of Castor?"

"That's right. Clodius uses that temple as a kind of headquarters. They say someone sneaked up during the night and painted this poem there. Clodius is furious."

"Who did that?"

"I can't imagine," Caelius said with an air of large innocence, and went away again, grinning to himself.

The rumble of thunder grew louder in everyone's ears. At meetings of the

Plebeian Assembly the disorder was so great, and the threats so naked, that business could not be transacted at all. At one point the disturbances were so serious that Caesar had his colleague in the consulship, Calpurnius Bibulus, thrown bodily off the platform. Cato, protesting this, was ill-treated by the mob—a basket of ordure was dumped on his head, and he was punched and kicked. It did not prevent the thin, sour, courageous little man from returning to the platform to finish his speech, until he, too, was led away and the meeting broke up.

Business in the Senate came to a halt. Bibulus, shaken and angry from his treatment—he was said to have bared his neck to Caesar's men and demanded that they kill him on the spot, if they were brave enough—barricaded himself in his house, from which he issued bulletins every day, saying that he had read the skies, in his capacity as consul, and the omens were unfavorable: no meetings of the Senate could therefore take place. Caesar announced that this was fine with him, he would not trouble the Senate any further, and asked the Plebeian Assembly to pass the land bill. They did, adding, at his request, several provisions so radical that Cicero blinked when he heard them.

"By Hercules," he said to Pompey at a meeting he had requested to discuss the matter. "They're giving land to every poor man in the city who asks, whether he has ever fought in the army or not. It must be thousands, tens of thousands, of extra people. I warn you—it's a bad idea. It's Flavius' bill all over again." He was angry, and Pompey knew it. The great man blinked and looked blank. "Will you oppose it, Marcus?" he asked. "I'll have to," Cicero said sadly. He had seen, behind all the disruptions, the small, aggressive, beautiful figure of Clodius, his enemy.

He was always there. He stood among the rough-handed men in the street, head back, fists resting on his belt, jeering and shouting, when Cicero approached; he followed him through the Forum, and when he went out in the evening. Sometimes Cicero would see him, late at night, leaning against the wall opposite his house, glaring at the windows on the second floor. Cicero did not sleep well, knowing that the hard black eyes were out there; they might have been trying to pierce the walls. Anyone who tried to visit Cicero was harassed; his friends began to avoid his house, unwilling to pass through the mob Clodius kept in front of Cicero's door.

"Prosecute him, then," Caelius recommended, coming in one afternoon, angry and hot. He had climbed over the garden wall, a fact which he was anxious to keep from Cicero, who, he suspected, would not have liked it. "It's against the law to offer violence to a Roman citizen."

"He hasn't."

"Oh, surely—"

"Think about it. There have been incidents of violence, of course, but in which of them was Clodius involved?"

"He's behind them all," Caelius shouted. "You know perfectly well—"

"Can you prove it?"

"I...yes, of course...I mean—"

"Just so," said Cicero, getting up and peering through the shutters. He did not go into this garden now himself and he avoided the rooms in the front of the house. "Pompey has kept his word. He's keeping Clodius away from me."

"This is intolerable," the boy said. "I feel like going out there and..."

Cicero turned slowly to look at him. His nose twitched and his eyes narrowed—he might have been angry, but when he spoke it was in a gentle and friendly growl. "Caelius, I don't want you to come here any more."

In the dimness the shuttered light fell across the boy's face. It was white. "Why?"

"I'm not punishing you," Cicero said. To prove it he rang for a servant and told him to bring refreshments. "It's simply that it's not safe any more."

"But that's exactly why I came," the boy protested. "I don't want your wine. I came to protect you. I'm your friend. At least I thought I was."

"Of course you are. But you are young—"

"Young?" Caelius shouted. "What do you mean? I'm twenty-three."

Something seemed to amuse Cicero, but he did not say what it was. He looked down at the papers on his desk. "You're just starting your career," he pointed out peaceably. "I meant 'young' in that sense. You haven't had time to develop a group of supporters and clients and so on. In view of that, I think it's unwise to involve yourself in anyone else's political problems. Especially mine. Even men with much more behind them than you have are beginning to think twice about that." He rubbed the bridge of his nose with his thumb and forefinger, as if that were where this infidelity hurt him.

"I'm not thinking twice about it. And I'm not starting my career. I'm not doing anything except watching the government fall apart, and you with it."

"You are now," Cicero said, handing him a sheaf of notes across the desk.

Caelius studied it. How intelligent he looks, Cicero thought, bent over the paper with the concentration of a fox on a trail. He seemed to quiver in his intensity, and his eyes shone. "It's an indictment," Caelius said, without looking up. "A prosecution brought against a former governor for corruption while he was administering his province, which was...Macedon, it appears."

"That's right. His name is Gaius Antonius Hybrida, and he's as guilty as a dog in a meat larder."

"And you want me to—"

"Prosecute. I've already said I'll defend."

"Why, if you think he's guilty? Why not prosecute yourself?"

"Gaius Antonius Hybrida was my colleague in the consulship, before he went out to Greece. I never thought much of him—he's a venal and rather stupid creature at best—but I have some kind of obligation to the man I shared the most important office in the state with. Besides—" He smiled. "I haven't the temperament for prosecution. I always think of the poor fellow in the witness chair, with all the established power of the rich and aristocratic classes against him..." The truth was, he always thought of poor Roscius, looking up at the heads on poles in the Forum and turning blue with terror.

"It sounds as if this Hybrida deserves to have them against him," Caelius said, going through the notes again.

"That's a prosecutor speaking." Cicero laughed. "Take that home and look at it. It hasn't been filed yet, and you'll probably want to rewrite it, but it will give you some idea of the case."

"I don't want to oppose you. Aside from the arrogance of my appearing against your...against you...I want to stand by you, not oppose—"

"You haven't been listening," Cicero growled. To Caelius he suddenly looked rather fierce. "I don't want you around me now. This will provide a reason, if anyone wants one, and I'll be free to act. Now, get out of here before I change my mind and give the case to someone else. And don't come back, by the garden wall or any other way, until I tell you it's all right."

Cicero made his preparations: he wrote a speech for Hybrida—it wasn't much, but there wasn't a lot a reasonably honest man could say in the ex-consul's favor anyway—and he did his best with it. But he went farther—so far out on a limb, he said, it made his head swim to look down.

When the speech was finished he began to canvass his supporters. Pompey's known friends were helpful and interested—but more important, he also spoke to Pompey's growing number of enemies in among the aristocrats. One way or another he discussed his plans with nearly every member of the Senate. He argued and flattered, promised and bargained. It had been true what he told Caelius: he wanted to clear away the underbrush so that he could move freely. Most of the conservatives seemed happy to see him, and he went home well pleased and much reassured for the future.

He wrote about it to his brother, who advised him to follow his conscience, reminding him that long ago, when they had been students in Greece, the oracle at Delphi had told Cicero the same thing. The last call he made was on Pompey. "I owe you a lot, Marcus," the great man boomed. "You've brought up the reinforcements for me over and over. I'm not going to pay you back by letting the enemy inside the walls now."

The day was dark, choked with fog so thick that an hour after sunrise it was as dim as nightfall. The fog curled slowly through the shutters and under the doors; out on the street, where it was mixed with the smell of smoke, it clawed the throat and brought tears to the eyes. Buildings loomed, unrecognizable, distorted, vast, but when Cicero passed they gave back the footsteps of his servants as hollowly as if they were only facades with nothing behind them. On the Palatine Steps the stones were slimy with water and the air was so thick he had to pick his way down like an old man. The Forum had disappeared in the acrid darkness; only the first steps were visible, going down into a pit. Voices rang up from it, of invisible men.

Near what might have been the Rostra, the praetor who was going to preside was waiting for him, his togaed figure glimmering as he appeared out of the murk. Beads of water had congealed coldly on it. "They're bringing more torches." His voice seemed to go on chiming like bronze long after he had turned away. The damp was so icy Cicero could feel it under his clothes, as insistent as an animal scraping at him; water dripped from his hair down the back of his neck. He shivered, and knew he was afraid.

It was not for himself that his bowels slid and his stomach clenched, he thought some time later, sitting on his bench next to his client while Caelius took a witness competently through a tangle of financial testimony. He had never been afraid for himself, not once he had made up his mind to do what was necessary. He suffered agonies of anxiety before, but by Hercules, he was Roman enough to think that the end he worked for was more important than his own safety. And in all honesty, action absorbed him, lifted his spirits, occupied a mind otherwise a little too given to imagining horrors. No, it was not for himself he feared. But the darkness of the day oppressed him, the harsh flare of the torches, the gleam of wet paving... Out of the corner of his eye he seemed to see heads in the Forum, looking down from poles. Hercules, he would be paralyzed, unable to speak, when the time came. He moved his dry mouth in prayer, but he did not think there was any god to hear.

Caelius was making his speech now; Cicero jolted upright on his bench, forgetting everything else. The boy was pacing over the glittering wet stones; the torchlight caught him, emphasizing his height and his graceful gestures. Where had he learned them? He, Cicero, had taught him the motions, but Caelius was making them elegant and vivid, and all his own. His voice was clear, and powerful, though perhaps a little shrill; his leaf-shaped eyes sparkled with anger which for all the world looked real. He was describing Hybrida's behavior when the people of a the neighboring tribes, whom Hybrida had attacked wantonly and without provocation—he was hoping to kill enough of them to merit a triumph—returned the compliment and marched on the governor's headquarters. Caelius was making a meal of the scene, enjoying every morsel.

"Well, then," the boy was saying, his own freshness a contrast to the picture he was painting, "they stumbled upon him, this degenerate, lying in a drunken stupor, snoring from his chest, and belching all the time. The most distinguished of his tent-mates—because, let me tell you, women, not army officers, were his—What should I call them?—his, ah, comrades-in-arms. The most distinguished of them were stretched out on the couches, and the rest lay scattered around nearby on the floor.

"Nevertheless, when, half-dead with terror, they became aware of the enemy's approach, the poor creatures tried to rouse Antonius. They lifted his head, they called his name—in vain. Another whispered seductively in his ear. Someone else went so far as to slap his face—hard.

"At last he recognized their touch and their voices. He reached out to embrace the closest around her neck. He couldn't sleep, they cried too loudly, and he couldn't stay awake, he was too drunk, so he lay prostrate in a drunken doze in the arms of his centurions and concubines."

"Wonderful," Cicero muttered involuntarily and Hybrida shot him a murderous look.

The jury thought it was wonderful too; they listened with gaping mouths as Caelius, flushed now under his peach-like skin, went on with the sordid story. It scarcely mattered now what he said; they would not forget the drunken and debauched governor, and his terrified women. Hybrida was as good as convicted. He knew it too, he was jerking frantically at Cicero's clothes as he rose to make his own closing speech. He blinked and set his toga squarely on his shoulders. "Gaius Antonius Hybrida has had an outstanding career: he has been an officer in the army, a tribune, a praetor, a consul..." He was trotting through it briskly, it was better if the jury didn't think too much about Hybrida's career. And he didn't want to waste time on this petty business himself. He had other things to get to... "His service to the state..." he went on, hardly hearing his own voice. Blah, blah, blah. "Invaluable help to me during the rebellion of Catiline..." Blah, blah. "Poor reward for a lifetime of..." Blah, blah, blah. Now for it. "But Gaius Antonius Hybrida cannot be blamed for his lapses—which are minor, gentlemen, minor, I assure you—when an example is being set for him by our present consul, Gaius Julius Caesar, a man from a far more important family than Hybrida's, and backed by men even more distinguished—can run riot in the city like a slave on a holiday, even going so far as to push a consul—a consul, gentlemen—down a flight of stairs, and to let his bullies dump a basket of night soil on the head of a senator, who is a Cato as well. A Cato." He shook his head. To his secret amusement he saw the jurymen shaking theirs in sympathy. "And why has he done this? Because they disagreed with him, because they did not vote the way he thought they ought to. Beside this destruction of our liberties, this willful attempt to abrogate our constitution, what Gaius Antonius Hybrida has done, or not done, is nothing at all. Nothing at all, gentlemen."

Through the dirty air he could see some men in the back slipping away. They seemed to fade into the fog. Going to tell their masters, no doubt. Going to let them know what he had said. But he was angry now, and well into his speech, and the thought did not frighten him. He grinned. He would have liked to call after them, wait, there's more.

"What do you say to Publius Clodius Pulcher, gentlemen, if your verdict here says to Hybrida that he must go into exile? Will you thank Clodius and his rich patron, whom I do not need to name, for the corruption of our courts and the loss of that ancient safeguard of our freedom?" More men were leaving now, he was surprised to see how many. "Will you bow to Clodius in the streets, as he and his gangs swagger past you, driving you off the pavement and into the gutters? Will you shove past armed men to denounce Clodius in the Senate—if the consul, his friend, will allow you to speak when you get there? Will you go to the other consul—why do we have two every year if not to prevent just this sort of danger?—and ask him for his protection? Good, honest, upright Bibulus. He will want to help you, but he will still be barred in his house, in fear of his life, as he is already; it will not be long before you, and all law-abiding citizens, will be, too."

More men had gone, but a number had appeared in their places, hanging around the edges of a crowd that not even the day could discourage—large men, looming across the cold swirls of the fog. No doubt they were armed too. From farther down the Forum among the buildings there was a noise—shouting, and running feet. The jury heard it, too. They were sitting up and looking around, judging the distance, perhaps. Only Caelius was smiling, grinning with joy; he winked at Cicero across the intervening distance when his old teacher's eye fell on him. Cicero turned away.

"A moment more, gentlemen," he said, making his voice calm and beautiful, and the jurymen, who had partly risen to get away from the threat around them, returned trustfully to their seats. "We are Roman citizens. Our ancestors rebelled against the Etruscans and their kings, they defended us against Carthage and the power of the oriental despots, they made and preserved a city in which we could live as free men. Do not throw away what they built. Rebel again. Resist, as your fathers did. Vote, argue, stand up against the power which is being brought against you. I do not disguise from you that it is dangerous: death may well be your reward if you fail. But the powerful men who would destroy us count on your believing that death is worse than living in our own country as slaves, worse than being forced into exile. It is not—our ancestors knew it, and in your hearts you know it too. We are free men. May the gods remember us, and help us to remain so."

He waited a moment to see if the jury had understood. They had. They looked like a line of battle on a field, waiting for the enemy to appear.

It was not slow to come. The noise was louder now, cries and shouts of something that sounded like orders, in the din. There were men hurtling toward them, flickering whitely in and out of the torchlight as they came. He saw the glint of bronze.

The praetor had taken him by the arm and was leading him into an odorous passage between two buildings, dark as a cave and ringing with the splash of water. His feet slipped into the icy gutters and the cold gripped his legs. Then he was out in the thinner, chillier fog of the Sacred Way, hidden from the Forum by the bulk of the jewelers' shops. "Go around and get up the Palatine Hill by the back way," the praetor was whispering. "Clodius keeps a lot of men by the Steps, in the Temple of Castor. It isn't safe that way." His own men were around him, a press of warmth and strong bodies. They murmured agreement, preparing to lead him off. He could not imagine how they had found him in the dark.

There was noise in the street all the rest of the morning: men tramping up and down, voices calling. At noon, when he ate his meal with his family in the dining room, which was at the back of the house, he heard it. If his wife and little son did too, they said nothing, though Terentia ate with white lips, sitting very stiffly, as if she had set herself to make a demonstration of eating in front of a hostile crowd.

When they had left he stayed on in the room, working until Tiro came in. He gave the effect of swimming through the fog, which had thickened so much that even inside the house the lamps were circled by globes of their own fuzzy light, and drops of water condensed on every surface. Tiro was shaking a spray of it out of his tunic. "Have some soup," Cicero said, spooning him out a bowl. "There's plenty left."

Tiro was a slave and did not recline on a couch to eat, but sat in a chair like a woman. Cicero thought: I've never noticed before how uncomfortable that looks.

"Young Marcus Caelius won his case," Tiro said between mouthfuls. "Hybrida was convicted, nearly unanimously."

"That's good."

"Everyone's talking about it. He's made a sensation; some patrician hostess has invited him to dinner tonight and is telling everyone she's got a young lion to show them."

He was glad the boy was well launched, and if the aristocrats were taking him up, so much the better. Much the same thing had happened to him when he had achieved his first successes.

"They're talking about your speech as well," Tiro said, pushing a piece of bread around the bowl.

"I dare say they are."

"They're afraid—" He stopped: the noise from outside was suddenly louder. Both men stood up; a servant was panting in the doorway. "Marcus Tullius," he was crying. "The doorman says to come. Something's happened, out in the street. A young man—"

Caelius, Cicero thought.

Out on the street it was nearly as dark as night, though there must have been two or three hours left of whatever daylight they were going to have. Black water trickled between paving stones, the gates of Crassus' house dripped like icicles in the melting dimness. A crowd had gathered down the way, toward Metellus'— Metellus' widow's house. They were bending over something on the ground. A slave was holding up a lantern.

The figure sprawled on the cobbles, half hidden by a kneeling passerby, his hand thrown out as if he were running after something, the fingers curled open. Blood seeped out around it, glittering in the lantern light. "Caelius?" Cicero whispered.

"Yes?" a familiar voice answered, and the tall boy was standing beside him. "Here, watch out. You'll fall."

Someone was yanking the tunic down over the knees of the figure on the ground. "What happened?" Cicero said, recovering himself.

"I don't know. A fight, I think."

The crowd moved a little, the man who had been trying to straighten the tunic stood up. Cicero could see the face now, lumpy and pale, the reddish hair plastered down on the high forehead.

"Catullus," Cicero cried, remembering the boy in the Forum.

"That's right. Here, come away and get a bit of air."

"Is he dead?"

"I don't think so," Caelius said. "But he's badly hurt. Some men—Clodius' gang, I think—seem to have set on him in the street. The doctor's coming. We'll know just how bad it is then."

"Oh, gods, Caelius. I thought it was you."

"No." The tall boy's color had come back and he was laughing a little as he looked down at Cicero affectionately. "I'm safe, thanks to you. I won my case, and Clodia Metelli has invited me to dinner."

XII

There had been a meeting at the Temple of Castor. The result had been that Publius Clodius Pulcher was transferred from patrician to plebeian status. In rumors that went around the dinner parties somewhat later, it appeared that he had been adopted by a plebeian named Fonteius. What made it spicy enough for dinner was that Clodius' new father was twenty years old—some ten or twelve years younger than his adopted son. "But some large amount richer than he was before," Cicero commented when he heard the news.

Someone, too, had taken advantage of the weather and the small turnout to push the adoption through the Plebeian Assembly the same afternoon. "We all know who that was," Cicero said when he heard. "Caesar has owned the Assembly for the whole of this past year."

So few voters had been at the Assembly that word of what they had done did not get out for a month. By then, Cicero had been out of town for some time, visiting a house he owned in Sicily, where he hoped to work on a book about geography and get in some mackerel fishing. He didn't—the weather was too good for one and too bad for the other—and presently he moved on to Formiae, then to Arpinum, where he stayed with his brother.

He had told everyone that he was taking a rest—indeed he tried to convince himself that this was so—but the truth was he had not liked the thought of violence so close to his house; it was perfectly plain what Clodius' men had been doing in the street: they had been waiting for him to come out. That he hadn't, he supposed, had been only luck. The poor boy who stumbled on them had only gotten what Clodius had intended for him instead. And it might have been Caelius, or Terentia, or even his little boy, whom they attacked.

"Terentia," he had ordered. "Pack up the household. We're going to the country. I'm going to forget politics." White-faced and ill from a lingering weakness that kept her to her bed, Terentia had agreed; he knew the same thought had occurred to her, but she had been too brave to say so. Pompey, too, had thought it a good idea. "I don't like it, Marcus," the great man had said. "I don't know what's going on. I feel like a general in a town under siege, and there's someone tunneling under our walls—you know what I mean? I hear it, but I can't see it. Perhaps it's better if you get away until I find out who it is."

In Arpinum Cicero's letters caught up with him: one from Caelius, telling him of the strange and uneasy atmosphere in the city, another from Pompey assuring him, a little mysteriously, of his continued support and friendship, and a third, which went some way to explaining the other two.

FROM GAIUS VALERIUS CATULLUS, IN ROME, TO MARCUS TULLIUS CICERO, AT HIS COUNTRY HOUSE IN ARPINUM.

May 1, 695 years from the founding of the city.

Greetings. If you are well, I am well. I must apologize for the brevity of this note: I have to dictate it to a secretary, and am not yet well enough to talk very long. On the day I was set upon by men in the street, I was coming to tell you that Clodius had been adopted into the plebeian class. The ceremony was performed in the Temple of Castor according to the forms. I am no expert but it seems to have been quite legal. Julius Caesar presided as consul, and Gnaeus Pompeius Magnus, Pompey the Great, represented the College of Augurs. It was done less than three hours after you made your speech at Hybrida's trial...

Less than three hours. He put the two letters, this one and Pompey's, side by side and looked at them for a long time, trying to make sense of them, but nothing came to him. Or nothing he could bring himself to believe.

A few days later he had another, and a further explanation.

TO MARCUS TULLIUS CICERO, IN ARPINUM FROM MARCUS CAELIUS RUFUS, IN ROME.

...now that I am the celebrated young advocate I go to all the best parties, and hear all the choicest news. And the latest is—are you ready for this?—I heard it at Clodia Metelli's, and by the gods, she should know—the latest is that Pompey is marrying Julius Caesar's daughter. She's twenty-three, and Pompey is...whatever age he's calling himself today. I make it forty-seven. Isn't he the same age as you? Yet it's a love match, they say...

Quintus, reading this over Cicero's shoulder, said, "A love match?"

"That's right." Cicero set down the letter. "Pompey's love of prestige, and Caesar's love of power." He had turned pale, and his eyes seemed to be hurting him, for he was pressing the space between them so hard the bridge of his nose was white. "I have to go back, Quintus. I should never have left. But that young fellow's beating upset me. I imagined—"

"Go back? Now? It's more dangerous than ever."

"This isn't politics. This is something worse." Cicero had already called to Tiro to start the servants packing. "I thought that in their discord those three powerful men would tear Rome apart. I was wrong. It's their harmony that's going to destroy us. Unless I put a stop to it, what they are preparing for us is tyranny."

He saw Pompey as soon as he came back, not at the wedding, which was so private that he only heard it had taken place several days later, but at the games, where the two of them were cheered and the crowds, pleased to see two popular heroes together, made one name of their two, calling them "Gnaeus Cicero." Secretly Cicero was gratified that the more important name was his; Pompey may not have been, for his red face flushed a fiery purple and he held up his arm in a military salute with more than his ordinary brusqueness. Still, he seemed impressed by their reception, and exerted himself to be very pleasant to Cicero. He might have been recognizing that Cicero had as much to offer him as Caesar and Crassus. Indeed he hinted that he did once or twice. "Oh, yes," Cicero said. "We could go down in history as the men who saved the republic, even at the expense of our own careers. A very honorable way to be remembered, isn't it?"

"Yes," said Pompey, licking his lips as if he could taste honey there.

Cicero congratulated him on his marriage. The huge eyes blinked as Pompey smiled. Sleepily he announced that he and his wife—he rolled the word around on his tongue with pleasure—would be going out to his place in the Alban Hills for a while. It was a very satisfactory arrangement. Very satisfactory indeed. Of course, while he was gone, Cicero needn't worry; he would keep an eye on things in the city and make sure his old friend—his oldest friend, really—was safe. If he wanted anything he had only to call on him; he was always at Cicero's disposal. He hoped his old friend knew that. Cicero assured him that he did.

XIII

I n July, Clodius, who had married his heiress Fulvia after all, was elected tribune. Though Metellus had banned most of the clubs and temple sodalities during his consulship, Clodius had found ways to see that quite a lot of money
went to his supporters among the plebeians all the same. Though much of the
money came from his new wife, a certain amount came from Clodia too; every
night the house on the Palatine Hill was lighted and filled with music. Crowds of
men, young aristocrats going through their inheritances, elderly senators with
unusual tastes, rich knights hoping to improve their social positions—trooped
between the black and silver gates. Chairs with silk hangings brought courtesans
from the lower city; there were caterers, acrobats, actors, dance troops, mimes, all
come to add to Clodia's entertainments. No one left without making some contri-
bution to Clodius' campaign; no one seemed displeased or reluctant to do it.

"Government by money," Caelius said, disgusted. He had been to a few of the
parties.

"And by women." Tiro had dumped a stack of unanswered letters on Cicero's
desk and was eyeing his master commandingly.

"A deadly combination," Cicero said, and, sighing obediently, picked up his
pen.

Women, and money, and the violence that was everywhere now, even at the
polls... Bibulus, the consul, ordered the elections for the consuls for the new year
postponed, issuing an edict from his barricaded and defended house that the omens
were unpropitious and the voting could not be held. There was talk of trying to
burn him out, but nothing much came of it. Pompey was working hard behind the
scenes to get a friend of his into the office, and perhaps he had been in favor of the
postponements; in any case, they stood, and no consular election was held for more
than a month. Cato, in a speech, called Pompey's methods "dictatorial," and there
was nearly another riot over that.

"You'd better prepare yourself," Hortensius said at a boating party he gave one
sweltering afternoon at the end of July, not long after the elections. They were
cruising on the river below the city, listening to a small group of musicians and
watching the burnt brown banks slide past. The ladies chattered among themselves; he could see Terentia, animated and enjoying herself, but looking a little

anxious and pale as if she had heard bad news or were coming down with something. There was no breeze, and the rowers were sweating over their oars. "There's going to be trouble," Hortensius insisted. "Clodius is going to be coming after you as soon as he can."

"What kind of trouble could there be?" Cicero asked, smiling. It was a pleasant day, and he was enjoying the party—well, he loved all kinds of social gatherings, and the river was beautiful. It hummed with life, insects buzzed, fish rose, small boats paddled past; out in the main current a row of barges toiled up from Ostia toward the Tibur Docks. A submerged log just under the tawny water caught his attention. The current rippled around it, flexing its long muscle to embrace it. "No trouble. If Clodius tries violence, I have my friends—" he nodded toward them and gave them his wide, intelligent smile. "I almost hope he does try something like that. It would give us a case for a prosecution."

"Clodius is a tribune now, he's immune from prosecution," Lucullus the general said from his couch.

"Not forever."

There was a murmur from the men under the awning on the deck. It was true. He would only be tribune for a year.

"Perhaps you haven't thought of other forms of aggression against you," Hortensius persisted, so worried that his red face glowed with sweat like the rowers'.

"A court case, do you mean? An accusation of wrongdoing when I was consul, or some such thing?" Cicero's large nose was twitching and his lips curved in a smile. The others smiled with him, and Lucullus chuckled under his breath, a little sound like bees on the summer air.

"No, not a court case. Even Clodius wouldn't be so foolish."

Cicero grinned. "You never know. We can only hope he tries." The rest of the party laughed.

Only Hortensius refused to be cheered, "I wouldn't hope for that if I were you." The men on the couches, catching his disquiet, looked uneasy and oppressed. Perhaps it was the heat. He was glad, at last, to get back to the quay and go home for a bath.

On the eighth of August Cicero received a note inviting him to Pompey's place in the hills for dinner. Curious, and rather pleased, he dressed himself with care, and packing a jar of his best wine in a basket, trundled out the cart to the vast yellow house in the country. This time Pompey himself was waiting at the door; he led Cicero out to a pretty courtyard, entirely Roman in style, where a fountain played among oleanders and a fig tree nodded gracefully over the table. Pompey's new wife was not in sight—except indirectly, Cicero thought, watching the big man stretch out with lazy and contented pleasure on his couch. From time to time as they ate and chatted, Pompey's blue eyes clouded over and he dreamed, a small, unaware smile playing over his face. But when it came to the wine and the dessert, and the reason for the invitation, the great man was as present and alert as he had ever been on a battlefield.

"Marcus, you know that bill for land to compensate my veterans?"

"Of course," Cicero said, with reserve. He still thought of the violence of Julius Caesar with disgust and dismay, and he did not care for the radical new provisions of the law.

"Perhaps. You may be right. But some of those provisions have a certain interest. They're going to use public land, you see—property the city owns—grassland and farms and so on. They plan to divide it among the soldiers, and some of the poor from the city."

"Yes, I know. Gnaeus, it's a terrible idea. It's going to do a lot of harm—the city can't afford..."

Pompey waved his way with a gesture of his cup. "That's all past now," he said.

"Well, at any rate the bill has passed now," Cicero replied crisply.

Pompey laughed. "What I want, my old friend, is for you to take a place on the commission that's going to administer the transfer of this land."

He couldn't have been more surprised if Pompey had reached across the table and popped one of his stuffed figs into his mouth; indeed, he found he had opened his jaws as if to receive it, but Pompey had not noticed; he was still talking.

"I need a man like you," he was saying, bending forward and directing his stare persuasively in Cicero's direction. "I," Cicero thought. That's interesting.

"There's a lot of feeling in the city about this now," Pompey said. "Bad feeling." He seemed puzzled, perhaps upset. His large eyes were hidden behind his heavy eyelids, but Cicero could see the pupils moving back and forth uneasily.

"Well, what did you expect?"

"I don't know. Not this, anyway. Not this violence."

"Gnaeus, that's the way things work here. If you put yourself in the hands of two entirely unscrupulous men like Caesar and Crassus, they will use your name and your prestige for their own ends."

"I think I know as well as anyone how politics works in Rome." But that was doubtful, even to him. He looked around the pretty courtyard with an air of desperation, as if it were too bare, too small, too confined. Cicero, remembering how happily he had reclined on his pillows in the tented room indoors, thought: why, he wishes he were still in the East, with his army. He's sorry he came back to Rome at all.

"Look," Pompey said. "I want you on that commission. You're a man of integrity; people admire you, even if they don't agree with your ideas. You have a following among all the classes—senators, knights, plebeians, everyone. They'd all have more confidence in this law if they knew you were serving on the board. Do you see what I mean?"

"Oh, I think so." I think I see better than you, he added silently. You're not used to being unpopular, are you? You're used to obedience, and foreigners walking back-wards out the door when you dismiss them. It must come as a shock that Romans have minds of their own.

"You see, Marcus, it's a complicated business, administering this law, and I need someone of your intelligence to do it. Quite frankly, that's at the bottom of my request: no one else could manage it as well. I know you don't agree with all the provisions, but, you know, from a place on the commission you'd be able to modi-fy things as they came up. If you thought it was necessary. And it might be—I admit that. The bill isn't perfect. I'd back you over any changes you'd care to make."

"I'd carry out the law as it was written."

"Oh. Oh, of course. Of course." The wine cup was in play again; Pompey was not to be worried with details. "You'll be compensated for your trouble, of course. Rather well, as it happens—the law is generous on that point. As it's written."

"I would serve without compensation," Cicero said, feeling like Cato.

"It's a position of honor," Pompey said, managing to ignore this too. "It's wor-thy of you. And as such it would offer you a certain amount of protection from…"

"From Clodius? I thought you were protecting me from him already."

"Oh, I am. I don't care for this violence, as I said. I've seen it happen before, in the army. I've seen commanders who were lazy or weak let this sort of discontent get out of hand. Terrible thing when it does. Morale falls apart, discipline dies…" He shrugged. "What Rome needs right now is strong leadership. That's what the trouble is. The Senate hasn't the foresight, or the unselfishness, to lead—they haven't for a generation or more, if you ask me."

"That's true enough."

Pompey sighed and smiled a charming grin at Cicero. "Well, until the city gets the leader it deserves, you can be sure that I'll see to it that you're left alone. It's just that with your support for the land law it would be so much easier. Do you see what I mean?"

He did see; he closed his eyes and the image was still in front of him: Clodius, head thrown back, hand on the knife in his belt, and behind him the tall, thin, ele-gant consul, the hollow-eyed financier.

"I can't," he said. "I appreciate your generous offer, and I'm flattered that you want me—" Well, it was a sign that he still had influence and power if Pompey needed to bribe him with a job, so perhaps he was flattered after all—"but I could not accept a position administering a law I opposed in the Senate, nor could I do anything that would appear to condone, much less support, the illegal methods of the consul."

He paused, but Pompey was saying nothing; he was watching Cicero with an intensity of concentration that suggested he was looking for something hidden in the words. Cicero had a strong temptation to turn and see if there was someone standing behind him.

"Gnaeus, we're old friends. I can speak frankly to you; you won't misunderstand. I've done a lot for the sake of politics in my career, but I have always stood for the law and the republic; I have always argued that they were our best, indeed our only protection. In all that I was perfectly sincere. But if I accept this position, not only will it do nothing to help your law, it will destroy what reputation I have. People will say I was as cynical as any other politician. I just can't do it."

"I see," said Pompey, getting up. "Well, I hope the law and the republic will protect you, as you say." He smiled and put his arm across Cicero's shoulders. "I really do. I wouldn't want anything to happen to my oldest friend."

"As long as we're friends, nothing will."

"Of course we are," Pompey beamed at him. "Of course we are."

In the next few days Cicero's friends took to spending a lot of time with him, as if they were sitting at the bedside of a man who was sicker than he knew. They came early in the morning, neglecting their own business, and stayed until late in the day; after a while he realized that they did it to keep him from going out. Annoyed at first, he gave in and let them take care of him. He was glad of the time; he spent it preparing a defense against an accusation in court if Clodius brought a suit against him there. He did not tell the others for fear of worrying them. It was a foolish precaution; they were so anxious they could hardly speak to him in a normal voice. All the same, they tried to help. Lucullus suggested tentatively that a voyage might be beneficial—he did not say for what; Hortensius urged him solemnly to remember his philosophy; Pompey, on the one occasion when he called, swore that he would never allow harm to come to Cicero. He seemed to mean it, and Cicero felt better while he was there, but as soon as the great man left he began to worry again.

Caesar sent a note and followed it with a military tribune, carrying a message. If Cicero would like to travel for a while, it could easily be managed: Caesar had a position on his staff in Gaul that he would be delighted if Cicero would take up. A man of Cicero's brilliance would be invaluable; Caesar found himself unable to express how honored he would be by this arrangement. Cicero could consider himself his lieutenant-general.

Cicero sent this messenger back without a word, and two days later another—this time one of Caesar's friends from the Senate—arrived with a proposal that Cicero might like an appointment as a kind of honorary legate. He could travel anywhere in the empire for a year, at the Senate's expense, of course, and bring back reports on whatever problems he thought important. Or no reports at all, if he found writing them too disagreeable a task. This man also Cicero dismissed, confirming his friends' opinion that he was not quite well. "But I could not accept," he wrote to his brother Quintus. "What would history say of me in six hundred years, if I took a bribe to alter my convictions now?"

Caelius came often, always at night and in secret, so that Cicero could not really object. He brought morsels of information which he fed to Cicero, watching him all the time with anxious eyes, as if he might see signs of fever in his face: Caesar had been given Metellus' province in Gaul, and the appointment had been extended for five years; someone had tried to assassinate Pompey, but before he could be questioned he had died in prison—no one knew how. Clodia knew something about it, he added; he had come on her in her bedroom, sitting before her mirror with her hand on a yellowish piece of stone—some sort of keepsake or reminder, of what he didn't know. She was muttering over it like a village wise woman; he had been positively frightened of her. He gave Cicero a look out of his clear hazel eyes: he looked frightened now too. "It's all right, Caelius," Cicero had snapped. "I'm fine. There's nothing wrong with me." And the boy had cheered up a little.

Quintus wrote to him every day, in a tone of unmistakable anxiety, urging him to prepare himself if Clodius attacked him through the law courts, and begging him to take care. Even Terentia began to look hunted and nervous, and took to feeding him soups and porridges and plates of stewed beans, which he hated, as if he were an invalid. When he tried to reassure her she retired to her room and did not come out again. Tiro said nothing, but his craggy face grew gray in the hollows, like a man who looks on an empty and frightening future.

Then in December, Clodius took office as tribune, and the illness everyone suspected was revealed as mortal.

XIV

It was the first of January, and though it was dangerous, this time Cicero went out. He had had enough of sitting at home, he said, and besides his presence was required in the Senate for the installation of the new magistrates. He assembled, therefore, all the men of his household and as many friends as he could find—it was gratifying to see that there were nearly two hundred people walking with him. Caelius had made a point of coming, though he had told him not to, and now, in the first cold of the new year, the boy smiled at him over the cloud of his own breath, which trailed blue-white through the sunshine as they went.

His friends kept by him anxiously, but there was no trouble at the temple. The magistrates took their oaths quickly enough, and he was willing to go home. "I've made my point," he said. "Clodius hasn't kept me from my duty." Relieved, Caelius took his arm. "Come on then," he urged. "The sooner you're behind stone walls the better I'll feel."

But out in the Forum Clodius had seized the occasion to make a speech—his first as tribune. There he was, like a shining statue of himself, on the Rostra; the Forum was packed with his poor, uneducated followers, idle and looking for trouble as always, and with his bullies, making a space around the fringes. They all let out a huge cheer as the small man talked. Cicero stopped near the back of the crowd.

Up on the Rostra Clodius stared back at his audience, mocking and insolent. Then he threw back his head so that his black hair rose like a wing into the sunlight, and his voice flew out to them. He made no effort to speak well; he used no rhetoric, no flourishes; it was as if he scorned such devices. Nor did he modify his sneering aristocratic drawl. Let them dislike him, he seemed to say: he knew more about dislike than they would ever learn.

"All right," he said, as if continuing a remark that the cheering had interrupted. "All right. Enough of that. Now we'll get down to business." They yelled for him again, but he ignored them. "All right. Listen: in a few days I'm going to call the Assembly—our Assembly—and propose some laws. First, that the government subsidy of the price of grain will stop." There was a gasp and some of his supporters raised their arms in a threatening way. Someone shouted, "We're poor men. We can't afford the price as it is. Do you want us to starve?"

"I know," Clodius said. "Shut your mouths and listen, you fools. I said the subsidy will stop. Stop it will. Bam! But any man who is eligible for it now will get his ration free from now on."

"Well," said Caelius, under the roar of the crowd, "that ought to insure the passage of that law."

"Yes," Cicero said, depressed. He seemed to be counting the heads of the crowd. "And whatever else he proposes as well."

And there was to be more. Clodius, grinning at the crowd, had raised his hands over his head like the winner of a boxing match in the Arena, but he brought them down again, palms outward, silencing the noise. "Yes," he drawled, as if he were alone with them in a room. "Next: all workingmen's clubs will be legal again. Bam! We will have our rights back, and our poor men's pleasures."

"And the base of our power," Cicero said tartly. "He'll organize them; they'll do whatever he wants."

"They do already," Caelius said.

"Well, now he won't be hampered by a little thing like the law." The great nose twitched, but Cicero was not amused.

"He hasn't been very badly hampered by it up till now."

Clodius was shouting, to the continued tumult of the Assembly. It sounded like the chariot races or a popular gladiatorial match. Cicero's men moved closer around him; some of them bunched their fists and swore under their breaths. Clodius screamed in a voice like the caw of a crow over the storm of noise. "No one will be allowed to take omens or watch the skies on days when they're voting on our bills. They can't use that trick on us again. Last," he whispered hoarsely, like a man confiding his secret wish, "anyone who executes a Roman citizen without a trial will be subject to the fullest penalty of the law."

The cheers of the crowd were puzzled, but they did their best for him. A wedge of his burliest supporters, ex-gladiators by the look of them, cut through and up the steps to the tribune; they raised him up as if he were the image of their patron god and carried him on their shoulders around the square, over the waving arms and the voices crying his name.

"What was that about, that no one can condemn a Roman citizen without a trial? No one can do that anyway," Caelius said. "Oh, Hercules, what is it?"

Cicero had crumpled: his face had drawn down around his nose and mouth until it looked like an animal's muzzle, his heavy shoulders sagged. "Are you hurt?" Caelius shouted, looking for the knife, the wound.

Cicero was staring at him as if he had spoken in a language he did not understand, as if like a beast, he understood no language at all. Even his voice had failed him: in a thick mumble he said something unintelligible. His trapped eyes gazed out at Caelius.

"What?" Caelius cried, frantic with fear. He could not look at those eyes. Cicero was leaning his weight against his arm, as if he could no longer support it himself. "What? What did you say? What's the matter?"

"Hortensius was right. It wasn't a court case, after all," Cicero said, and closed his eyes.

Somehow they got him home. Someone brought him wine, which he drank, someone else a sponge with hot water, which he shoved away. He sat, slumped in his chair, and would not look at anyone. Perhaps he could not see them; there was something about the pulled skin around his eyes that suggested that he had gone blind. They kept asking him, did he want a doctor? A priest of Asclepius? A blanket? A drink? Perhaps he had gone deaf too, for he did not answer.

At last Terentia ordered them away. She put out her arm to Caelius, however, to keep him; she had noticed that when Caelius spoke, Cicero's head had swung toward him slowly, as if he scented something on the wind. "Is he ill?" Caelius whispered to her, hiding his voice under the noise of the others' departure.

"I don't think so, but it's possible." She shook her head. "Did something happen in the Forum? Is that what it is?"

But that was what Caelius could not tell her; he did not think anything special had happened. One moment Cicero was crisp, acerbic, angry at the demonstrations around Clodius; the next moment he was like this. So Caelius sat on a cold stone bench in Cicero's atrium, afraid to take his eyes from the motionless man in the carved pear-wood chair, and he had to clasp his hands tightly between his knees to keep them from tearing at his hair.

The day faded in the opening in the roof; the sky grew pale, blushed, retreated into darkness. A servant came in to light the lamps but Caelius waved him away. He did not want the sudden brightness to startle his friend. Under the columns the shadows drew together and tangled themselves into a forest of darkness. The slumped figure sat motionless in the depths of it; only the silver gleam of his eyes showed that he was still as alert as ever.

At last he spoke, so quietly it was like a breath of wind stirring among leaves, the whisper of a forest creature moving in his haunts. "I want to tell you a story, young Marcus Caelius."

Tears sprang behind Caelius' eyes, he all but lept to his feet to run to Cicero, but he held himself back. "I'm listening."

Cicero did not answer. He seemed to have retreated deeper into the tangle and the dark.

"I was consul," Cicero said at last. "I ran a clean campaign. I had to—" the eyes flickered once, an unreadable message— "I had no money to buy votes, or to bribe men who could." You didn't need to, Caelius said in his mind. You were a great man, and everybody knew it. But he held himself tightly in the bonds of his watchfulness and said nothing.

A breath stirred the shadows around the seated figure; Cicero sighed. "Catiline did."

"Who?" whispered Caelius.

"Lucius Sergius Catilina, my opponent. They called him Catiline. He was an aristocrat, and he had all the money in the world. He spent it, too. But it did him no good. He was defeated." His voice said that he had been defeated himself, though Caelius knew that he had won that election, as he had won every other he had ever entered. "It made Catiline bitter—yes, I think it did. He was, as I say, a patrician, and he had lost the consulship to a knight; he was born in Rome, and I am from Arpinum. He had money, and he lost to a poorer man. He had talent, courage, charm-it was peculiar how everyone liked Catiline. Even when you knew what he was, you liked him. I always envied him that. That ease, that confidence. People were attracted to him, he had the gift of making you feel he cared about you. Perhaps he really did. He had intelligence, too. I never met a man with more. It was a pleasure to hear him talk. He was brilliant." I know, Caelius managed not to say. I used to hear him too, when I was young. The whole city did.

"It did something to him to lose that election." Cicero's voice was stronger, the gusts and sighs that had shaken it were passing off. "Yes, Catiline couldn't understand how he had failed. He had everything; he had done all that he was supposed to do. He thought that if he had not succeeded it must be because there was something wrong with the way things worked. Something wrong with the state, the laws, in fact with the Republic. It never occurred to him that the trouble might have been with him, with his character—or lack of it—with his soul. Voters can see that, you know. They're very hard to deceive, for any length of time—unless they want to be, but that's another story. No, Catiline was sure it had to be something outside himself. Well, once a man decides that, he is lost. Because when he looks around he can see that there are others for whom the Republic does not work as well as it might—as it should, if you like. There always are."

The dark shape moved, the light of the eyes went out: Cicero had turned his head to look over at him. "It is important to remember that. Under any form of government, kings, tyrants, oligarchs, democracies, there are always people who flourish and people who fail. The question is who, and how many, and what kind of changes will help the unfortunate without damaging the others. There is no perfect system; though we dream of it, there is no ideal republic. There is only this sad, difficult, discordant state of conflicting desires among men, and we must do the best we can to bring some harmony to it."

Caelius sat still. He was not sure if Cicero knew that he had told him this many times before, when he was a pupil in his house, but he did not want to interrupt. Besides, he was remembering that Catiline's rebellion had coincided with certain rebellions of his own, and for a time he had gone to the meetings, listened to the speeches. He knew about Catiline's fatal charm, as he knew about his intelligence. He was certain, too, of something he was not sure Cicero believed: Catiline had had passion, as well as his other qualities. His speeches showed it: he had owned an incandescent belief in the impoverished and desperate men he had tried to lead.

"He gathered some of these people to him," Cicero said. "Though many of them have reappeared in our lives as Clodius' followers, not all of them were as bad as you might think. One of them was actually a praetor at the time, and several of them were sons of good families..." He sighed, and for a moment Caelius had a glimpse of his profile against the lighter darkness of a doorway. He had raised his head, as if he heard some sound not present to other ears. "Well, Catiline never cared about the poor. He used them when he thought they could help him."

"I—Didn't he? I thought he did. I mean—"

Perhaps Cicero heard him, for his head was shaking. But perhaps it was no more than that he was following his own thought. "He never troubled about the poor until he needed their backing, and then, of course, he went too far. He began with a proposal to abolish all debts, not caring what destruction this would bring to our trading, our banking, all our commercial life. I say not caring, for surely he was too intelligent not to know, though perhaps his followers were honestly misled.

"From there he went on to plans to arm the slaves, turn loose the gladiators, set fire to the city. Oh, yes, it's true. He planned to raise the countryside, too, and create what chaos he could there. He intended to step into the office to which he could not be elected over the charred bodies and broken buildings of a city that had already rejected him. We put it down, of course. We had to. I had to; I take the responsibility for it; I'm glad to take it. Catiline tried to have me murdered, you know. I was the consul; I was his enemy. Hybrida was a friend of his—I had to buy him off with the province of Macedon to keep him from interfering. Yes, it was I alone who stopped Catiline. I consider it the greatest glory of my life."

There was a long silence, through which the sound of breathing came sadly to Caelius' ears. "Catiline got away," Cicero said. "I let him go, because I didn't have enough evidence against him; he joined his ragbag of an army—he had thousands of men by then—away in the north. And I waited. I am good at waiting: a lawyer learns it, if he's going anywhere. And a boy from a country town knows all about it from his birth."

An old bear in the forest knows it too, Caelius thought: he could see Cicero's face now, the flexible mouth, the large, intelligent nose. He seemed to be looking around the room. His voice had changed again: it was the voice of the consul now, judicious, weary, strong. "All around me the city was in a panic, the Senate pressed me for action. They had declared a state of emergency, and gave me power to deal with it. They passed what is called their 'Ultimate Decree'—'The consul shall have full authority to do whatever is necessary to see that the city comes to no harm.' Whatever is necessary, without constitutional restraints. They urged me to move against the plotters, they came to me and argued, pleaded even, but I refused. The timing was wrong, the mood of the city—

"Once Catiline had left," Cicero said after a while, "his friends lost all control. They got drunk and bragged to their women, they talked too much at all the wrong parties. Then one day they tried to suborn the embassy of a disaffected tribe of Gauls who had come to Rome to get help with their problems. Well, the tribesmen came to me; they knew there was something wrong with what they were being asked to do. And that was what I was waiting for."

Caelius remembered those days, too, though he had long since left the con-spiracy—indeed his involvement did not survive the knowledge that that was what it was. He remembered. The old hunter had put out his paw and swept his prey into it. "I went back to the Senate," Cicero said. "They passed another decree, naming the plotters individually, because by now I knew who they were. They designated them Enemies of the People. That meant again that I had full power to deal with them as I saw fit. That's what it means. Full power." He sighed, and his hand went up and hid his eyes. Whatever it meant it was no satisfaction to him now.

"So at last I moved. I sent Metellus, who was my praetor, north with an army after Catiline. I told the other praetors to set up an ambush, out on the Mulvian Bridge, where the Via Flaminia crosses the Tiber, because the Gauls were going to pass that way. And they did. We took them all, Catiline's friends, their letters, weapons, promises, everything. When they were brought back to Rome I had them up before the Senate and showed them the evidence. Every one of the conspirators confessed. What else could they do? We had them, and if their hands were not yet red with Roman blood, it was only because I had moved on them so fast."

It was the end of the story; Cicero had turned away, retreating again into the thicket of shadows. "They voted you the Father of Our Country," Caelius said soft-ly, to call him back. "I know because I went to the service of thanksgiving in your honor at the Temple of Jupiter. They told me that no other civilian had ever been given that title before. They were grateful, you know. They realize what you've done for them, and they'll stand by you now."

"They do," Cicero said, "but they won't."

Suddenly there was movement in the room. A lamp was burning, the columns and statues stepped forward out of darkness, the paintings on the walls breathed. Cicero was standing, on the point of a stylus he held a coal from the brazier poised over the flame. His eyelids fluttered slowly; his head drooped forward against his chest. "I can't say this in the dark."

"Say what?" Caelius cried, but fortunately Cicero did not hear him. He stood by the pillared lamp, listening to the past. "Great Gods," he shouted, throwing up his massive head. "I had them executed."

The sound went around the room, trapped against the walls, infinitely dis-tressed.

"They were guilty," Caelius said.

"You don't understand. There was no trial." He had turned his head away. "There wasn't time. We didn't know if we had them all. Rescue was possible, armed uprisings, deaths. Catiline still had his army—Metellus hadn't caught up with him yet."

"I understand. Anyone would."

He wondered where the servants were; he thought Cicero looked bad, his color was bluish and he seemed cold. Heated wine might help...

"I asked the Senate for advice," Cicero said. "They voted for death. There was only one dissenting vote."

"Then it's not your fault. It wasn't your responsibility."

The head came up, the dark brown eyes looked into his. Behind them something flashed out: a glance, noble, authoritative, proud. "It *was* my responsibility. I was the consul."

XV

Cicero would not give in, not so easily. He would let them see that he still had all his teeth and claws. He told Terentia, who pressed her lips together and retired to her room, he told his servants, who did what was necessary. Dressed in a dusty black toga, with his cheeks unshaven and his hair uncombed, according to the custom, he went, a man in mourning over his disgrace, to the knights.

One by one he called on them, waiting patiently in their anterooms while they conferred in panic with their advisors and their friends. When they agreed to see him he reminded them in a voice that would rather have kept it secret of all he had done for them in the past: it made quite a list. There were tax contracts they had overbidden and he had gotten canceled for them, there were their dignities lost under Sulla the dictator, which he had restored. There were law suits defended in court, places for their clients and dependents, advancement for their sons.

Some of them agreed with him and even came with him to the next man on his list; a few pressed money on him and turned away; a few argued; a few looked as if they feared that someone might hear them and muttered about the violence in the Forum. But he had not lost his eloquence, it seemed, for all of them, the entire order of knights, put on the black toga and followed him out to the Campus Martius, where, standing on a block of marble meant for a theater Pompey was building for the city, he talked to them. All the young bloods of Rome were there, too, led by Publius Crassus, Crassus' son—there must have been twenty thousand men, crowded among the buildings, all in mourning. A field of faces bloomed above the black cloth, turned toward him, listening. When he had finished they cheered him until the stones rang and the very fabric of the city seemed to offer its support.

There was violence. In the streets Clodius' men threw stones and filth at him. Sometimes he arrived at his destination looking even worse than he intended, blotting a scratch on his forehead, a splash of blood from one of his injured men, water from a fountain where he had stopped to clean himself from these expressions of the small man's disapproval. Caelius, wincing at this, tried to keep him at home, explaining that what he was doing was undignified, but Cicero only smiled and in his new, humbled, apologetic voice, insisted that he had to go, he had to save himself if he could.

In the Forum Clodius harangued a huge crowd one afternoon for several hours, claiming that Pompey had approved the bill to condemn to exile all those who had put Roman citizens to death. "He will use force if he has to." He added that Crassus and Caesar—"the leading men of Rome—"were in favor of it too.

Perhaps they were, though Cicero denied it to the friends who crowded into his atrium to see him. There was evidence on his side too: Publius Crassus, who had once been his student, came that night and sat at Cicero's rather dusty feet with half the younger aristocrats in his train; it was possible that he was acting on his own, but then again, as Cicero maintained, he might have been standing in for his father. In any case no one could disprove it—the elder Crassus was out of town on an extended visit in the country. Caesar, asked for his opinion two days later, outside the walls where he was waiting with his army to go north, admitted that though he had opposed the executions at the time-his had been the sole dissenting vote in the Senate—he did not think anything would be served by trying to punish a man for what was already done.

"Well, that's something in our favor," Cicero said, but he spoke in the voice of man who had hoped for better.

"Really?" Caelius said. "It's the first time anyone's said in public that Clodius' bill applies to you. Do you think that's a good thing?"

Cicero did not answer. "And why is Caesar here to be asked in the first place?" Caelius demanded. "Why isn't he in Gaul? Does a man really need an army eating its head off just outside the city walls to remind us that he didn't vote for the death penalty but he's too magnanimous to hold it against you?"

Cicero had gone deaf again in that convenient way he had developed in the last few days, and he did not answer. He was remembering Pompey—generous, openhearted Pompey—a little slow, perhaps, a little brash, but loyal and good. He would not forget his friend. Others might—it seemed to be the fashion in Rome these days—but Pompey never would. Fretfully he demanded of Caelius, "What does Clodius mean, Pompey will use force? Does he think Pompey intends to murder me?" Neither Caelius nor any of the others who came to see him in those days—Hortensius with his distracted wisps of white hair, sheep-like Curio, Lucullus the general, Cicero's brother Quintus, bleached under his olive skin, and very anxious—could tell him, though Caelius supposed that these men knew as much about politics among them as there was to know.

"Of course not," Cicero said, answering his question for himself. "Pompey would never allow harm to come to me. I have his promise on that."

"Let him say so now then," Caelius shouted furiously across the room, but from the villa in the Alban Hills came only silence.

The Senate tried to rally, and to pass a decree in opposition a few days later—an uneasy meeting, choking with anxiety, for Clodius had come in surrounded by thirty of the worst-looking toughs anyone had ever seen outside the Arena. He had to be reminded that as a tribune his person was sacred and no one would dare to touch him, before he would consent to leave them outside. Even then he marched his echoing heels up to the platform with a military swagger which showed the hilt of his sword under his toga as unmistakably as if it were naked. "No one could miss the meaning of that," Hortensius said afterwards. "How dare he? In the Senate," Metellus Nepos raged.

When, shortly after, Clodius introduced his law to the Plebeian Assembly, it went further than he had originally said it would, too: now it proposed that anyone who put a citizen to death would be "forbidden fire and water."

"An old phrase," Tiro whispered to Caelius, eyeing Cicero with disquiet. "It means that no one may give him any food or shelter, no slave may serve him, no friend take him in. He must leave the city, you see, or he will die. Exile. Exile is what Clodius has in mind."

"It still doesn't mention him by name," Caelius protested. "He doesn't have to agree that it means him. After all it's the Senate that acted."

Cicero turned on his bench and gave him that strange, proud glance again. "Let's face the facts. It means me."

The knights got up a delegation to the Senate, but Gabinius, the consul, a friend of Caesar's, grinned through his teeth at them and would not let them speak, though they had taken the precaution of getting Hortensius and Curio, as members of the Senate, to go with them. Angry at the insult and the infringement of their rights, both Hortensius and Curio tried to address the city from the Rostra, but Clodius' men were there, and they were driven away. A senator who was with them was killed in the fighting.

Caelius brought the news to Cicero; he had been in the crowd himself and had a swelling over one eye to show for it. "It's getting very stormy out there," he said, easing himself into a chair. He had pulled a muscle in his thigh running after an ex-gladiator named Gorgias, whom in any case he had failed to catch.

"A killing." Cicero's face was white. He had come in from the back of the house, where he had been sitting at the bedside of his wife. She had collapsed that morning with what she insisted was a minor attack of asthma, but he did not believe her; though he did not tell her so, he thought it was something more serious than that, brought on by the strain. With difficulty he brought his mind back from his anxiety for her. "A killing. And a senator. Let's see to it that it's the last."

"What do you mean? Will you organize some kind of defense for yourself now? Something to reinforce the knights?" But his voice trailed away when he saw Cicero's eyes.

"No. I'll tell the knights to stop what they're doing. Now. Enough is enough."

But it was not enough for Clodius, and two days later he asked the consuls in public for their opinion. Piso, whom no one forgot was Caesar's father-in-law, merely answered that no cruel or barbarous deed commended itself to him, but

Gabinius, taking on his hero Pompey's blank-eyed stare, announced that the knights and senators were responsible for the violence because they had interfered.

At that the Senate united, and to show its feelings it too adopted the black toga, the unshaven jaw, the disordered hair of mourning. "It looks as though the whole city has died," Caelius reported, and Cicero lowered his head and squeezed his eyelids tightly shut with his fingers.

That night he wrote to Pompey. He had no pride left; he begged him to put an end to the agony of Rome. "Do not let one tribune destroy us," he wrote. "I will do whatever you think necessary; my life does not matter against the danger we are all in now." To Caelius' secret surprise, Pompey actually answered this.

"Got himself out of bed with his new wife, did he?" Lucullus asked when Cicero showed the reply to the council of war that met every morning in his house now.

"It wasn't worth his trouble if he did. He just says he won't let any harm come to you," Hortensius observed, straightening his black toga over his arthritic knees and sighing gustily. The senator who had been killed was a friend of his—he had been at the funeral, and his clothes still smelled of incense and wood smoke, giving a mournful and peculiar note to the meeting. There were still bruises on his own face from the beating he had received at the hands of Clodius' slaves in the Forum, too. They were purple and black. Caelius had an hysterical wish to ask him if he had chosen the toga to match.

"Well, that's something, if Pompey says that," Cicero said.

"Yes, but what?" Hortensius demanded, but no one had an answer for him.

The crisis dragged on. There were letters all over the atrium, stacks of boards that clattered when anyone moved among them, drifts of folded paper or parchment like the leaves of a forest floor. "They're supporting me," Cicero said, looking up from them and smiling like a skull. "All over Italy they're writing to tell me I can count on them for men, money, votes, whatever I need. I have only to ask."

"Ask then," Caelius whispered, but Cicero was listening for Lucullus and the praetor Lentulus Crus, who had gone to Pompey, and he did not raise his head. The sun spilled through the opening in the roof; outside it was spring, birds were making an uproar, the sky was as blue as an eggshell, and as fragile. Inside it was autumn, and the tedium of waiting, while long splashes of light fell across the disorder of the room. Caelius had tried to urge him to sit outdoors—in his mind then Cicero was like an invalid, and needed care—but no one had moved. They want to be near the door, Caelius thought. They don't want the news to travel one foot farther than it has to.

The afternoon grew dusty and threadbare, the men in the room had aged in the fading light. Hortensius' mouth had fallen slackly open, and his eyes were closed; Cicero's brother Quintus played angrily with a dish of fruit, as if he suspected his appetite of having deserted its post; Cicero was slumped gracelessly in his chair. But when the noise began he was the first to lift his head. His eyes gleamed in the shadows. "There they are," he growled, hope filling out his voice and making it rich.

Lucullus marched into the room; behind him Lentulus Crus slipped like a servant in his wake, grinning as broadly as a dog, as if he feared the general might turn on him. Perhaps he would, for he was looking for something to fix his anger on. He rattled out a chain of oaths; Hortensius surfaced, snorting the sleep out of his ears; Quintus had put down the dish; Cicero laughed softly to himself.

"What did Pompey say?"

Lucullus opened and closed his mouth several times before he succeeded in renouncing his mission. "I shouldn't have gone. I'm the wrong man. It never does to humble yourself to someone you hate. They can always tell if you don't mean it. He had my command in Asia, he knows I'll never be his friend."

"It was good of you to try," Hortensius said.

"He ought to realize that this has gone beyond party, or class or faction, if someone like you was willing to go out there and talk to him," Curio said with less than his usual tact, but Cicero was not offended; he was listening to another voice, and presently they fell silent to hear it too.

Lentulus was whispering, "Pompey told us to go to the consuls."

"We've already been to the consuls," Quintus shouted; Caelius, sick with rage, leaped to his feet. His bad leg crumpled under him and his sword clattered against a chair.

"Hush," Cicero murmured.

Lucullus was still standing in the middle of the room, waiting to finish his report. "Pompey says he can't do anything against an armed tribune without the express authorization of the Senate, because it is a sacrilege and therefore a crime to touch a tribune. So we must make an application to the consuls, and they will put it before the Senate, if they approve."

"He's joking," Quintus said. "He must be."

"No," Cicero said, so quietly that they all turned and looked at him. "He means exactly what he says. He hopes we will go, he wants the Senate to declare a state of emergency."

"Why?" Hortensius cried. Lucullus swore again, louder than before.

"Lucullus has seen the reason," Cicero said, smiling grimly into the gloom where the general stood. "Haven't you?"

"Yes," said Lucullus. "Because then he can do the one thing he has wanted to do all along. Then he can bring his army into Rome."

An argument had developed between Curio and Hortensius, but Cicero was not listening to it. He supposed that they were deciding his fate: Curio wanting him to stay and fight, Hortensius fretting anxiously about a civil war. He had picked up a handful of the letters and was waving them under Curio's nose. Lucullus seemed to be counting them, Caelius was shouting angrily. Blind Diodotus, his old teacher, had come in and was sitting in a corner on the floor, smiling faintly to himself. Pompey, Cicero thought. Pompey. My oldest friend.

They had left after a while, taking the reluctant Caelius with them. He had been that young once; the world had seemed as simple to him then as it did to Caelius now. What a pity that he had ever learned differently, that he had ever forgotten that shining certainty, and the energy it gave.

He had gotten to his feet to see his friends to the door. From here the disordered room looked worse. The papers seemed to rise and float down to the floor, carried on a wintry little draft. It chilled him, in any case, no matter what the season was; he thought it would be a long time before he saw the sun again.

So strong was this feeling that he pulled on his winter cloak when he went out and ordered a box of hot coals to be put in the wagon to warm his feet. To his surprise, the night was pleasant. The stars were large and close, a little breeze whispered among new leaves. Out on the road toward the hills, drifts of white floated across the beams of the lantern, but they were petals from the flowering trees, and not the snow he mistook them for at first.

The villa stared out blankly over the valley, its windows illuminated; on the balcony lamps cast yellow spears of light upward to the arches. He could see the statues along the roof, gesturing to the sky.

At the gate he gave his name and, respectfully, they let him through. "Yes, Marcus Tullius," they said, bobbing in time to the lanterns on the wagon. "He's at home." The servant at the door, however, asked him to wait. Cicero sat on a bench by the entry, looking out through the open doorway. The night wind brushed its hand over the grass on the hillside; a bird awoke and called, like the barking of a small, bronze dog.

Pompey, he thought. My friend.

The bench had grown colder and harder; he supposed he had been sitting on it for a long time. Well, perhaps Pompey was at dinner, or working, and couldn't come right away. Still it would have been polite to send him out a message, a cup of wine.

No one came. He sat patiently, remembering the bronze-haired boy, the young hero, the triumphant general. Pompey. The little wind passed over the hilltop, sighing for absent friends. Out on the drive, where it curved from behind the house, a horse clattered, going fast toward the gate.

"Oh, no," he said aloud, getting stiffly up from the bench. He could not explain his feelings to himself. He had a little pain in his chest that might have been anger, or fear for his future, but mostly what twisted his heart was grief, as if a friend had died. Not Pompey, he thought. But from out on the terrace he could see the gate, the rider pulling impatiently on the reins, while the servant hurried to the doorway to unlock it. The light fell on the horse, the bulk of the man on its back, the bright, metallic hair. Oh, no, Cicero thought. Not Pompey.

The servant had come out on the terrace, but Cicero was already climbing aboard his wagon. Over the rumble of the wheels he heard the man anyway, calling apologetically into the wind. He had to shout, quite unnecessarily, to his horses, so that he would not have to hear the servant's explanation.

That night he packed, thinking of Hortensius' warnings. He could not risk a civil war. He did not sleep, but sat up writing in his study: letters to his supporters, instructions to his bailiffs and managers, a long and painful letter to his wife. He spoke with old Diodotus for a while; he left word for Tiro to prepare for a journey. When dawn came he took a small silver statue of Minerva and hurried with it through the deserted Forum. The air was cold and black; in the east a band of crimson showed where the sun would rise, but the Forum was still dark and the buildings colorless. Beneath his feet pebbles slipped from crumbling paving stones; there was a noise in his ears—a long, aching sigh. He saw himself, head down, scuttling across the empty, open space like a crab on a seabed that some natural disaster had left unnaturally exposed. It seemed to him that it was not so much that he was leaving the city as that the city had already abandoned him.

In the Temple of Capitoline Jupiter he left the statue with the priest, giving instructions that it should be engraved. "To Minerva, the Protector of This City." He said a prayer and left a coin, but he felt no better. Like the sea, the gods seemed to have retreated, and there was no answer in his mind, only a long sighing whisper, which, a month later and hundreds of miles away, he realized suddenly had been the wind.

BOOK THREE

XIV

I t was dark. He blundered around the room, trying to put his hand on a spill to light the lamp, but the place was unfamiliar, and he struck his thigh against a table. It made a dull pain, like the others, the ache in his chest that had been with him for a month, the weight that bowed his neck so that his forehead throbbed and his shoulders were stiff with fatigue. He bumbled on. "Light," he muttered, but speech was a mistake. He might never see Rome again. The pain in his chest grew sharper.

I am exiled, he thought. Like King Oedipus, he was sent out into the world alone and defenseless, and in the dark. "Oh, gods," he cried, roaring like a wounded animal, and the tears on his cheeks were as warm as blood. He had to sit on the edge of the bed, choking and coughing while he cried. After a while he put out his hand and took his sword onto his lap.

King Oedipus had gone out from his city with his daughter to keep him company; he, Cicero, had been sent alone. His daughter was still in Rome, widowed and anxious, waiting to know if he would ever return. His little boy, his wife were lost to him. He could see their faces, there in the dark before him, helpless and uncomprehending. "Gods," he bellowed, "it would be better to be blind." His hand felt the sharp edge of the sword. It would be better to be dead.

He had lifted the sword and poised the point against his breastbone, feeling it prick through his clothes. A moment, a moment, and there would be no more pain, the dark would dissolve in light.

"Marcus Tullius, please, don't," someone was shouting, distracting him. Another voice said, "Marcus, you really shouldn't frighten us like this." There was light after all, lamps were burning, hurting his eyes, Tiro and his host were staring at him with the most tender concern. He blinked and set down the sword. There was light, but he was still in pain. "Gods," he said, and turned his face away, so that they would not see the agony in his blinded eyes.

In letters he could say something of what he felt.

MARCUS TULLIUS CICERO TO HIS FORMER TEACHER, THE RHETORICIAN DIODOTUS, NOW LIVING WITH CICERO'S FAMILY IN ROME.

Travelling between Vibo and Brundisium
April 13, 696 years from the founding of the city

I hope I may see a day, someday, when I will thank you for forcing me to live;
so far I regret it bitterly...

TULLIUS SENDS A FATHER'S GREETINGS TO HIS TERENTIA, TULLIA, AND LITTLE CICERO.

Brundisium, April 29, 696 A.U.C.

It's true that I send a letter to you less often than I might, because all my days are a misery to me. In fact, either reading or writing a letter brings tears to my eyes, and I cannot bear it. If only I had been less anxious to live, without a doubt I would have seen little or no trouble in life. Well, if fortune holds in reserve any hope of getting back some day, the mistake I made is not so serious. But if this evil is irrevocable, truly the first thing I want is to see you, Terentia, my life, and die in your arms. For neither the gods, whom you have always worshiped so devotedly, nor men, whom I have always served, have given us the smallest sign of gratitude.

We are in Brundisium, at the house of Marcus Laenius Flaccus; we have been here thirteen days. He is an excellent man, who ignores the risk to his own fortune and to his life to show his concern for my well-being. Nor is he deterred by the penalties of a most unscrupulous law from providing everything that the duties of friendship and hospitality usually require. If only some day I can show my gratitude to him. I will always feel it.

I will leave Brundisium on April thirtieth. It is not safe here, so close to Rome. How can I ask you to come here, a woman exhausted in mind and body? What if I don't ask? Does that mean I must therefore be without you? I think I will urge this: if there is any hope of my return from exile, help it and encourage it as much as you can; if, as I fear, it is all finished, do what you can to come to me. Only this I want you to know: if I have you I will not feel entirely lost.

But what will happen to little Tullia? Now you will have to see to her future; I have no advice to give. And little Cicero? What is he to do? He will always be in my thoughts, and in my heart.

I can't write any more now—my sorrow prevents me. I do not know if you have managed to keep possession of anything. What I fear is that you have been stripped of all our property and are in want...

MARCUS CICERO TO HIS BROTHER QUINTUS IN ARPINUM

Thessalonica, June 13

My brother, my brother, my brother, did you really think that in anger I sent a messenger to you without a letter? Or that I actually didn't want to see you? I, angry with you? Could I be angry with you? But surely you have always been honorable and pleasant to me; in me you would see no anger, only sorrow for my suffering, dread for you, longing, grief, deprivation. I did not want to see you? Rather, in all honesty, I did not want you to see me. For you would not have seen your brother: not the man you left when you went home to Arpinum; not the man you knew; not the man who accompanied you with tears when you set out for your province years ago. No trace of him, no image. A ghost, a dead man breathing. And if only you had seen or heard of me dead before you left! If only you could look back not only on my life but on my honor untouched.

If by my love for you, my brother, I have brought you and all of mine down with me, do not attribute my downfall to any dishonesty or wickedness on my part, but to a miserable lack of foresight. My only mistake is that I blindly trusted those whom I thought the gods would not allow to deceive me. In fact, I thought they would see that it was against their own interest to do so. My closest friends, the most congenial and familiar and devoted, turned out to be either afraid for themselves or jealous of me. Thus there was nothing wanting to bring me down but faithful friends and my own best advice.

I should never have taken Clodius' bill seriously. If I had seen that the thing to do was to support it when it was proposed, or to ignore it, it would never have done us any harm. I must have lost the use of my wits, or rather, I used them to bring about my ruin. It was blind, absolutely blind of us to put on mourning, to appeal to the crowd—a fatal thing to do before I was attacked by name. But I keep going over in mind something that's settled, finished, done with...

Answers came. Cicero read the first, sitting in the sun on the terrace of his friend Plancius' house in Thessalonica, with a cup of wine and a plate of olives at his elbow. He did not notice them; when he looked up from the paper it was to stare out over the blueness of sea and sky, the purple of islands, the soft, vacant, dreaming distances toward Rome. His face was empty too, as if his mind had gone as blank as the sky. "Tiro," he said, "they've torn down my house."

"Which one?" Tiro said looked up from a stack of letters he was sorting for his assistant to file.

His beautiful villa at Tusculum, his house in Rome... Thank the gods Antium and Formiae were all right. "The eyes of Italy" he called them; they were as dear to him as his sight. "Tusculum and Rome," he said aloud, choking a little over the last word. His house, which he had built to show the world that he had succeeded and was a Roman as good as any other, a consul, an aristocrat in his own right. "That Pretty Boy has had it burnt to the ground—to build a Temple to Liberty on the site. As if I were a tyrant, and the city might be glad that I left..." He turned away, blinking hard.

Oh, gods, thought Tiro. I thought we were past that stage. At first he had had to sit up with Cicero all the time, fearing what would happen if he left him alone. In those days Cicero could not speak without tears coming to his eyes. But for the last half month or so he had seemed a little stronger. He had had a dream, he said, that the old hero Marius, his ancestor, had told him not to lose hope. Perhaps the sunshine and sea air had done him good, too, and the letters. But now, there he was, blinking like a bear in the daylight, and his heavy shoulders had begun to hunch.

"If it's dedicated to a god, you won't be able to rebuild it when you are recalled," Tiro said briskly.

"If the dedication is legal," Cicero snapped, and Tiro, bending over his letters, smiled to himself.

Caelius, in Rome, had a letter, too. His servant brought it as he was preparing to go out, and he set it, unopened, on the table, among the objects there: the silver bowl of shaving water, the straight razor, the pumice stones, the chewed twig with which he had cleaned his teeth. He knew the seal, and he did not want to open it now. He was happy; why should he spoil his evening? "Philo," he said, holding out his arms for the tunic. "I'm a famous man. Did you know?"

"Yes?" Philo was directing the slave who jerked the tunic over his master's shining, autumn-colored hair.

"Well, I am. Everyone knows me, everyone invites me out. It was my speech: they all say so." He began to recite his denunciation of Hybrida; Philo, caught in the slippery length of the toga, paid no attention.

"Turn, please," Philo ordered, wrapping the white wool around Caelius. Obedient, Caelius shifted his body, and his eye fell on the letter again. "Do you know where I'm going tonight, for instance? To Clodia Metelli's." He shot a defiant glance at the square of folded paper propped up against the bowl. "She's invited me again. It's a great honor."

"I'm sure it is. If you will just remember to keep your hands away from the sides, here, and here, it shouldn't slip off your shoulders. You remember the last time."

"Yes, yes. Don't worry. And don't wait up. Clodia's parties sometimes go on all night."

"So they say." Philo stood with his hands folded in front of him, pleased with his work. His young master was as handsome a man as any in Rome, he was thinking, and as well dressed. The crimson bands of his tunic were particularly fine; they had given him a lot of trouble at the fuller's shop—he had had to make the cleaner press them three times. Well, it was worth it; his master's looks repaid the effort. His oblong, flat-planed face with its flush of soft pink on the cheeks, his light brown eyes, like a winter leaf, glowed back at him. Philo smiled. If what he had heard was true, Clodia Metelli was going to enjoy this evening.

"Well, I'm going," Caelius said, giving one uneasy glance at the table.

"Have a pleasant time."

"Yes. Well... Don't wait up, Philo." He seemed to be hesitating, poised on one foot by the door.

"No, I won't."

Caelius gave him an uncertain look. How young he still is, Philo thought. "Goodnight."

"Goodnight."

Caelius pulled his toga around him, yanking it at the sides, just where Philo had warned him not to, and swept out the door, leaving behind a scent of balsam and mint from his bath, and the faint scorch of wool from the pressed toga. In a moment he was back, blushing to his eyes. He would not look at Philo, but reached over and grabbed the letter from the table, thrust it into his belt under the toga and disappeared again. This time the front door of the house slammed behind him. Philo smiled and turned to put away the objects on the table.

He wished he had not brought the letter. All evening he had felt it against his side, where it was tucked into his belt, a little square, folded and sealed with a gob of black wax. Everyone must know it was there. When he leaned forward on his couch in Clodia's elegant dining room, he thought it crackled so that the other diners must hear it. It made him blush so hard his cheeks burned, and he could not watch the acrobats who were performing in the space between the couches, though they were all girls, and they were naked. Under cover of the applause he fingered the letter; he could almost read the seal through the cloth. A sprig of some kind of plant, with beans or peas or berries growing from it. He knew it, of course. It was Cicero's seal. And here he was in the camp of the enemy.

Clodia was looking toward him, giving him a smile and a tiny glimpse of the creamy flesh above her breasts. "Marcus Caelius, could we possibly prevail upon you to give us again that brilliant speech you made in the Forum? We all enjoyed it so much."

There were important men at this party—praetors and other magistrates, distinguished jurists. There were rising young men too: he saw Licinius Calvus, Crassus' student and assistant, sprawled ungracefully on a couch talking to the elder Curio's effeminate and buck-toothed son; across the way two aediles he recognized from the market were arguing about water rights. Well, I suppose I'm a rising young man too, he thought, and flushed with pleasure.

"Marcus Caelius?" Clodia had a wonderful voice, low and musical, intimate, friendly, and warm. It managed to suggest that they were alone together, and that she... He swallowed hard.

"Yes?" he said.

"Won't you recite the speech?" Her huge black eyes were resting on him; he could feel them on the skin of his face like hands. He got to his feet without taking his eyes from hers. He could see the whites, milky blue under the curve of her lashes, the tiny, tender spot of rose at the inner corners. Gods, he thought, Cicero didn't appreciate her. He must have been blind not to realize what she is.

The dining room had grown quiet, the important men on the couches were all looking at him. He jerked his toga to straighten it, suddenly remembering the letter. Resisting an impulse to take it out and wave it in their faces, he raised his left hand, fingers up, as he had been taught, and began. "They stumbled upon him," he said, "this degenerate, lying in a drunken stupor—"

Someone was coming in the door—a bustle, a clatter, a metallic clanking. The men on the couches turned to look, and Clodia removed her gaze from him, leaving him with the odd feeling that he had been stranded. A rush of arms and legs rattled through the entrance between the marble columns. Publius Clodius spilled into the room, very disheveled and very obviously drunk. "Has anybody got a chisel? I've got a prisoner here, and I want to take off his chains."

"Chains?" Clodia said.

Caelius was still standing; he was tall, and could see over the crowd around the door. There was indeed a prisoner there, a young man around eighteen years old, with skin as dark as a walnut and black shining curls in ringlets around his ears. His wide eyes stared at the company with shy incomprehension, and his wrists and ankles were linked by a heavy bronze shackle. He was no Roman, he wore some kind of robe like a woman's dress that fell to his feet; it was patterned with swirls of dark, brilliant colors, with bits of mirror winking in it. It was very dirty, and the hem was ragged.

"Who is it?" a praetor asked while a servant brought in a chisel and a hammer, and presented them to Clodia on a silver tray.

"Prince Tigranes of Armenia." Clodius knelt over the chains, taking up the hammer. The boy, recognizing his name, gave a startled and tentative smile. Then he put his hands together with a clash of metal and bowed over them to Clodia. "Hold still," Clodius muttered.

Caelius sat down. He knew who this was. Prince Tigranes of Armenia was one of the captives Pompey had brought back from Asia and decided not to sacrifice at his triumph. Caelius had seen this boy walking behind the models of the captured towns, his eyes dilated with fear but his head high. "Where did you get him?"

"He was in custody, with a praetor called Flaccus who was keeping him in a back room of his house. Pompey asked him to. He's supposed to guarantee the good behavior of his father the king, out there in the East." The hammer rose and fell. "There. You can move your feet now."

The letter crackled under Caelius' clothes as he shifted on his couch. "But if Lucius Flaccus was keeping him, how did you get him?"

"I stole him." His mouth was curved in a grin and his chin was raised. "Come on in," he said to the prince. "Join the party. Gods, I'm thirsty. Clodi, get them to find us something to drink, will you?"

He had brought his friends with him; they were standing in the doorway now as Tigranes took a few careful steps forward and gazed in wonder around the room. The friends followed, a very heterogeneous assortment. A few aristocrats like

Clodius, young men notorious in the city for their free spending and dissolute lives, a couple of social-climbing knights, a large group of freedmen and slaves, bowing and grinning anxiously at Clodia. One or two of them wiped their feet before crossing the threshold. "Stole him?" Clodia said, smiling.

Clodius tossed the hair out of his eyes. "I was at dinner at Flaccus'. He was trying to impress me—he had out his gold dinner service; you know the one, Clodi? He'd have done anything I asked. So I just said I wanted to see my friend here and we walked out together. Flaccus can't touch me—a tribune's person is sacred. Give us a cup of wine, will you? I didn't get much at Flaccus' house, I can tell you."

He was laughing, and his sister, like him, had put her head back; her slender body shook and her hair came loose from its pins. It fell down her back, as thick as a waterfall, and as glossy. "Gods, Pulcher, you took a risk. All right. Let your friends join us." She signaled to the musicians, and presently the room was filled with dancing men; a line of them snaked between the couches and curled itself around the dark figure of the bewildered young prince.

Caelius sat uneasily on his couch. He knew what Clodius had done couldn't have been legal; he also knew that if Cicero heard about it he would be furious at him for being there.

"Come on, Marcus Caelius." Clodia swayed past him in the line. "Don't you like to dance?"

She had put a wreath on her wonderful hair; it made her look like a child going up to the temple for the first time. Her dress had molded itself around her body as she moved; he could see the outline of her breasts under the thin material, the curve of them, the weight, the tiny rise of the nipple. Yet her face glowed with the most innocent pleasure. "Come on," she whispered, bending down and giving him her hand.

It occurred to Caelius, sometime later as he swung through the complex figures of the dance, his hand in Clodia's, his eyes on hers, that the real danger was not going to be that Cicero might find out about his presence at this party, but that he was going to have to conceal the letter from Clodia when he finally took off his clothes.

"Listen to this," Cicero said. He had picked up a folded sheet of paper from a stack of his correspondence and was holding it close so that his near-sighted eyes could make out the scrawl. Tiro could see the edge of his cloak, the corner of his nose, could make out beyond him the white square of the letter cutting into the blue of the horizon and the sky. Out on the water a boat with an eye painted on its hull made its way toward the harbor.

"It's a letter from Caelius."

"Listen," Cicero said; he had wiped his eyes surreptitiously with the edge of his toga. Gods, Tiro swore silently. Is he crying? Not again. "It's about Prince Tigranes." His master turned, and Tiro was relieved. The massive face was creased in a grin. Well, that's something, Tiro thought.

" 'Flaccus seems to have conquered his scruples about the sacredness of a tribune's person,' " Cicero read. " 'Because he went to Gabinius the consul and got him to send all twelve of his lictors to Clo—to the Pretty Boy's house. But the tribune's men held them off, and the Prince escaped. Flaccus is saying that the Pretty Boy took a bribe from the King of Armenia to release his son.' Well, I imagine it takes a lot of money to maintain an army of criminals," Cicero said.

"No doubt."

" 'It didn't help,' " Cicero went on, reading again. " 'That the Great Man, the Conqueror of the East, is furious at the insult to his prestige, or that half the city is holding its sides with laughter, or that the tribune and the prince go everywhere together and no one can do a thing about it...' "

The Pretty Boy, the Tribune, the Great Man, Tiro thought. He can't even bring himself to say their names. "Pompey is furious," he repeated, thinking it over.

"Of course he is. He doesn't like to be interfered with." Cicero's sadness had come back and was sitting on his shoulders, bending them down. "Caelius is right. Pompey will take this as an insult."

"Let's hope it makes him see what a mistake he's made supporting Clodius."

"Yes," said Cicero, looking away again. "Lets hope it does that."

If only he didn't feel like a traitor, Caelius thought, stretching his long legs in the bed. The woman beside him murmured in her sleep and buried herself further under the pillow. Her body made a shape like a landscape, the cliff of her shoulder falling in a long curve to her waist. The slope of her thigh and calf lay under a snowfall of white linen, muffled and mysterious; one delicate foot, intricate and beautiful, poked through the whiteness to rest against the distant horizon of the end of the bed.

The woman sighed in her sleep and Caelius went on with his reflections, drowsy and comfortable in the rosy lamplight. There was no reason for his sense of having betrayed someone. There was no one to betray. He was a grown man now, with his own way to make. No one, least of all Cicero, who had sent him here—really it amounted to that—expected him to behave as if he were still a pupil in his old teacher's house. Clodia, the woman in the bed, and her brother were the real powers in Rome now. He needed them—he had had a patron in Cicero before, but now that he was gone, his influence destroyed—He winced away from the thought and did not allow himself to finish it. If he, Caelius, were going to prosper-no, survive-He had to ally himself with someone. And Clodia had been so persuasive.

He must have moved, shifted uneasily in the discomfort of his thoughts, for the woman had opened her eyes and turned toward him. He could see the lamplight shimmering on the curve of her breast, the nipple, still soft from the warmth and sweetness of her sleep. Her mouth curved in a smile, the lower lip stretching so that its fullness gleamed. He bent to kiss her. "Nnn," she muttered. "Asleep," and turned back, seeking the depths of the pillow again.

Grinning, Caelius ran his hand along her ribs; her skin was so fine-grained it felt powdery under his hand. He slipped his hand over to rest it on her breast. Sighing again she arched her body against his. Under his fingers the little nipple rose in excitement; his own much more insistent erection answered. He turned her over on her back and pressed his belly against her, finding the opening between her thighs, pushing himself home. "Asleep," she objected again, but he had put both hands on her breasts and was pinching the nipples until she groaned with pleasure; the rhythm of his insistence was repeated in the involuntary arching of her hips. "Gods," she cried as he moved his hand down her belly, thrusting his fingers through the tangle of hair to rest in her damp and folded flesh. She had put her head back and opened her mouth; her beautiful dark eyes stared at him. "Gods," she cried again. A long tremor went through her, which he released himself to meet, letting his passion spend itself in a shuddering tumble into darkness and quiet, and the returning light of the room. "There," he said, a little anxiously. "You wanted me to do that, didn't you?"

"No," she said, mocking him. Gently she pushed him aside, sliding her wet and shining body out of bed. "You're a nice boy, Caelius." She was hunting for something in the mess on her dressing table. A stack of papers sifted to the floor, the rosy lamp in front of the small statue of Venus hung with jewelry guttered as it tipped. She put out her hand to steady it; every movement she made was graceful, he thought. She was no more capable of an ugly gesture than of...but he did not know what she was capable of. He had never met a woman like her before.

"Here," she said, turning back to him. From her hand trailed a tangle of gold and gems.

"What's this for?"

"Take them. They'll fetch a good price."

"I don't need money." He had pushed himself up on one arm: he was posing for her, showing off the muscles of his shoulder and chest.

"I've heard that you have debts."

"No, I don't," he said quickly. He feared a lecture; when they raised this subject his father was inclined to shout, and Cicero to look troubled and sad.

"That's all right. All young men have them. You should see what my brother owes. It's natural; and since we're allies now, political friends as well as—" She smiled at his naked torso. "I'm glad to help."

He made her a bow, half serious, to thank her. It was true he had debts—he owed money all over town, for clothes, parties, visits to the country, furnishings for his apartment. He had entertained his friends, and his hoped-for friends, very lavishly. It was all much more expensive than he had imagined it would be. This kind of spending was expected of him; he really didn't see why his father could not understand... Or Cicero, for that matter. He winced again, and hid the jewelry under the bedclothes.

Clodia was smiling down at him. "Now, go home, Caelius."

He grinned and reached for her, but she dodged away. "It's time for you to go home. I'm serious."

But he knew better. He reached out his arm and pulled her to him.

XVIII

I t seemed to Cicero that it was months since he had slept the whole night through. He would wake, always at the same time-about two hours after midnight—far too early to get up. His first thought was always of death; he longed for it, crying out in his mind at the cowardice that had prevented him from taking his life when Clodius first attacked him. Then, he thought, his death would have been a protest against his humiliation, it would have repaired the insult. Now it would only end it.

From there his mind moved to the people who had wanted him to live: his wife, his brother, his friends. Slowly his anger against them subsided, and lying awake in the dark, he told himself he ought to get up and work—read a little, write... Really, he was very lucky, he told himself briskly. He had always said he wanted to leave politics and do some serious work: resume his studies in philosophy, compose a few dialogues himself. His teachers in Greece had thought he had something to say.

"Cum dignitate, otium," he had told people—peace with honor—were the greatest happinesses a man's life might provide, as they were the best things for a country. Now he had them, and he was doing nothing to take advantage of them. Plancius had no library to speak of—a few volumes on estate management and the breeding of horses and dogs seemed to suffice for his intellectual requirements, but he was a fine host according to his lights, and provided Cicero with secretaries, quiet, time, and an agreeable place to work. It should have been enough; if he had been himself, it would have been: he could have written volumes out of his own reflections and experiences—indeed, he had always planned to do just that. Plancius was generous with his own company too, though as governor of this province he was naturally busy. All the same, he seemed to be trying to turn Cicero's stay with him into a country-house visit. It was charming of the man, and Cicero was very grateful, but the fact was he was lonely, for what or whom, he didn't quite know. His family, of course. His friends. But what was hurting him was not that. He didn't know if he would ever see Rome again.

Lying in bed in the dark thinking of this, he saw the city, its streets repeated endlessly, its squares empty, its houses abandoned, as if all the inhabitants had fled, and was visited by a vast sense of desolation. He had never been so alone in his life.

In his mind he counted his friends.

Metellus was dead, as dead as old Lutatius Catulus; he would never have expected to miss the pompous, gray-faced man. All his troubles had come from

Metellus' death. He should never have died; he was young—well, not old anyway—healthy, strong. He wondered how it had happened. He knew that Clodia... But it was useless; the idea that had glimmered faintly in his mind had gone out. He was left, as he had been from the moment Metellus' breathing had stopped in the suddenly silent room, alone and without allies, and sure that a great wrong had been done. Well, he could not think about anyone else's wrong—his own required too much of his strength just now.

Hortensius, whom he had trusted, might as well have died too, since he had betrayed him with his advice to run away. Why had he listened to it? He had trusted it, and now where was he? Cato, upright and old-fashioned, of such proverbial integrity that people said of some particularly incredible news, "I wouldn't believe it if Cato himself told me so," Marcus Porcius Cato had accepted an ambassadorship from Publius Clodius' over-white and over-elegant hands, and had gone to Cyprus. Not that it wasn't wise for him to get out of Rome. After all, look what had happened to Metellus. But still, an ambassadorship—

Even the boy Caelius, famous now since his victory in the courts, had been taken up by Clodia Metelli and added to her collection of influential young men. At least Caelius had written to him about it himself, full of protestations of continuing affection and support, full of apologies and explanations. In the middle of the night they reminded Cicero forcefully of Pompey's reassurances, which were the hardest to bear of all.

He had a new anxiety that disturbed his sleep, too: Quintus also was under attack. Clodius was trying to get an indictment against him for what he called Quintus' malfeasance in his province. Malfeasance. At night he dreamed that he was defending his brother in court; he could see the jury, all attention and sympathy. Clodius was not visible, but Cicero knew he was there, crushed and humiliated by his eloquence. Destroyed by it. Unable to hold up his head in Rome ever again. Cicero awoke full of happiness and confidence to the chorus of the birds at dawn: he knew that he would make a wonderful speech, the best of his career. The city would talk about it for months. He knew he could save Quintus and ruin his enemy—he had done such things before. It was fitting that his greatest moment would come in the defense of someone who had always been loyal and loving. Then he remembered that he would not be allowed to try.

"As the gods are my witness," he wrote to Quintus, "the one thing that kept me from death was that everybody said that so much of your life was bound up in mine. And so I behaved like a fool and a criminal. For if I had died, it would have been proof of my brother's love for you, but as things stand now, my mistake has deprived you of my help while I am still alive, and made you look to others for their aid. My voice, which has been able to save the most distant strangers, will be forced to silence when the danger is nearest..."

XIX

W ith the summer there was hope. Several of the tribunes for the coming
year, and Lentulus, one of the new consuls, were his friends, though
many of the returned candidates were not. Still, even a few were something. Pompey was growing cooler to Clodius, too. He had not liked the Tigranes
business, as Cicero had predicted, but he had let it pass; now Clodius was interfering with treaties Pompey had signed out in the East as well.

Perhaps Pompey was disgusted, too, by the shifts his new friends had forced on
him; Caelius reported that Pompey had accepted a large bribe from the deposed
Pharaoh of Egypt to put him back on the throne of his country. The rumor in the
city was that it was more than fourteen million sesterces, and that Pompey had
been pushed to accept it by Crassus and Caesar, with whom he had had to split it
as well. No doubt some of it had trickled down as far as Clodius' outstretched hand.
The story had somewhat tarnished Pompey's shining reputation in the city; the
conservatives in the Senate and among the old families were saying that it proved
how little even the son of a New Man could be trusted. "As if they had never taken
a bribe themselves," Caelius wrote, but Cicero, reading the letter, thought it
unlikely that any of them had ever been offered fourteen and a half million sesterces.

There were other rumors in the city too. To Cicero's surprise, the young poet
Catullus wrote to tell him one—that Metellus' death had not been just the stroke
of an evil fate, though at first the city had accepted that it was. Now, the boy said,
in the bars and brothels and baths they were saying openly that Clodius had murdered him. "Down there," was the phrase he used for the poorest and roughest parts
of the city, and reading it on Plancius' pleasant terrace in the glittering Aegean sunshine, Cicero had a vision to match the city of his dreams: he saw a Rome submerged, with streets as dark as the passage to the underworld, where the souls go
down to King Hades and his shadowy fields. "Down there," Catullus wrote, they
said that Metellus had been poisoned. He, Catullus, was looking for the men who
had so badly beaten him; when he found them he would force them to tell him
more.

A few days later Cicero had a letter from Caelius, describing an incident in the
Senate: a slave had drawn a knife on Pompey, to the shock and horror of the legis-
lators, who heard it clatter to the floor and saw Pompey's bodyguard thrust itself for-

ward with a sudden flurry of movement. Pompey had turned around and gone straight home, Caelius said, refusing to come back to the city until public order had been restored. "A chance for a long holiday with his new wife," Caelius wrote, and added some bawdy details. The slave, under torture, admitted that he had been sent by Clodius.

There was an immediate consequence of this news; Pompey, when he heard it, sent one of the new tribunes to Gaul with a letter to Caesar, suggesting it was time to recall Cicero. He himself wrote to tell Cicero about it—an odd document, as formal and stiff as a new toga, and nearly as blank—and he did not say what answer, if any, Caesar had sent from Gaul.

On the twenty-ninth of October, eight of the new tribunes proposed a bill in the Senate to invite Cicero home to restore order; the two serving consuls, Caesar's father-in-law, and Pompey's closest friend, had it vetoed without discussion. "Still," Quintus wrote, "it's a sign of a change in the wind. Be patient, my brother, it may still blow you home to us." But to Cicero, hope was now a torment that patience could not soothe. He spent his days pacing the terrace of Plancius' house, his eyes on the Western horizon. "I am waiting for the event, or else for the end of hope," he wrote back.

XX

I t was a big party: nowadays Clodia's usually were. Caelius had enjoyed himself: he had talked politics with a Spanish businessman named Egnatius, and military matters with a tribune called Attilius Serranus; afterwards he had had a long conversation with Clodia's dignified elder brother Appius Claudius, who had just been elected City Praetor. Caelius had then drunk several cups of wine, and danced all the dances. Now, feeling relaxed and comfortable and not really very drunk, he was looking for Clodia. It was getting late and most of the guests were calling for their outdoor shoes and cloaks; he wondered if she would ask him to stay. Often after such a party she did. If not, there was a woman he knew in the Subura who would be glad to see him, even on such short notice. But he preferred Clodia, if he could find her.

She was not in her bedroom, though she had been. The dressing table had received a new snowfall of powder; there were hairpins scattered at the feet of her little statue of Venus like an offering; a lump of soft gold stone had been set on top of the filmy shawl she had been wearing, to hold it down. A pretty thing. The room smelt of roses and honey. He took a deep breath, feeling it in his belly and his thighs. Her maid had been in earlier, and the bed was turned down, waiting.

There was no one in Metellus' abandoned study, which was dark, and gave out a breath of dead charcoal fires and dusty papers, nor in the storerooms which he peered into in passing. In the kitchen the servants were washing up; they looked up from the clatter and the steam. "Your mistress?" Caelius asked, and one of them jerked his head toward the back of the house.

The night air outside sobered him; he felt foolish and inopportune, and he wished he had brought a cloak. He stood under the colonnade, surprised by a sudden sense of size in the darkness; the wind seemed to blow from a great distance away, sighing thinly in the bare branches, the stars overhead were tiny and high. Out in the garden, in a corner behind a row of cypresses, a lantern glowed softly on the gravel. Clodia sat on a bench, carved by the lamplight into black and white. She was watching her brother pace up and down, head back, fists on hips. He was arguing with someone hidden in the vast shadow on the trees. The wind caught the words, tossing them towards Caelius. "...Money...?"

The other voice rumbled unintelligibly.

"Twenty thousand," Clodia said as clearly as if he had been standing next to her.

The rumbling went on; Clodius cocked his head, then laughed.

"Thirty," Clodia said.

What are they buying? Caelius wondered, and looked to see if he could move closer, but the open space around the fish pool was between him and the trees. Clodius was facing him; it was a good thing the lantern was at his feet and casting its light upwards: he would not be able to see much beyond it.

The voices had reached agreement; the hidden figure leaned forward and the light fell on his features. Attilius Serranus. They were buying a tribune.

And at a good price, too, for Serranus was grinning as he offered his hand to Clodius to shake. Caelius turned and went quickly back into the house. He would not wait for her, he decided. He would find the woman down in the city after all. He had a lot to think about, and a thicker letter than he had planned for Cicero in the morning.

Three days later, on the first of January, he went to the Senate, where he stood in the back to watch the installation of new magistrates. The senators took their places quietly; he thought they looked nervous and unhappy, as if they did not expect much good from these officers. The day was dim, and the lamps on their hanging chains did little to illuminate it; to Caelius the white faces of the senators huddled in the gloom, like the faces of children fearful of the dark. They all clumped together as if for protection; infected by the atmosphere himself, he leaned forward from his place in the back and scanned the crowd for people he knew. He smiled at Quintus Cicero sitting with a group of ex-praetors like himself, Lucullus, the general, caught his eye and bowed to him, the younger Curio, standing beside his father, gave him a sheepish grin and swayed gracefully over to stand beside him. Hortensius had come in, his red face set and determined under his white hair. Caelius had an impulse to go up to him, but he was talking to Lentulus Spinther, the new consul. From outside, Caelius could hear Clodius' men making an uproar as someone else came through the Forum to the Curia. Clodius was no longer tribune, his term had expired and he had no place among the magistrates inside. Well, he was making his presence felt all the same.

A brief rustle, a dying hum, and the Senate settled down on the shadowy benches; the doors to the lobby were closed. The new magistrates repeated the oaths they had taken at the Temple of Jupiter earlier, Lentulus as senior consul last. When the others had taken their seats he stepped forward to make his speech. There was a pause, a hush, a sudden sense of tension, through which the shouts of Clodius' men came, distant but clear, in spite of the heavy bronze doors. Lentulus filled his lungs, glanced at the nearer rows of senators, and said, "We are in a pitiable state. It is time for every man who loves it, no matter what his politics, to help our country—"

In the dimness every eye was on him, every breath stilled. "We are a mockery of what we were, powerless, humiliated, bought and sold like slaves. Rome is on the brink of revolution, or of something even worse and we must save ourselves if we can." The silence was absolute; even the noise from outside was stilled, as if Clodius and his men were listening too.

"To this end," Lentulus said, raising his voice and speaking very clearly as if he did not want anyone to miss a word, "I propose to recall Marcus Tullius Cicero from his unjust and illegal exile. Once before, when he was consul, he rescued us by his energy, his understanding, his courage and force of character, from a danger like this. Remember how he steered us through his consulship, how he preserved our lives, our homes, our liberties. Let all men who care for the safety of the Republic put aside their differences and come together now. Let us bring back the one man whose leadership we can trust, and whose care has never failed us."

The senators were on their feet, cheering. Caelius, tears stinging his eyes, was laughing and hugging the man next to him. It was Curio, grinning around his huge, herbivorous teeth.

There were people who wanted to speak now and the Senate made itself quiet again to hear them. First Lentulus recognized Metellus Nepos, the other consul, Metellus' brother. He had no objection to the proposal, he said. The praetors, all except Appius Claudius, kept silent and would not look at anyone, but eight of the ten new tribunes spoke one by one in favor of Cicero's recall.

"What about the other two?" Curio bleated in Caelius' ear. "I m-mean, I can understand why Appius doesn't want to speak against his own brother, no matter what he may feel—f-family loyalty and all that—but the tribunes?"

Caelius rubbed his thumb against his fingers. "Oh, I see," Curio drawled. "How do you know?

"It stands to reason," said Caelius and turned away, not wanting to spoil his happiness.

Now a distinguished old ex-consul was rising shakily from his place to propose an amendment, crying that the Senate ought to vote honors to Cicero instead of merely recalling him. There were cheers for that too, and Curio wrung Caelius' hand so hard the knuckles cracked.

Down in front a bulky figure was lumbering from the left side benches. Pompey. His heavy-lidded eyes slid over the crowd while his thick tongue flicked, snake-like, across his lips.

In the silence Curio whispered, "He's g-going to support it."

"Well, he might be going to. He doesn't like to be unpopular," Caelius said doubtfully, watching the large, reptilian head swing back and forth. Pompey's face was gleaming with sweat and earnestness.

"Excellent proposal. I have always been a friend to Marcus Cicero, as I have been a friend to every man with the best interests of Rome at heart, however mistaken any individual policy of his may be."

Curio asked. "Is the f-fellow joking, do you think?"

"It ought to be the other way around—he owes most of his career to Cicero.

And he wouldn't lift a finger to help him ten months ago."

Down in front Pompey boomed, "I look forward to working with Marcus Cicero again to restore the city to her greatness and to bring back the benefits the constitution designed for us. Although I warn you, order cannot be restored without the discipline our ancestors bequeathed us. Well, that's a big job, and I'll be very glad to have his help with it."

Down on his bench Quintus was shaking his head in disbelief; Curio had raised one eyebrow until it nearly touched his curls. "Cicero's help? But m-my dear, it's the other way around, isn't it?"

"But I do think," Pompey was going on, "and I suggest to you, just to be on the safe side, and entirely for your own protection, that your bill—which I'm sure will pass now that you've heard me out so graciously—should be submitted for ratification to the Plebeian Assembly. It would be better for my old friend to know that the city is behind him to a man."

"But... I m-mean, Clodius controls the Plebeian Assembly, doesn't he?" Curio said, with obvious bewilderment.

"I know." Caelius could hardly speak for rage. "And Pompey knows it too."

The Senate it seemed had seen nothing behind Pompey's remarks, for they were voting, quickly and efficiently, for the amendment. It passed with no dissent: within twenty-five days a bill would go to the plebeians.

"Now for the recall itself." Caelius leaned over to touch the wooden railing. He was promising in his mind to make offerings to every god he could think of.

"It's going to pass," Curio said happily. "Look at those faces."

It was true, the senators were beaming with relief as they sorted themselves out to vote. The first of them had already come forward when Attilius Serranus leaped to his feet, shouting, "One moment, gentlemen. One moment. I want to ask you for one night to consider this bill. Just one night."

"No," Caelius cried aloud.

"They'll have to agree," Curio said. "If they don't he'll just veto the whole thing. I m-mean, he's a tribune, he has the right."

That was why Clodia and her brother had bought a tribune, of course—because he could do precisely this. Caelius admired the economy of the move, so much simpler than trying to bribe a majority of senators, for example. And so much cheaper than bringing in an army of hoodlums.

In his cracked and beautiful voice, Hortensius was begging Serranus to reconsider. To Caelius it sounded like the piping of a small child in the dark. Lentulus looked fatherly and said something inaudible among the cries of distress from the crowd; a very old man shuffled down the aisle and knelt at Serranus' feet.

"Who's that?"

"Attilius Serranus' father-in-law," Curio said in awe.

Even the old man's humble pleas did no good; Serranus insisted. "Just one night," he said, staring in embarrassment over the head of the suppliant. "I swear that tomorrow I will not oppose a vote. All I ask is one night to consider it." And through all the cries and speeches and appeals he remained standing composedly, refusing to catch anyone's eye, deaf as an egg. At last, seeing that it was futile to go on, Lentulus extracted a promise of non-obstruction the next day from him once again, and adjourned the meeting.

The promise was a lie, of course. Caelius had to write Cicero that. During the next month or so, though the Senate continued to press for Cicero's recall every day—even going to so far as to pass a resolution that no other business would be considered until it was done—Attilius Serranus did not withdraw his objection. Every morning the senators trooped down to the Curia amid the threats and jeers of Clodius' men, who surrounded the building. Every morning Lentulus Spinther opened the debate, every morning Serranus said he had not considered the bill sufficiently yet. Occasionally he varied this by claiming to have been watching the skies, but the omens were always unfavorable. The Senate ground its teeth in rage and waited for the meeting of the Plebeian Assembly on the twenty-fifth.

XXI

I t was a grey afternoon, weeping and cold. The laurel hedge in Caelius' garden dripped, though if there was rain in the air it was falling invisibly. Caelius was working in his study—there didn't seem to be anything better to do. Across the desk from him, his servant Philo swore as the paper, swollen in the damp, bled the ink. Caelius put down his board and stylus. He supposed he ought to have gone to the meeting of the Plebeian Assembly, but he had not seen the point. All that would happen was that Clodius and his bravoes would prevent the vote. It had not seemed worth facing the weather for that. Now he was sorry—at least he would have been outside and moving around.

Philo had looked up. In the doorway stood Quintus Cicero's freedman, a man called Teucer. "I beg your pardon," he said aloud. "I didn't hear you come in. What can I do for you? Does Quintus need anything?"

The man was disheveled and out of breath; there was a mark on his forehead that might have been the beginning of a bruise. "Marcus Caelius," he panted. Unable to say more, he beckoned urgently.

"Yes," Caelius said, guessing. "I'm coming. How bad is it?"

"Very," Teucer gasped. His skin was greenish, as if he had swum through the day to Caelius' door, and it was filmed with an unhealthy-looking moisture.

Caelius was picking up the short, thin-bladed knife he used for sharpening the reed pens and putting it in his belt. "Philo, get a message to Curio and the others. Something's happened. Tell them we'll need men—as many as they can get together on such short notice."

"Armed?"

"I don't know. Yes, if possible. But the main thing is to get them there quickly."

Outside the day was worse than it had seemed from the study. Clouds pressed low over the street, the wind blew water as fine and stinging as sand into his eyes. It was so cold he shuddered even as he ran.

"All right," he said through his rattling teeth. "Tell me what happened."

Teucer shot him a frightened look. It was definitely a bruise on his forehead.

"This morning one of the tribunes who is friendly to us went to the Forum before dawn... He was going to propose the bill when the Assembly convened."

"Yes." Caelius clenched his jaws and moved faster. It didn't help, he was still cold and the street seemed to drag on forever.

"He wanted to get there early...but Clodius and his men were already in the...Forum and the Curia. Thousands of them. Thousands."

They had passed the place that had been Cicero's house, a black and broken gap smelling of ashes and dust, now more melancholy than ever under the rain. So as not to have to look at it, Caelius stared at Teucer. The little man was shaking so hard his clothes were moving, even heavy with damp.

"There was a fight."

"I gathered that. Come on, man. What happened?"

"They killed...I don't know. Lots of men."

Clodia's house. He didn't want to look at that either; he had lost his taste for the pleasures she provided, and he did not go to her parties any more.

"They were the City Praetor's men," Teucer said. The ex-slave was sobbing. From running? No, the moisture on his face was tears.

"Appius Claudius supplied the men?" Caelius cried, suddenly understanding what Teucer was saying. "He lent them to his brother?"

Teucer nodded. "Gladiators. For some games...Appius is going to put on, now that he's...City Praetor. I recognized them."

The top of the Palatine Steps, the Forum below, nearly invisible under the gray sheets of rain. "My patron, Quintus Cicero, got up on the Rostra to give his speech anyway," Teucer panted proudly. Then turning to Caelius he cried, "He's dead. He must be. I can't find him anywhere."

The Temple of Castor, gaping pathetically: Clodius had removed its steps to make it defensible. Instead it looked vulnerable, like an old man who has lost his teeth. None of Clodius' men anywhere. Now the Forum, set around with wooden railings for the vote that had never taken place.

For a moment he thought someone had struck him under the heart; his breath stopped, and he swayed on his feet. Under the dripping sky the Forum looked like a battlefield. There were bodies everywhere, sprawled on the stones among the wooden bars. An arm moved, fingers crawled over the ground like crabs searching for the sea, the wind ruffled the edge of a toga and let it fall. Crimson blood lay in pools around the bodies, darker than the bricks of the buildings. Oh, gods, Quintus was out there lying dead somewhere; how would he ever tell Cicero?

Someone was groaning in a corner, a sound mixed with the crying of the wind. "Look over there. Are those the men who did this?" he whispered to Teucer from behind a pillar of the Temple of Vesta. The little freedman peered out timidly. He was a librarian, or a tutor, or some such thing—not made for this. "Yes. Those, by the prison. What are they doing?"

He saw a group of men—twenty or thirty of them he thought—in leather armor and heavily armed, moving among the bodies, eyes on the ground. Behind them came a squad of slaves, loading the corpses into a wagon. They were heaped in there already, higher than the sides. Now and then the armed men stopped and looked closer; some of them turned over one of the limp figures. Once they jerked up a head by the hair; Caelius could hear the cry of pain from where he stood. A gladiator drew his sword and the cry ended, the corpse fell back on the stones. "Oh, gods," Caelius said, unaware that he had spoken.

"What is it? What are they doing?"

He didn't want to say, but the little man was scrabbling at his hand with his nails, weeping and shouting. In a moment he might be heard. "They're looking for someone."

Teucer fell back as if he had struck him. "For Quintus Cicero."

"Yes, they must be."

The little librarian looked at him with horror. "What if he's not dead?"

"I thought you said he was."

"I—I don't know."

Of course, Caelius thought, swearing silently. He stood under the exiguous shelter of the curved temple porch, shifting his weight from one leg to the other. He had never been so conscious of his body before, not even in love. Every hair seemed to stand up on his arms and legs, every vein to hammer, every part of his skin to crawl over his flesh. He could feel his toes in his shoes, his scalp under his hair. His breath whistled with unbearable loudness, and his feet seemed to scrape over the stones like boulders in an avalanche. Oh, gods, they would hear him, out under the rain that rattled down like javelins... His fingers clasped the little knife. A pen knife. One man. They were twenty or more, some had swords, tridents, spears, he couldn't see what—

"Wait here," he said to Teucer "Keep an eye out for Curio's men. Tell them where I am."

"But, Marcus Caelius—" Teucer cried, but he had to raise his voice to call, for Caelius had leaped down the temple steps and out into the rain.

He had not forgotten caution, all the same. He kept to the darker grayness among the jewelers' shops, working his way around the edge of the Forum. If Quintus had been making a speech, he was most likely to have been cut down near the Rostra; though the rain was drawn across the Forum like a curtain now, he could see bodies scattered under the platform and down the steps. He went slowly, his heart catching in his chest. Once something struck him on the back of the neck; he whirled around, his ineffectual little knife in his hand, but it had only been a drop of water from an overhanging roof. Once, much worse, someone clutched his ankle with an icy hand, nearly unbalancing him, so that his heart shot into his mouth and his skin froze. But it was one of the injured men, blind-eyed and open-mouthed, his face covered with blood that the rain could not wash away. "Water," the man moaned, though the rain was falling into the black circle of his lips.

The party of gladiators had come closer to the Rostra, followed by the slaves

away down the man's grayish neck, fading to pink as the rain diluted it. "No," he said, wonderingly.

"Yes, he did," Quintus said.

Milo whistled through his yellow teeth.

"I did? How?"

Quintus pointed at the sword he still clutched in his hand.

"What happened to the others?" Caelius was beginning to feel very peculiar; his vision wobbled and his knees shook like seaweed in a tide. He wondered if he were going to be sick. It was all he needed.

"Ran away," Milo said with satisfaction.

Perhaps he had better sit down; he thought he might have to. He didn't want to look like a weakling in front of this flinty man. Gods, he prayed, feeling his stomach heave and his mouth fill dangerously with water.

"Well, it looks as if you're the hero of this engagement, Marcus Caelius Rufus," Milo said.

"Yes," Quintus breathed, wringing his hand. "I'll always be grateful to you, Caelius. I'll write to my brother right away. I know he will be, too."

Someone had grabbed his other hand and to his horror was pressing it to his mouth. Teucer. "Marcus Caelius," the little ex-slave was bubbling and weeping. Caelius shot an appalled and unhappy glance at Milo.

"Buy you a drink," Milo said, and clapped him on the back.

XXII

FROM A LETTER FROM QUINTUS TULLIUS CICERO
TO HIS BROTHER MARCUS

...fight in the Forum was not the end of it by any means. Publius Sestius—you remember him, I'm sure: he's the tribune who went to Gaul to talk to Caesar on your behalf—took it upon himself to speak to Metellus Nepos, the consul. It was a brave thing to do, but perhaps it was foolhardy just at this stage.

In any case, Clodius has established a sort of headquarters in the Temple of Castor; he and his men spend all their time there, and the rumor is that they have stored a lot of arms in the temple treasury, too. Sestius went to call on Nepos there. Trusting his tribuneship he went alone, and Clodius' men beat him so badly he nearly died of it...

Caelius, hearing about this incident from Milo, who had come to call on him, thought that Clodius' gladiators must have believed that they had in fact killed Sestius—otherwise, surely, they would have finished the job. The penalty was no worse for murdering a tribune than for beating him up.

"See what it means?" Milo said in his curious, clipped way. "Clodius was there."

"Yes," Caelius said, pouring Milo another drink. He was beginning to like this man.

"He can be prosecuted for this. It's a serious crime."

"Are you going to do it?" He was getting used to being a hero; he was enjoying it, in fact. Men like this came to call on him. Milo was a New Man, but he was a kind of aristocrat, too: he was the Hereditary Dictator of some small town out in the country. Caelius, listening to him talk, felt older, more mature.

Milo was grinning at him. "Help me with the speech? That is, if Clodia will let you."

"How do you know about that?"

"Asked around. Heard a poem—epigram, really: 'In the dining room, a whore; in the bedroom, 'No more.' ' That yours? They say it is."

"Well, yes. I made it up."

"Clever."

"Thanks. That's all over now. Anyway, I wouldn't let a woman dictate to me about a thing like this."

Milo was looking at him out of his stony eyes, an assessing look, giving nothing away. "Sorry to have asked about you—had to, to know whom to trust. You'll help then?"

Caelius smiled happily at him. "I'm your man."

FROM A LETTER FROM QUINTUS TULLIUS CICERO TO HIS BROTHER MARCUS IN THESSALONICA.

...Milo has brought a prosecution against Clodius for using violence in the city. If he can get a conviction, it means exile for Clodius. He has reacted in typical fashion, as you might guess, with an attack by his gladiators on Milo's house. Milo's wife repelled it with great courage, directing her servants like a general. The violence in the city is growing worse: Clodius' men have burned a temple in the Campus Martius where the censor's records are stored...

FROM ANOTHER, THE SAME TO THE SAME

...and pulled down the arcade Lutatius Catulus built next to his house to commemorate a victory by our army, I forget which one. Clodius, by the way, has announced that he is running for aedile; if he can get himself elected he will be immune from Milo's prosecution. So it looks like a race between Milo's case in court and election day...

FROM A LETTER FROM MARCUS CAELIUS RUFUS TO MARCUS TULLIUS CICERO

...The city is so fed up it's ready to spew back Clodius' poison in his face. Metellus Nepos—get this—has decreed that no case can be tried until new magistrates are elected, the old ones in his opinion not being properly qualified to do the job or something. Can you believe it? Milo is so angry he looks like a boulder with an embolism. He's hiring gladiators of his own from all his rich friends. He says he's "going to fight fire with fire." Let's hope he doesn't burn down the whole city while he's at it; he's angry enough to try...

Cicero had been forced to leave Plancius' pretty villa; the new governor of the province was a friend of Clodius', and he would no longer have been safe. A knife in the back, poison in his dinner—who would have known, or been able to object if they had guessed? Feeling hunted, he had debated in his mind where to go: he could think of no place that was certainly safe. Finally he had given up and rented a small house in the free city of Dyrrhachium, just across the Adriatic from Italy. He believed he could see the distant shore from the upstairs study. In any case the fishing boats in the harbor went there every day, and the merchants called regularly from Rome.

Sitting in the stuffy little courtroom in the town, where he had taken to spending his mornings listening to the provincial lawyers arguing their cases, Cicero smiled to himself as he read this letter. He could see the boy's bright eyes open, hear the freshness of his laughter. The airless courtroom seemed cooler for a moment, and it occurred to him that he had not laughed in months. Not since he had left Rome. A pain pierced him like a javelin; he must have cried aloud. The jury and the witnesses turned toward him, the counsel for the defense frowned in his direction. Ashamed, he drew the edge of his toga over his face and left the room.

FROM A LETTER FROM QUINTUS TULLIUS CICERO
TO HIS BROTHER MARCUS

Rome, June 27

...Milo's men have held off Clodius', and the Senate was able to get up to the Temple of Jupiter, which Milo thought would be easier to defend than the Curia. There were some disturbances outside, of course; we could hear them. But we could also hear Milo's men fighting back. The Senate refused to be intimidated and voted a number of decrees proposed by Lentulus, the consul. They are: I) to commend you to all foreign peoples you may be travelling among; II) to thank our allies for taking care of your health and safety; III) to hold all provincial governors personally responsible for your welfare; IV) to empower the consuls to send letters to every municipality in Italy, summoning the citizens to vote on your recall. On Pompey's suggestion, they added that no one should be allowed to delay the proceedings by watching the sky for omens, or by any other means. If anyone tries, he will be declared a public enemy, and if the bill is postponed for more than five days for any reason, your citizenship will be restored to you without further action by the Senate or the Plebeian Assembly, and you will be able to come home in perfect safety. When we had finished voting, the whole Senate broke out in cheers and cries of happiness and relief...

FROM A LETTER FROM MARCUS CAELIUS RUFUS
TO MARCUS TULLIUS CICERO

Rome, July 8

...Broke out in cheering when the senators appeared. I thought the theater was going to collapse under the weight of the clapping and footstomping and the shouting. There were tears in people's eyes—in mine too. Lentulus put on the games this year, so when he came in the noise was even wilder. People left their seats to go and kiss his hand, they were so glad he had proposed the vote for your recall. You do not need to doubt your popularity among the ordinary people of this city. Clodius, however, was hissed, and curses were shouted at him. In the course of the play the tragic actor Xanthius came to the line, "our greatest

friend, in this our greatest need," and the audience cheered him to the skies. He waited—a very artful pause, I thought—and added his own words: "Endowed with the greatest genius." I'm not ashamed to say that like everyone else I yelled myself hoarse and the tears ran down my cheeks...

FROM A LETTER FROM QUINTUS CICERO TO HIS BROTHER MARCUS

Rome, July 17

...I went to Pompey to discuss with him the feeling that is so apparent in the Senate, and to see what he intended to do about it. Whatever we'd like to think, my brother, supporting us to the extent of not liking this sacrilegious abuse of watching the skies is not the same thing as actually bringing you back. He received me with the utmost cordiality, out in his grand place in the hills. "In view of the Senate's decrees," I said, "do you think you could see your way clear to helping my brother come home?" He gave me a very peculiar look—I don't know how to explain it. He was alone, of course, but you would have thought there was someone listening behind the door. He kept looking over his shoulder as if he expected someone to be there, and passing his tongue over his lips—you know the way he does. But when he spoke he was the same Pompey he has always been. "Very well," he said. "I'll do what I can. But I can have no repetition of what happened before. If I'm to keep order in the city I have to have certain assurances." It struck me as strange—why does he think he is obliged to keep order in the city? He's not a praetor. And surely the Senate doesn't think of appointing a dictator or anything like that; if they did, the most logical person to appoint would be Milo, wouldn't it? Naturally I asked Pompey what assurances he had in mind, not wanting to argue the point. They were nothing: just that you would support his programs and not, as he said, "stir up trouble against his two good friends"—you-know-who, and you-know-who. Of course I told him you had always supported his programs, and had never stirred up trouble against anyone, but he insisted, so I agreed. It didn't seem like much, and in the hope of seeing you again, my brother, I would have promised much more. If I was wrong, forgive me...

In any case, Pompey did his part and came into the city to make a speech in the Temple of Jupiter (where the Senate is still meeting). He said you had single-handedly saved the republic when you were consul, and that we needed you now to do it again. Once it was Catiline, now it was Clodius, and you were as capable of taking on one as you had been the other. I do think, my brother, that you would have been pleased...

He had been trying to answer this letter all evening; the day had faded and gone, the lamp had been lit; there was paper in front of him and a pen, freshly cut. But he could not bring himself to write. He supposed he had been sitting here thinking for hours. Around him his house was asleep—the little seaport town itself had packed up its day and gone to bed. He had no answer for his brother. The assurances worried him. Quintus, he thought, was being remarkably vague. Support Pompey? He had always supported Pompey. The great man knew that perfectly well.

Anger shook him, as sudden as a pain, and as overwhelming. Pompey displeased with him? He was the one who had been betrayed, abandoned to his enemies. He reached for his wine, but his hand shook so badly it distressed him to see it. Pompey wanted him back, did he? Well, he should have thought of that the night he left him to wait alone in his villa in the dark. Let him whistle for his old friend now, let him make speeches, write letters, come crawling... In the dark, alone, he laughed a little to himself.

It was true that Cicero had argued against the land bill as it had finally been presented to the Plebeian Assembly. Could Pompey be thinking of that? Had he felt wronged by Cicero's opposition? Is that why he had not prevented Clodius from exiling him? But really, that bill—Metellus had been right to oppose it. Pompey knew that: Cicero had explained it very carefully. Pompey had listened attentively, too. He had thought Pompey had understood, had agreed.

Clodius had made a mob of the poor and desperate men the land bill had endowed so extravagantly: Pompey ought never to have stooped to using such weapons. He had warned Pompey then that the sword would turn and cut its master. He had been angry, and had said harsh things—he could not remember now exactly what they had been, but he knew that Pompey had not minded. Not really. He had known, Cicero guessed, that his old friend had been thinking only of his own good. In any case they had made up their friendship-Pompey had told him specifically that he understood... Of course he understood. He was not a fool.

On the desk the flame of the lamp fluttered like a moth. He could hear the sea scraping the pebbles with somnolent calm, drawing in and letting out its breath. Go. Stay. Pompey, he thought, we've been friends since we were boys. And now Quintus has bound me to you like a slave.

His head sank down on his chest and his eyes closed. He might have been asleep, for presently he began to inhale and exhale with deep regularity, like the Adriatic outside; his mind wandered into images that were like the landscape of a dream. After a while he awoke. In the dark—the lamp had gone out and he did not bother to relight it, for the stars were fading into the now-paler blackness of the sky—he reached for the water jug and drank from his host's fine pottery cup. He closed his eyes again.

Immediately he saw the face of his brother. Poor Quintus—hot-tempered, ambitious, less gifted than he was himself and all the more desperately determined to prove he was as good as his brother all the same. Yet Quintus had never reproached him for the ruin he had brought on them, though he must have seen his own hopes collapsing at his feet. No, Quintus had not reproached him; he had stood by him instead, with great loyalty and courage. He knew that he owed Quintus something for that.

And his wife. Well, there was nothing he could do to repay her devotion, though he would of course do his best. She had looked after his money, his farms, his investments; she had taken care of Tullia and his little boy. Under his closed lids his eyes stung with longing for their faces. And there was Caelius, who was like a son to him, reckless, generous, brave... He hadn't liked the idea that the boy was growing closer to Milo: it was dangerous. He saw the young man, lying on the stones as the boy Catullus had lain, bright scarlet blood on his fading features; he saw his head, blind-eyed, on a pole. He has no idea what he's letting himself in for, he thought. But I do. Oh, yes, by Hercules, I do.

He began to think of the Senate, calling the roll in his mind, summoning up the faces: who would support, who be against. He had done it a thousand times, planning a speech, an argument, a bill. Now he was doing it to save himself. And the Republic, which was more important than one New Man from Arpinum. He hoped he was Roman enough to believe that.

His head fell forward on his chest and he dreamed. He must have been consul again, for he was trying to summon the Senate, standing in the shadowy Curia. Up among the rafters here and there lights picked out winking bits of gold and scarlet in the dimness, the mosaic on the floor stretched away to the darkness by the invisible entryway. The door hammered and shook; someone was trying to get in. "Stop them," he cried. "They will burn the Curia to the ground, the whole city..." The noise of the pounding bronze was louder; a crack was gleaming at the edge. He threw himself against the cold metal; the door shuddered and rang; he felt the panels press against his cheek. "Help me," he cried again. The door rocked on its hinges. He began to call the names of the senators, but no one answered, and after a while he saw that the benches around him were empty.

He jerked himself awake again. He was trembling and sweating; his heartbeats shook him. They had left him to do it alone, he thought, still confused by the dream, and anger moved in him, mixing itself with his fear. Even though it meant that he lost everything—home, honors, family, country. They had left him to bar the door against the return of the chaos that had threatened them once before. He was the lock they had fixed to the city, like the great bolts of the gates that were closed against bandits and wolves at night. Bandits and wolves; for a moment the faces of these men—Pompey, Crassus, Caesar—rose before him, seeming to bare their teeth as if they were animals indeed.

He shook his head to clear it. They were men, like anybody else. Still he could not deny the danger; he doubted that the Senate had guessed, in spite of everything, how perilous the situation was. His dream was true: if his strength did not hold the gate, the city itself would fall.

He was awake now, and very angry once again. Well, if he had to do it alone, that is what he would do. He would keep out these three ambitious men. He had been born for this task—to save Rome from its enemies, in spite of its deepest wish.

XXIII

Some letters:

FROM QUINTUS TULLIUS CICERO
TO HIS BROTHER MARCUS IN DYRRHACHIUM

Rome, July 29

My brother, the Senate rescinded the order for your exile today, by a vote of four hundred and sixteen to one. I don't have to tell you who the one was. His own brother-in-law Metellus Nepos spoke for the bill himself. That makes it as nearly unanimous as anything could be. The whole city seemed to be waiting outside the Temple; they cheered us to the skies when we came out. Now for the vote in the Plebeian Assembly. Let us hope that everything goes well there. Clodius and Milo may come to a confrontation; there may be violence...

ANOTHER LETTER, THE SAME TO THE SAME,
NOW WAITING IN BRUNDISIUM

Rome, August 4

...Pompey brought his veterans in from the country to help Milo and his gladiators keep order. They packed the Forum this morning; there was no trouble, and the Plebeian Assembly voted to rescind the order for your exile.

BOOK FOUR

XXIV

At the Appian Gate there were so many people that Caelius could hardly get through. He used his height to advantage, and his elbows, and finally he achieved a place on the steps of one of the temples, where, over the heads of the crowd, he could see the road. It ran away across the golden fields; the trees—cypress, parasol pines, oak-emptied their arms over it, splashing the brick tombs along side it with wine-colored shadows, the white stones of the road with deep sea-blue.

For a long time nothing happened, and the road remained empty. Caelius didn't mind; he talked to the people around him: a trader in Greek pottery, a mason with his fat little son on his shoulder, a couple of slaves given the day off from the textile factory where they worked. It was like a holiday; everyone had come out. In the city behind him the shops were closed and the temples draped in bunting.

He bought a sausage and a slice of bread from an enterprising vendor and washed them down with wine the trader passed around. He watched the road. Far away where the horizon melted, chalk-blue and violet, into the sky, a cloud of dust appeared. It grew. It shone silver in the sunlight. A noise came with it, like a distant swarm of bees, swelling to a mutter of thunder approaching through the hills. The cloud seemed to take a long time to come closer. For a while it disappeared into a hollow, and the road was blank again.

Caelius waited. Presently, over the road, a lark rose, shedding the petals of its song as it went up into the sky. As if the bird had announced it, the crowd which had made the dust cloud came immediately into sight. It was vast; it stretched away down the road so far that it too melted into the haze on the horizon. In the van, children were throwing flowers down over the stones; after them came a flute player, calling a reply to the lark. Behind him walked a man, slope-shouldered, heavy-headed, solid. The shadows passed over him; he seemed to appear and disappear, blending with the trunks of the trees as if he were able to lose himself amongst them. He put his feet down steadily on the flower-strewn road; the bird seemed to call to him, but he was looking straight in front of him; his massive and handsome head moved slowly from side to side as he walked. The crowd by the gate, catching sight of him, called his name, a huge breathy roar of love and happiness. "Cicero. Cicero." He looked up and smiled. As he came toward them, trudging out from the shadow of the last of the tombs, the sunlight shone on his face. From the steps Caelius could see the quick glint of his smile.

He came closer. A deputation of senators marched out from under the gate. At Cicero's shoulder his nomenclator bent to whisper their names in his master's ear; a young married woman who resembled him-his daughter Tullia—pressed closer to his side. "Cicero," Caelius shouted, making it carry over the crash of voices around him. "Marcus Tullius Cicero," As he passed under the steps of the temple, the great man looked up. He surveyed the crowd massed to greet him; he gave a long, deep, speculative glance to the city just visible beyond. The strong head turned. Over the top of the cheering crowd, Caelius gazed into Cicero's fine, brilliant, dark brown eyes. Then Cicero was gone, swallowed under the arch of the city wall, and the tens of thousands of people who had escorted him across Italy from the sea filed slowly after him. The crowd around the gate let out a long, happy sigh, and followed after.

For a long time Caelius sat on the steps of the temple alone, watching the shadows lengthen on the road as the sky turned to gold. "Cicero," he said once or twice to himself. "Cicero." Over his joy there was a sifting of sadness like the dust settling on the road, falling from silver and gold in the air to ashy purple among the shadows on the stones. "Cicero."

He was older, for one thing. Sixteen months had grayed his hair and cut lines of grief and weariness around his mouth. His shoulders had bent further, his sturdy tread had become something like a shuffle. He had kept his endearing resemblance to a bear, and the sense he gave of being at home in the city as if it were his natural habitat; he was still very strong, and he had looked at the city he knew so well with his familiar intelligence and good humor, but the eyes he looked from were now wary and alert. To Caelius, stiff from sitting so long on the granite steps, came the reason: the eyes had seen the forest, just as they always had. What was different now was that they had also seen the trap.

To Cicero, passing under the Gate into the City, it seemed that all of Italy had come to welcome him. Truly, if he had wanted to start a civil war, he could have raised the men to do it on the spot.

All along the way to the Capitol, where the consuls took him for yet another service of thanksgiving—like the ones the towns had held for him along his road, but bigger, of course, and far more splendid—the crowd was as thick, and in the Forum afterwards people had packed so tightly there was no space anywhere; even the monuments were covered with bodies waving and crying like wood pigeons on a rock. He had to be lifted over their heads to be set on the Rostra; his speech was drowned in shouts of approval and rejoicing. When he had finished they carried him back, all the way to his brother's house, where his friends waited for him, jammed into the atrium, and his brother beamed at him from across the room. When he had finally worked his way through the press of bodies to Quintus' side, he was exhausted and elated in equal measure. His hands burned from the squeezes of congratulation, his ribs were sore from embraces, his feet had been trampled flat into the ground.

"A bath, Quintus," he gasped. "Hercules, I need a whole lake of hot water. This is wonderful, but..."

"Not yet. Come into the garden. I've got something for you."

"Oh, no, you shouldn't have. I don't need anything . This is enough."

"Come," Quintus said, ignoring all of this.

Quintus' garden was small, but whatever it was remained invisible. At some time—when? He had never noticed—night had fallen, and the place was dark. But Quintus led him happily, talking over his shoulder as he went, toward the back where among the topiary and the fishponds he had built a pavilion to hold a stone table and three couches. They had often dined there when Quintus was in Rome.

Someone was there now, and he had been dining too. The lamplight shone on a greasy plate, a piece of broken bread. Cicero could see nothing but a hand on the table; it was motionless; the manicured nails gleamed back at him, reflecting the light of the single small lamp like tiny suns. Behind them a dark figure watched him from among the columns and the leaves. Cicero stepped forward, the figure bent; a vast face, scarlet and gold, floated into the lamplight, smiling.

"Pompey," Cicero cried, surprised by a sudden and furious anger.

"Hello, Marcus," Pompey said. "Welcome home." He was hanging back, unsure of Cicero's reaction; well, that's something at least, Cicero thought, feeling savage. I wouldn't have credited him with even that much sensitivity.

"Hello," he said biting back his rage. His arms and legs were trembling, and he was drenched with sweat, as if a cloud had opened on his head. Hercules, he said to himself, I thought I was over that.

The big man had come forward to put his arms around him; he was thumping Cicero's aching shoulders and saying to Quintus, "So he's back. Sixteen months, and he's finally back."

"Yes," said Quintus, passing around cups of wine. For a moment they stood in solemn foolishness, watching Pompey pour a little wine on the path and mutter a prayer. Then they were sitting down, and Cicero leaned back against the cool stone of the couch.

It was a simple supper: bread, olives, salad, and cheese. "In all the time I was away, I never ate anything that tasted as good as this," he said.

"Friends," Pompey announced with his usual sententiousness. "Friends are the greatest of all the gifts of the gods."

Friend? What friend? Where were you when they were about to send me into... But even in his mind Cicero could not say that word.

"Well, we owe some of this to Pompey." Quintus was giving him a warning look. "He brought in his troops to keep order so that you could be recalled from exile."

That word, Cicero thought.

"It was the least I could do," Pompey said around a mouthful of bread.

"By Hercules you're right about that," Cicero burst out, unable to hold himself back.

There was a moment of shocked silence, then Quintus began to gabble. Pompey's great blue eyes blinked. "I...I know, Marcus," he said with difficulty.

"Sixteen months away from Rome, without my family, my children... And all that time thinking I might never see them, see Rome, again-"

"I know. I... But I thought Caesar... Crassus..."

"You thought they and their tame dog Clodius would be better friends to you than I was. After all these years."

"Yes," said Pompey simply. "I...I made a mistake."

"Yes, you did," Cicero said, still angry, but he knew what it had cost Pompey to say that.

"I didn't want to hear..."

"You didn't want to be told that what you were doing was wrong, bad for the city."

The great eyes blinked. "That's true, Marcus."

"Well, you'll have to listen now."

"Yes, I will," Pompey agreed humbly, and all of a sudden, Cicero's anger, which had been such a flood a moment before, evaporated like a puddle on a windy day. Pompey was blinking unhappily in the lamplight, bewildered and contrite, saying, "Marcus, I need your help."

You always did, Cicero thought.

"I always did," Pompey said, wondering and sad. "I hope you can see your way...I mean...to forgive..."

"All right. Of course I can. Many things are more important than a misunderstanding between friends. Forget the past: what kind of problem are you having now?" Cicero smiled into that vast, red face.

It was Quintus who answered; Pompey was busy with his wine cup. "Marcus, we've got a famine on our hands in the city now. The price of grain has been going up steadily for a month, and yesterday in the market it nearly doubled. The poor are already feeling it, and the city supplies are getting low. If someone tries to exploit the situation..."

"So many strangers in the city now," Pompey said as if it were a personal injury. Cicero stared at him, wondering if he realized that his own veterans must constitute most of them.

"We may not be able to go on giving out the free grain much longer," Quintus said. "Then people will starve by the thousands."

"Which will make the disorder so far look like a parade ground exercise by comparison," Pompey said. "We'll have unrest, riots, revolution, the gods know what."

"I see." Cicero thought about it while Quintus watched him over the lamps and Pompey ate another piece of cheese. Out in the dark garden, a frog broke the surface of the pond with a hollow plop. "We've been giving out subsidized grain for many years."

"It's free now," Quintus said. "Thanks to Clodius'...reforms."

Pompey swallowed his cheese. "A lot of men freed their slaves when that bill passed. It was cheaper to let them collect the grain themselves than to feed them at home."

"Not that many," Quintus said, and a small argument developed between them over it.

"Clodius' grain distribution is costing the city one fifth of its revenue every year," Quintus said.

"That much?" Cicero said. "I hadn't realized."

Pompey lowered his head and confessed to the table in an inaudible voice, "Neither had I."

"Well, it's odd that we never put any of this on a rational basis. We buy grain abroad, from Sicily and North Africa mostly, I believe, but we do it in a very unsystematic way. We've never tried to do anything to stabilize the price, or the sources." Cicero's old friend Caelius, young Marcus Caelius' father, used to argue about it with him. Old Caelius had made a fortune out of the fluctuations of grain prices.

"We ought to have someone to take over the administration of the whole thing," Quintus said in a voice that meant he knew who should do it.

"Big job," Pompey said. "Needs a man with lots of backing, lots of prestige." His lids had come down over his eyes; in the lamplight the thick folds seemed to glitter slightly as if his face were a mask beaten out of gold.

"I see," Cicero said, amused. "Well, no one would do a better job—"

The huge face widened in a smile.

"—Than the general who's having such a success in Gaul these days. I mean Gaius Julius Caesar, of course." Pompey's face fell and the blue eyes iced over and looked blank.

"No," said Cicero, instantly sorry. "It was just a joke. It's a bad habit of mine. I'm sorry. You would do a wonderful job. Your talent for administration, your popularity, your immense abilities would be invaluable. I think you ought to do it, Gnaeus, if you're willing to take it on." All the same the little joke had repaid him just a little for what he had suffered. Well, he was sorry now, too.

"My duty," Pompey said, gratified. "Help the city."

"We thought... We wondered..."

"I'd be glad to propose it in the Senate, if you think that would help," Cicero offered. Quintus nodded in relief.

"Thank you very much," Pompey boomed. "I'll be glad if you do. And we'll have to do something in return, for you. Would you consider a position with the commission?"

"I have to see about getting my house rebuilt," Cicero said quickly. Long ago he had learned to make himself seen in the city. "Rome has no ears, but it has eyes." He had told Pompey that himself once, but he did not recall just when.

Yes, he did. It was in his house, the tent-like room wavered darkly around them, the servant lay down on the floor... Well, he had not come back to Rome to accept a gift at Pompey's hands. He would be no man's slave; instead he would turn Pompey toward what was right and good for the city. "Of course, if you prefer not to go, I understand." The big man was giving off heat and light like a sun shining with pleasure. "I think I can do something about your house for you. They ought to vote you some kind of compensation..."

"And declare the dedication of your property for a temple illegal," Quintus broke in quickly.

"Of course." Pompey's face had retreated into the shadows again. Is he offended? Cicero wondered. He might only have been watching, ill-at-ease and hidden behind his reserve, as before. Cicero, seeing the glints off his jewelry—he wore a lot of it, rings, a band around his arm—the richness of the folds of his clothes, thought: Pompey doesn't really understand how things are done here. He shook his heavy head, and his nose twitched with good humor. Well, he thought, if he did, he wouldn't need me.

Pompey's voice came out of his retreat. "Of course. Anything to help a friend. 'Hand washes hand,' as they say." He had left behind his own two immense ones, twisting together on the table. The polished nails winked at Cicero over the dirty plates and the broken meal.

"Marcus," a voice said softly in the dark of the upstairs hall. Peering, he made out a white face, a blur in the night. "Terentia, my dear."

She came forward, smiling. "Marcus, while you were away there were a number of things that happened..." She was anxious: her voice vibrated like a lute string in the dark, her hands were cold. "Publius Clodius tried several times to sue us. I didn't know what to do. I was at my wits' end. He was claiming that some of our income—most of it—was from illegal sources... I know that's not true, Marcus." Her voice was a little stronger: she was sure that he was honest, at least, and taking confidence from that. "And there were other things, too. I didn't know how to deal with them—"

She was a good woman; she had tried to defend his home for him while he was unable to look after it himself. It wasn't fair that this burden had fallen on her. "Of course you didn't know how to deal with them," he said, patting her chilly shoulder. "Why should you? You're a woman. Your province is the household, and the children: it's intolerable that you should have been forced to take it on."

"But Marcus, what if something happens again? Don't you think I ought to know how to deal with it?"

"I think you can leave that to me." He put all the warmth of his affection in his voice. She must have been reassured, for she looked uncertainly into his face for a moment, then, gave him a little, bitten-in smile. He did not know why, but he had had the impression she was disappointed in him.

XXV

Men were running in the Forum, heading for the Curia, dodging among the buildings and monuments, careening into the railings that divided the Forum from the Comitium. As they went they wailed, a sound like a wind tearing through the opening of a cave. "Hercules," Cicero said. "I thought we'd finished with all that."

"What is it?" Quintus cried, but no one knew. They pushed on, ignored by the running men, probably not even recognized, for they were walking in a cluster of their own servants, among their friends and supporters.

"Where are they coming from?" Cicero asked. "Tiro—?"

But he had no need to send someone to ask, for Marcus Caelius was loping up to them, breathless and unhappy. He drooped where he stood, catching his breath; they waited, watching him in fascination. "They were at the theater."

"It must have been quite a play," Cicero said.

Caelius' head came up and he laughed. "Oh, it was. It was called, 'Cicero, or The Reason For The Shortage of Food,' and it was written by one Publius Clodius Pulcher."

"Indeed," said Quintus, frowning with anger.

"Really?" Tiro asked. "I didn't know Clodius wrote plays."

"Of course not," the others said all together, and Cicero added, "He means there's been a demonstration of some kind at the theater."

"That's right." Caelius, stretched his broad grin. "Clodius and his bullies interrupted the performance—"

Cicero, looking at the boy as he talked, thought how much he'd changed. He looked surer of himself, and more elegant. He didn't think, for instance, that he'd ever seen a toga quite like that—the wool so white, the borders so beautifully woven. And the boy stood up straight, with so much confidence. Cicero supposed it was his success in the courts and his affair with Clodia Metelli, that had given him this air of distinction. Well, perhaps the woman was good for something after all. He supposed he ought not to think of him as the boy any more.

"This play," he said to Caelius. "They're hoping to see the sequel now, in the Curia, are they? What do they expect, that Clodius will be appointed to regulate the grain supply instead of Pompey?"

Caelius nodded. "Seriously," he said, falling into step beside Cicero. "It's a bad situation. Clodius has been telling them that it's your fault they're hungry. I think they believed him."

"I can take care of Clodius," Cicero said.

And he could. When they reached the Curia the mob yelled and called to him happily. The running men let him through, shouting at him to save them; hundreds of them tried to follow him inside the already overflowing lobby and aisles. He did not see Clodius anywhere.

It was plain that the grain commission was the only business that was going to be transacted, though half a dozen reddish-brown Egyptian ambassadors in gold collars and short white skirts were waiting in the visitors' gallery for a chance to present their credentials; the crowd, and many of the senators as well, were already calling on Pompey, but no one came forward to open the meeting.

"Why not?" Tiro was muttering. "These people are anxious for action. Why are they making them wait?"

"Look," said Quintus. "None of the former consuls has come."

"They knew there was going to be a vote on this appointment, and they didn't want to vote for Pompey, nor to be on record as opposing him," Cicero said. Caelius, next to Tiro, gasped. "Do they hate him as much as that?"

"Yes," said Cicero, rubbing his eyes. "I think they do."

At last the meeting began, but before they had gotten through the opening prayer and the call to order, a new name was being shouted in the aisles and from the seats in the back. It grew in rhythmic strength— "Cicero, Cicero"—until the flames trembled in the lamps and the benches shook. Under it came another shout, like an undertow, rising to a swell that broke into a thunderous call.

Pompey must have had an excellent system of spies, Caelius thought, for it couldn't be coincidence that he was coming through the door just when the noise was loudest. He smiled modestly and sat down in his place, pretending to ignore the shouts; the ex-consuls, who had caucused in the back of the room, came down the aisle to shake his hand. When he was called upon he stood up in his place, though the crowd shouted at him to take the podium.

"No," he said. "I won't trouble the consuls to move. I only want to say that whatever you ask me to do I will do gladly"—he held up his hand to prevent the cheering—"on one condition." There was a sudden silence. "Marcus Tullius Cicero must help me. He will be my second self in everything..." They wouldn't let him finish, they were shouting with such enthusiasm. You clever old fox, Caelius thought. Taking over Cicero's popularity like that. It may not be honest, but it was very well done.

"Well done," Cicero was saying, coming back to his place. "He realizes he will need some help and is too wise to exceed his limits."

It was strange, Caelius thought. Cicero could find his way around Roman politics in the dark, but about Pompey he was blind.

Down in front the consul was calling on the caucus to propose their bill. It gave

Pompey the direction of the grain supply from its sources in the colonies to its distribution in the city for the next five years. "Very good," Cicero said. "Effective, but not too radical—"

"Five years is how long Caesar's command in Gaul will last," Caelius said.

Someone was shouting from the floor, crying that they had given Pompey a burden but nothing to carry it in. Someone else was standing up—to cheering at the back of the room, which he obviously appreciated—proposing that Pompey be given a fleet. And authority over the local officials in the colonies, the second man added. "Give him control of the Treasury," the first man shouted. Obligingly, the second added that to his bill. Pompey has more than a network of spies, Caelius thought; he has a network of backers as well.

The Senate, uncertain, was looking over at Pompey, who managed to look as if he had not noticed these proposals at all. Doesn't he want them? Caelius wondered. If not, what does he want?

"Well," said Cicero disgusted by this excess. "At least the conservatives will think our own plan was very moderate, after this." He stood up and gathered the folds of his toga around him.

"Aren't you staying for the vote?"

Cicero's dark, intelligent eye rested on him. Perhaps there was something he knew that he was not saying. He certainly did not look blind now. "That's not a vote. That's a double suicide. Tiro, let's go. Bring your notes." He was gone before the consuls had called the Senate to order again.

Cicero ran into Pompey a few days later at a garden party Lentulus gave for the performance of some new music. "No, no, my friend," Pompey protested, beaming into Lentulus' fishpond as they drew apart from the others during a break. "I have no desire to exceed whatever the Senate wishes. Why should I need an army and a fleet—much less authority over the provincial governors?"

Cicero could think of several reasons, but Pompey's scarlet face was never very readable and his thick, papery lids reduced his blue stare to slits.

"I don't feel, myself," he said carefully, watching the reflections from the pond net Pompey's ruddiness in a mesh of gold, "that I ought to vote on this. I'm not in a position to do it yet. I know my brother promised, but the Senate still has to vote on the compensation for my house. I'm sure you understand. I don't want to antagonize anyone just now."

"Oh, I understand," Pompey said genially, resting a hand as heavy as a statue's on his shoulder. "You get your life in order; then we'll do great things. But I do hope you'll agree to serve on the commission to administer my grain program when the time comes?"

Lentulus was waving them back to the chairs for the second half of the concert, shepherding the twittering ambassadors with him. "If you don't mind," Cicero said. "I think I'd better stay in Rome."

"So you said before. But I want you with me, Marcus."

Cicero laughed. "No." He moved out from under Pompey's hand and bowed across the lawn to the Egyptians. He was not sixteen any longer, it was a long time since he had had to obey an order, even from Pompey. "I need to be here. I have in mind that I might run for censor. That would be something, wouldn't it?"

"For a New Man it would be unheard of."

"That's what I thought. But you saw that demonstration in the Senate the other day. With my popularity as high as if is now, and my prestige and good character vindicated, why not?"

"Why not indeed, Marcus."

The last of the guests was taking his chair. "There is someone I could recommend for the commission," Cicero said. "My brother Quintus. He had plenty of administrative experience in that province of his. It has never been so well run, before or since."

The blue gaze was fixed on him like the beam of a lighthouse. "You want me to offer the job to your brother?"

Cicero thought of Quintus' loyalty and devotion during his exile, the blow to his own career he had suffered so patiently. Never a reproach or a moment of anger, only love and help and kindness.

"Yes," he said, staring blindly into the blueness. "I would. I'd like to repay him in some way."

"Very well." The reflections had trapped Pompey again; he was studying a large tame mullet in the pool as if he planned to have it for his dinner. "Quintus it is. Anything to please a friend."

XXVI

I t was a good thing he had not pushed too hard for Pompey's bill: it passed anyway, without his support, or the extra amendments, and he himself was having trouble with the conservatives over his house. "The men who clipped my wings," he confided to Quintus, "are not pleased to see me taking flight again."

He made a speech to the Senate. Tiro had it copied and posted all over town almost as soon as he had finished speaking, but even so the award was grudging: two million sesterces for the place on the Palatine Hill, half a million and a quarter of a million respectively for the villas at Tusculum and Formiae.

Clodius tried to prevent the bill from passing by talking the time away, but was shouted down; Serranus, the tribune the Clodians had bought, tried to veto it, and failing that, to ask for a night to consider it, but the Senate, shuddering to remember the last time Serranus had tried this trick, refused. Cicero, thinking about it afterwards, doubted that without the opposition of the Clodians the award would have been even as large as it was. To make up the difference between it and the cost of his new house he sold part of the lot on the Palatine Hill to his brother—it would be agreeable to have Quintus and his family next door, and cheaper to build two houses side by side. They engaged the architect together.

"Did Pompey really want the grain commission at all?" Caelius asked one morning not long after this.

"Well, he said he did." Cicero looked up from a pile of correspondence that never seemed to get any smaller.

"Did he want the army and the fleet as well?" Caelius was thinking of the meeting in the Curia, and the impression he had had of subtlety, even of trickery.

"No." Then, catching Caelius' eye, he added, "or so he said."

"Nor control of the Treasury?"

"No one minds getting control of the Treasury." He laughed. "The truth is, I have no idea what Pompey really wants. Even after all these years he remains a mystery to me. You ask him, and he tells you. He seems as open as the day, but you find you have to keep adding, 'so he says,' to everything, like the refrain of an old song."

"I hope we like the next verse when we hear it," Caelius said.

Pompey went to Africa for a short time. A story went around in the city that his sailors had heard there was a storm and were refusing to leave the harbor. Pompey had stood up to them. "It is necessary to sail," he was supposed to have said. "It is not necessary to live."

"Very brave," Caelius said when he heard this. He was not sure he believed it.

"Very Roman," replied Cicero, who did.

Quintus had left, putting his wife and son under Cicero's protection and his building site in his care. Pompey had returned, and Quintus was going out in his place, first to Sardinia to organize the wheat crop there, then perhaps to Sicily and Africa. "Write," Cicero said, embracing him on the quay. Pompey stepped up with some last instructions and Quintus disappeared. On the way back from the docks Cicero walked with Pompey. "You're not going back out there again yourself?"

"Not quite yet." The force that usually radiated from Pompey had gone behind a cloud that morning, leaving the great man cool and dim. "Quintus can manage without me. I have a lot of work to do here. I'm sure you can see that."

He didn't see; surely nothing was as important as this commission. It was a puzzle, but a small one, without any great significance, and he forgot it quickly in the press of business over the building. Quintus' house, which was smaller, was progressing faster than his own; the walls were nearly finished, and the tiles for the roof had been delivered. His own lot was still a wilderness of square-cut stones and unassembled rounds of columns, but the architect kept reassuring him that the walls would go up any day. "Good," he said, thinking that if he were going to plan another election campaign—and this one for the censorship—he would need the place to be ready.

On the third of November, Publius Clodius tried to destroy the new houses, launching stones from Cicero's plot at the walls of Quintus' with a great crash of rubble and dust. By the time Cicero arrived the torches had been brought out and the back of Quintus' house was blackening slowly under the invisible acid of the flames. It was some time before Milo and his men arrived, and the destruction was nearly total. Cicero, shaking his head, spent most of the day assessing it, turning over stones on his plot and wondering if the Senate would compensate him for this outrage too. Milo watched over him with his pockmarked face expressionless and grim, but there was no further trouble.

In the Forum the next day, Milo asked for an indictment against Clodius for using violence in the city. "I've got a good case," he confided to Cicero. "Everyone saw him. He won't be able to say that other people did it this time. Or that he didn't know. Not this time."

"You won't get much help," Cicero said, and sure enough when the question of Clodius' violence was raised in the Senate, no one spoke. Appius, Clodius' older brother, sat in one of the dignitaries' chairs, glaring at the men in the benches, until the silence prolonged itself into refusal and the Senate took up another matter.

"He's got friends on his side," Milo admitted. "But I've got justice on mine."

"Let's hope that's enough."

"Of course it is," Milo asserted, revealing a vein of endearing innocence in the stony soil of his personality. "For a Roman that's always enough."

But Clodius had more than friends, he had a kind of cunning as well. A few mornings later the street down to the Forum was painted with signs announcing his candidacy for the aedileship—a junior magistracy, but one that would confer on him immunity from any prosecution except for bribery—"Which no one has any hope of bringing home to him," Cicero said. "Though he must have been pouring money out like a proud father at his daughter's wedding. Look at this. 'THE FULLERS' GUILD SUPPORTS P. CLODIUS PULCHER FOR AEDILE. A FRIEND OF THE PEOPLE.' What are the rest of us, enemies? And this one. 'THE TEMPLE SODALITY OF THE GREAT MOTHER PROPOSES P. CLODIUS PULCHER FOR THE AEDILESHIP.' Those people aren't even citizens, the Great Mother is a foreign goddess. What are these organizations?"

"Those are the clubs that Metellus banned," Caelius said. "Because he got the members free land from Pompey's bill, Clodius has been able to organize them. They're practically private armies of his now."

"How do you know?"

To Cicero's secret amusement, Caelius blushed as red as a beet. "I found out from Clodia," he admitted. "She did a lot of the work of organizing, going to meetings and religious festivals all over the city—I went with her a couple of times, in case they got rough. Some of them were very strange, too. She said since she was a woman no one would notice what she did, and she would be effective. She was. They're behind her brother to the last man, now."

"I see. And are you still her lover?" He expected another blush, and he got one, Caelius staring at him until his eyes nearly popped.

"How did you know about that?" he gasped, remembering the letter and the way it had crackled against his skin.

"It wasn't hard to guess."

"No, I suppose not. It was only while you were gone, and not all of that time either. It wasn't disloyal, really; as soon as I knew what they were up to, I broke it off..."

There were footsteps behind them, running down the Sacred Way. Cicero's bodyguard was shouting. A stone landed nearby, shattering on the pavement, another whizzed past and struck the wall of the house in front of them. One of his own bodyguard cried out and dropped his sword, clutching at his arm. "Quickly," Cicero said, grabbing Caelius. They were in front of Tettius Damio's house; he had been to dinner there a dozen times. He threw himself at the gate, forcing it open, while he dragged at Caelius. "Let me go," Caelius was shouting, but the bodyguards were piling in after him, pushing him through. Damio was calling his own servants. The gate screamed on its hinges, but it closed, the iron bar crashed down. Outside, Clodius' men were beating on it with clubs and swords. It rang like a cymbal, it shuddered, but it held.

"Come out, coward. Come out." Clodius was swearing, shouting at the top of his voice. They could hear him as if he were with them in the hall.

"Let me go," Caelius said. "I'll take ten men. This can all be over this morning."

"You mean you'll kill Clodius."

"If I get my hands on him, I will."

He couldn't let him do it: a murder in the streets. His beloved Rome, its stones red with blood he was responsible for shedding. And besides, it might be Caelius' blood. "No. Come away. Leave him to the law, or the gods, or whatever powers protect us."

"Are there any?"

Cicero made the sign against evil. "So far there have been."

"Do you intend to allow this to go on?" Cicero demanded, watching Pompey pour out a cup of wine. In the chilly air the flask steamed gently, and Pompey seemed reluctant to put it down; he had already drunk quite a lot of it, and had called for more. How much he likes warmth, Cicero thought; there were at least four braziers of charcoal in the room, and though the November morning was gray and cold, the dining room of Pompey's townhouse on the other side of the Palatine Hill from his own was as overheated as an oven. At least it was a thoroughly Roman room, with plain dust-blue walls and statues in the corners—not that hideous tented place out in the hills.

"You must protect yourself, my friend," Pompey said. "Please believe me, I am on your side. Something must be done about that little man."

"Just so," said Cicero, wondering what was bothering Pompey. Something plainly was—he kept glancing uneasily at the corners of the room as if he expected it to be some other place. "What exactly are you going to do about helping me?"

Pompey's sleepy eyes widened. He was not used to being challenged so directly. "Marcus," he said, and the deep voice had a warning in it, "I don't know that there's much I can do. Crassus and Caesar both support the man."

"You're not Caesar and Crassus' man, remember? You're Pompey the Great."

"I can't turn my back on them." The blue eyes were closed, the voice, under its vast boom, was upset. He clutched the cup tighter in his huge red hands. "My wife... And they've helped me, you know. I couldn't have gotten my land bill without them."

Considering it, he could not feel that it was prudent just then to point out to Pompey what a disaster the land bill had been. "But they used you so ruthlessly," he said instead. "It's true that they got you the land, but they took advantage of your quite reasonable need to do something for your men and turned it into a quite unreasonable piece of demagoguery for their own purposes."

Pompey put out his hand to push away this idea.

"Gnaeus, are you all right?" Cicero could not have said why, but he felt suddenly sorry for Pompey.

The big man gabbled hastily, "I had a letter from your brother. He's doing very good work in Sardinia. He says he'll be able to arrange for ten thousand tons of wheat, as a preliminary. Here, I've got the letter somewhere; let me get it for you. You'll be very pleased."

Pompey was looking at him like a nervous horse. "Gnaeus, are you sure everything's all right?"

"Perfectly," Pompey said heartily.

They've promised him something, Cicero thought, suddenly sure of it.

A servant was bending over Pompey-not, thank the gods, bowing and prostrating himself, but simply speaking as one civilized person to another—murmuring something in the great man's ear. Pompey's face glowed; it might have been with relief. "My friend," he said. "Something is happening. Milo's house has been attacked by Clodius' men."

"Is Milo there?"

"No. Marcus Tullius," the servant said. "But his wife and children are."

"Hercules," Cicero said.

"Milo's house is where?" Pompey said, half out of his chair. But a thought occurred to him and he sank back.

"It's too far. We'd never get there," Cicero said, taking pity on him.

They sat in silence while the man went to find out more. Pompey began to sweat. "His wife and children," he muttered. Cicero said nothing.

Somewhere in the house a fountain dripped in an unsteady rhythm, like a waterclock in an intolerably slower world. Finally the servant reappeared. "Yes?" Pompey snapped before the man was fully in the room.

"Quintus Flaccus, Milo's friend, arrived in time. He had armed men with him, and they drove Clodius away. There were some casualties—I don't know how many, but one of Clodius' men is dead."

"He's got to be stopped," Cicero said.

"Everything is all right now," Pompey said, avoiding his eyes.

"Yes, but for how long? Next time—"

Pompey licked his lips. "His wife and children. What is Milo thinking of? He ought to protect them, get them to the country."

"We ought to protect them," Cicero said. "You see, Gnaeus, no one's children are safe if you go on sheltering Clodius."

"Don't say it." Pompey had closed his eyes.

"Then you'll stop Clodius?"

"Milo's doing it. He and his friends."

"This time. But Clodius has many more men than these. He just didn't expect opposition this time—he thought it would be a simple matter to burn out a woman and some children. Next time he'll be better prepared."

"Why did he do it?" Pompey cried. "Everything was going so well."

"Why not?"

"The law... He'll be tried, exiled, declared an Enemy of the People, I don't know what. You're the lawyer. Why did he do it? There were witnesses, too."

"Oh, my dear old friend, I've been trying to tell you. None of that matters any more. He can do whatever he likes. If he can be elected aedile, he's immune. If Milo brings him to trial first, well, he's done enough already to justify the most extreme penalty of the law. He might as well add the murder of as many men—and women and children—as he likes now. He can only be exiled once."

"He won't be elected aedile," Pompey said firmly, but spoiled the effect by adding almost at once, "Will he?"

"He's got plenty of backing. In the Senate he still has the many of the families he's related to, and among the people he can raise an army any time. He's done so much for them, you see." He tried to keep the bitterness out of his voice. "The clubs, the free food, the land..."

"Yes, yes. You don't have to go through it again. I understand."

"Then you will help?"

Pompey shrugged and looked blank.

"At least you won't stand in the way? Protect Clodius, I mean?"

"No," said Pompey at last, as if a team of oxen were dragging the words out of him. "You don't know what you're asking, but I won't." And on the way out he gave Cicero a smile so radiant, it was as if the sun had come out of the clouds of his unhappiness and shone for a moment in the deserted, wintry street. "We'll be a team together," he said. "Two outsiders against those three aristocrats."

"Two of us should be sufficient," Cicero said. They had always been sufficient; between the two of them they had remade Rome. He took the big man's hand in his own warm grip.

"Achilles and Homer," Pompey said happily, and with his free hand clapped him on the back.

XXVII

I t was a council of war: Milo, Sestius, Quintus Flaccus, a man called Philippus, who was one of the consuls-elect, several new tribunes, Caelius, silent as a shadow in the back of Quintus Cicero's atrium, as if he hoped to pass unnoticed. Cicero had Tiro with him, but the slave was not writing anything down.

"I delayed it as long as I could," Milo was saying. "The omens were bad, and I said so, and the elections were postponed." Caelius in his corner smiled to himself. Did Milo really believe that? No one else did; no one cared.

Milo was explaining some trick Metellus Nepos had tried to play on him— telling him a meeting would be held in the Forum when it was really to be in the Campus Martius or some such thing. Milo would not have been able to serve his notice about the omens if he were in the wrong place, and Clodius could have been elected, his immunity secured. But Milo was a good soldier, he understood the value of speed and surprise: he had caught up with Metellus in time.

"But you're out of office now yourself," Philippus, the consul-to-be, said. "And so is Sestius. Who will keep track of the omens now?"

Everyone looked at the new tribunes. "Of course," one of them agreed.

"That's all right," Milo said. "I'll kill Clodius soon now anyway."

Someone smiled uneasily.

"Why not?" Milo demanded in a voice like gravel. "It wouldn't bother me at all. It would be like spearing a mad dog. A public service."

"It may not be necessary," Cicero said, speaking for the first time. His fine brown eyes blinked unhappily. "Naturally, Milo is upset by the danger to his family, as well as to the rest of the city. We all are. But violence? There has been enough already. I think we can approach the problem in another way. We have enough votes, I believe, now that we have Pompey's help, to get a ruling in the Senate that the trial should take place before the elections. People are badly upset by the disorder. It should swing some votes our way."

The consul was nodding his agreement. "Clodius is threatening to take revenge on the whole city if he's not elected aedile. Everyone knows what that means."

"Arson, riot, murder," Milo said. "It would be simpler if I just killed him."

"Perhaps," Cicero said patiently. "But what kind of example would that be? How could we say that we were defending the republic and the laws if we used the same methods as his? And, in the end, why would it matter if we won, if we were no better than he? Rome would never survive the conflict, not the Rome we know.

No, what we want is to cut their power off at the root from which it all grows..."
They were watching him expectantly. "The way to do that is through the law that
gave them that power in the beginning."

"The veterans' land," Sestius said.

"That's right. We must reopen the debate on that law."

They were smiling, nodding their agreement. A tribune called Rutilius Lupus
said, "I'll be glad to propose it. I never cared for that bill." Pompey had sent this
tribune with a recommendation: "A very steady man." Cicero thought he probably
was.

"Fine," said Cicero. "That's settled then."

"And Pompey won't object?" It was Philippus, putting his finger on the issue,
as the others must have realized, for they buzzed uneasily.

"I've spoken to him," Cicero soothed them. "I don't think he will."

"That's all right, then. If he told you he didn't mind, he won't. He's your friend,
after all."

"Yes," said Cicero, glad it was true again. "He's my friend."

He made the rounds, calling on people, sounding them out. There were a few
surprises: Hortensius, for instance, insisted on talking about something else. "So
much for old friendship," Cicero muttered to Caelius when they were outside again.
"It throws a new light on his telling me that I should accept exile rather than start
a civil war." He looked depressed, sinking his massive head on his chest and with-
drawing into his thoughts.

Cato, away in Rhodes, wrote that since he had accepted an ambassadorship
from Clodius it would be immoral for him to do anything against a man who was
now his patron, or to direct his friends to oppose him. "Immoral?" Cicero cried.
"What does he call what Clodius is doing to the city—a philosophical symposium?"
Cato must have meant it, whatever he thought he was doing, for none of his friends
and family would agree to vote with Cicero. "They stick together, don't they?"
Caelius said, but Cicero, growing angry and determined, growled shortly, "You
leave that to me."

He pursued Lucullus out to his country house, where the general sent out word
that he was too ill to talk. Furious, Cicero left, shaking his head. His shoulders
looked clenched somehow, as if he were about to lift up his arms and fight.

If he were, it wasn't clear how. He spent the next two days alone in his study—
"Hibernating," Caelius said-but he came out from time to time to go down to the
Curia to talk to individual senators. One of them was Lentulus, whom he caught
up with during a break in the debate.

"Well," Lentulus said. "Normally, I'd be pleased to help, but I'm very busy these
days. The Egyptian ambassadors are here; when they present their credentials
they're going to ask for assistance in restoring the Pharaoh to his throne. There's
opposition in the country itself, I understand, and it will probably mean sending an

army to establish him with his rights again."

"And you'd like to be the one to go and take care of it?"

"Yes. Why not? I'm an ex-consul, I've got as much right to the job as anybody."

"Why not indeed?" Cicero rumbled genially, trying not to let Lentulus see his contempt. He succeeded—his patience in those days was inexhaustible.

"Then you'll support me?" Lentulus' eyes opened in surprise. "I thought that…"

"That what?

"Doesn't Pompey want it?"

"He hasn't said so to me."

"Well, that must mean he doesn't. You're his friend—you're the one he would talk to."

"Yes," Cicero said, "I'm his friend." He knew he had won.

All the same he thought he ought to check with Pompey. "Why should I want to go to Egypt? I'm very busy with the grain supply."

"Then you definitely don't want to?" Cicero asked, pressing for a commitment. It was like trying to press a drop of mercury into a mold.

Pompey's eyelids came down. "Why should I?" he repeated, and, slapping Cicero on the shoulder, walked away to his place on the benches.

"He didn't discuss it," Cicero said the next morning in the Forum as he wound through the crowd toward the Curia with his friends. "Something about it was making him very uneasy."

"He took a bribe from the Pharaoh," Caelius said. "Possibly he's feeling uncomfortable about that."

"He's nervous about something," Cicero agreed, easing past a large group of loungers around the Temple of Saturn. It was a few days before the Saturnalia; the Forum was already decorated with garlands of greens, there were people up from the country and in from the suburbs, setting up booths for food and wine, toys, souvenirs, and the special wax candles people gave as gifts for the holiday. The Forum was already crowded, noisy, and full of smells.

"Well, perhaps that's why he won't say if he wants it," Caelius said, but Cicero had stopped on the fringe of another group. He was watching a Phrygian flute player with a dancing bear. The bear was old and rather scruffy, like an elderly tapestry. Its powerful arms were shackled with a chain from which tassels bobbled as it shuffled through its steps. The chain had worn patches in the dusty fur, and its small, intelligent eyes looked sadly over the straps of a muzzle.

"Even though he's in chains, he can still dance," Cicero murmured.

"Well, perhaps he enjoys it; he was trained for it, after all. The poor old thing."

"So was I," Cicero muttered. "So was I."

Summoning a coin from one of his retinue, he tossed it at the feet of the flute player. The man gave him a low bow, which the bear, grinning through its muzzle, imitated. The crowd laughed, but Cicero, smiling sadly, bent his head to the animal in return. "Egypt would mean an army for Pompey. Caesar has eight legions in Gaul and is using them with great success. Perhaps Pompey would like some legions he could command too. It would put him in a stronger position against Caesar, and go some way to blunting the force of Crassus' money."

"And make Pompey the sole real power in Rome?" Caelius asked.

Cicero shook his head, reminding Caelius so strongly of the bear that he almost forgot himself and laughed. On the whole it was fortunate therefore that Cicero was so deep in thought that his eyes were blind with it, though it meant that Caelius did not get an answer to his question.

XXVIII

T he Curia was nearly two-thirds empty. Under the flickering lights about two hundred senators had seated themselves. "Not bad for so near the holidays," Cicero remarked to Rutilius Lupus, who had come down the aisle to meet him.

"No. Not bad. And a fairly good mix of our people and theirs. We ought to do all right."

"It will be better if Pompey comes."

Lupus must have thought so too, for he complained about Pompey's absence several times in his opening remarks. But the bulk of his speech was a serious, careful, remarkably detailed exposition of the problems that the veterans' land settlement had raised—political, social, legal, and constitutional—and a very sober assessment of the damage it had done. The Senate listened in vibrating silence. Caelius, watching Cicero, thought that he was pleased, but his massive head kept turning to the door, and he did not seem to be concentrating on Lupus' words. Well, he had written most of them, late at night in his study. Pompey did not come.

"Senators," Lupus was saying, "I think I can infer how you are feeling from your silence now. It is quite a contrast with the protests of this body when the bill was originally passed." There were a few smiles at this, a few shaken heads. They were remembering the violence and discord of that meeting, when Caesar shouted that he had no need of them any longer. "That is all I have for you today. If I may have a motion to adjourn? Yes?"

"Just a moment." It was Marcellinus, the consul-elect.

"Of course," said Lupus, but Caelius could see him grinding his teeth.

"You, Lupus. You have no right to judge anything by our silence, certainly not whether we approve or disapprove. I for one—and I think others as well—are not saying anything because I don't think it's right to discuss this without Pompey."

Lupus smiled smoothly. "Of course. When we meet after the holidays could he be here? His opinion would be invaluable." The same senators nodded and smiled, the same few shook their heads, but they all looked relieved that there was not going to be a vote.

"Well, if that really is all," Lupus said, smiling easily at Marcellinus, "I'll take that motion—"

"Just a moment." This time it was a young tribune. "I just want to say that I think...I think we should talk about the elections and the trial...I mean if we're not going to meet again until after the first of January, it might be too late then..."

"Are you proposing a motion?"

"Yes, I propose that we, the Senate of Rome, decide today which shall take place first, the elections for the office of aedile, or the prosecution of Publius Clodius Pulcher for violence in the city which is to be brought by Titus Annius Milo."

Marcellinus was on his feet. Lupus, who had not lost his smoothness, said, "Gnaeus Marcellinus has the floor."

Marcellinus was on the right side after all; his voice was full of anger and grief as he spoke of the burnings, the deaths, the terror in the streets. It turned into a speech, which the Senate listened to with cries of outrage and distress. "I move that the City Praetor should be empowered to draw lots for the jury immediately, and the elections be postponed until after the trial. I further move that we pass a resolution that whoever, in any capacity, should obstruct the trial in any way shall be declared an Enemy of the People, and punished according to the law." The shouts of approval and consent broke over his head, and he sat down without attempting to finish his speech.

The sense of the Senate was plain. All the same, when, as leader of the senators who were not also magistrates that year, Cicero was called upon to speak, he stood up willingly. In the first place, it relieved the burden on his heart to speak of the destruction of Clodius; in the second, he did not like to leave anything to chance that he could tie down.

How he thunders, Caelius thought, listening to the beautiful voice modulate itself through all the human emotions. He is like some protecting god speaking for us; he is the tongue of the city itself. The very stones might be groaning in their agony, rousing themselves to righteous anger at his command. They will never resist him; the Senate will give itself to him simply for the pleasure of hearing him talk. And leaning forward he let himself be swept away in the tramp and triumph of the city's glorious march to freedom and order. It was some time before he was aware of Clodius' men, bursting into the Curia to break up the meeting.

BOOK FIVE

XXIX

It was a season of omens: on the Alban Mount a small temple to Juno turned on its foundations from east to north; a blaze of light shot across the sky; a wolf came into the city by the Flaminian Gate and wandered through the streets. There were earthquakes, and rumors that out in the suburbs people had been killed by thunderbolts. On the first of January the statue of Jupiter, seated on its throne in the forecourt of the temple from which it gazed out over the city it protected, was struck by lightning and badly damaged.

The city felt the shock of these events in its bones, and staggered. People hurried through their business, looking frequently toward the sky as if they expected it to drop on them, and went home as quickly as they could. The baths were nearly empty, and the streets as quiet at noon as at midnight. Only the temples were crowded, and the space in the Forum near the Curia, where people waited to learn what the augurs would say. But here too the mob was silent, and when the augurs came through the crowd they drew their togas over their heads as if they were praying, so they would not see or hear anything unlucky.

There was a poem going around the city:

> Who can stand by and watch this—
> unless he's an adventurer, shameless,
> insatiable, himself?
> Mamurra to have what long-haired Gaul had before,
> and distant Britain.
> And you, you pervert, you queen—you'll see this,
> and suffer it?
> Then you're an adventurer, shameless,
> insatiable yourself.
>
> And now this strutting cock-pigeon
> makes the rounds of all the beds in Rome,
> like some Adonis on leave from his goddess, his queen.
> And you, you pervert, you see this, and suffer it?
>
> Was it for this, oh, glorious general,
> that you marched to the ends of the earth?
> So that Mamurra—that prick—could blow, not only you,

but thirty million sesterces as well?
What is this but generosity, perverted?

Why do you nurture this human pest-hole?
What is he good for, except to devour fortunes?
Was it for this, oh matchless son
of a magnificent father-in-law,
that you two combined
and swallowed the whole world?

"Who wrote it?" Cicero asked Caelius, who had brought it to show him.
"Catullus."

"The red-haired boy?" Cicero was working on a speech in support of Lentulus Spinther's application to go to Egypt. He seemed glad of a chance to rest, and yawned and stretched his arms. "Mmm?" He rumbled from deep in his chest.

"He's in Asia with the praetor Gaius Memmius now. He sends things like this back from time to time. There's a very beautiful one about his brother, who died out there." He was working on a letter, copying it out for Tiro.

" 'Oh, glorious general,' " Cicero read. "I suppose we can guess who that means. And the father-in-law is Pompey, I suppose."

"Well," said Caelius, laughing. "Isn't it?"

"Not everyone agrees with this," Cicero said. He held the rough paper out as far as he could to see it. "Most people think Caesar is doing a splendid job up there in Gaul."

"Do you?" Caelius' leaf-shaped eyes glowed in the winter light. He's entirely too fond of action and heroic events, Cicero thought, worrying about him. He hasn't any sense of proportion, or self-restraint. The responsibility for this weighed on him, and his shoulders slumped.

"I don't suppose Pompey's any too happy about Caesar's success," Caelius said, laughing to himself. "And I'll bet he doesn't like being linked with this kind of scurrility either."

Cicero caught his look. "By Hercules, you had this copied and sent around yourself."

"I thought it couldn't hurt," the boy admitted, giving him a mock-modest grin.

"Couldn't hurt what?"

"I thought it might help to widen the breach between Pompey and the other two."

"And you think that this will do it?"

"Well, it couldn't—"

Cicero took up the paper again. "You'd be surprised how much a thing like this can hurt. You stay out of this business. I don't want you involved in it in any way. Is that clear?"

"But—"

"Is that clear?"

"Yes, Marcus Tullius," Caelius said, and bent his head unhappily over his letter.

A scandal was going around the city too. As soon as the people of Egypt had heard that their deposed Pharaoh was in Rome asking to be restored to his throne, they sent a delegation of their own with their side of the story. It was led by a prominent citizen of Alexandria named Dio. For a few days Rome seemed full of dark-skinned men in thin white skirts and gold collars, carrying palm-leaf fans that scraped against the cold December sky. They were strange to look at: they had tucked their hair into headdresses that resembled siege-towers, and circled their eyes with paint. They spoke Greek in a rapid, liquid accent which few people in the city had ever heard before; they smelled of spices that Romans did not use. One of them led a leopard on a leash through the Forum, to the amusement of the idlers and the alarm of the shopkeepers, but it was perfectly well-behaved, as were its slender, dark-eyed masters.

Then, suddenly, at the end of December, they seemed to disappear. Within a few days the bodies of seven of these graceful men were found floating in the winter-swollen river near the Tiber Island; the priests of the Temple of Asclepius fished them out and laid them in a row on the stones of the temple precinct. There the aediles visited them, and consulting the priests, determined that they had died by violence. Soon it was rumored that the Pharaoh had had them murdered, but this was impossible to prove, since the remaining delegates would not speak. An explanation of this went around the city, as well—they said that the Pharaoh Ptolemy had bribed or threatened them to keep them quiet. No one had any guesses about what happened to the leopard.

Pompey, particularly, was disturbed by these events. He behaved in characteristic fashion, retreating to his house in the hills and no longer appearing in the Forum. He came out only once, to speak to the Senate in favor of Lentulus' commission to go to Egypt—"as eloquent, energetic, earnest, and enthusiastic a speech as anyone could have made" Cicero called it. Certainly the Senate was relieved. "They're so glad they don't have to vote for Pompey to go out there with an army," Tiro whispered to Caelius, but Cicero overheard. "They're so jealous of him," he said.

The Senate sighed, settled down, and passed a decree empowering Lentulus Spinther, in his new capacity as governor of a neighboring province, to restore Ptolemy to his throne. It was possible to see in this a strong desire to be rid of the whole business.

If that were indeed what the Senate wished, it did not get it: the issue refused to die. Shortly after he took office as tribune, Cato let it be known that he had seen a prophecy in the Sibylline Books; it was illegal to repeat it without the authorization of the Senate. Cato, virtuous as always, would not break that law. So the city whispered and the rumors grew louder. One day a crowd collected in the Forum and demanded to know what the omen said. The next day they were there again. At last a relative of Marcus Cato came out to speak to them, leading the augurs. This Cato was a tribune: when he insisted that they read the passage, they could not refuse.

The omen was read and duly translated into Latin. "The city was warned, that if the King of Egypt comes asking for our help, we must not aid him with a multitude, or we will bring down on ourselves great toils and dangers."

"Pompey is an augur," Caelius said, but Cicero shook his head. "Don't look for plots everywhere. It isn't true. Remember, he supported Lentulus." He was short-tempered these days, and Caelius did not argue.

As soon as the prophecy was announced, there was an outcry, and the Senate withdrew its commission to Lentulus. The Pharaoh Ptolemy sent a letter, which was read in the Senate by a tribune, asking for Pompey himself to escort him back to Egypt with only two lictors for protection, and many were in favor of this—"Well, no one could call two lictors a multitude," Cicero said—but the debate was prolonged and indecisive. On the twentieth of January Publius Clodius was elected aedile.

66 "The Senate didn't care about the omens." Cicero pulled at a stalk of ivy that had come loose from a topiary ball. Behind him Tiro made a note.

"It didn't?" Caelius asked. "I'd have thought the old conservatives would have the greatest respect for the omens."

"Of course not. They were just glad of a pretext to refuse something to Pompey."

"Yes," said Tiro, pulling back his lips in an unhappy grin. "They pointed out to him that he was much too busy organizing the grain supply to go to Egypt."

The air was cold; Tiro's rugged face was as gray as bark. Out by the pool the bare twigs of the almond tree scraped like dispirited musicians; the leaves of the ivy and oleander looked pinched and blackened. From the back of the house came the voice of Diodotus, ill and confined to his bed, asking for something to drink. They could hear the stoic courage of the blind old Greek, who was plainly in great pain.

"Well," said Caelius. "Does Pompey want to go?"

"He seems to. But I talked to him—"

"And?"

Cicero raised his head and his clear eyes looked proud and fierce. "Oh, I told him very seriously that what he was doing, if he was trying to get himself sent to Egypt, was self-seeking, and self-serving. It wasn't Roman, I said; he was behaving like an Eastern despot with nothing but his own power and enrichment in mind. He wasn't thinking of the good of the city at all. And I told him that he didn't need to add to his prestige at the expense of the people of Rome—in fact he would have more glory in refusing that appointment than accepting it."

"He must have enjoyed the lecture. What did he say?"

Cicero was smiling at him. "The thing is, Pompey may not say so, but he has always listened to me."

"You're his conscience."

"More like the slave at the triumph, who reminds him he is mortal." He laughed, and in a moment Caelius laughed too.

"And does he really want the appointment?"

Cicero shrugged. "No. But you remember the old song—so he says." Caelius laughed. From the room under the colonnade came Diodotus' voice, incomprehensible now, saying something in long sentences that rose and fell like music.

Perhaps he was rambling in his mind.

"What are you going to do?"

Cicero shook his head. "First I must see this through. Then it will be time for other matters." He pulled his toga around him and hurried into the house.

"See what through?" Tiro bent to pick up the sprig of ivy from the grass. He gave Caelius a deep, bitter look. "The restoration of Ptolemy, or the death of his old teacher and friend?"

"I don't know," said Caelius.

Milo was a good soldier. When Clodius, a few days later, brought an indictment against him—"For what?" Caelius cried. "For defending his life and his family against Clodius' toughs?"—the flinty man presented himself promptly and dutifully to answer the charge. The Forum was packed with Clodius' men; the senators kept themselves carefully to the middle of the space and walked in groups, the shopkeepers were already pulling the shutters across their doors. "It's a good thing I let you persuade me to come," Pompey said to Cicero, looking around over the heads of Cicero's friends at the mob. "They need someone with authority to keep them quiet."

Cicero was thinking that it might have been better if instead of his authority Pompey had brought more men. They were badly outnumbered, even with his own escort and Milo's gladiators—Clodius must have hired the contents of every training school in the provinces. Presently it became obvious where the money to hire them had come from, for across the way, standing next to Clodius, was the financier Crassus, as lean and hollow as the tower of a tomb, looking out over the mob with dead eyes. He appeared to be counting the men. Clodius grinned, said something to him, and strode away.

There was some activity while the aediles discussed the arrangements, during which more men came into the Forum and took their places with Clodius' gangs. A small crowd of senators watched from near the Curia, ready to run if necessary. They eyed Cicero and his friends, they noted each arrival of ex-gladiators and slaves with nods and whispers, and their eyes shone in the pale light of the February sun. By the time one of the aediles came over and asked Pompey to make his speech from the Rostra, the open space was clotted with Clodius' men, hard and hostile, with mouths like knife blades. As soon as Pompey climbed the steps they began to yell.

Nothing disturbed Pompey. He spoke calmly and clearly in Milo's defense until he had finished, then stepped down with no more fuss than if he were going back to his seat in the Curia.

"This is the first time I've ever admired him," Caelius said. He had spent most of the speech organizing a response among their own men, and was a little out of breath from his exertions.

A dirty little wind had come up and was kicking the dust around their feet.

Overhead the clouds had begun to pile themselves on top of each other, the weak noon sun was fading behind them. Clodius took Pompey's place on the speakers' stand, giving his usual effect of having popped up there, dwarfed by the statues and the decorative urns.

A woman had come into the Forum, getting down from a closed chair and standing beside Crassus among Clodius' friends. The wind toyed with the hem of her black cloak; it pulled a strand of her dark hair from under her hood, and blew it across her pale, oval cheek.

From Cicero's escort there was a low buzz of comment and question.

"What is Clodia Metelli doing here?" Pompey asked, coming up.

"I don't know," Caelius heard Cicero say. "Splendid speech."

Up on the Rostra Clodius took a step forward and flung up his head; his own black hair, so like his sister's, rose in an arc above him. Clodia, mouth slightly open, took a rapt step towards him; Crassus reached out his hand to hold her back. "Citizens," Clodius shouted. "Citizens, I have come here today—"

Caelius turned toward their own men and shouted "Now!" as loudly as he could. The word caught the woman's attention, even from across the way. Her huge, dark eyes widened in her face. "She's recognized you," Cicero said to Caelius, but the noise from his own men drowned him out.

They yelled, they stamped, they clapped, they whistled; someone had brought a copper washtub and was hammering on it with the hilt of a sword; someone else had climbed the plinth of a statue and was using it launch abuse at the small man on the Rostra.

Clodius didn't seem to like it. His face had gone white with rage and his gestures had grown wilder. They could see his open mouth shouting into the noise, though they could no longer hear him. Down below, Crassus had taken Clodia's arm and was escorting her, plainly much against her will, to her chair.

Clodius threw himself forward on his toes. "Who wants to go to Egypt?"

"Pompey," his men shouted.

"And who do you want to go instead?"

"Crassus. Crassus. Crassus."

"What?" Pompey cried.

It might have been a signal, for suddenly Clodius' men were massed and running toward them over the paving stones. Pompey looked bewildered. Milo braced himself, Cicero gestured to his slaves to come closer, Caelius reached for his knife. "No," Cicero said, and the boy dropped his hand.

Clodius' men had halted and drawn up into rows a few feet from them. Clodius was screaming from his perch. "Get them out of here. All of them. Now."

At last Pompey understood. Calmly he raised his arm. "Forward, men," he said, and stepped out at a stately pace toward Clodius' gang. Milo let out a roar, and, drawing his sword, he dodged through an opening in the railing to follow; Sestius leaped the barrier after him. The three soldiers did not look back, but Cicero could see the rest of his men waver and lean after them, looking to him.

"Yes," he said. They let out a cry and ran after Pompey. For a few moments the Forum was full of flying men, like some extravagant gladiatorial game. Someone had climbed up on the Rostra and thrown Clodius down; he sprawled across the lower steps, then picked himself up and hobbled off. Cicero, grabbing Caelius by the arm, hurried him out into the Sacred Way. "Anything might happen in there now."

"Let me go," Caelius begged, panting with excitement.

"No," Cicero said. "No." But the boy was so wild he did not think he could hold him.

"See me home." Cicero put all his authority into his low voice. "I can't go alone."

From the Forum they could hear shouts and screams and the voice of a tribune—he must have taken Clodius' place on the Rostra-convening the Senate in the Curia in half an hour.

"Don't you want to go back?" Caelius asked hopefully.

"No. Take me home; they won't do anything today, you know. They're much too shocked."

"Well, so am I." Caelius' eyes were glowing.

"What are you so happy about? You like to see the city in danger, do you?"

"Milo asked me to speak on his behalf at his trial."

Cicero closed his eyes.

"Aren't you happy for me?" Caelius cried. "He said he admired my speech against Hybrida. He says his trial will be as important as any ever held in the Republic. As important as when you defended Roscius against the dictator Sulla, he says. Look—I'll be famous, I'll make history, just for this one speech."

"Perhaps the trial will never be held," Cicero said wearily. "We can always hope for that, I suppose."

It certainly seemed unlikely to take place. Clodius was the only one who wanted it, and though the Senate feared to oppose him, they did manage to delay first the debate on it, then the trial itself. They met in the Temple of Apollo outside the walls, for Pompey was refusing to come into the city unless the Senate could guarantee his safety.

"I thought he was a brave man," Caelius complained. "He is," Cicero said, but he looked doubtful.

The Senate passed a resolution that what had been done in the Forum at Milo's indictment had been against the interests of the Republic. Cato had seized the occasion to speak against Pompey, denouncing Pompey's treachery to Cicero when Cicero had been forced into exile.

"Gods," cried Caelius, "why bring that up now?"

"Look," Tiro whispered. "They love it." He was right, the Senate was listening to Cato with greedy attention.

"They'd like to see us fall out," Cicero whispered back over his shoulder to them. "They've never felt safe with an alliance between two outsiders like us—they've always been sure it must be an alliance against them..."

But Pompey, when he rose to speak, was as impressive as ever, and did much to diminish the force of what Cato had said. The trial was postponed.

That night Cicero had dinner with Pompey. He took special care of his appearance, asking his wife to lay out his best toga and making sure the barber shaved him closer than usual and trimmed his hair. While the man worked he read the invitation over several times. He thought the little note sounded distinctly nervous.

When he arrived this impression was confirmed. Pompey met him in the atrium and hurried him through to a room he had never seen before—a dining room with paintings of trellises and vines, peacocks, fountains and lawns, so that it was like going out into a garden. It was a very Roman, and a very reposeful room. But there was no repose in Pompey, who picked at the first course—leeks in egg sauce—with every evidence of anxiety, and talked of trivial things, all the time keeping his shielded gaze on Cicero. He pressed food on Cicero as if he feared he might be starving—as if, Cicero thought, he hopes I am—but only once did he show any real interest in the conversation. "Your brother?" he said, repeating something Cicero had said as if he had not heard it clearly.

"Yes. My brother's house is being built next to mine. I'd like to consult him about it, because there are some problems that are delaying the work."

"You'd like to see him?" Pompey asked, leaning forward so intently that the hem of his toga trailed in his plate. "You'd like to have Quintus back in Rome?"

"Well, yes, of course I would," Cicero said, taken aback by this sudden interest. "But I know he's very busy in Sardinia with the grain business..."

"I'll bring him back. I'll do that for you, if you like." He was watching Cicero; he was smiling, but the blue eyes were studying him anxiously, as if he feared that this might not be what Cicero really wanted, as if he might not be able to use it to his purposes.

What purposes? Cicero wondered, but aloud he only said, "Thank you, that's very considerate of you," and smiled cheerfully at Pompey. "Delicious dinner."

"You like it? Have some more. Have some—no, I know. They've got some mullet in the kitchen, I'll get them to bring it out. And some Old Falernian to drink afterwards, with the fruit. Yes. You like mullet, don't you?"

"Everyone likes mullet, when they can afford it." Cicero was beginning all the same to enjoy this. He wondered what Pompey would have offered if he'd said he loathed mullet. Pheasant? Oysters? With pearls? Swan? "Look," he said. "You didn't invite me here to ply me with your no doubt excellent fish, did you? What's really on your mind?"

Pompey gave him a look of sky-blue alarm. "Crassus is trying to have me killed."

"Oh, surely not."

"Yes, he is. Clodius is getting money from somewhere, you know."

"Not necessarily from Crassus though. He's got a rich wife, Fulvia."

Pompey looked doubtful. "She must be richer than I thought, then. He's bought a house on the Palatine Hill, did you know? He's paid almost fifteen million for it."

"Fifteen million?" He had to take a bite of the sweet white flesh of the fish, though it choked him. "Fifteen million?"

"That's right. And that egregious Gaius Cato, Cato's nephew, or whatever he is. He's got a lot of money too, all of a sudden..." He put down his bread and leaned forward again. "It's those old conservatives; Bibulus, Cato, Hortensius, Metellus Nepos, Appius Claudius. They hate me," he confided in a whisper, as if they might be listening.

"I know," Cicero said. The corners of his warm eyes crinkled as he grinned. "They're none too fond of me either."

"Why? I've done nothing to them. I only want..." He did not say what it was that he desired, but it was something that mattered to him terribly, for his eyes were glazed with longing for it and his tongue passed several times over his lips as if he tasted it.

"Well," Cicero said, watching this with fascination. "They don't like having to share their power with people like us. It's a new idea to them, and I suppose we ought to give them time to get used to it."

"I've given them time. And they've used it to turn people against me."

"Oh, no, surely not. You are so deeply loved and admired in the city. I'd give anything to have your popularity."

Pompey had sheltered his thoughts again behind his puffy eyelids, hiding them in a glimmer of blue hardly visible through his flesh. But Cicero, to his surprise, found that he could read them anyway. Pompey was thinking of the crowd in the Forum shouting, "Crassus. Crassus. Crassus."

"But that was a hired gang," he said gently. "You can't take that as any indication of how the city really feels."

"Can't I? They'll swallow anything a cheap speechmaker tells them. Anything at all. The Senate is prejudiced against me, the patricians and nobles despise us, the young men think of nothing but clothes and women. Have you seen that young fop, Marcus Caelius Rufus? They're all like that now. No wonder they admire Julius Caesar—he's just like them: no principles, no ideals." His mutter trailed away into silence. Suddenly he was angry, his huge face was stained with scarlet, a vein stood out in the thick flesh of his brow. "I won't lie down for it," he shouted. "What do they think I am? Some terrified girl who'll spread her legs for them as soon as they scowl in her direction? Not Pompey the Great. I've got plans."

"So has Clodius."

"I'm training four centuries of soldiers for Milo's trial. I'll have that aristocratic son of a dog so badly outnumbered he'll think the whole of Italy has come in to fight him. And I've got more, coming in from Picenum, and from Gaul. That trial will be held honestly, let me tell you."

"It must be expensive," Cicero murmured, shocked by the size of this plan.

"I can afford it," Pompey said simply. "They owe their farms and homesteads to me, after all." He was passing a dish of apples and pouring out the wine. It was Old Falernian after all.

"Kind of you to give me this wonderful wine," Cicero said, smiling.

"My old friend," Pompey said sentimentally. "My oldest friend," and Cicero heard behind it the words that Pompey did not say. "The only one I can trust."

XXXI

C lodius was no fool. Caelius, knocking on Cicero's door just before day-break four days later, had a moment of sharp appreciation of the small man's determination, though he had never thought much of his mind before. Perhaps he hadn't much of one really—it might be Clodia, his sister, behind this latest move: she had intelligence enough for both of them. Yes, it must surely be Clodia who had thought this one up.

It was dark in Cicero's house, and though the lamps had been lit in the atrium, there was no one there but a servant sweeping the floor. He gestured to the back, and Caelius ducked his head, hurrying out.

Tiro was setting out writing materials for the clerks in the study, but he did not know where Cicero was either. Out in the garden, chilly under the fresh March wind that shook the crocuses in their newly turned beds, there was no one at all, but the smell of baking bread was collecting in an invisible cloud under the colon-nade at the back. And there, sitting at a scrubbed pine table in the kitchen, was Cicero, eating a bowl of gruel and talking to his architect.

"Clodius is bringing an indictment against Sestius this morning," Caelius said.

"An indictment. And what is this one for?"

"It's really two of them: one is the usual 'using violence in the city.' The other is for bribery. Clodius got some informer—I mean perjurer, don't I?—to bring the bribery charge, but the two are going to be tried together."

"Really? I'd better go to Sestius."

But partway to the door he stopped and looked over his heavy shoulder at Caelius. His brown eyes had widened with surprise. "He knows. That's what this means. Clodius knows that I've seen Pompey and won him away from the other two."

"Oh, no. That's not possible. He's just trying to revenge himself on Sestius for helping you."

"Oh, yes. You'll see. He's trying to make sure that no one will ever dare to stand up for me again." The big, squarish head was shaking. "Poor fool. He'll need a lot more than that to frighten Pompey."

The doorway stood empty, a bright patch of garden and sunlight. Cicero ducked back inside it. "You'd better be careful yourself. You might wake up one morning in the same position."

"I? Why should I?" But Cicero had already hurried out the door again.

Could he really find himself in the same position, as Cicero had said? It was not that he was afraid, of course; he was confident that he could defend himself against any charge that Clodius might bring. He had never run for political office or governed a province, so it would be difficult to indict him for bribery; he had not, like Milo and Sestius, brought his men into the city to fight Clodius' gangs—though he would have liked to—so a charge of using violence in the city was unlikely to stick. He didn't see that there was much that Clodius could do. Besides, he could speak as well as anyone in Rome; from his first speech, against Hybrida, he had been famous, and Clodius knew it. His own sister had taken him up, made him her lover, because of it. No, he didn't think Clodius would risk anything, he didn't see anything Clodius could risk.

He had a case of his own to prosecute, and he was working on his cross-examination for it, when, late that night, Cicero stopped by. "It's all set," he said. "I'm going to defend Sestius. What are you working on?"

"Some notes for the prosecution of a man called Lucius Calpurnius Bestia," Caelius said, stretching his arms over his head and yawning.

Cicero stared thoughtfully into his winecup. "I'd better appear for the defense."

"But you don't even like Bestia," Caelius cried, dismayed. He had seen this case winning for him the same praise that his first one had. Now, if Cicero defended...

"It doesn't matter." Cicero's eyes looked shadowed in the darkness outside the circle of lamplight, but his mouth gave a small, nearly imperceptible twitch, and he seemed to be smiling sadly. "The main thing is that you and I should be seen to be in opposition to one another. I don't want the Clodians to get any ideas about you."

"But the trial is tomorrow."

Cicero was certainly smiling as he lumbered to his feet. "Well, then, I'd better get busy, hadn't I? In the meantime, between now and Sestius' trial, I want you to stay away from anything controversial. And don't appear in public with Milo for a while. Is that clear?"

"Yes," said Caelius, too depressed to resent his tone.

Of course, Cicero wouldn't have much time to prepare—that was a consolation. And in the Hybrida case, when Cicero had had as much time as he needed, he, Caelius, had managed to beat him anyway. Perhaps it wasn't as bad as he had thought. This idea lifted his spirits, and when he went down to the Forum the next morning accompanied by his secretaries and clerks, he was in a cheerful frame of mind.

And of course the trial was a disaster. Not that there was any trouble—Pompey had brought in his men; the Forum was packed with them, and though there was some shouting and shoving, Clodius and his gangs were unable to prevent the trial's orderly progress. Cicero's speech appeared, like all of them, to be entirely extemporaneous, and in this case it probably was—a detailed summary of the evidence, a moving plea for the client, a few very funny and damaging jokes, and the whole thing was over. Caelius' own speech attracted mercifully little attention, except from the Clodians: when he got home, still half-angry, half-laughing at his defeat, he found a note from Clodia inviting him to dinner. It was not the first such note she had sent him since the end of their affair: he had not paid much attention to the others, but this time he thought he ought to go. He ought to see what she wanted. It was plainly no more than polite.

So, bathed, perfumed, shaved and curled, he presented himself at her door late that evening. There was music, which he could hear from the street, and there was Clodia, standing behind the doorkeeper, looking at him gravely out of the most beautiful eyes in Rome.

"Good evening, Clodia."

"Marcus Caelius." He had forgotten how wonderful her voice was—it was like the aulos, the deep-toned flute; it made him feel a little dizzy, and in spite of himself he smiled at her. She looked up under her eyelashes and gave him a tentative and heartbreaking curve of her strange, sad mouth in return. "I'm glad you came."

It was a splendid party—hers always were. She knew everyone: he talked with a legate recently back from Caesar's campaign in Gaul, and with a couple of aediles in charge of weights and measures in the city's markets and the registration of prostitutes. He listened to the poetry reading and the musicians, he ate the elegant food, he danced. He loved to dance as much as Clodia did herself. Sometime not long before dawn he wandered into her bedroom, following the instructions on a tiny folded note she had pressed into his hands when she passed him, cheeks brilliant, eyes shining, in the line of a dance.

The room was as he remembered it, honey gold and rose pink, glowing with the light of alabaster lamps on gilded stands. The great black and silver bed floated on a sea of carpet; a drift of linen so fine it was transparent lay across it. The dressing table was littered, as it had always been, with bits of every part of her life: hairpins and jewelry, letters and bills, a child's broken amulet, a half-finished cup of wine. A stack of reports from a farm manager was held down by a golden stone, a necklace was draped around the neck of a small gilt statue of Venus. Nevertheless, a candle burned faithfully in front of the image. The whole assortment had received a dusting of powder and smelt of her perfume. He smiled as he touched the objects on the table, remembering the pleasures he had had in this place.

"Just what are you doing?" It was Clodia, in the doorway, as angry as a snake disturbed in its lair.

"Sorry if I've done something wrong." His own quick anger rose in him. "But you did invite me."

Her breasts moved under her dress as she drew her breath to speak again. With a pang of regret he watched them. "I didn't ask you to spy on me."

He could not calm her down; indeed he made her more angry, for he didn't understand what had upset her. Presently he left, as mystified, and as irritated, as before.

The attacks on Cicero's friends continued. "Clodius is trying to pick them off one by one," Cicero said. The small angry man was not deterred by Sestius' unanimous acquittal—"in a case like this it must be unanimous," Cicero said. "Anything else and they will see it as a sign of weakness. We sober men, plebeians, knights, and patricians, must be seen to stand together"—and a few days after the verdict Clodius brought an indictment against another of Cicero's political friends, Publius Asicius, one of the chorus that followed him every day in the Forum. This time it was an accusation of murder: Clodius claimed to have evidence that Asicius had assassinated Dio, the envoy from Alexandria, who had come to Rome to protest the restoration of the Pharaoh. "Well, that's original, anyway," Cicero remarked. "It's a wonder he didn't come right out and accuse him of murdering the leopard too."

This case Cicero also won, though he lost the next one. Pompey, encouraged by these results, had conceived the idea of using the courts to their own advantage; he and Milo cooked up an indictment against a freedman of Clodius' called Sextus Cloelius, who was Clodius' chief henchman in organizing the riots. "Well, he deserves the prosecution," Caelius said. "He deserves to be exiled, at the very least."

"Of course he does," Cicero said, shielding his eyes wearily from the lamplight. The sweet rain of the spring equinox fell musically outside the door, drawing out the smells of new wood and plaster, wet earth, and the sad undertone of an old fire; the petals of an almond tree—not the original one, which had been uprooted by Clodius' bullies, but one as nearly the same as Cicero could find—lay pasted to the ground. "But Pompey doesn't realize that you can't use the courts that way. Clodius will pack the jury and bribe the rest. You'll see. He won't allow a man as close to him as Sextus Cloelius to be condemned."

"But the city hates Clodius."

"Not all of it," Cicero said. "And a lot of people don't like Pompey much better."

He was right. He was always right, Caelius thought, despairing of ever knowing as much. The jury, whether it had been bribed or not, split along the lines of class, the plebeians voting against Sextus Cloelius, the knights half for half against, the senators all for acquittal. "The case was lost by three votes. Three," Caelius cried, raging up and down in the garden. "How could it happen?"

"Because the senators stand by their own," Cicero told him patiently. A little wind was teasing the irises by the pool, their bearded heads nodded sagely to the rippled surface. "And they hate Pompey."

Caelius was as restless as the garden. "Do they think murder and arson are better?"

"Yes. They do. A small part of them, anyway." He made a soft noise in his throat; presently Caelius realized that he was amused.

"What are we going to do?" Caelius cried, throwing himself into a chair. Even there he was unable to keep still, and his fingers drummed on the arm, his long legs crossed and recrossed in front of him.

Cicero smiled. "I don't know about you. I'm going to wait. Our chance will come."

XXXII

C icero was good at waiting; he thought that no one in Rome practiced that discipline better than he. He had waited when he was a young man and his enemy Sulla had died; he had waited when he was consul and the evidence he had needed to put down Catiline had come into his hands. Even then he had delayed and, against the clamor of his friends, he had not opened the captured documents until he stood before the Senate—though he had had no way to be sure what was in them. It had been the hardest restraint he had ever practiced on himself, but it had been the wisest as well—the impact of his confidence had carried the Senate with him, swept the old men off their feet.

The clamor of his friends—he seemed to be surrounded by it now again. Hortensius came every morning, Lucullus and Bibulus and Cato nearly as often, full of plans and enterprises that came to nothing; they brought their own friends, who derived some hope or consolation just from being in his presence. Or he supposed they must have, for he had nothing more concrete to offer them. In any case, his house was so full of nobles that the Senate seemed to be meeting as often in his atrium as in the Curia and the temples. He could hardly work at all—just when he needed quiet, and time. Just when he had to think. Pompey seemed to bellow constantly in his ear; he was anxious and upset, and the big pink tongue moved constantly over his lips. Well, Pompey was no fool, he understood what the verdict on Sextus Cloelius meant as well as anyone did. As well as that chorus of worriers in the atrium all day long...

Pompey was full of plans and countermeasures. "We could assassinate Clodius," he proposed one night at dinner. Fortunately they were eating alone at a table the servants had put out in Cicero's garden, where no one could hear. Around the pool lamps had been set out, each one made a little round frontier in the dark.

"That's the worst thing we could do. Gnaeus, you can't—we can't abandon constitutional government, not to mention ordinary morality, at the first setback. Besides, if Clodius is killed the whole city will be plunged into anarchy. The only hope we have is to undercut their power by a return to law. And the only way to do that is to show ourselves the defenders of the constitution, not its worst opponents."

"Yes." But Pompey was looking at the half-replanted garden, the unfinished section of the roof across the way, with a dimmed and disappointed expression. He did not really believe it.

And there was Caelius, who did not argue, but went around looking nervous and miserable. Something was worrying him; Cicero could not tell what it was, and the boy was too old to ask. Indeed, he wasn't really a boy any more; he was—twenty-seven years old. No, surely that was wrong. But when he counted up the years, a decade had passed since Caelius had come to him as a pupil. Well, when he was ready to speak, no doubt he would. In the meantime, he, Cicero, could only wait.

On the thirtieth of March, a parti-colored day, half sunlight, half shadow, full of blowy movement and sailing clouds, Caelius appeared at the door from the house into the garden, shouting Cicero's name. Cicero led him to a seat under the arbor. "Ran all the way," he gasped. "Need your help."

"What is it?" Cicero said; studying his young friend slumped and heaving in the chair, he thought that he was not merely winded, he was shocked. His skin had a green tinge not entirely due to the shade of the new grape leaves, and his eyes were staring in his head.

"It's Clodia. She's brought an indictment for murder against me. Murder, and attempted murder, and robbery and—"

"Here. Calm down. Start at the beginning. Clodia can't have done anything to you—women can't accuse anyone in a court of law."

"No, of course not. She's got someone to do it for her. But she's behind it."

"No doubt. Calmly now. Who is actually making this accusation?"

"The son of the man I prosecuted. He's called Atratinus. Cicero—"He was furious, his hazel eyes were stretched wide in his tight face—"Atratinus is seventeen years old."

"I see." Cicero leaned back in his chair. He moved slowly and his shoulders were bowed under his thoughts, but he rumbled out his beautiful voice easily, making it weave a kind of pattern under which Caelius slowly began to relax. "Now, let's see. Whom are you supposed to have robbed?"

"Clodia."

"Really?" What are you supposed to have taken?"

"Gold. A purse of gold coins."

"And did you take it?"

Caelius looked up. "No. She lent me money—she insisted. I don't know how we'll prove that though. There weren't any witnesses." For some reason this made him blush, and the wave of color travelled up his neck to his troubled eyes.

"You leave that to me," Cicero said trying not to laugh. "Let's get on with this—just whom are you accused of murdering?"

"Dio and the other envoys from Alexandria."

"That again," Cicero said.

"Well, perhaps it is an old accusation. So, just to be sure, they've accused me of trying to poison her."

"Poison whom?"

"Clodia."

"Oh, for the Gods' sake," Cicero cried, and laughed so hard his chair creaked.

The noise seemed to sober Caelius, who, after all, was an excellent lawyer himself. "That's the one they'll make stick," he said, looking at the ground.

"Really?" Cicero had gone very still. His large body seemed to have blended into the deep forest green of the shadows. His eyes looked out, dark and watchful, as if he were hunting. "Why? Are you guilty?"

"No," Caelius replied without looking up. "There was a time, a year or so ago, when I would have liked to kill her, but I didn't."

"Look at me."

Caelius raised his eyes.

"All right," said Cicero after a time. "Tell me about it." In the luminous shade, he was grinning.

"What are you so pleased about?" Caelius' always touchy pride flaring up like a torch.

There was a long silence, filled by the rustling of the leaves and the slap of little wind waves in the pool. "They've gone too far. The Clodians have overreached themselves." Cicero sighed, a rumble of content. "That's what I've been waiting for."

What he had been waiting for. He had his chance. Into his hands a weapon had come, like a gift from a god. A chance to ruin the Clodians, destroy their credit in the city forever. By Hercules, he thought, he had been waiting long enough. If only the gods gave him this chance, this time he would not let it escape.

Why "this time"? It nagged him—he did not remember when he had had such an opportunity before. Later that night it occurred to him, and he paused as he ladled out the soup to his family at supper, that he had indeed had such a weapon in the past—Metellus, with his conservative friends, his old-fashioned outlook. With his help, Metellus had managed to keep his wife and her lunatic of a brother from their hopes. But since he had died there had been no one, and Clodius had run as wild as a flame over the city...

Metellus. Ever since Metellus had died. For the next two days he thought about the old consul and his surprising death. He paced in his garden without seeing the new hyacinths by the pool, the flutter of returning birds in the grass. Tiro had ordered the workmen out of the garden, but he might have saved his breath, for Cicero did not notice. His eyes were on the past, on Metellus in his bed long ago, while the doctors watched and his wife sat in her chair, her bleak eyes waiting for the moment of her liberation. Gods, he had known even then that there was something wrong with that death.

She had never touched her husband, except to give him his medicine. Any wife—any good wife—might have done that. But Clodia was not a good wife. Why then, had she... He paced again, and sat down on a bench, his eyes unseeing on a group of lotus trees, their roots wrapped in linen, waiting for the gardeners to return. The bench bit into his legs, he grew stiff and chilled with sitting on it. She had even taken a sip from the cup, he remembered. That certainly proved there was nothing wrong with it. The oddness of that gesture struck him: why would she drink her husband's prescription? His mind went away from that and he saw Metellus looking pale and ill, heard him complain of his indigestion... Indigestion indeed. And Clodia, with insane economy, had accused her former lover, Caelius, of wishing to poison her.

It was going to be tricky—no Roman jury was going to like rough treatment of a married woman, especially not one from a distinguished house like Clodia's. He was going to have to be very sure of his facts, and he hadn't a single one to go on yet.

"Tell me everything you can remember about Clodia," he said to Caelius, seating him in the clients' chair in his study that night. "Everything about her house, her friends, her servants. Anything at all that you might remember, whether it seems important or not."

It took two more days, but in the end he had it: a small irregular oblong of gold-colored stone which she kept on her dressing table among the pots of Egyptian rouge and the powder and perfume. Caelius had seen it there more than once. She seemed to use it for a paperweight. Cicero, going back through his memory of the one evening he had spent with Clodia, was sure it had not been there then.

"You didn't hold it to a flame by any chance, did you? Or smell it?"

"Smell it? Why would I smell a stone?"

"Why indeed? Well, it doesn't matter. Do you know what it is?"

"No."

"It's a form of arsenic. It's called orpiment—'gold pigment'. My wife used to inhale the fumes to relieve her asthma. I thought I recognized the odor—like garlic. But the stuff is a deadly poison, especially if it's swallowed. The Greeks call it 'masculine' because it's so strong. Only a little is fatal."

"Are you sure that's what it was?"

"We'd be more certain if you'd smelled it."

"But how could she have given it to him?" Caelius burst out. "She never touched him, and she drank his medicine herself."

It was an insoluble problem. He knew she had done it, there was no doubt in his mind at all. It was simply that he could not see how. It irked him to think that a woman might get the better of him, he didn't want to think that Clodia Metelli might be cleverer than he was himself. Besides, he hadn't much time; the trial was scheduled for the third of April. He hadn't enough time at all, for there were five charges in the indictment, some of them silly, some of them not. He took his pride on his bowed shoulders and went to Crassus.

"You know Caelius well," he began rather tentatively, when he was sitting in

Crassus' clients' chair. "He was your pupil too for a while."

"Yes." Crassus' hands were folded on a magnificent red porphyry desk. The rest of the house was all marble; Crassus was the only man in Rome who could afford to build a whole structure with that stone. The room gleamed whitely, like a bone; the few ornaments—a lamp, a box for writing materials, a bust or two on the shelves—were gold or bronze. But it was cold, a chill seemed to come up off the floors. It had risen to his chest so that it was difficult to draw a breath.

"I wonder if you would agree to speak on Caelius' behalf," he said, wondering rather a lot more at the same time. Pompey had turned against Clodius: that much was clear. Had Crassus had a change of heart too?

Nothing in the financier's demeanor gave any hint. He did not even seem to have heard—he sat perfectly still and his black eyes did not blink. Really, Cicero thought, he goes with this tomb-like mansion. He's cold, and his eyes are as dead as a corpse's.

"There are five charges against Caelius," Cicero said. "I can't prepare a defense for more than a couple of them in the time I have left."

"How much time is that?" Crassus asked; it was the first sign of interest he had shown.

"Four days."

Crassus was emitting a peculiar sound, a creaking, as if something were turning on a winch inside him. His mouth was opening. Hercules, Cicero thought. The man is laughing. He grinned back at him across the desk.

"That makes it April fourth," Crassus said. "April fourth is a holiday."

"So it is. That's the opposition's doing—they've chosen a charge—attempted murder—that can be tried on a holiday, when other courts are not in session, and they've scheduled an early date, presumably to prevent us from preparing a case."

"I've heard from a mutual friend that you and he patched up your quarrel, Marcus Tullius," Crassus interrupted.

"A mutual friend? Do you mean Pompey?"

Crassus' nod was the smallest, least provable acknowledgement.

"Yes. Well, that's true enough," Cicero said cheerfully, trying not to let Crassus see how badly shaken he was. "I don't know that we ever actually quarreled, though. There was a time when we didn't see the political situation in exactly the same light."

"It's enough if you see it the same way now," Crassus said.

"Oh, certainly, certainly," Cicero said, choking back his rage. Pompey can't like this man any better than I do, he thought, and was consoled. He even managed a graceful and confident smile more or less in Crassus' direction.

"Good," said Crassus. "I'll take it on then. So glad you asked, Marcus Tullius." And he closed his eyes again, very slowly, like a door creaking shut.

He hadn't much time, even with Crassus' agreeing to speak on three of the charges. He hadn't enough, for instance, to figure out how Clodia had poisoned her husband, though he sat up the next three nights trying to work it out. Finally he gave up; he would write his speech without it. He would speak last, as he preferred to do: perhaps by then something would come to him.

He was halfway through his remarks, and he was still without inspiration, two days later. The afternoon sunshine flooded across the Forum, picking out details with unnatural clarity: the sudden glow of a leaf turning on a branch, the scaffolding of the new Basilica Aemilia where the jewelers' shops had been, edged in gold, as if remembering their origins; Marcus Caelius' polished cheek, visible where he stood, half in sunlight, half in shadow, leaning with crossed arms against the translucent granite of a statue's pedestal, nodding to his father, stooped like an arthritic tree over the witnesses on the defense bench. The old man stare back at his son with hazel eyes rinsed pale by feeble anger.

The prosecution bench was jammed with lawyers and friends of the accusers; on the pavement, a little way behind it, Clodia Metelli, her evidence given, sat in a chair surrounded by her relatives, grave and pale. Pompey's veterans stood in clusters nearby with their hands on their swords. Cicero smiled at them from time to time as he spoke, and their centurion nodded in return. A crowd had collected, as always; further down the empty space seats and awnings had been set up for a theatrical performance or a gladiatorial combat in honor of the holiday: banners snapped over the now-deserted site, but from the Circus, invisible behind the bulk of the Palatine Hill, the sound of cheering drifted intermittently as the last chariot races were run. It struck him as a good omen, as if they were cheering for him.

He had been speaking for nearly an hour; he had already, with Crassus' very effective help, gone through the charge of murdering the envoys from Alexandria. Now he was describing Caelius' character, his upbringing, his education, excusing his wildness as high spirits, his recklessness as the impetuosity of youth. Why not? It was probably no more than true anyway. And one or two of the jurymen hadn't much to blame anyone for—they had once, he remembered, been rather high-spirited and impetuous themselves. Not that it helped. They were not with him. They looked like a panel of censors, getting ready to strip the boy of his rank—and they were anxious too. Caelius' father smiled grimly, remembering no doubt the expense of his son's way of life. Clodia looked bored.

Anger flooded through Cicero, lifting him above his words. Bored, are you? he asked her in his mind. Perhaps you don't think it's interesting to try to ruin a young man's reputation and career? Well, we'll see about that. His scruples about exposing a woman disappeared, his sense of the power of her family connections, swamped in his fury at her. You won't get away with it, he swore silently. You murdered that poor old man; I'll see you destroyed for it as surely as you tried to destroy an innocent young man today.

"Gentlemen," he said in a loud voice, calling the jury back to attention. "There are two charges here—one about some gold, one about some poison—and the same person is the fountainhead of both. The prosecution says the gold was taken from Clodia, the poison acquired to give to her. That is all we need to be concerned with: all the rest of the accusations are not criminal charges, they are taunts and insults, hurled by an angry accuser, who is..." He shrugged. He would tell them later what she was.

"Look at it yourselves. Caelius wanted gold, they say; he took it from Clodia, took it without witnesses, kept it as long as he wanted it. Well this is strong evidence, all right, just as the prosecution claims—strong evidence of—"

He paused; the jury was watching him. His nose twitched and his mouth bent slightly.

"I see it as strong evidence," he said, "of a quite remarkable...intimacy."

He had expected a laugh. Instead the jury looked shocked. This was going to be difficult. Evidently they didn't like an attack on a woman. Especially not one from a family so exalted.

And Clodia, he had to admit, had known how to play to that sentiment. She looked magnificent. Beautifully and discreetly dressed in mourning for her husband, she was sitting as quietly as a vestal, her eyes on her decorously folded hands.

"In the same way, the prosecution says, Caelius wanted to kill Clodia. He searched out some poison, bought it, prepared a potion of some sort—" What kind of potion? he wondered. A pity they hadn't said; he might have known from that how she had done the job herself. "This time, gentlemen, I see a fountain of violent hatred spewing out of this charge, and it comes as a result of a rupture in a...in a personal relationship."

Again no laugh, and the uneasy glances. He took a deep breath. "All in all, in this case, gentlemen, we are concerned entirely with Clodia. She says she lent the gold to Caelius, she says the poison was bought to kill her. There are no other witnesses. Without her, the prosecution has no case."

The jury had all turned to stare at Clodia, who stared at them down her nose and turned away.

"Gentlemen." He could see that the look Clodia had given them had further shaken their confidence; he was going to have to scramble to restore it. The first step was to let them see that he was on their side. "You yourselves in your wisdom will understand that this is a woman not only of noble birth but of great notoriety in this city. If she had not brought these charges, if she did not say that she lent Caelius gold, if she did not allege that he tried to poison her, we would be acting disgracefully—using a Roman matron's name in any other way than such a lady's virtue demands."

He was going to have to try something to discredit her, to make them see what she was. He hadn't any idea how if what he had already said hadn't done it. Well, he thought, it doesn't matter—any mud will stick to a wall.

"But what can I do? What other course is open to his counsel than to refute the attack on him? And that I should do with all the more vehemence were I not hindered by my personal dislike—"he gathered his toga in his hands and leaned toward the jurymen—"hindered, I say, by my personal dislike for her husband—I mean for her brother—I always make that slip."

The spectators got it first; they roared with laughter, drowning out a cheer from the distance. The jury, still a little unsure, first snickered, then laughed. The president of the court looked at Cicero warningly, but he pretended not to see. He was watching Clodia.

Her calm was gone. Why? What had he said, to get such a reaction? But there it was. White as marble and swaying on her feet, she clutched the hand of an elderly relative. Well, whatever he had done, he had better follow it up.

He spoke to her in the voice of her ancestors, standing stiffly and chastising her in the archaic style. "Woman, what had you to do with Caelius, a youth, a stranger? What was he to you? A blood relation? A connection by marriage? An associate of your husband—?" The jury loved it: it was as good as a play.

And when he had them again, he spoke of Metellus. "Poison? I saw, I saw—I drank the bitterest sorrow in my life the night Metellus was taken from us. Will a woman who comes from such a house dare to speak of poison? Isn't she afraid the house itself will burst out in accusation against her? Doesn't she tremble to think that the walls know her conscience, her memory of that night polluted by murder and grief?"

The chariot races must have finished. Her brother was standing beside her. Clodia, still pale, leaned toward him and whispered. Clodius reached his arm around her, glanced uncertainly at the jury, glared at Cicero and shouted into the streaming crowd. "To me, Clodians. Get him. Get him." A knife appeared in his hand in that magical way the Clodians commanded. But when he turned to look for his slaves, Pompey was standing behind him, smiling and bland, with half a century of soldiers at his back.

Of course the case was won. Cicero scarcely noticed. All through the rest of his conscientious argument he was staring at Pompey, gorgeous as always in his scarlet and bronze, trying to remember what it was that those colors reminded him of.

That night he walked down the street to Metellus' house. He told no one where he was going, and he went alone. In the street, treading through the pools of shadow and starlight, he had doubts about the wisdom of this course, for anyone might have been lurking there. A knife in the ribs, the splatter of running feet, the slow bleeding away into darkness from which no light would rescue him...

But in the street starlight fell, and presently a lamp added its gleam—a feeble thing, flaring on its bracket beside the black and sliver door. The doorman peered out, reluctant to let in a man he couldn't see. "Marcus Tullius Cicero. The former consul. Let me in." The man's head disappeared, the door swung open. Surprised at the success of this maneuver, Cicero smiled to himself, taking care that the man did not see. He had passed through the courtyard before it occurred to him to wonder if the doorman had had orders to admit him, to let him walk into a trap.

The house was dark, there were no lights anywhere, contributing to his uneasy sense that something—someone—might be waiting for him. The pool by the atrium gave back a liquid silver glint from the hole in the roof. A good thing, he thought. Otherwise I might have fallen into it. And how would he find his way anywhere in this barracks of a place? No one, of course, had thought to send a servant to show him the way.

Well, perhaps it was better that way; he might be less likely to walk into whatever was waiting for him. He paced through the frigid rooms, his footsteps pursuing him; it was like walking through a cave, pitch black, and chilly. It smelled of damp. He began to wonder if the house was deserted.

He went through a little garden, recognizable by the pale square of sky above, the smell of plants; he remembered it from his first visit. Going more confidently, he passed the niche with the statue—dark now—and the shell-shaped fountain, silently giving out a breath of cold water. Ahead, down the long corridor, a thread of light lay across the darkness. It grew wider as he approached; he could see that it was showing from under a door. He raised his hand, hesitated, drew himself up, and knocked.

If she answered, he did not hear. He didn't much care. He pushed open the door and went in. A shock of color and warmth struck him, and he blinked in it. He had an impression of rose and gold; he could smell smoke and perfumed oils. The walls seemed to move gently on a current of air. He opened his eyes wider, seeing more clearly now. Clodia was standing at the dressing table, wrapped in a white gown from her bath. Her pale face was twisted in scorn, her eyes stretched with anger. "Well, Marcus Tullius," she said. "Do you make a habit of breaking into women's bedrooms like this?"

"Only when the women are whores," he said. "And murderesses."

She had courage; in that respect her ancestors would have recognized her for one of them. She threw up her head and her long hair sailed out behind her. "I have no servants tonight. Otherwise you may be sure, I would have you thrown out. As it is you will have to go of your own accord. Good night, Marcus Tullius." She turned her back and picked up a comb from the litter on her table.

"No you don't." In two steps was across the space between them. His hand reached out and clamped down on her wrist, and the small piece of gold stone fell out of her opened fingers. "That, my girl, is destroying evidence." He looked down from very close into the pleated darkness of her eyes, aware that he was still holding her wrist; he could feel the pulse in it, shuddering like an imprisoned animal. "What were you going to do with it?" She was so beautiful. The shape of her cheekbone was shadowed by her lashes, the curve of her nostril and lip repeated it in the most moving way. In the hollow of her temple a thin blue vein showed, the color of a line of mountains far away in a country he would never visit. "Were you going to swallow this?" he said, pitying her now.

She ignored him. "Get out of my room, Marcus Tullius. You are revealing your origins. No gentleman would have come here."

He was not even angry any more. "Oh, Clodia," he said, between tears and laughter. "It's too late for that." Then he was pacing, holding the little stone in his palm, looking at it. It was a pretty thing for such a deadly one: bits of amber shone in it, and a vein of coppery green wound through the soft, dull, antique gold. "How long have you had this, I wonder? How long did you pare it into your husband's food and wine? He never guessed, did he? Well, he wouldn't have. His sense of his family would prevent that, his pride in it. Did you count on that? Did you care? I liked him, you know, though it took me a long time to realize it."

"Really? He disgusted me." He looked up to see her staring back at him, her lips curled in rage.

"Is that why you killed him?"

He could not panic her by the speed of the question. "I didn't kill him," she said calmly.

"Then you are a liar, too."

"Prove it."

"A long time ago," he said, "when I was just a boy, my teacher, the great jurist Scaevola, taught me one simple lesson about crime. "Cui bono?" he always asked. 'Who benefits?' It's a good question; I've taught my own pupils to ask it too. And the answer is plain here, isn't it? You did."

"Don't be ridiculous. What benefit? Do you know what it's like for a woman alone in Rome?"

"But you haven't been alone, have you? You had lovers, and with your husband dead, you were free to enjoy them. And you did enjoy them, didn't you? Didn't you?" he shouted.

She was not the least ashamed. "Yes, I did. But I had a lover before my husband died. I didn't need to kill him for that."

"There were other profits, though, weren't there? There was your brother's marriage to a rich woman—you didn't like to see your husband blocking that, did you?"

"I arranged that marriage. Before he died."

She was so clever, he found he admired her for it; she was an opponent far more worthy than her brother, that pathetic drunk, had ever been. "Did you? I might have guessed. Why did you take the trouble?"

"For the sake of my brother's career."

"His career. His career as a murderer and an arsonist, a rioter, a looter, a criminal."

"He is a Claudian." She smiled as if that explained everything. Perhaps it did.

He remembered that Metellus had prevented Clodius from becoming a tribune, too. "Your husband never should have died," he said sadly.

"Well, I didn't kill him. Now are you satisfied? Will you leave?"

"Oh, no. Not yet. You see I have proof. You did kill him—with this." He opened his hand to show her the golden stone.

She was so sure of herself she did not even deny it. "When?" she challenged him. "How?"

In sorrow, in anger, he said, "All along, I suppose. He often complained of indigestion. Indigestion. I should think he would with this stuff in his food, but the time that did the trick was the last, wasn't it? When he was on his deathbed. That's when you murdered him, when he was already sick, already dying."

"He ate nothing on his deathbed. How could I, how could anyone, have poisoned him?" Her white nostrils flared with contempt, and she turned away. Oh, by Hercules, she was superb; it was a pity she was so dangerous, too.

"He had his medicine."

"Which I tasted. There were witnesses to that. Everyone saw me."

"Yes," he said very quietly, watching her. "And how long had you been doing that?"

"Doing what?" she whispered. She had fallen back a step, pressed herself against the table to hold her body upright. He had thought she was pale before, but he had been wrong.

"Taking this," he shouted, shoving the arsenic under her nose. "Taking small doses of it, accustoming yourself to its effects. I saw it when Pompey came into the Forum—I haven't seen him in armor since his triumph. Yet there he was. It brought it all back to me—King Mithridates, who feared poison all his life, did just the same thing—he took small amounts of it regularly. He developed such a tolerance for it that when he wanted to die—when Pompey was on the point of capturing him— he couldn't. A normal dose would not kill him any more. You knew all that, didn't you? I daresay you heard it from your brother. He was out in the East, wasn't he? Or at the triumph. I heard it there myself. People were all talking about it."

He had not defeated her yet; her head was still up, and she was forcing her lips to speak, though her eyes were blank with shock. "You'll never prove it."

"Yes, I will," he said softly. "You know who I am; you know there isn't a jury in Italy that would fail to convict you on my arguments, my evidence. I'm not sure what the penalty is for murdering a husband. Burial alive? Stoning? Do you know?"

"A jury?" She was swaying on her feet; he rushed across to help her to sit down on the bed.

"Look, Clodia," he said gently, kneeling so that she would see his face; she wouldn't lift her head. Or perhaps she couldn't, just then. "It doesn't have to be a jury. It never has to happen."

She said nothing, but stared down into his face.

"All I want is to be left in peace," he said. "I didn't look for this quarrel with you or your family, I haven't been the one to prolong it. But I must continue it as long as your brother prevents me from doing my job. You see that, don't you?" She made no response. "So," he said. "I'll make a bargain with you." He was talking to her as he sometimes spoke to his little boy, explaining things very simply, as if she had lost the power of understanding as an adult. "A bargain. You tell your brother to let me alone, and I will say nothing about this discussion, nor will I bring any prosecution. Nothing will return Metellus to us—and perhaps he would not have liked the scandal of a trial anyway. He protected you while he was alive, just because you were his wife. Let us protect him now that he's dead, shall we? How will that be? Do you accept that?"

"I—I don't control my brother."

"I think you do. He has so few friends left. Pompey has turned against him, the Senate has sent Milo after him, Crassus defended Caelius and lined himself up with me. Tell him it's over, tell him it's useless to go on. Even the poor are getting nothing out of this."

"No," she murmured, but he knew she meant yes.

"Do it, Clodia," he said, getting up. "Tell him. If you do, I will say nothing about Metellus. Here, I'll give you your evidence back—an earnest of my good intentions." He smiled and put the piece of gold stone on the table; he saw her eyes flick toward it as he was going out.

Poor animal, he thought in the cold dark hall; if she's really been taking small doses of it all along, there isn't enough left of that stone to kill herself with now.

XXXIII

When he went down the hill the next morning, it was to find the Senate so well disposed to him and pleased with his victory in the courts the day before, that it welcomed his proposal for a grant of forty million sesterces to Pompey to pay for grain in the colonies. In fact the bill passed virtually unopposed, in less than half the morning.

"Astonishing," Cicero said to Pompey during the break while they strolled outside the building for some air, much to the dismay of their bodyguards.

"Clodius hasn't been able to mobilize his reserves." Pompey surveyed the empty Forum with satisfaction. He beamed with pleasure, weighing down Cicero's shoulder with his meaty hand. "You've done me a good turn today, my friend."

"When are you going back out to Sardinia?"

"Sometime around the middle of the month. I'll tell you what. I'll do something for you."

"You needn't. I'm happy to get what I can for you."

"I know. I'll send your brother home on a visit."

"Well, I would like to see him. I'd like that very much."

"I owe you something," Pompey said, watching Cicero from under heavy lids. "And I'll see you get it."

Cicero dropped a word to the consul, and as soon as the speaker was finished was given the floor. "Gentlemen, your indulgence, please, for a very brief time—I know you're as interested in a recess as I am." They were happy with him, they laughed easily. He smiled back, expanding a little with pleasure. "I have only one more point to raise. Clodius' power is not yet destroyed. You might say that yesterday Clodius lost a battle, but given time, he may yet bring up reserves—" He looked over at Pompey, who seemed to be studying his shoes. "I ask you to head them off, to make sure that they never reach Rome.

"Gentlemen, you know as well as I do where these reserves will come from—from the poor and discontented of this city. Clodius has exploited their misery, and led them into folly—and worse, into crime. They follow him because they believe he can help them." The attention of the Senate was absolute; the men on the benches could not have watched him with more fascination if he had been a Gaul in trousers, or a dancing bear.

"It is we who have allowed this," he told them, meaning it was they. "We, who, fearing for our lives and the safety of the Republic, passed the laws that enabled him to take advantage of these men. We were threatened by powerful men our-selves." He did not have to tell them whom he meant; they remembered as well as he did the riots when Julius Caesar proposed his laws, the attacks on Cato and Bibulus, the crowds outside the Curia and on the steps of the Temple of Concord. "We were threatened, and we gave in. We believed—" you believed, he told them in his mind—"that death was worse than slavery and exile. Well, we were wrong."

From the benches came a little sigh of sorrow and remorse. He raised his head to sniff at them, angry, proud, wounded by their weakness. "Yes," he said softly. "We gave in. We passed, for example, the law that let Clodius settle his men on land that belongs to the city, though they in no way deserve this gift. They were not sol-diers, who have offered us their lives; they have no claim on our generosity. On the contrary. For their attempt to destroy all we believe in, they ought to owe us com-pensation, not the other way around."

The Senate had divided itself; a large number of the senators were shouting at him, rising from their seats and waving their fists in the air. As many more were defending him, and his right to speak. Some, less aware of the challenge he was offering to Pompey and Crassus, merely gaped at him in shock. He couldn't tell how many were really on his side. He might actually have a majority—it was hard to tell in that waving sea of arms. "I propose, therefore, gentlemen, that in the next full meeting of the Senate—say, on May fifteenth, if that is the date—"

"It is," Marcellinus, the consul, called, heartily on his side. He caught sight of Crassus, getting up and hurrying out. Pompey continued to stare at the ground.

"I propose that on the fifteenth, then, we reopen the question of the bill for the Campanian land which was passed with so much illegal pressure some time ago." He looked around but there was no need to elaborate. He saw that they remem-bered the tactics of Caesar and his men. Several senators in fact were looking over at Bibulus, who sat with grim authority in his seat, like an old tribal chieftain ready to vote for war. "I think," Cicero said, "that we don't have to give in to pressure now. Indeed, we have already begun to resist it. Milo and Sestius, working for you, I myself, whom you brought back from exile, have done our best..."

At the back: a tribune—one of Clodius'—was standing up and pointing a blunt finger at him. "Exile him again. Exile. Exile." Behind the finger his face was con-torted with hatred and rage. "Sit down," Marcellinus shouted back, and over the rising din a hundred voices answered him. "Sit down." The tribune disappeared in a sea of heads and togas, to reappear a moment later, sitting on his bench, his mouth snapped shut and his eyes white.

"Gentlemen," Cicero said. "The time has come to reassert your ancient rights as senators, and your present wisdom as the guardians of the laws and constitution of Rome. On May fifteenth you will have the opportunity to do both."

The voting went quickly, though not without considerable interruption and a violent stew of noise. He was outside in the glare of the April sunshine sooner than he expected; his guards had to come running after him. Pompey, too, hurrying in a brisk swirl of toga and good humor, clapped his hand on Cicero's back. "They're willing to reconsider the land law, then."

"Yes." He could not keep the triumph out of his voice.

Pompey said nothing. He had retreated behind the ramparts of his eyelids, where his blue eyes moved secretly, like sentries. "Well," he said at last. "So you did it. You've blocked the most powerful forces in the city. Well, congratulations." He was moving off, beaming over his shoulder like the sun. "I meant what I said. I'll send your brother to you."

It was a triumph, like the night of his return from exile, like, even, the night of Pompey's return from war. Senators packed themselves into his house, talking, gesticulating, shouting their pleasure and admiration to him. Pompey had sent him a note inviting him to dinner; Crassus rattled out of town in an empty wagon, leaving his family and his treasure behind. "He knows that when the land law is reconsidered, the Senate will smash it up," Marcellinus said, making a gesture to break the tablets on which the law was engraved. "It's all over for them," Tiro exulted in his ear. Caelius was grinning from the back of the room, Hortensius, red-faced and white-haired, was shouting unintelligibly, Lucullus, gripping him by the hand, said over and over, "They're on the run now. They're on the run."

Towards the end of the evening, someone proposed his health: "To the Father of His Country." They all repeated it. "To the Father of His Country." He went to bed that night with the chorus of their voices still ringing in his ears. He wished Quintus had been there to see it, or Tullia. The surprise of the Senate, the admiration of those great men. Well, Pompey, he said in his mind before he fell asleep, it took me thirty years to prove it, but I was as good a man as you.

BOOK SIX

XXXIV

I n spite of the celebration and the admiration he enjoyed, Cicero left the city two days later. Pompey at dinner had urged it on him, pointing out that Clodius was still at large and more dangerous than ever. "I wouldn't want anything to happen to you," he said, moving his wine cup forward with the back of his finger, and considering its new position.

"Not before the debate on the bill, anyway."

"Always joking, Marcus."

"I know your veterans are deprived of their reward if we break up the land bill," Cicero said some time later, and much more seriously. "But I don't think you need to worry about that. The Senate will be so impressed by your willingness to oppose the other two that they'll pass you something in another form—perhaps a monetary settlement. I know them; I know how they think."

"Of course you know them," Pompey said, pulling the winecup back. "That's why you must be present at the debate on the fifteenth. And safe between now and then."

The month had turned and it was May when Quintus arrived in Arpinum. From the terrace of his house in the little country town Cicero could see the trail of dust on the road, a line of silver under the unbroken arch of the blue sky. There were flowers in pots on the terrace; he stood among them, looking out, for a long time. The hill fell away in wide, stony steps, planted with olive groves and vineyards. The blueness of the sky had gotten into everything, so that the sun seemed to come up from the bottom of a sea of air. A strip of reflected sky in the deeper ultramarine of shadow and the soft sea green of fields, travelled across it, purposeful and empty. The road. A trail of dust, twinkling as it moved, was the only object in motion in his view.

As he watched a smaller cloud of dust detached itself from the main one and floated out ahead. It disappeared around a bend in the hills, leaving the longer, slower one to follow. Wagons, thought Cicero. And one rider, hurrying as fast as he can. Presently he heard the drumming of horse's hooves down by the main gate, and the shout of welcome. Quintus, then. He was always very popular in the village. They would bring him up here, of course; Quintus would be eager to see his brother. He was grinning with joy as the door from the house flew open and Quintus, still booted and cloaked from his ride, strode out. Letting out a shout,

Cicero ran to embrace him.

"Don't," Quintus said, holding up his hand. "I'm all dusty."

"That doesn't matter," Cicero said, stepping closer, but Quintus had not lowered his palm.

"I'm sorry, my brother," Quintus said, kneeling down like a suppliant, like a prisoner pleading for his life.

"What? What are you talking about?"

"I have ruined everything. I have destroyed your chance. I came to tell you—"

It was not dust, then, that made Quintus' face so gray, that pulled his lips back from his teeth in grimace. "But, didn't Pompey send you here? He told me he was going to."

"Yes, he did. And he told me to give you a message."

"A message?"

"If you bring up the land bill in any form on the fifteenth of this month-or at any other time—he will ruin me. He will destroy my career, prosecute me for corruption, swear I diverted money he gave me for the grain. He will drive me out of Italy, he said. I would be forbidden food and water. Exiled..."

Cicero blinked. His surprise was like a sharp little knife in his chest, just below the breastbone; he had to catch his breath around it.

"My brother," Quintus said. "I have come to tell you that I will do as Pompey says. I will go into exile, or whatever is necessary. I will not allow you to suffer..."

He considered it. Anger gripped him—the land bill was crucial: Pompey, Caesar, Crassus all depended on it for their power. Without it they would be cut off from their support. Quintus would understand. By Hercules, he would have to. If he weren't clever enough to avoid the trap...

But of course, he wasn't—Quintus had never been a notably clever man. He was only Quintus, his brother, who had their father's gentleness and their mother's eyes. Cicero supposed that was going to be enough.

Briefly his conscience spoke to him: surely the good of the state outweighed those claims? But he knew he was not so ruthless, nor so Roman.

"Never mind," he said aloud, looking out over the vast blue space below him. "Don't distress yourself. It will never happen. There's no point in it now."

"But Marcus, your life's work..."

"It's too late. If Pompey prefers Crassus and Caesar to the constitution, or the Senate, or me, it doesn't make much difference what we do."

"Surely it must matter. You can't give up now."

He turned and smiled at Quintus, who still knelt on the flagstones, amid the bright indifferences of the flowers. "Never mind," he said again, putting his hand under his brother's elbow and lifting him to his feet. "I'll go into exile again myself before I let anything happen to you."

"No, you can't do that."

"Of course I can. Why not?"

"They won't allow it."

"They won't allow it? What do you mean?"

But he had to make his voice very gentle, for Quintus had gone to the edge of the terrace, where he stood looking out into the gulf of air below.

"Pompey told me. He wants you to withdraw your motion. Instead, you must make a speech in favor of whatever they're doing, he and Caesar and Crassus. He said you gave your word when he allowed you to be brought back from exile. Or I gave it for you."

"And did you give it?"

"Maybe something I said sounded like that."

"And did he say what the speech was to be about exactly, or am I to be allowed to write the text myself?"

He would have gone on, for it was intolerable, but something in the way Quintus stood, a black figure poised somehow insecurely against the huge empty arch of the sky, alarmed him. He seemed to be rocking back and forth on his feet. "No," Cicero whispered. "Don't."

"Why not?" Quintus said in an angry voice. "If they can use me to hurt you?"

"Because, my dear brother, if you do, I will too," Cicero said, and Quintus turned from the edge of the terrace to embrace him with tears in his eyes.

He had a letter, just as he was preparing to go back to Rome. It had followed him out from the city and was consequently delayed.

GAIUS VALERIUS CATULLUS SENDS GREETINGS TO MARCUS TULLIUS CICERO

Luca, in the Province of Cisalpine Gaul, April 17

...passing through this little town on my way from Verona back to Rome. Luca is the winter quarters of the legions from Gaul, since it is the southernmost town of this province, but it is not otherwise interesting, even to a man like me, who hails from the region. Today, however, it has taken on a sudden attraction for senators and magistrates from Rome not apparent to lesser men, for there are at least two hundred of these distinguished persons here. Outside Caesar's headquarters there are so many lictors you cannot get by on the street. The local people say that Caesar is passing out loot he gathered in Gaul in the last few years. Perhaps it is true, though they also say that they have not seen any of it themselves. Certainly Crassus must think so, for he is constantly in attendance on Caesar—an odd reversal; I remember when Caesar owed his career to Crassus. Pompey is here too; I saw him myself, arriving at the main gate of the town in a litter, to the cheering of the crowd...

Two hundred senators indeed. Nearly a third of the Senate. The land law would never have been revoked in any case. It was just as well that he saved his breath and did not bring it up on the fifteenth of May. As for the speech he did make that day, he never afterwards remembered it, and if Tiro had not taken it down in his shorthand, he might have come to believe that he had never delivered it at all. Oddly enough, technically it was one of his better efforts, and many people congratulated him on it. He thought, when he looked into their faces, that they must have been among the two hundred at Luca.

The conspiracy of three—for that was what it was, there was no longer any question of that-had cemented itself closer than ever; by summer everyone in the city knew it. Pompey and Crassus announced that they would run for consul in July; mysteriously, the elections for that joint office were postponed over and over.

"They're waiting for Caesar to bring his legions down from Transalpine Gaul for the winter," Cicero said.

"They're waiting for enough time to bribe every voter in Italy," Caelius snapped. He had been trying to borrow money, as usual, but had found that the interest rate had climbed from four to eight percent and was difficult to find even then. One of the moneylenders had told him why, and he passed it on to Cicero. "Pompey and Crassus are borrowing to finance the elections. And all they need is time."

Probably both explanations were true. And Crassus and Pompey were preparing a lesson for the city as well. They had suborned a tribune—Gaius Cato, a relative of Marcus Porcius Cato the Younger—to postpone the elections by vetoing the date. The Senate, outraged, had to go along: any tribune could legally veto any law. But the senators had put on mourning to show their disapproval; their unshaven faces showed under the edges of their black togas, which they had pulled over their heads as if someone had died.

"Not someone," Cicero said, seeing them file out from the Curia into the Forum. "Something."

Milo muttered beside him and pushed back his own fine woolen hem. "Well, it's beginning to stink, and the Senate doesn't like it."

It didn't matter much what the Senate liked—Clodius was marching in his troops. At the end of the day several people lay dead, and the Senate had to put off its dark clothes. In that battle—"Because really," Caelius said, "you can't call anything so deliberate a riot, can you?"—"Clodius had been struck by a javelin and had to be carried from the scene on a stretcher, to the cheers of those of Milo's men who saw it. "Will he die?" Tiro asked. "No," said Milo, depressed. "I've heard that he's recovering."

"A javelin," Cicero said, shaking his head as if it hurt him. "In the Forum. This is Pompey's fault." He went away muttering to himself. Pompey, who had been standing beside Clodius, had been spattered with blood so badly he had had to give his cloak to his servant and send him home with it for a new one. His pregnant young wife, Julia, seeing the bloody garment, had fainted; the shock was so great that she miscarried.

"He's paying a high price for this," Cicero said when he heard, and he could not prevent himself from sending Pompey a note of condolence. He did not tell Caelius if he had gotten an answer, and Tiro would not let himself be questioned about it.

Cicero was writing a book on the techniques of speechmaking, and staying away from the Forum and the Curia. He seemed older, grayer. His mouth was hard under his large, sensitive nose. He shook his head from side to side, as if something were bothering him, and his eyes had withdrawn so far into his thoughts they seemed to have abandoned the outside world altogether. Caelius, waiting for him one morning, had caught sight of him when he did not know and felt his heart squeeze in his side.

"What's wrong with him? Why isn't he down there? It's killing him not to be involved with politics," he told Milo; they were patrolling the alley behind Cicero's house, their naked swords under their arms. If Cicero had known that he, Caelius, was with Milo he would have sent a letter to Caelius' father. But he didn't know, he didn't seem to be very aware of much around him now. "He just works on that book."

"It's a very worthwhile project. Passing on his knowledge to the future—"

"Gods," Caelius cried in rage, and dropped his sword.

Caelius hoped that Cato's return from his mission in Cyprus would rouse Cicero—Cicero admired Cato, though he sometimes thought him unrealistic. But it did no good. Though Cato came to call, he went away again, his narrow face drawn and his lips pursed in disapproval. A few days later Cato's brother-in-law Domitius announced that he would be a candidate for consul when the postponed elections were finally held.

"If Cato can do something, why can't we?" Caelius demanded, leaning over the desk in the now rather disordered study. "Why don't you run for consul again? Or let me join Milo?"

"Domitius is a good man," Cicero said without looking up from his writing.

"Let me—" Caelius tried again, but Cicero, contemplating him for a moment with angry eyes, got up, and putting his finger in his book, rolled it up and walked with it out of the room.

It was January before the elections were held; Cicero, bundled up in extra tunics and cloaks against the wind, which he seemed to feel more nowadays, went down to the Forum under heavy escort to vote. Milo and his men were already there, having arrived before the brief scarlet winter dawn and taken up positions at the entrances, to keep the paths to the voting urns clear. The aediles in charge of the elections seemed to have had much the same thought, for the table was surrounded by lictors lent by other magistrates; only their capes moved in the fretful wind, and their nervous eyes, which scanned the Forum from under their helmets. Except for the lictors, and Milo's men, the place was nearly empty.

Before the sun was fully up Cato and Domitius came in, followed by a large number of their clients and slaves. They stood around, stamping with the cold, while the voters slowly assembled and the open space came to life under the spreading stain in the sky. The buildings began to take shape, here and there a torch flared in the shadows, picking out a face or a gesture.

From around the corner of the raw new bulk of the Basilica Aemilia a troop of men marched in, then another, and another. They were certainly soldiers; they kept their formation and the rhythm of their march all the way across the Forum.

"Caesar's troops from Gaul," Tiro whispered in Cicero's ear as the tramping stopped and the squads took up their positions. Milo's men watched uneasily, outnumbered. Under the torchlight Domitius had gone pale and Cato was glaring with fury at the armor and the swords.

A laugh floated out from under the Portico, mocking and a little mad. "I know that voice," Cicero said.

As he spoke the small white figure stepped out into the gray morning light. His white clothes shone, his black eyes blazed at Cato over the heads of the troops between them. It occurred to Caelius that the two men were about the same age and came from the same sort of family. Odd that they had turned out so differently. Clodius tossed back his head and was laughing again. Perhaps it wasn't so odd, the laugh sounded insane, chilling on the cold morning. Clodius raised his arm, then, his eyes still on Cato, let it fall. Immediately the soldiers moved a few steps, gathered speed, and, drawing their swords, ran forward, a mass of movement in the dimness, like a wind. Someone screamed, and the torch that had lighted Cato and Domitius flew into the air, flared brightly, and went out.

"What was that?" Caelius cried, and Cicero put his hand on his arm. "I warned him."

There was shouting now, as Milo's men bravely rushed the soldiers; over the noise they could hear Cato crying shrilly, "Stand. Stand. Even if they kill you. Let them see you. Domitius, stand I tell you." But Domitius, his torchbearer already dead at his feet, had turned to run. Cato, unmoving, shouted after him.

"It's heroic," Cicero said. "It's the most purely Roman thing I've ever seen."

Cato, furious as a spitting lion, was facing his enemies, unarmed except for his voice. "Murderers. Murderers. Call yourselves Roman soldiers—" Blood was running from a cut on his forehead over his eye.

"They'll kill him," Caelius said, trembling. His hand on the sword hilt felt hot with sweat.

"Oh, yes," Cicero said. "They will. Go and get him out of there."

Caelius' mouth had fallen open. "Do you mean that?" he cried.

"We can't stand here and watch a murder. He's a good man, and a Cato, too."

Caelius gave a shout and turned on his heel, pulling his sword from its sheath as he ran. "But nothing else," Cicero shouted. "No fighting. Nothing else." Caelius raised his arm in acknowledgement, and dashed into the crowd.

Caelius reported later: Cato had been persuaded only with the greatest difficulty to leave the Forum. Milo had urged him, pleading that he could not protect him, that it would be a waste of the lives of his men, and the shame of Cato's death would be on him forever. Finally Cato had given in and allowed Caelius to lead him away. The soldiers had reformed their units, the dead had been carried home; as the sun rose, Pompey and Crassus had come into the now orderly Forum, looked complacently around, and permitted themselves to be elected consuls for the year. The soldiers had cheered, but the rest of the spectators had not made a sound.

"But the best thing of all was Cato," Caelius said, stretching out his legs. He was still dusty and his right hand had a stain on it that Cicero did not want to look at. "He insisted on going back after the election and making a speech, directed at Pompey. It was wonderful. He told him that he would have Crassus and Caesar on his back now, and would never get them off."

"He's right," said Cicero. "Poor Pompey. If the Senate had been less prejudiced in the beginning..." But it wasn't worth thinking about. They would never open their eyes, not even to see what happened to one of their own. Not even for him.

The consuls were making themselves felt in the city: Pompey had built a new temple to Venus and a huge stone and marble theater with gardens and a colonnade attached. It stood among the low buildings near the Campus Martius, its perfect round dome visible from many parts of the city. It was the first permanent theater the city had ever had; Pompey inaugurated it with games so spectacular they were the talk of the city. Hundreds of gladiators had been trained for them, thousands of wild animals sent from Asia and Africa.

But in the event the games were not an unqualified success. It was the elephants that destroyed the day. When their time came to be led out for slaughter, they seemed to understand what was happening. As, one by one, their fellows were killed by the javelin throwers, they lifted up their trunks and cried so piteously that the audience wept and shouted in sympathy.

"They're calling on heaven to punish the oath-breakers and avenge their deaths," Marcellinus said to Cicero from his seat beside him in the section reserved for former consuls.

"What oathbreakers?" said Cicero. On the stage another elephant sank to his knees, crying out in a vast, mournful voice.

"Before they would get on the ships in Africa, their drivers had to swear to them that they would not be harmed in Rome. Now they are protesting, calling on the gods."

"I see."

The crowd was yelling now, demanding that the remaining elephants be led away. Pompey sat, imperial and unmoving—what is wrong with him? Cicero wondered, remembering the pardoned hostages—but the great general would not listen, and the killing of the great gray beasts went on. Cicero stayed to the end, his eyes on Pompey, wondering again what was passing in that huge, dignified, impassive shape. When the dismal afternoon was over, he had not arrived at any conclusion.

Pompey behaved regally in other ways too. In spite of the Senate's vote for inaction, he sent his friend Gabinius to Egypt to restore King Ptolemy to his throne. When the news broke in Rome, the scandal was immense: Pompey was blamed for going against the Senate's express wish and the rumor of the fourteen-and-a-half-million sesterce bribe was revived. Pompey did not seem to care. He appeared every day in the Forum as if nothing had happened. After a while it began to seem that nothing had.

Crassus, too, used his office to please himself. Without even waiting for his term to expire, he assembled an army and set out for Parthia.

"Why?" Caelius demanded, stretching his legs out toward the first brazier of autumn in Cicero's study. He was frowning, his straight brows were creased with the effort of thought, his hazel eyes glowed with interest. "The Parthians have never done anything to us. We have no quarrel with them at all."

Cicero shook his head. "We had no quarrel with the Gauls either, but Caesar has been there for five years, and will be there for five more, sending back treasure and slaves, and making himself a reputation as a general. We don't need quarrelsome neighbors to go to war nowadays, all we need are rich ones."

Others must have agreed with him, for there were several meetings at Cicero's house, to which Caelius was not invited. On the day when Crassus was appointed to leave for Asia, a crowd collected outside his door, shouting at him. It took Pompey all the charm and dignity he could still muster to calm them down enough so that Crassus could depart.

Even so, at the city gate, a tribune named Ateius had set up a brazier. "Haven't I seen him at your house?" Caelius whispered to Cicero, where, from far back in the crowd, the two of them were watching. Cicero said nothing, but kept his brooding eyes on the tribune. When Crassus appeared, walking with Pompey in front of his chariot, Ateius leaned forward over the brazier and, pouring incense into it, shouted curses and imprecations through the aromatic smoke. Crassus, hollow-eyed, stared at the tribune, and seemed to hesitate as he passed. Around Cicero and Caelius the crowd was groaning in fear, for the curses were so serious that Ateius himself would pay for them. The tribune knew it, too—he was as pale as a man being led to his execution, but he continued to mutter and shout, calling on the dark gods. "The city is going to suffer for this," a senator beside Caelius muttered, looking a little green around the jowls.

"It already has," Cicero snapped.

On the road Pompey was putting his hand under Crassus' elbow and helping him into the chariot. It had rolled away in a trail of dust before Ateius finished his curses and the crowd dispersed.

There were more meetings: after them, Caelius noticed, objects began to disappear from Cicero's house. The statue of the nymph in the entry hall, which Cicero had bought to celebrate his return from exile and which was worth a small fortune, the gold and alabaster lamps from the dining room, a few of the rarer volumes from his library—all were gone. Caelius wondered, but Cicero was so closed from him, so deeply hidden in the forest of his thoughts, that he did not dare to ask. And Cicero seemed to be living as he had before, doing Pompey's bidding when the great man asked. He defended a villainous former tribune named Vatinius, though he hated him: the man was a friend of Caesar's, and Cicero as usual got him off. The victory gave him little satisfaction, and he would not allow Tiro to publish his speech.

The elections for the next year were bitterly contested. The interest rate was at ten percent, and even then money was scarce, though the candidates had plenty of it; they splashed it around the poorer quarters of the city like water from a broken aqueduct. The Senate quite openly had joined the funds of its richer members to the flood. "Why not?" Hortensius demanded from the floor. "There are some cases where bribery must be justified. If it brings good government and protects us from violence, it will have been spent on the side of the gods." Even Cato agreed, and contributed a large sum from his surprisingly extensive fortune. Caelius wondered if a marble nymph and a pair of lamps had been added to the stream.

Finally the elections were held, and Cato's brother-in-law Domitius was elected, but so was Publius Clodius' elder brother Appius Claudius. "They might as well have saved their efforts, and their money," Cicero said heavily. "They cancel out, like figures in a demonstration in geometry. Two opposing consuls equal no consul at all." All the same he was a little more cheerful, and when Pompey asked him to defend Gabinius for restoring King Ptolemy to the throne of Egypt without authorization from the Senate, he refused. Gabinius was furious, and stood up in the Senate screaming, "Exile, exile," but Cicero, to Caelius' admiration, faced him down quietly and did not answer. Gabinius was acquitted but the outcry was so great that fresh charges were prepared against him. The men who brought them went around the city with eager faces, as if they were certain of winning this time.

Indeed, everywhere the city seemed to take heart. The Forum was quiet, and Clodius and his toughs seldom visible. Cicero, however, still seemed worried.

"Why?" Caelius asked. "It's what you wanted, isn't it? Things are finally going back to normal."

"I wouldn't be too sure of that," Cicero said. "It's possible, I suppose, but I think it's the wrong kind of quiet—it's not the silence of a contented house, Caelius, it's the stillness of the tomb. That's despair you see out there."

All the same he smiled and admitted under Caelius' questioning that there was hope for the elections of the following year. "If the gods remember us," he said, and could not be induced to say anything stronger than that.

The gods, however, must have forgotten the city. There were no elections, Publius Clodius having seen to preventing them with his usual success. His brother, Appius the consul, had helped too: Clodius went everywhere with a long train of Appius' gladiators to swell his normal retinue. Milo was unable to do much; he sent to the country for more men, but they were slow to arrive and had to be trained when they came. The months went on and Clodius kept the Forum undisputed; on the first of January there were no new consuls to take office, and the Senate had to appoint a caretaker. He served five days, as the law decreed, and another was appointed after him.

"Far from buying us good government," Cicero said, "our efforts have brought us no government at all." There was talk of a dictatorship for Pompey, as if the city were at war, and even Cato looked assessingly at the large figure striding through the rain.

"Perhaps even bad government is better than none," he said bitterly.

The weather made things worse. In November the rains had begun, but they were not the usual winter showers, they were huge drenches that came down on the city as if the sky had fallen open. They did not stop; day after day water poured down. The sewers rose, then the river. There was standing water in the streets, weakening the unbaked brick foundations of houses and apartment blocks. All over the city these began to collapse, leaving thousands homeless and hundreds dead in the rubble. The grain in storage from the harvest rotted, and people began to go hungry. Here and there a few of the poorer ones starved. Clodius went around the city saying the rains were a sign from the gods that there were disloyal men in the city, and though he did not name them, everyone knew whom he meant. If their names were not mentioned, Pompey's was—it was everywhere in the city now, repeated in hope, in despair, in apathy. Within a month misery had locked up the city like iron; the grain supply was so badly depleted that now there were people starving in every street.

In January the cold became so intense that people weakened by lack of food began to die from that as well. The poor burned their furniture and tools to keep warm; apartment blocks, flimsily and hastily constructed, caught fire and were reduced to ash in no time. "It's a punishment for the acquittal of Gabinius," said Cicero.

If so, he made up for it, for shortly after he was forced again to defend Pompey's friend—this time on a second charge relating to the adventure in Egypt. He failed—Caelius wondered if it had been deliberate—and Gabinius had left Rome. Cicero should have been happy that Gabinius, who had threatened him with exile, was the one who had to go—at least Caelius derived a lot of satisfaction from it on his friend's behalf—but Cicero did not seem to be enjoying it. He had felt the whip and danced to Pompey's tune, like the well trained performer he had become.

The whole city seemed to move to Pompey's commands now; the great man was plainly determined to tighten his grip. He put forward a list of candidates of his own, not even troubling to conceal his interest in the elections. Among them was Publius Clodius Pulcher, running for praetor.

"Praetor," Cicero said with contempt. "It used to be a position of honor."

No one answered him; Caelius was away in the north at the funeral of a friend of his, the poet Gaius Valerius Catullus, who had been one of the victims of the cold. Even the rich were dying now. The Forum was nearly abandoned, the Curia vacant and echoing on the icy mornings. Cicero missed Caelius; his own house seemed deserted, the home of drafts blowing under doorways, billowing curtains, silence and dark. It was really empty—he had sent Terentia and his little boy Marcus to the south to keep warm; his old teacher Diodotus, who had lived with him since his own youth, had died, going with stoic heroism uncomplaining to his tomb. Saddened and lonely, Cicero gave Tiro his freedom. He had been meaning to do it for some time, but had not gotten around to it. Nothing was changed, except that Tiro's new name was Marcus Tullius Tiro, and he went around the house whistling as he worked. He confided to Cicero that he was saving to buy a farm. Quintus wrote from Gaul, where he was serving as Julius Caesar's legate: "How wonderful. Now we have a friend instead of a servant." It was the one break in a year that seemed to be covered with a dense cloud.

On the ninth of June, Crassus was killed in a battle far away in Parthia. The news arrived quickly in Rome, though at first it was not believed. "Crassus is too good a general for this," Hortensius said, handing Cicero a letter from a military tribune with the army.

"It says there are twenty-five thousand Roman soldiers dead or taken captive," Cicero read, holding the letter close to his near-sighted eyes.

"I know. It must be some kind of lie. If I get my hands on that tribune—"

But it was not a lie. Slowly, a few hundred at a time, the names came back to Rome, and funeral processions wound through the streets, under the low, cool sky. Clients came to Cicero every morning, begging for news of their fathers or sons. In his pity and helplessness, he could not look at them; he felt blinded by pain, as if he had suffered a blow himself and the blood had run into his eyes. At night he dreamed of long lines of marching men, Roman soldiers, brave under their standards and the calls of their trumpets; when they came closer he saw that they were chained together, like animals being led away to a brutal sacrifice. He awoke, unable to move in his bed, feeling the shackles around his own neck and arms. He grew reluctant to go to bed and when he forced himself, he could not sleep. His old trouble with his stomach returned.

At last he called for his wagon and had himself driven out through the gates toward the Alban Hills. The day surprised him; it was full summer, the air at once brilliant and soft, full of the cawing of rooks and the clatter of magpies. There were poppies in the grass; a breeze ruffled the cypresses and played among the leaves of the olive groves.

On its hillside, Pompey's golden house grinned toothily against the smoky blue of the mountains, but on its gate there was a spray of dark leaves, tied with a black ribbon as a sign of mourning. At first he thought it was some sort of symbol for the lost army, but when he came into the house itself he saw that it was more than that. The family altar was draped in back cloths, the statues in the atrium wrapped like a procession at a funeral.

"My wife," Pompey said, levering himself out of a chair where he had been sitting with his eyes on the altar. "And my child. She died giving birth to it, and it only lived a short time after her."

"I'm sorry." Cicero came forward and took Pompey's hand. "The gods take the best of us first, I'm afraid." Red-eyed, Pompey looked back from a face that grief had made sallow and shapeless. But behind his eyes there was another emotion. He's surprised, Cicero thought, considerably startled himself. He looks like a man who has just been struck by an entirely new idea.

"Gods," Pompey said. He sat in his plain military chair, staring at the opposite wall. From time to time he reached for a sweet from the dish beside him, but his thick fingers hesitated. Finally he pushed the dish away.

"What do they want?" Pompey said at last, forcing the words out. The muscles beside his mouth had bunched into an angry cluster, pulling his lips into lines of disappointment and frustration.

"Who? The gods?"

"The Senate. Who else?"

Cicero said nothing.

"I should have had that command in Egypt," Pompey said. "It was mine by right. But they wouldn't... The Senate let itself be intimidated by that..." He was very angry. "They have driven me to this, by heaven. I have given them gifts that a god would not be ashamed to endow his city with, gifts that have cost me in life, in force, in blood. I'm fifty-three, my youth is gone in their wars, my strength is wasted with this quibbling. They've spilled out the substance that made us great like wine on the sand while I've cooled my heels outside the city. I could have put out my hand and taken what I wanted—" He reached for the dish of sweets forgetting that he had thrust it away. The huge hand clutched at air.

He let out a bellow of rage. "Ah, gods," he shouted, so that the curtains shook and a servant opened the door to see what he wanted. "Gods. My wife is dead, and my child. And still they keep me waiting, still they refuse me. What do they want? What more do they want?"

"What have they driven you to?" Cicero asked quietly from his own chair, but Pompey had turned away. "I'm alone now," he said sadly.

"I know. It's very terrible. I know how you feel. When I was in ex...in Dyrrhachium, I thought I might never see my family again, and it was like a knife in the dark. Sometimes we don't realize until after they're gone how much we depended on our them, even if they weren't very close to us before—"

"Gods, not close before?" Pompey shouted. "I loved my wife. I married her for the good of the city, to make an alliance—"for a moment he looked proud, like a king with dynastic aims—"but she was so sweet, you can't imagine..." His voice fell away, muffled and thick, and he wiped his red eyes. "I'd have loved that child, too."

"You are young, still. I'm the same age myself, and I know. Fifty-three isn't old. You might have another."

From under his lids Pompey shot him a sharp blue glance. "What have you heard?"

"Heard? Nothing. Is there anything I should have?"

"No, of course not. I can do all right alone. Better, in fact. If I'm not hindered, I can do great things."

"You won't be now." Cicero was remembering that Pompey's wife had been Caesar's daughter. Well, he was certainly free of that connection now.

"No, I won't." Pompey's face was redder than ever. "It worked out very well, didn't it?" Pompey said. "Crassus dead, Caesar in Gaul for five more years. Who would have expected it? Some god must be smiling at me."

His bitterness was shocking, and Cicero snapped at him, "He's frowned on Rome then. Twenty-five thousand killed or captured. The tribune's curses came home, didn't they?"

"I told you, a god is working here. I will be repaid for this, I'll make the Senate see what's good for it—" His words were thickening; he must have been drinking, alone in his atrium, a long time before Cicero arrived. Cicero wondered just how drunk he was.

"It's the Senate's job—with the people, of course—to decide what they want to do for the city."

Pompey laughed. The sound fell away among the drapes and wreaths, muffled and sorrowful. "They'll want what I tell them to."

XXXV

Cicero wrote to Caelius, and early in July the young man was back. He looked fit and hard, as if he had been doing some demanding physical labor rather than attending a funeral; he was tanned, and his light brown hair had strands of yellow in it. There was a new maturity in his handsome eyes too. He stretched out in a chair, completely at his ease, reminding Cicero irresistibly of Pompey, but when he smiled his eyes creased pleasantly, his mouth curled, and Cicero found himself for the first time in days smiling in return.

"It was very interesting," he said with reserve, having told Cicero about his stay in the north. "I'm glad to be back. Are we waiting for someone? Because I have something I want to talk to you about. An idea I had up north—"

"Yes. I'm expecting Milo."

Caelius nodded. "I've had a lot of time to think. I'd like to talk to you—"

"Why don't we wait for Milo?"

"Look, I don't want to be put off. This is important. I'm thirty years old; it's time to start a political career. It's the legal age, and everyone begins then. You did. But for the past five years I've been kicking my heels, waiting while you and Clodius fought it out, because you didn't want me to be involved. Well, I am involved; I want to be. This is the most important time in the history of the republic, it's the crisis, you know, and I want to have my say in it. I've decided. I'm going to run for tribune."

Cicero did not seem to hear. "Let's wait for Milo."

"By the gods," Caelius shouted, getting angry. "I've been put off long enough."

"In the meantime, I have some things to tell you." Cicero held up his hand. He looked so grave and preoccupied that Caelius fell silent to listen to him. "I've been to Pompey. Caesar has offered him a second marriage alliance, but he has turned it down. My guess is that he has plans, now that he is free of the Julians, and Crassus is dead. He intends to—"

"To take over the city," Milo said briskly, coming in.

"Yes, that's what I was going to say. He's using Clodius to mobilize support for the idea."

It struck Caelius as funny. "So they're friends again, Pompey and Clodius." He laughed so hard he tilted back the chair at a dangerous angle. "The last I heard, Clodius was trying to assassinate Pompey. Or was it the other way around?"

"Pompey needs Clodius," Cicero said. "I didn't realize that. He's very bitter just now, and he wants his own way. He needs Clodius to frighten the Senate, so that they will not oppose him." He handed around some wine.

"Well," said Milo, drinking his off in one gulp, "he's got to be stopped."

"Of course," Caelius said, resisting the temptation to drink his the same way. "How do you propose to go about it? I have some ideas myself. I've been trying to tell Cicero; I plan to run—"

"By running for consul myself," Milo said.

"That's right." Cicero was smiling, but it only made his eyes look more trapped and unhappy.

"Milo has been doing very well," Cicero said as if he were announcing a disastrous defeat. "There's a lot of support growing in the poorer sections. They see that Clodius hasn't helped them as much as they hoped..."

"I'm spending millions," Milo said grimly.

Cicero's grin had widened until he had bared his teeth in a grimace. Now his sorrow was plain for anyone to see. "The Senate is helping him, going into debt to do it."

"You had something to do with that," Caelius said to Cicero.

"Of course he did," said Milo in a voice like pebbles grating together.

Cicero flinched. "Yes. I've called in my debts."

"Why aren't you running for consul yourself? Not that Milo wouldn't do a good job, but you are famous. The Father of Our Country..."

"It's his brother, in Gaul," Milo said. "Legate to Julius Caesar."

"Oh," said Caelius. "It's an honor of course."

"If a javelin in the back some dark night is an honor."

"I see. And who arranged this?"

"Pompey," said Cicero. "My friend."

There was a little silence. When it became apparent that Cicero would not speak again, Caelius said, "Well, Milo will be a very good consul. I don't know what I can do, but I'd like to help. I'd contribute some money, but I'm going to need it myself. You see, Milo, I've been trying to tell Cicero, I'm going to—"

"Save your money," Milo said. "You'll need it. Cicero and I want you to run for tribune."

Cicero was showing his teeth in that ugly smile again. "Why not? You're eligible. You're thirty years old, and getting well known in the city."

"And not of a patrician family," said Milo.

Caelius was laughing, and they had to assure him that it was no joke. "Here I thought I'd have to persuade you. And all the time—" But Cicero was not amused now, even in the unhappy way he had been before. His eyes seemed to be bothering him, for he was rubbing them with his thumb and forefinger, pinching his nose as if he had a headache.

"Don't be pleased," he said; it was an order, and very angry. "It's dangerous."

"He knows that," Milo said. "He doesn't care."

"No," said Caelius happily. "I don't."

"Then you should."

"If you feel that strongly about it, why do you want me to do it? You've always tried to prevent me from getting involved."

"It's too late for that. If we don't stop this, no one will be safe. There will be heads on poles in the Forum, and lists of names posted on the walls..."

They knew what he meant. Milo remembered, and Caelius had heard.

Savagely, Cicero smiled at them. "It's Pompey who has brought this horror back to Rome."

"And Publius Clodius?" Caelius asked. "What do you propose to do about him?"

"He must be stopped."

"Yes, but how?"

Cicero would not answer; he was sitting so still he might have been hoping they would forget he was there.

"How?" Caelius said again.

"Kill him," Milo answered, and Cicero, eyes turned away, nodded.

Caelius was thirty years old, not a patrician, and well known. It was a good thing he was rich as well, for the election was the most expensive ever held in the city. The interest rate was still ten percent, and even at that price he had trouble finding bankers who would lend to him. His expenses were fabulous. He had to bring in slaves from the country to go with him everywhere; he had to make gifts to the workingmen's clubs, entertain important senators, help influential knights. He did it all, and he made speeches too, standing on improvised platforms in the poor parts of town with his bodyguard around him; he spoke in the Forum so often that he knew it better than his study at home.

Milo campaigned with him, adding his gladiators and slaves to Caelius'. They needed them, for there were several clashes with Clodius and his men, and more than once bodies were left on the paving stones, staring thirstily at the sky while life seeped out of them. A young man named Mark Antony, on leave from Caesar's camp in Gaul, tried to assassinate Clodius, but both of them escaped, Clodius from the young patriot's knife, Antony from Clodius' toughs. The incident passed practically unnoticed in the general atmosphere of murderous violence that hung over the city.

The elections were held on the earliest propitious day, without much trouble. Milo had packed the Forum, as he was becoming expert at doing; Clodius, it appeared, had decided on a dignified show of strength without provocation. He came into the Forum at the head of a large crowd of what were mostly respectable or semi-respectable citizens; if there were criminals and violent men among them, they were scattered discreetly throughout the mass of the others and not visible to the spectators. Caelius, swaggering in at the head of several hundred of his most enthusiastic supporters, bowed ironically to him as he went up the gangway to drop his ballot in the huge painted urn. When the votes were all counted there were two new consuls for the remainder of the year, Clodius had become a praetor, and Caelius, grinning with happiness, had launched himself on a political career by a nearly unanimous election as tribune. Milo escorted him home, humming with satisfaction under his breath.

When it was Milo's turn, however, the situation had changed. Clodius' men were out in force—"Naturally," Cicero said. "They know that if they don't do something Milo is certain to win." Clodius' people and Milo's met in what amounted to a pitched battle, and Milo was struck on the arm by a stone. Caelius received a scratch over his ear that bled copiously into his tunic until someone else bound it up. One of the new consuls took a sword thrust in his leg. In the end, three of Milo's men were dead, and two of Caelius' so badly injured that they died later. Clodius' gangs carried off their own wounded so that it was not possible to tell how many of them had been killed. It was certainly a large number, but Clodius announced that no one at all had been harmed, a lie that no one in Rome believed but which served to create a certain amount of confusion for a while. Milo and Caelius were left in possession of the Forum and the urns, but by then the Senate had taken fright, and the elections were postponed again.

The first of the year came and went without new consuls or praetors. The Senate met every day, but did no more than choose caretakers for five days at a time each. "We have no government at all," Cicero mourned, thinking of what the government of Rome had once been. "Good," said Caelius, thinking what it would be if there were one now.

XXXVI

On the eighteenth of January, Milo came out of the Curia, looked at the sky, then at Caelius. "I have to go out to Lanuvium this afternoon. They're installing a priest there. I'm the dictator of the town. Inherited the honor, I'm afraid." He seemed embarrassed by this rather inflated designation. "Doesn't even mean anything. Not like Rome. Not a war leader or anything—just chief magistrate. Nuisance more than anything else. Ninth hour of the day, getting dark, wind coming up, and I have to drive out to the country. Want to come? I'd be glad of your company."

"All right. But you'll have to smuggle me out; I'm not supposed to leave the city while I'm in office."

"Not a problem. I'll put you in the back of the wagon. But let's get going. I don't like this wind."

In the end it took them an hour more to leave: Milo had to fetch his wife and organize his men. A band of nearly eighty of them set out on the Appian Way, clinking with armor as they tramped through the gathering grayness of a winter evening. Milo drove the wagon, Fausta Sulla, his wife, on the seat beside him. Her maids, and four young singing boys she was taking to her sister-in-law, sat on benches in the back. Caelius rode half-standing up among them all now that they were out of the city, his naked sword under his arm.

Slowly the day waned, a few lights appeared in the little towns as they drove through; ahead the trees scored black letters across a bitter, sulphur sunset. The wind fretted and tore, tangling the reins on the backs of the mules, snapping the edges of tunics and cloaks against chilly flesh, making the men of Milo's escort swear. Fausta Sulla drew her hood over her face and turned her streaming eyes from the wind; on the seat of the wagon, Milo put his hand over hers and smiled at her.

Up ahead there was darkness on the road, a shadow under the reddening fringe of the sky, which revealed itself as they approached as a squad of marching men, led by several others on horseback. "Watch out," Caelius muttered to Milo, who took his hand from his wife's and set it more firmly on the reins. "Saufeius," Milo said softly to the captain of his bodyguard. "Who is that?"

The marching men were closer now, and though the day was darker, they could see the white figure on a shadowy horse, glimmering through the murk against the angry scarlet word stretched out on the horizon. The pale figure advanced; they saw it toss up its head and the hair, black as the calligraphy of the sky, flew up and caught the light.

Milo glanced at his wife, then at Saufeius. "Pull over to the side," he said quietly. "Let them pass. I don't want any trouble. Not now."

Saufeius moved his men against the stone coping of the road in a jangle of armor and a mutter of angry curses.

The two groups came closer. Over Milo's rigid back Caelius could see Clodius turn and laugh with a companion, ignoring the oncoming crowd. His voice had a raucous edge; like the call of a crow it tore across the wind. "Please, gods," Caelius muttered. Milo swore under his breath and clenched his fingers on the reins. Clodius came closer; they could hear his horse snorting in the cold and see Clodius' knees grip the burnished sides. He kept his face away as if he had not seen them; he was still talking to his companion. Caelius started in surprise—beside Clodius rode the little rat-faced knight, Gaius Causinius Schola, who had testified at Clodius' trial so many years before. Won't Cicero be interested in that? Caelius thought, holding his sword tighter in his slippery palm.

The horsemen were passing them; Clodius had leaned back over his thoroughbred's rump to say something to his men. As he swung back his eye caught Caelius' for the space of a heartbeat. It widened in surprise, the dark pupil seemed to open like a flower in the shining white. A jolt went through Caelius and he almost dropped his sword. He's insane, Caelius thought. He had to fumble for his sword; when he looked up, Clodius had gone past; he had become a small figure on an elegant horse, riding down the road toward the lights of a tavern, pretending not to see Milo's muttering men as they stepped out of his way. His own gang followed, marching under a stiff frieze of upright javelins glinting in the last crimson glow of the sky.

"They're well armed, for a simple escort," Caelius said in Milo's ear. Milo shrugged and pulled up the reins, urging the mules into a trot. "Just so long as they don't start anything." His voice grated more harshly than usual. They were passing a little shrine, a fistful of pallid columns in a grove, now nearly swallowed by the night. Milo's lips moved; Caelius wondered if he were praying. It seemed unlikely; probably he was swearing at the slowness of their progress. The last purple of the sunset picked out a gleam of sweat on his shoulder like spilled wine. Fausta Sulla patted Caelius' hand and whispered, "So glad you're here, Marcus Caelius. Such a reassurance."

Down at the end of the line of men a sharp noise rang out, its echoes mingling with the sudden clang of metal. "What was that?" Caelius jerked around with his sword in his hand.

Someone was shouting, unintelligible noise in the sudden tramp of running feet. Armor clattered. He saw Clodius wheel his horse back; the white face shone, the black hair flew. Clodius had drawn his sword, raised it. A long cry came from him as he sat suddenly bolt upright on his horse. From his chest a javelin protruded, vibrating. Slowly his hands went to it, grasping feebly at the shaft. A look of astonishment had come over his face.

He leaned over backwards, bent nearly double; his horse reared up. For a moment they hung on the darkening night; then Clodius' back arched further, bending impossibly, until he was only an excruciating white curve over his horse's back; the shaft floated over him. Then he was down, disappeared.

"Gods," Milo shouted, dropping the reins. Caelius was shouting for someone to guard the women; leaping down from the wagon, he hit the ground so hard his teeth jolted shut. Pulling himself together he got up and ran after Milo.

It was too late; there were bodies on the road already, a horse was screaming, men grunted and cried as they fought. They had spread out over the whole way: Milo had to stiff-arm them out of his path as he ran toward the center of the brawl. Saufeius was shouting orders, unnoticed in the noise. His javelin was missing, a triangular tear in his leather breastplate showed like a diagram of flesh. Around him the fight surged. Milo paid no attention. He had grabbed the captain by the throat, choking him; Saufeius' eyes rolled and his head snapped back and forth as Milo's fist struck with a thump that Caelius heard as he came on. "Are you the one?" Milo shouted. "Did you start this?"

"No, no," Saufeius was groaning. He was on his knees, his mouth was black with blood. Milo must have hit him, very hard, perhaps more than once.

"Then who did?"

"It was Birria. One of the ex-gladiators, Titus Annius. One of ours."

The horse that had screamed was shrilling into the night, louder, intolerably louder; up ahead a small group huddled over a white figure, scrambling away with it, toward the tavern.

"It's Clodius," Caelius cried.

"He's still alive then." Milo dropped Saufeius, moaning in the dust, and ran for the little group.

"It will be worse if he lives," Milo panted, as Caelius came up to him.

"Yes," Caelius said under his breath.

Milo looked back. Someone had taken the wagon into the grove; it stood abandoned. "Your wife is in the temple," Caelius told him, remembering now that he had instructed someone to do this. When? His sword weighed heavy in his hand too, as if he had been thrusting with it.

The road was full of bodies, and weary men, gasping and sobbing as they snatched at their breath. Here and there some still fought: a sword flared redly against the darkness of the sky, catching the light from the tavern; a man choked and slid to his knees. "Come on then." Milo snapped his fingers, and several of his men fell in behind him.

There was light in the tavern; it spilled across the dusty yard and over the edge of the road. Around it night had fallen; the word on the horizon was blotted out, the brawl on the highway covered decently by darkness. In the little temple a lantern had been lit; it trembled as the wind moved the trees back and forth. Night scents—cold stone, evergreens, the dust of the road—flowed down to Caelius, along with the smell of distant snow. He took a deep breath and pushed open the door of the tavern.

Clodius lay on a table in the middle of the cheap, stuccoed room; someone had wadded up a cloak behind his head. They had removed the javelin: the wound had begun to bleed, making a pool under his ribs that shone scarlet in the light of the one overhanging lamp. One hand lay on his chest, the signet ring on his finger flashing with a barely perceptible motion, red and gold like the blood. A film of dust seemed to have settled over him, dimming him: his skin was gray. Only his hair still shone, so black in the lamplight that it looked nearly blue. His eyelids moved back and forth, but his beautiful stony mouth was still.

A little group of his friends stood around the table; they looked up when Milo came in, and Caelius, behind Milo, recognized Schola again. No one spoke. The only sounds were the sputter of the flame along the wick of the lamp and the labored cough and choke of Clodius' unconscious breath.

"All right," said Milo. "Take him outside."

The little rodent-man had courage when cornered, at least. He bared his teeth at Milo. "That will kill him. It will be murder then, if it isn't already."

"That's the idea," Caelius said with ferocious good humor; he was overheated and excited from the fight, and thought he might have killed someone with his sword.

Milo only shrugged. "Stand aside, Schola." Repeating his order to his men, he went out into the night as if he did not care whether he was obeyed or not. His gladiators tramped in through the door he had left open, and the little group, seeing them, lifted Clodius from the table. Groaning, Clodius opened his lips—the movement must have hurt him—but his eyelids stayed down over his eyes. He did not seem conscious. His friends slipped a little under their burden, but they carried him out. Behind him, in the room, Caelius could hear Schola squeaking in protest.

"Put him down," Milo said out of the darkness. He had taken out his sword. Caelius watched, unable to turn aside. His good humor had left him; he felt cold and the wind snapped at him.

Clodius lay on the road; his eyes open. The deep shadow of the lashes curved away in an arc so perfect it was a grief to see it. As he struggled to breathe, his fine black hair slid softly from his forehead, a tiny movement like a gesture of renunciation or farewell. His eyes were looking up at Milo, wide and unmoving. Perhaps they could no longer recognize their enemy. Caelius found himself hugging his body to keep warm, hoping that they did not. Gods, he thought, at least he'll die here, and not in that sleazy tavern. Then he remembered that taverns like that were where Clodius had found his power. He drew his own sword.

The noise seemed to rouse Milo from a dream. He knelt down and grasped Clodius' hair, pulling back his head. A pulse beat in Clodius' white throat, a shadow crossed it—Milo's hand with its short square knife, flashing amber in the light from the door. Clodius' throat seemed to open, blood and froth pumped out. He stretched, his back arched, his head fell back. Milo let go of his hair and stood up, wiping his blade. Transfixed, Caelius stayed where he was, unable to move. Clodius' head had turned, the wide black eyes were staring into his.

"Gods, it's a shame to kill anything so beautiful," Caelius whispered, awed. The eyes, silver and black, looked at him, full of understanding, perfectly sane. As he watched they changed, fixing themselves in Clodius' pale head.

"He's spoiled his looks now." Milo raised his voice. "Someone take him away. Throw him in the ditch. I don't want any of the slaves to get at the body. They'll rob him, and that's bad luck." He looked down at Clodius' heavy scarlet and gold ring. "Dispose of him," he said finally, then took Caelius by the arm. Behind them a wailing cry went up; Caelius twisted to see what it was.

"Better not to," Milo said, his voice harsher than before.

"But what are they doing?"

"Witnesses," Milo said, as if that were an explanation.

"But you can't just—"

Milo's grip tightened on his arm. "Let them do what they must. Our business here is finished." He turned on his heel and ran toward the temple. Caelius glanced back before he followed, but there was nothing to see. Under the dark sky the road was bare.

XXXVII

The wind tugged bitterly at the corners of the house, a shutter banged, making Cicero sit up quickly in his chair. For a moment he thought it had been Catiline's friends, coming to murder him again. He sighed and rubbed his aching eyes.

He must have been asleep; the lamp on his desk had burned down to a glimmering husk, the book he had been writing in had rolled itself up, leaving a blot where his pen had fallen. Wearily he straightened it, annoyed by the hammering of the shutter. Why doesn't someone fix it? It must be waking the whole house. Picking up the pen, he held it poised over the paper. "On the Republic" he had written. He looked at it a moment, then, making a small grunt of disgust, set down his pen again. His head throbbed, and his stomach felt frayed and knotted like old rope.

On his desk Terentia had left a cup of some infusion of herbs she believed in. He had drunk some of it, but it was cold now, and an unpleasing scum had formed on the top. He shoved it from him; it hadn't done much good anyway. He would tell her that it had, of course, if he remembered to empty the mess in the garden before he went to bed.

"Someone fix that shutter," he muttered as the noise echoed through the house. His eyeballs seemed to swell and pound with it. Ah, that was better. Someone had gone to see to it. The silence was a blessing. He did not know why he felt so ill; something was bothering him, but he could not decide exactly what. It wasn't Pompey; he knew too much about the great man ever to be upset by anything he did again. It wasn't Milo; Milo would do what he must, and the responsibility was his. Milo was strong enough to carry it. No, he couldn't imagine what it was, but it had bothered him for months. His mind wandered, and his stomach heaved; his bed at night was as unquiet as a ship in a storm.

Tiro was at the door to the study, looking white and rather disheveled, with his beard beginning to show in his puffy night-time skin. Cicero ran his hand over his own prickle of stubble. "What time is it, Tiro?"

"Almost midnight."

"Are you the one that fixed the shutter?" He had picked up his pen again, he didn't know why, except that he disliked Tiro to see him idle.

"It wasn't a shutter, it was the neighbor's servant at the door. Hortensius Hortalus' man. There's a disturbance down the street..." He seemed reluctant to go on. "Something is happening at Publius Clodius Pulcher's house."

Caelius, Cicero thought, and his hands were suddenly cold.

"What kind of disturbance?"

"Clodius has been killed."

"In his house?"

Tiro shrugged. "A crowd is collecting. They've got the body laid out in the courtyard."

"Where is Caelius?" Cicero was lacing on his outdoor shoes, calling for his black toga.

"I don't know, Marcus Tullius."

"And Milo?"

Again the shrug. "All right," Cicero said. "Send someone to find them—I want them here in half an hour, not a moment more. When they get here, have someone come and tell me."

"You're not going out there," Tiro cried, waking up to Cicero's preparations. "You don't understand. There's a mob out there, ready for anything. Their hero is dead; if they catch sight of you—"

"I do understand," Cicero said grimly. "The republic is in danger."

Tiro was crying; there were tears glinting on his cheeks. Cicero stopped and stared at him. "It's all right," he said awkwardly. "I have to go."

Tiro shook his head angrily. He seemed to deny that he had ever wept in his life. "It's just foolishness. I'm tired."

"Get some sleep," Cicero said, patting him awkwardly on the shoulder. "We're going to need all we can get."

Down the street a dense crowd had collected, blocking the way. The voices of its members went up into the windy sky, wailing and groaning. Pulling the edge of his black toga over his face, Cicero pushed his way through. No one did more than glance at him as he worked his way forward. Tiro need not have worried: if he kept his head down, no one would recognize him. They were all preoccupied with their anger and grief. He could see tears on some of the rough, sun-darkened faces, and many clenched jaws and glittering eyes. Once he caught a glimpse of Hortensius, surrounded by his servants, making an island in the press of bodies; once he thought he had seen Lucullus, standing with Cato—but that was very unlikely, it was far too dangerous. He did not see Caelius anywhere, though he kept his eyes moving over the crowd, looking for the tall, bright-headed figure.

The gates of Clodius' house stood open; it would not have been possible to close them against the weight of the crowd. Perhaps no one had tried. A movement was going though the mass of people like sluggish current; he let it carry him toward the courtyard. From inside he could hear a single voice, rising and falling. Someone is making a speech, he thought, pushing a little further. His motion carried him through the gates.

Inside the courtyard the mob was thicker than ever; he could smell the bodies, the coarse garments, garlic, wine, sweat, smoke. On a bier, Publius Clodius lay, covered with a cloth; his sandaled feet showed under it, and his pale withdrawn face. His black hair lifted and fell as the wind tugged at it and let go; his eyes stared up at the stars, full of the black night sky. Over him torches flared; his body seemed to stir a little under them.

The speechmaker had finished; he climbed down from the box he had been standing on.

"Clodius Pulcher looks as if he's still breathing," someone muttered to him. Gaius Vibienus, a senator who had come often to his house.

"What are you doing here?" Cicero whispered.

"Same thing you are, I imagine."

The wind had caught the edge of the pall and was snapping it back and forth, shaking the cloth where it covered Clodius' body. He might have been trying to get up.

"How did he die?"

"Seems to have been killed out on the Appian Way, early tonight. Someone who was passing saw the body in a ditch and sent it to Rome in his litter. It was near the Temple of the Good Goddess, in a village called Bovillae."

"The Good Goddess?" Cicero said, shocked.

"Yes," whispered Hortensius, coming up to them through the crowd with a swimming motion. "Bizarre, isn't it? It was the Festival of the Good Goddess that he desecrated when he broke into it all those years ago, disguised as a woman. She has waited a long time for her revenge."

"Who killed him?" Cicero's hands were cold, and he thrust them inside his toga. He had an idea that someone in the crowd might guess he was a senator if he saw their manicured elegance; besides, they were trembling. "Who killed him? Was it Marcus Cael—"

A cry drowned out his question. From the house a procession was entering the courtyard: a woman, escorted by a small cluster of black-togaed and heavily cloaked men, all with a certain resemblance to the face on the bier.

"Here come the Clodians," Vibienus whispered.

"Who's the woman?"

Hortensius stood on tiptoe. "Fulvia. Clodius' wife."

"Widow," said Vibienus.

The woman caught sight of the body, and immediately her own jerked upright and a long, shrill cry came from her, very horrible to hear. It went up until it seemed to splinter against the sky; the wind blew shards of it over the crowd, which groaned in sympathy, swaying toward her. She went forward and looked into Clodius' face. "Oh, gods," she screamed. "They've murdered him." She grabbed the pall and yanked it; the wind caught it and with a great crack like the breaking of a tree in a forest, it billowed up, then sank to the ground. Clodius lay on the bier, completely naked except for his sandals, his too-white flesh shining. A dark line of hair divided his arched ribs; running down to his belly, spreading like a river at his groin where it cast up the pale, slender sandbar of his slack and defenseless penis. All over his body there were marks like shadows, as if the night itself had put violent hands on him. Black trails of blood went down from them, curving over his shoulders, his flanks, the long, smooth swell of his thighs. His hand was mutilated—someone had hacked off the fingers; a pool of shadow had collected under his chin; his jaw and neck were drowned in darkness.

"What did they do to him?" Vibienus cried; the crowd had seen the wounds too, and was moaning and shouting.

"They robbed the corpse," Cicero muttered. "See? They stole his ring."

"Oh, gods," Vibienus cried, making the sign against evil.

In the open space by the bier, Fulvia had fallen forward, arms outstretched over the corpse of her husband, weeping hysterically. Her hair trailed in his cuts, it blanketed his damaged body. She shrieked and sobbed, and the crowd, intolerably worked up, sobbed with her.

Women were leading Fulvia away. He thought one of them might be Clodia Metelli, but the wind was twisting the flames on the torches so that they lay flat out, and the shadows leaped eagerly forward to devour the cloaked and togaed figures. Probably it was someone else, anyway; all the Clodians looked alike.

The men had come back and were looking down at Clodius' pale body; one of them, a tribune, climbed up on the box left vacant by the speaker and began to harangue the audience. Cicero did not listen; he had gone back to looking for Caelius in the mosaic of faces, turned now to watch the tribune with angry, glistening eyes.

The crowd was moving before he fully realized it; several of the men had lifted Clodius' body—he lay as straight and as stiff on their shoulders as he had on the bier—and were carrying it toward the gate. The tribune—no, it was another one, he recognized this one too before the crowd swept him along with them after the corpse—was shouting unintelligibly into the noise of the mob. Borne along with them, he could not resist the pressure of their bodies. Yet he tried to, struggling toward the side nearest his own house. He had left word for Milo and Caelius, he had to get back.

"Watch where you're going," someone snarled in his ear. "Who do you think you are?"

"Sorry." He was attracting attention. He put his head down and pulled his toga closer so that he would not be recognized, and abandoning hope of getting home, he let himself be drawn out through the gates and down the streets.

At the top of the Palatine Steps, he paused for a moment. He had to, otherwise he would have fallen onto the heads of the men in front of him. He was looking directly down at Clodius, who was now being carried into the Forum. The fine, night eyes looked up at him, staring into his, jolting him, as if a bolt of lightning had passed through him. He stood rooted to the ground and the hair rose on the back of his neck. That was my enemy, he thought. He was so beautiful he might have been a god.

Hortensius and Vibienus were gone, separated from him by the movement of the mass of men. Around him were strangers, men with hard faces, lumpy with sorrow and pale with rage. If they guessed who he was... As he put his foot to the first stair his eye fell on Clodius again, passing into the Forum between the Temple of Castor and the Hearth of the Goddess Vesta.

"Hercules," he muttered, unable to refuse Clodius this last, dangerous tribute. "What a tragedy."

"They'll pay for this," the man beside him swore, giving him a glance from under a clouded and suffering brow. Cold with apprehension, Cicero pulled his toga further over his head and turned his attention to the steps.

They had laid Clodius on the Rostra where everyone could see him, and the tribunes, one after another, had stood up to make speeches. It was as if this were the normal funeral of a public man, except that it was the middle of the night, and Clodius was still naked. Why don't they cover him? Cicero wondered, but he knew perfectly well why they had left him exposed. It was just that Clodius looked so small and so cold up there under the vast black rush of the wind.

The tribunes were shouting about Milo. Intermittently, when the wind died, he could hear them. So far he thought they had not mentioned Caelius. At any moment they might, of course. Where was the boy? If he came would anyone from his house be able to find him? Most likely not; the Forum was packed, they were standing pressed very tightly together.

The men around him let out an enormous cry, angrier than any that they had made before. Someone on the Rostra was lifting Clodius up. The blue-white skin shone, the arms hung straight out from his shoulders as if they were heaving him down from a cross. "Oh, shame." The man beside him sobbed. "They've treated him like a common criminal."

Once, years before, he had said to Clodius that he was being saved, not for a public career but for a public disgrace. The little wasp of a man had sneered, but it had been true.

"What? What did you say?" the man beside him cried, but Cicero, shaking with the chilling fear, pulled his toga further over his head and ducked deeper into the crowd. One or two workmen muttered in complaint as he went, but he thought they were really unaware of him and had forgotten him as soon as he had passed. Like the rest they kept their eyes on the leaders, who had hoisted Clodius onto their shoulders again; now they were carrying him down the steps, across the Forum. The men around him had swept him up again, following the small white figure where it bobbed and floated on the darkness up ahead.

The leaders had arrived at the Curia—the doors gaped like a black mouth wailing in the night, as if the building embodied the voice of the mob. Clodius' body passed inside, devoured by the darkness. Then the torches followed, the crowd hesitated, shuffled, let out a huge soft, animal bleat of uncertainty and dismay.

From inside noises were coming now, crashes of overturned furniture, cracks, thumps, shouts. The torchlight flickered; Cicero could see figures running back and forth, a heap of benches, desks, stools, lamps. He could see Clodius stretched out on top of it, still gazing upwards to the sky, but now his eyes were blocked by the painted ceiling.

The men inside gave a shout and ran out. Behind them the torchlight fluttered like a captive bird. With a loud crackle it soared up over the heap of benches and chairs. The crowd let out a roar as a great wing of it went up to cover Clodius as if it were lifting him on its curve.

The crackling had become a steady drumming, the flames were pouring out the door and curling up over the front of the building. The heat was intense; the leaders of the crowd were backing away. Even where he stood, near the Jewelers' Portico, Cicero could feel it, blistering his face and hands.

The flames were unfolding over the Curia like the petals of a rose; the building was enveloped in them, hidden from sight. The wind caught them and tugged them this way and that, so that the light flooded and danced over the Basilica nearby, and the shadows leaped after it. Down in front, black figures ran; several of them had clustered by the railings of the Comitium. They heaved and tossed, and the railings went hand over hand into the pyre. From the next street there were crashes and shouts as the mob tore open the booksellers' shops and threw what they could find toward the flames.

The fire curled tighter over the Curia. The paving stones of the Forum were growing hot, the acrid smell rolled down toward him on a cloud of smoke. All at once sparks sprayed up into the sky; the roof had crashed in. In the relative quiet that followed he could hear the people in the Forum as they pressed all around him: they were singing a hymn for the dead.

The long night of chaos and destruction wore on. All over the city buildings were burning. In the Forum the Basilica Porcia next to the Curia had caught and one wing of it was gone, though the fire still blazed too high for anyone to see how badly it had been damaged. Further out, the house of the caretaker of the government had suffered heavily, and black smoke was pouring out of the windows of the second floor. Milo's place was besieged by a yelling mob, which had set fire to a row of shops next door in the vain effort to force the inhabitants out, but the house was still defended. From time to time a volley of javelins rattled into the street in testimony of the fact.

Milo was not there. Cicero, tramping wearily around the city, had managed to establish that. He had been back to his own house two or three times, but there had been no sign of Caelius or Milo, and no message had come. The first time he had appeared Tiro had come to the door and begged him to come in. "Hortensius Hortalus was found an hour ago, beaten up in the Forum, Marcus Tullius. If they recognize you—"

"They won't," said Cicero catching sight of his smudged and blackened face in the polished bronze of his door. Not even his own family would know him now. He limped, his ribs were sore; between the bitter smoke and the cold of the wind his eyes burned and watered; his toga was as ragged as a beggar's. Still, he went out, wandering around the city, unable to keep quietly at home and wait for news. He could not forget Clodius lying on his bier; he saw the phosphorescent body with its many wounds. I told them to do it, he thought. This is my responsibility.

Now he was trudging through the streets behind the Forum, looking for someone to tell him where Caelius was. He had been walking a long time; he was no longer sure exactly where he was. The stars were gone; the wind had pulled a pall of smoke and cloud over them which glowed on its underside with dull scarlet light. From time to time the flames and sparks shot up into it, splashing the dark mass with ocher and amethyst, as unnatural as dyes. Everything looked different, as if he had wandered into a city he did not know; at the end of a street a looming shape which he had taken for a hill rising out of a wood turned out to be no more than a shed propped against the wall of a brickyard; what looked like the entrance to a cave showed in a sudden flare as the foot of the Esquiline Hill.

Everywhere the wrong parts of things were exposed, the interiors of doorways, the undersides of arches and balconies, the walls of rooms high up under the eaves of tenements—it was as if the city had been laid open by the stroke of a sword; all its little secrets, shabby or shameful or pathetic, were thrown open to everyone's eyes.

From another street he could hear screams and cries, shouts, the clash of metal. Bands of running men careened past him; as he backed into the shadows he saw the crimson glint of their swords. They passed, baying like a pack of dogs, on their terrible errands, unaware of him where he hid, his breath caught in his chest, his blood whispering in his ears.

Up on a hill—which one he had no idea—he came upon a grove of trees. The light struck upwards from below—a quick blaze showing bare branches tossing and blowing. He could make out figures ducking among them. The ground was dark; he tripped and his knee went down on something soft. A body lay stretched out, face in the dirt; it was not the first he had seen lying in a street or kicked out of the way into a dark alley that night. Sick with fear, he turned it over. The firelight off the clouds made a faint glow around him. He could see the face—

It was not Caelius; it was Gaius Vibienus, the senator who had stood beside him in Caelius' courtyard. A long scratch clogged with pebbles and grit ran from his eye to his chin; the back of his head had a spongy bruise. When he pulled his hand away from it, his fingers were wet and black in the lurid light. All the same he did not think the senator was dead. His body seemed warm enough, under his toga. "Vibienus," he said softly. The senator's chest moved under his hand.

Inside the grove men were shouting; he had thought they were dancing but now he saw that he had been wrong. Swords were flashing and someone cried out, a high, bubbling scream cut off abruptly. "Come on, Gaius Vibienus," Cicero muttered, trying to pull the body deeper into the shadow of the trees. "Any moment now they'll be coming out. We don't want them to see you, do we?" He was kneeling, heaving at Vibienus, who slid forward a little distance—not much. Praying that he had not done more damage to the injured head, Cicero pulled Vibienus' toga over his face to hide its pallor, then his own as far as it would go. He huddled close to the trunk, cursing the fact that it was January and the shadows were thin.

The men were coming out of the grove. There were about a dozen of them, dark figures hardly distinguishable from the trees, except where they stepped into a clear space, and the light of the sky fell on them. Straining forward to see, he thought he could make out the leaders, carrying something. Yes, they were: in their arms they cradled some kind of bundles, he couldn't see of what. At his feet, Vibienus groaned. In horror he put his hand over the injured man's mouth. Fortunately the men were making a lot of noise, yelling triumphantly as they shuffled and danced across the pebbled hilltop; as they passed he saw what they were carrying—long cylinders of sticks wrapped in bands of wool: the fasces, symbols of the magistrates' power and authority.

Shocked at this desecration, he could not think for a moment. Then it occurred to him that at least he knew where he was: the Grove of Libitina, the Goddess of the Dead. It was there that the fasces were stored when they were not in use. Well, it was appropriate. He got to his feet to follow, for the men had to be stopped, but Vibienus was mumbling something. Sighing, he turned to the more immediate of his duties, but by the time he had knelt down again, Vibienus was dead.

Delayed by the priests, Cicero had lost track of the mob, though he could still hear it yelling in the distance. It had left traces, though: injured men staggering by twos or threes with their arms around each other, in an open sewer a body lay tumbled—not Caelius', thank the gods. At least he had not seen the fasces abandoned in the street, or any sign that they had been destroyed. He could not imagine what might happen to the city if they were.

He wandered into the Forum. Here the light was brighter: a sulphurous glare and haze, mixed with roils of acrid smoke. The Curia was still burning; he could see the ribs of the rafters against the blaze. The Basilica Porcia threw streamers of flame into the sky from under its roof; long purple shadows leaped and jerked across the faces of the other buildings, so that for a moment he thought that they had caught too. Someone had tried to hold a funeral feast; there were tables near the prison, broken now, with their contents scattered; from under one of them came a high-pitched bubbling shriek. He moved a few feet closer, to see what it was, holding his eyes averted as long as he could, but by the time he arrived, the sound had stopped.

"Oh, gods," he said, and there were tears of pity and distress on his cheeks. He could feel them, like little tracks burning in the heat of the flames. A noise attracted him; he looked up from the mangled corpse along the length of the Forum, down past the Basilica and the Temple of Vesta. Riding through the fumes and the sprays of sparks came a troop—of cavalry, he thought, unsure of his eyes in the variegated light. He could hear harness jingling, the clop of horses' hooves. Behind them marched armed men on foot, javelins glittering over their heads.

They tramped into the open, seeming to unfurl themselves from the darkness near the Temple of Castor. The two leaders sat on their horses, straight and soldierly, looking at the destruction of the Forum with impassive faces. One of them raised his hand: a knife he held flashed amber and gold, a gravelly voice issued a brief command. The other leaned across the cropped mane of his horse and said something to him. "Caelius!" Cicero lifted his tired arms in a shout of joy.

They jogged through the Forum, following the mob. Cicero had been given a horse and was riding next to Caelius. "They've got the fasces."

Milo grinned cheerfully. "I've got three hundred men here. That ought to be enough to get them back."

Cicero turned to look. They were riding, it appeared, at the head of a column, half mounted, half on foot. It was like being sixteen again, and on campaign. "I went on to Lanuvium to get some of my people," Milo explained. "That's why we're so long getting here."

Cicero had lost track of time. "Is it so late?

"About three hours to sunrise," Caelius said.

Out in the streets behind the Sacred Way there were puddles on the ground reflecting the dull, rust-colored sky. The buildings looked odd, distorted, here as well. Cicero's eyes twitched with fatigue, making the street seem to jump. They had passed Milo's house; someone had come out to tell them that everyone was all right. Milo listened grimly. "If they think they can stop me this way, they have a lot to learn. I'll put down these dogs if it costs me everything I have."

Caelius, who knew how much that was, whistled.

He was lost again. Thankful for Milo and his troops, he rode on through growing bewilderment and unreality. Doorways seemed to gape at him like open jaws, windows stared, distances fell away into the livid haze; all they had to guide them were the echoes of their passage off the walls. They had caught up to the fringes of the crowd; one of the stragglers was walking beside Milo's horse, turning an earnest white face upward as he talked.

"He says they still have the fasces," Milo reported.

"Well, that's something."

"What do they want them for?" Caelius asked.

The man yelled something at Milo from where they had passed him in the narrow street. "First they went to the caretaker to try to get him to proclaim an election. When he refused—"

"Very proper," Cicero said. "Only the Senate can do that."

Milo was grim. "Well, they didn't think so. They set fire to his house. Then, this man says, they took the fasces to the two consuls from last year, to try to get them to take over the city. They wouldn't either."

"I'm glad to hear it. That would be illegal, too."

Ahead of them the crowd had thickened; Milo led them through as if he were riding through his own barley fields. All around him men scrambled out of the way, shouting and brandishing their clubs and swords, but when they saw the troop marching behind him, they let them fall. Milo passed through all this in silence, his eyes fixed straight ahead.

Finally they came to a place where the crowd, however willing to let them pass, was too tightly packed to get out of the way. They had to sit on their horses, moving slowly forward with the swell of the mob as it mounted a steep street.

"Where are we?" Milo looked around. They seemed to be up on one of the hills somewhere, though it was difficult to be certain.

"Come on," Cicero said. His voice was a growl, hoarse with smoke and aching with the weariness that had settled over him. He knew where they were going now.

The light in the street was poor, an acid wash of wine and lemon across the pitch darkness of the night, but they could make out the front of a house across the way. The door, carved with figures unreadable in the sickly dimness, was sunken into the wall beneath a balcony, all brushed with the baleful glare from the sky. The crowd had gathered there, shouting and singing. The noise was as bad as the roar from the fire, now far away in the Forum.

The cries of the crowd had become rhythmic, like a chant. A chant? What were they saying? Beside him, Caelius was mouthing the words along with them: "Consul. Dictator. Dictator." He was so tired he could hardly see, and the sound seemed to come to him from far away. "Dictator." They were demanding a dictator. No, he protested strongly in his mind. It couldn't be that. He would not believe—

The door was still closed; indeed it looked very solid and unusually firmly barred. Someone had let himself be raised on the shoulders of the men in the front of the crowd; they were hoisting him as high as the balcony. In his arms were the fasces; he was trying to thrust them onto the balcony while the crowd roared its rhythmic support. "Dictator. Dictator." It was possible to hope that the shuttered doors behind it would not open for him either. "Please, gods," Cicero muttered; he could not persuade them alone against all the other chants.

"Whose house is it?" Milo asked.

The shutters were opening; out onto the balcony a huge, dim figure stepped. Its armor flashed and glittered. The figure stepped forward. Far away in the Forum, a roof broke and crashed in, and the flames spouted upwards, streaking the edge of the cloud-mass with a feverish flush. At his feet the crowd was screaming, but the figure never looked down. It was Pompey.

He raised his hand. Light streamed between his fingers so that his hand was outlined against the surrounding darkness in purple and gold; its shadow, lengthened and distorted, fell across the people in the street. He stood staring out over their heads, seeming unaware of them. He was looking toward the city, showing dimly now in a glow like dawn, from the wrong quarter of the sky.

EPILOGUE

XXXVIII

For a month disorder lay over the city like the smell from the fires and the echoes of marching feet. Bands of men roamed the streets. When they met there was uproar and the sudden clash of arms; when they separated, to the clatter of the losers' escape and the shouts of the pursuers, the injured lay on the stones until slaves came to take them away. There were huge meetings in the Forum at which one after another the speakers got up to blame their opponents for the chaos in the city; the cries of the listeners went up into the low winter sky like the angry bellowing of animals trapped under its gray and lifeless light.

Aside from these meetings no one went out more than they could help. From early afternoon the streets were deserted and the shops closed and barred. Several men were killed; unlike Cicero they had forgotten to take off the gold rings of their rank, or if they had, their air of prosperity gave them away. Under pretext of searching for Milo, gangs broke into the houses of the well-to-do, looting and pillaging: the homes of prominent citizens burned in every quarter of the city. Once the mobs came so close to finding Milo and Caelius that they were forced to crawl into a space under a staircase for several hours, and had to sneak out the back disguised as slaves. They were lucky, Caelius said, that on that occasion Clodius' friends had not had torches with them.

All day there were crowds outside Pompey's house begging him to take control, but after the first night Pompey never appeared. Milo and Caelius, attempting to speak in the Forum, were set upon by a gang, and though they escaped, many of their supporters did not; even men who had no part in the disorder were killed in that brawl, merely because they happened to be in the Forum. The Senate, shocked and nearly unable to speak, appointed another caretaker, but he was unable to calm the city; fearing worse, they passed their Ultimate Decree—"the same one they passed to empower me to take action against Catiline," Cicero said, blinking his eyes. It called on Pompey to raise an army and do anything that he deemed necessary to see that the city was protected.

There was talk everywhere of the death of Clodius. Rumors shot back and forth from the Forum to the baths to the nearly empty squares, growing wilder all the time. Someone said that Milo had set out for Lanuvium that night intending to kill Clodius, someone else that after the incident on the Appian Way he had also tried to murder Clodius' young son, who was living nearby.

One day a man appeared in the Forum claiming to be a witness to the fight near

Bovillae, and saying he had been held prisoner by Milo's men until then. Indignant, the crowds demanded a reckoning, and two nephews of the murdered man, both called Appius Claudius, announced that they would bring an accusation before the praetor. To this end they demanded the slaves who had been with Milo that night so that they could be examined under torture and their testimony taken. Milo, unsmiling, stood up in the Forum and said that they could not be examined, as he had freed them all for saving his life.

After him, Marcus Caelius got up, and in his capacity as tribune, demanded the slaves of Clodius for the same purpose, and with the same result. One by one Milo's friends spoke for him: Hortensius, Marcellus, Cato, Cicero, his wife's brother Faustus Sulla. They were answered by as many friends of Clodius on the other side. A man named Marcus Brutus, an aristocrat whose famous ancestor had driven out the last of the Etruscan kings five hundred years before, published a defense of Milo on the grounds that Clodius' death was a service to the city; the mobs grew so angry at this that Brutus' house was attacked and he had to leave Rome for several days. Finally, amid all this violence and disruption, the date of the trial was fixed for the fourth of April.

Milo, however, refused to be deterred from running for consul and rode around the city making speeches and distributing money—it was said that he gave two hundred and fifty sesterces to every voter in Rome. Several conservative aristocrats denounced him at meetings, saying the money was to quiet rumors about the death of Clodius, not to advance his candidacy; there were brawls again over this.

At last Milo stood up on the Rostra, his back to the blackened rafters of the Curia, his face to the mob composed equally of his enemies and his supporters, and announced that if Pompey asked him he would abandon his efforts to get himself elected. Pompey, who many believed was supporting another man, refused to ask it, saying from his balcony where he appeared with a small squad of his newly levied soldiers, that he would not urge anyone to run or not to run for any office. He added, without a change of expression of any kind, that he wished Milo had refrained from asking him, since it made him, Pompey, look bad— "as if I were some kind of—dictator."

At this the crowd shouted his name and begged him to declare himself the ruler of the city. Pompey gazed out at them for a long moment, then turning on his heel, went back into his house, leaving behind him only the snap of his cloak on the wind and the ring of his departing soldiers' boots. The sound must have travelled as far as the Forum, for the Senate contemplated the crisp little sequence of noises for a few days. Finally Bibulus, the former consul, got up to propose that it would be safer to declare Pompey sole consul than dictator—although it was not an office that had ever existed before—since the dictatorship was for an indefinite term, but no man could be consul for more than a year. The Senate voted, reluctantly and silently but unanimously, to agree. Pompey was sworn in that afternoon.

XXXIX

The Senate was meeting in the Temple of Concord under the Capitoline Hill at the edge of the Forum. "Concord," Caelius said. "That's a pious wish."

"It's easy to defend." Cicero was looking glumly at the senators passing in among the rows of painted terracotta columns. His shoulders had a discouraged slump, a grim pair of lines went down from his nose to surround his unsmiling mouth. From outside came the tramp of heavy boots and the shout of a centurion as the guard took up its positions.

Presently Pompey appeared, flashing with bronze and gilding as he marched through the open door and his armor caught the early spring sunlight. He carried a helmet under his arm, and when he had arrived at the temporary podium he set it down with a musical clang that effectively silenced the men on the benches.

"Good morning, gentlemen," he said. "I have several items to give you today."

"What an unusual way to address the Senate of Rome," Caelius drawled, startled.

Cicero nodded. "He's talking to us as if we were his field officers."

"Now," said Pompey briskly; up on the podium he appeared to be sorting through some notes. "One: a modification of the procedure in criminal trials." In a tingling silence the Senate waited for Pompey to go on. "Especially in cases of assault," Pompey said. "I include particularly but not exclusively the incidents on the Appian Way, and in the Forum afterwards." The attention of the Senate could not have been diverted now if war had broken out in the temple precinct. "I propose that the procedures be shortened. Both prosecution and defense to speak on the same day-two hours for the prosecution, three for the defense—"

"Just a moment," Caelius shouted, leaping to his feet.

Pompey swung his blue gaze toward Caelius and looked blank. "You are?"

"Marcus Caelius Rufus, consul. A tribune of the plebeians." He had not been able to resist a fairly satirical "consul," though he was very angry. It made a good impression on the older senators, who took it at face value—he could hear their murmurs of approval.

Pompey could, too. "Go ahead, Marcus Caelius," he said with his usual geniality, though his tongue passed quickly over his lips.

"Consul, don't you think that this law you are proposing is a little...one-sided?"

"No. It applies to everyone involved in these incidents, on either side."

"But only Milo has been indicted. No one from Clodius' faction has been accused of anything at all."

Pompey shrugged. The senators were listening carefully; Caelius had no idea of whose side they were on.

"So the law, if it passes, would apply only to Milo?" he persisted, keeping a respectful tone, but Pompey blinked as if he had hit him. His tongue came out again, and disappeared, but he did not answer.

"Isn't it, in fact, a law directed expressly against Milo?" One or two of the senators muttered uneasily and there was some shifting on the benches.

"Well, consul? Isn't it? If it is, the Senate cannot pass it, however much it may wish to. A law directed at an individual is forbidden by the constitution."

Pompey's glance had swept the temple, but no one was helping him. The silence that greeted him was as blank as his own. "You are proposing, in effect, that Milo's trial for assault be rushed through," Caelius cried. "That he not be allowed to defend himself to the full extent—"

He broke off, for Pompey had decided to speak. The great man drew himself up, lifted his helmet from the podium, set it under his arm again and said loudly, "If this law is not passed I may be forced to defend the city with arms. Is that clear, tribune?" Without waiting for an answer he marched down the aisle between the columns and disappeared down the steps of the temple porch. Outside the centurion shouted another incomprehensible order and feet thudded together, then marched away after him.

The Senate, after some debate, approved Pompey's proposals.

"Well," said Cicero, rubbing his eyes. "You tried."

"And I'll go on trying," Caelius said.

They both did. While Caelius went around the city arguing against Pompey's laws, Cicero stood up in the Forum and in a series of speeches, denounced Clodius and his attempts at revolt. He praised Milo, who often stood at his side, for ridding the city of a great danger. When Milo was there, Cicero felt safer in his own person, for Milo had hundreds of men with him all the time now; Cicero's own bodyguard was barely adequate to protect him from assassination.

The other side made their speeches too, and to much better effect. The mobs that roamed the city came to hear them and went away angrier than ever, though largely because of Pompey's soldiers there were fewer incidents of violence.

There were other kinds of incidents though. A tribune produced a runaway slave of Milo's in the Forum one afternoon, claiming that he had been apprehended in the act of committing a murder on the Appian Way the night Clodius had died. One of the senators of the committee that dealt with capital offenses took the man into custody in his house, but Caelius, remembering the affair of the Armenian prince Tigranes years before, walked boldly in and managed to leave with the slave in his own possession, returning him to Milo the next day. There was laughter in the city over this, and a certain amount of feeling that a reversal was fair enough, but there was also a noticeable increase in the rage and bitterness of Clodius' followers. There were threats to bring prosecutions against both Milo and Cicero—Caelius was in office and immune—and insistent speeches in which men sympathetic to Clodius cried over and over that Milo and Cicero were plotting against Pompey's life.

"That's the most dangerous of all their moves," Cicero told Caelius and Milo when they came to alert him to it. "They're trying to drive a wedge between Pompey and me."

"Between Pompey and you? After all you've suffered at his hands, I should think the wedge would be about the size of one of the Egyptian pyramids by now," Caelius said.

Milo's stony face lightened in a smile, but Cicero shook his head. "We are on the point of complete collapse. Who knows what is in store for the city—terror, bloodshed on a huge scale, civil war, the breakdown of any form of law at all? Probably all of them. The Senate cannot resist alone; it has tried repeatedly, and it has failed. All that can save us is a man strong enough to rally the plebeians behind him, and, at the same time, satisfy the patricians that their claims are to be respected. That is Pompey. He's the best we have. Unlike Caesar, he has never used violence in the city. You know, there's no proof he has ever even tried to bribe anyone. We need him. I have my following, but I can't do it. The Senate has never trusted me quite enough for that." The deep brown eyes retreated into the forest of his thoughts. "In a sense, I am a failure. I have never formed a faction around myself, and without one, I couldn't overcome that prejudice—"

Presently his attention came back to them and he smiled. "But no matter how I feel, I will never allow personal considerations—personal considerations to stand in the way of the good of Rome."

"But you are not supporting Pompey now," Caelius said. "You're defending Milo."

"Of course I'm defending Milo. I have an obligation to him. It doesn't mean I oppose Pompey." With a kind of anguished pride he added, "He's my oldest friend."

"Let's hope Pompey still believes that," Milo said.

Caelius laughed. "You'll never know what Pompey believes. He hasn't the wit to conceal that it's something different from what he says, but he has too much to reveal what it is."

"Why, that's very clever, Caelius," Cicero said, but his eyes had closed and his mouth fallen into a shape of grief and distress.

Pompey certainly seemed to believe that Cicero planned some harm for him, since he moved out of his house and went to stay in his mansion in the Alban Hills, which he surrounded with an armed guard like a general's headquarters in war. He seldom came to the city, and addressed the Senate less often. Once, hearing a noise while he was speaking, he hurriedly dissolved the Senate and went back to his garden in the hills; on the next occasion that the Senate met, a friend and confidant of Pompey's called Cornificus stood up and announced that he had received information that Milo had come into the Temple of Concord armed with a knife.

"No, I have not," said Milo, standing up in his place and looking cool and very angry at the same time.

"Where is it, Cornificus? I don't see any weapon," Cicero called out. His voice, carrying resonantly from his seat near a statue of the deity, rang with amusement.

"Yes," several senators cried, taking heart. "Where is it?"

"He has it strapped to his thigh under his tunic."

Milo without a word marched down to the temporary podium and faced the senators. He lifted up the hem of his tunic to the waist. "Nothing there but what every Roman gentleman brings into the Forum," Caelius shouted.

"I wish all the charges against Milo were as—weighty as that," Cicero said, and the Senate, staring at Milo's unarmed nakedness, laughed itself sick.

Pompey, however, was not amused. He began to complain, loudly, whenever anyone was present, that Milo and Cicero were plotting to murder him; his friends urged this on the crowds in the Forum, and Pompey himself told the Senate it was true. Leaning over the podium, he stared blank-eyed at Cicero and whispered, "Whatever you try to do to me I will return to you—and your family—ten times over." Cicero looked back at him pleasantly, as if he were unaffected by this threat, but Caelius could see that his hands, held tightly in his lap, were trembling.

"Perhaps it would be better to back off a little," Tiro said, frowning with worry as they were leaving the temple that afternoon.

"Yes," said Caelius. "Possibly you could reassure him?"

Milo, striding along beside them, grated, "You've helped me enough, you know. It's time to think of yourself."

"And your brother," Tiro murmured.

"No," said Cicero. His eyes were hard. "I've said I'll defend you, and I will." And during the month that followed, though Pompey's attacks grew more and more violent, Cicero remained firm and continued his preparations for Milo's trial. Even when Pompey brought an accusation against him before the praetor, he would not consider abandoning the case.

"Look," said Milo, hard eyes shining so that Caelius, if he hadn't known better, would have said that he was moved to tears, "there are only three hours for the defense to speak. That's not enough time for everyone." He meant all the people who were helping with his defense: Hortensius, Marcellus, Cato, Faustus Sulla, Brutus.

"That's true," said Cicero. "Would you like me to make my remarks very brief?"

"No," said Milo. "I'd like you to be the only one to speak."

The tribunal had been set up near the Rostra and the president of the court was sitting at his table on it with the jury benches behind him. The president was Domitius, Cato's brother-in-law; Pompey had appointed him, perhaps as a gesture to the conservatives, perhaps to demonstrate his own impartiality. "Never mind why," Cicero said, seating himself on the defense bench. "He's a good man. He won't be intimidated."

Cicero's usual chorus murmured and glanced around at the Forum. "I see what you mean," Hortensius said. He had been injured on the night of Clodius' death, and was not about to be intimidated either. Cato puckered his mouth in disapproval; Marcellus and Faustus Sulla looked wary. "Nobody's expecting trouble, really," Marcus Brutus said.

The Forum was busy; the shoppers strolled among the booths, the priests went in and out of the temples, the clerks scurried on their masters' errands around the Basilicas and the Tablinarium. Everything was normal, everything was ordinary, except that the Curia was a mass of blackened rubble that slaves were carrying away in baskets, and there was scaffolding going up around the wing of the Basilica Porcia. And among the shoppers a large crowd of Clodius' supporters, prickling with arms, was converging on the court.

"How many of them are there?" Faustus Sulla asked.

Milo counted. "About a hundred."

Caelius pointed discreetly. "A lot more are coming in." Up on the tribunal the lictors had also seen them and were drawing themselves up, whispering to Domitius and clutching the fasces to their chests.

Domitius hammered on the table. "Call the first witness."

Across the way, young Mark Antony rose to his feet, beckoning to his witness. A small figure scuttled into the open space, looked around out of a pair of nervous eyes set too close to his huge, gray, pointed nose, and scrambled into the witnesses' chair.

"Well, well, well," Cicero said under his breath. "Gaius Causinius Schola of Interamna. So we meet again."

Antony, elegant in his long-sleeved tunic and gold fringes—"imitation Caesar," Caelius snorted from the defense bench—turned toward Schola. "What were you doing on the night of January the eighteenth of this year?"

"I was travelling with some friends of mine from the town of Aricia in the Alban Hills toward Rome."

"Ask him how far it is from Aricia to Rome," said Cicero in a tone that seemed to be private but which Schola plainly heard. He curled his gray lips at Cicero in a snarl, and the defense bench laughed.

"Whom were you travelling with?" Antony was studying his fingernails with absorbed interest. The jurors, listening from their benches, were not deceived; they were leaning forward to catch every word, every pause, of Schola's testimony.

Schola began a long list of the names of men from Aricia. "Who are those people?" Caelius whispered. "I never heard of any of them. If they were there that night, they must have been hiding." Schola also must have been hiding, to have escaped from Milo's men. Yet he had been in that tavern when Milo had sent his gladiators to finish the witnesses—perhaps, like the rat he resembled, he had found a hole and bolted down it.

The jury too seemed bewildered by Schola's list. Noticing this, Antony heard it out in silence. "That's everyone?"

"Yes."

"You are sure?"

Schola looked up at the sky, his perpetual source of help.

"There was no one else with you on the road that night?" Antony persisted, frankly disbelieving his own witness, and Schola gave him a panicky glance. "Publius Clodius Pulcher was with us."

At the name the armed men groaned aloud—there were well over twice as many of them as there had been before, Cicero saw—and Domitius pounded on his table. The lictors snapped to attention.

"Why didn't you tell us that at once?" Antony asked, unable to conceal his irritation.

"I didn't want to get Publius Clodius into trouble," Schola said, and the jury laughed.

This was too subtle for Schola; he drew up his face in a grimace of uncertainty that revealed his pointed, yellowish teeth. "His ancestor built that road," he remarked hopefully.

"Yes, we know," snapped Antony, losing his temper altogether. "That is not what concerns us. Just tell us what happened."

Schola began to narrate the events of the night, insisting on Clodius' entire innocence and saying over and over that Milo had plotted to meet Clodius with the intention of killing him. "They attacked us, praetor," he said, turning in his chair to Domitius, who said patiently, "Tell the jury."

Antony took him through it skillfully enough. "By Hercules, it wouldn't take much skill, at that," Cicero muttered. "It's a damaging story." But Antony was bringing out the most harmful facts: that Milo had taken a huge escort with him, that they had drawn the first blood, that the heaviest losses were on Clodius' side, that the bodies had been left abandoned and dishonored. The audience moaned and wept, looked angry or dismayed. Clodius' men kept their hands on their weapons and glared at Milo. "Antony is doing a good job," Cicero said, and up and down the bench the assembled lawyers nodded in unhappy agreement. "Very bad for us," Caelius whispered, but Tiro said loyally, "Wait until they've heard our side of it."

The sun had crossed the Forum and begun to descend in the sky; the shadows stretched out and embraced the crowd. "Look," Milo whispered, nudging Cicero. "Look how many men there are over there now." Cicero glanced across the way to the prosecution benches. It was true: the gang of toughs had swollen to three times its original size.

"That's all the questions I have," Antony was saying to Schola. The little man heaved himself upright out of the chair and started to scramble away.

Up on the tribunal Domitius slammed his hand on the table, and Marcellus, rising from the defense bench with a nod to his colleagues, called out, "Just a moment, Schola. I have some questions too." Schola shot him a look of alarm over his shoulder and dove for the witnesses' chair. Several of the jurors laughed.

"Good," Marcellus said. "Now. You were in Aricia with Publius Clodius Pulcher, you say, during the afternoon of January the eighteenth?" As soon as he said the name the men behind the accusers' bench began to shout. Schola was grinning. Marcellus looked up, startled. "Well? Were you?"

He never got an answer. Clodius' men were running toward him, shoving through the space between the benches or climbing over the seats. Schola had disappeared; the more alert of Milo's men had moved into a line in front of the defense benches. There was a lot of noise; shouting and overturning furniture, rumbles and cracks. Thunder was coming from the tribunal as Domitius called, "Order there. Order."

Cicero gasped. "Marcellus is out there alone."

Marcellus seemed confused by the noise and the disappearance of his witness; he stood in front of the empty chair in a late patch of sunlight. The first of the gang had not reached him yet. "Gods," Caelius said, leaping to his feet. Cicero's hand on his arm pulled him back.

Domitius had seen Marcellus and was crying over the clamor around them. Marcellus looked up and, dodging for the tribunal, sat himself beside Domitius. First the lictors, then the jury, closed ranks around them. Seeing their victims protected either by the tribunal or by Milo's gladiators, the gangs halted their rush, though they continued to yell. The spectators froze where they stood. And down the steps of the Treasury, where he had been sitting unnoticed all afternoon, Pompey strolled toward the court with an air of leisurely interest and an inquiring tilt to his head.

"He's agreed to bring his troops to keep order tomorrow," Domitius said later, calling at Cicero's house on his way home. The lawyers for the defense were all there; Milo had come too, posting his men in the streets and alleys around the house.

"Good," Milo said.

Cicero shook his head as if it hurt him. "I hate to see troops in the Forum." Like a chorus in a play, the others agreed.

"There's another prosecution, for corruption under the voting laws." Marcellus was hesitating.

"Yes," said Cicero. "Brought by the Claudians, too. They'd like to make sure that Milo is ruined as completely and finally as possible."

"Well, someone has to defend it," Marcellus said.

Cicero looked at him sadly out of his intelligent, dark brown eyes. "So they do. Would you like it to be you?"

"But you need me in the Forum. I have no intention of deserting—"

"That's very kind of you." The chorus murmured appreciatively. "But as you say, Milo must have someone to represent him in that court, too."

So it was agreed that Marcellus would handle the second defense, though he argued strongly against it, and they had to insist over his protests. All the same, when he left with the others at the end of the meeting, Cicero caught the expression in his eyes. He looked like a man reprieved.

Hateful as it was, the presence of troops did restore order. For the next two days the examination of the witnesses went on, undisturbed by anything worse than a few yells and an occasional threatening glare.

It was a slow business. There were the witnesses from Bovillae, the little town around the tavern on the Appian Way, one after another. "The Claudians must have brought the whole village to testify. I wonder what it cost?" Cicero was laughing. Indeed their testimony grew repetitive enough to bore the jury. "That's a good thing, surely," Caelius whispered. "They won't give it much weight when they come to consider the verdict."

"Perhaps." Several of Cicero's backers had disappeared, and the crowd around him on the benches was noticeably smaller. "Don't be too sure. They may get tired of hearing the same thing over and over, but that's because they already have it clearly in their minds. We're going to have to dislodge it, substitute our own version of events for something that may seem as real to them by now as if they'd been there themselves."

"That's right," Hortensius agreed, but he ran his arthritic fingers through his thinning hair so that it stood up around his head as if it were too energetic to rest quietly. "It's always more important to make a jury remember what you said than to get them to agree with it."

"Cicero will take care of it," Milo said, so decisively that no one argued with him, but on the other side of the bench Faustus Sulla muttered, "It's hopeless."

"Another one who won't be here tomorrow," Cicero said under his breath, and sank his head heavily onto his chest.

The next day the witnesses were women. Several of the Vestal Virgins from the town of Alba near Bovillae came down to the court in their ceremonial bridal dress, their long white tunics shining, their flame-colored shoes treading the gray paving stones. Awed, the jury gaped at them. One by one they took the witnesses' chair, lifted their veils, and reported a strange incident. A woman, wrapped in a man's toga so that they could not see her face, had come to their temple. She said she wanted to pay a vow. A common enough request, they said, their gentle voices twittering like sparrows in the afternoon sunlight. Many people made such vows. But the sum of money she left was so large they remembered it well. They remembered, too, her shadowed face, which they could hardly see, her shape thickly wrapped in the woolen garment; they recalled the name of the man for whom she was paying: Titus Annius Milo. They nodded to each other to confirm their impression. Only the Chief Vestal seemed to know more. Interested, she had questioned the woman. The money was to be paid because the goddess had answered a certain prayer of Milo's. What prayer? The woman had said it was for the death of Publius Clodius Pulcher.

It was Cicero who handled the cross examination: no one left on the defense bench wanted anything to do with it. He had the delicacy of touch, the tact. And in fact he asked very little, and that with great, and obviously unfeigned, respect. No, the Chief Vestal said, she had not seen the woman's face. A short woman, perhaps rather slender. That was all she could really say. There was one thing though; she had had an impression... No, it was too fleeting to mention, and she could not tell what had made her think... What? Oh well, it was just that she had been sure the woman was beautiful.

"Clodia," Caelius breathed as Cicero sat down again.

"Of course. She still had a little poison left, didn't she?" He was about to say more, but Marcus Brutus was standing up, muttering angrily to Cicero, "I cannot be associated with something like this," and he marched away down the row of benches without waiting for a reply. The rest of the defense, noticeably thinner and much more unhappy now, watched him go.

The prosecution had put up Clodius' wife Fulvia; she was pushing back her black mourning cloak to answer Appius Claudius' questions. No one could have said, even at the best of times, that she was a beautiful woman, and now she was far from that. Her sallow face was blotched and red from crying, her eyes looked out from hollows as dark as bruises. But she was very impressive. She began to sob as soon as Appius Claudius addressed his first question to her; her lashes lay clumped and spiky on her cheeks; her tears leaked out under her downcast eyes, making shiny tracks across her ravaged face. Answering the questions, she described how Clodius had been brought home the night of his death, in a stranger's litter. When she spoke of the condition of the body, her voice rose into a wild cry and her cloak fell back to reveal her hair flying in disorder around her face. She lifted her head and stared at the jury. Clodius' friends, unable to stand any more of this, shouted and rattled their swords against the benches; their clubs produced a drumbeat of anger and grief as they pounded the ground with them. A voice called an order, the soldiers marched in, and up on the tribunal Domitius hastily dismissed the court for the day.

"There were still two hours of daylight left when the court was adjourned," Hortensius said. He was explaining why Milo was not there to what was left of the defense panel, which was meeting in Cicero's dining room. "Titus Munatius, the tribune, called a meeting and urged everyone to be in the Forum tomorrow to let them know that they cannot get away with 'this cruel and dishonorable murder'. In all my years in politics I have never heard a more open incitement to riot."

"Yes," said Lucullus, grizzled and crow's-footed. He was in from the country for the night, and had stopped by to bring Cicero a basket of cherries, new fruits from the East that he was cultivating on his farm. It was obvious that he was glad he was going back to his villa near Naples the next day. "And he kept saying that they should be careful not to let Milo escape. Would Milo do a thing like that?"

"They don't think he'd try to run away," Cicero said. "They're hoping the mob will believe he might, though. It's worse than an incitement to riot—it's an incitement to murder."

"Well, Milo is in his house, which is surrounded by Clodius' mob," Hortensius said.

"And where are Pompey and his troops?"

"Keeping watch on the Forum and the Sacred Way," Caelius said. "They are going to prevent a repetition of the burning of the Curia, and keep the streets into the Forum open so the trial can resume tomorrow."

"Is Milo safe tonight then?"

There was general agreement that he was. "He has hundreds of men with him," Marcellus reported, coming in and taking his place. He had been in the court of a judge called Manlius Torquatus, who was hearing the other case the Claudians had brought against Milo—this one for corruption. "Ogh," he said, setting his helmet under the couch, for he had put on armor to go to the Basilica. "We don't have much to worry about. The Claudians didn't bring a lot of evidence. What they're depending on is that Milo will be condemned for murder. And since he'll be exiled for that, he won't be able to defend his case. He'll lose by default. They only brought this action because they won't be satisfied with exile for him—they want his property confiscated as well."

"Milo's a rich man," Caelius said. "No doubt the Claudians would like to pick over the bones of that fortune if they get a chance."

"No doubt. But they'll be disappointed. He has such huge debts, I doubt a sale would bring more than four or five percent of the value of his holdings..." Marcellus began to eat very busily, like a soldier on active duty; the others, less confident, picked at their meal.

"Well," Hortensius said after a pause, "the way to win the corruption case is to win the murder case. That much is obvious."

"Yes." Cicero's mouth twitched in a smile. "The only thing that isn't obvious is how."

"We have confidence in you," Hortensius said and around the pretty dining room the others echoed him.

"You'd better believe in me. Because since Pompey has obtained his laws about the time we may take, I'm all that's left to stand between Milo and the destruction of all he cares about in life."

"You're all that stands between that and the rest of the city, too," Hortensius said.

All that stood between the city and its destruction. He supposed that was true; it had been true before. Sitting in his study that night, he smiled at this thought. "Tiro," he said. "Get me the wagon. I have an errand to do."

"But, Marcus Tullius—"

"Get it." Silently Tiro bowed and obeyed.

Perhaps Tiro was right to worry, for Cicero went alone and in secret, not even taking a servant to drive him—he could not risk an indiscretion. He jolted under the arch of the city gate, smiling up at the huge reddish stones; it will be strong enough, he thought. It will hold.

Out on the road the lamp beside the wagon cast a circle of light; across it almond petals drifted, and once a small, frightened animal—he thought it was a rabbit—dashed through it, almost under the horses' hooves. Pompey's house stood alone on its hill, gleaming in the moonlight, the doorway open as it had been before, and the golden light spilling out.

This time the servant welcomed him in. Pompey lay on a couch, by himself, in the garden. Cypress trees pointed out the stars from a row along a wall, jasmine bloomed in the corner, thickening the spring night with its perfume. Over Pompey's couch a canopy was suspended; a fretted lamp glowed on the strange swirls of color. "Good evening, Marcus," Pompey said. His voice was full and rich; he had been eating from a bowl of fruits preserved in honey—some of the sweet seemed to have gotten into his speech.

"Good evening, Gnaeus." Without waiting for an invitation Cicero sat down. "I've come to speak to you about Milo's trial."

"Yes," said Pompey. "I imagined you would." The lamplight cut long shadows under the planes of his face; his blue eyes were lost in darkness, his glistening mouth a hollow of black. What expression he may have had was unreadable.

"Gnaeus, are your precautions really sufficient? I mean, to protect Milo? This is a dangerous moment, you know, perhaps the most dangerous the city has ever seen."

"I will do what I think best, Marcus."

"You do know that Milo was only defending himself?"

"Was he?" The big man had not moved—even his glistening face had not changed—but Cicero saw that Pompey was disquieted.

"Milo has never wanted anything but the safety of Rome."

"Is that so?" Pompey's indifference and unease were now apparent, though

Cicero could not have said how he knew. Perplexed himself, he watched Pompey reach for an apricot. The huge hand came out, took the topaz-colored fruit, slipped it into his mouth and disappeared into the shadows again. The night breeze poured out the scent of the jasmine, new leaves rustled. Everything was calm, tranquil. Yet he was sure...Pompey was too disturbed to listen to him, a thing which had never happened before.

"Gnaeus," Cicero said, suddenly guessing, "you don't really believe that I'm trying to have you assassinated, do you?"

Pompey said nothing, but behind his eyelids his eyes moved nervously.

"Really, that's too silly of you, Gnaeus. You've known me for nearly forty years. You know I don't do things like that."

"You do now," Pompey said. From the shadows he held out his hand; Publius Clodius' red and gold signet ring winked mockingly at him from the palm.

Late at night, he returned home. Tiro had gone to bed; in his study the lamps had been extinguished and the writing materials put away. It made him uneasy, as if his servants thought he would not need them any longer, as if he had died. He half expected to see a mourning wreath on the door... Dismayed by his thoughts, he found the flint and lighted the lamps. That was worse. The room was swept and bare, the books rolled neatly in their shelves. "Oh, gods," he muttered, sitting down heavily at the desk. Pompey had lost his confidence in him; he had thrown away the trust of forty years...

"What is it, Marcus? What's the matter?"

He looked up. At the door Terentia stood; her face was soft from sleep, her hair in braids on her shoulders, like a little girl's. A sense of warmth and comfort came from her, like the smell of her sleepy body, which he knew so well.

"Oh, my dear," he said. "I have forfeited Pompey's confidence."

"I can hardly believe that. He's been your friend for so long, and you have made such great sacrifices for him."

"Well, this business of Clodius has come between us, it seems." It was odd, his pain seemed eased as he spoke to her. Marriage, he thought. The gods have surely given it to us to console us for the rest.

"This business of Clodius," Terentia prompted him.

"Oh, my dear, it's so kind of you to ask. It's complicated..."

Her face changed, going cold and stiff; all the warmth departed from her body as she drew herself up.

"What's the matter?"

"Nothing, Marcus. You're right, entirely right—if it's complicated I wouldn't understand it." Before he could speak again, she was gone, so quickly that the breeze of her passage tossed the flames of the lamps; they stretched out after her, then snapped out. He sank his head on his chest. He was alone in the dark again.

XXXX

All day the silence hung over the city. The cool sunshine of an early spring morning splashed between the buildings into streets undisturbed by the passage of men or the movement of air. In the Forum the shops were still shuttered—"They won't open today," Tiro whispered to Caelius—and the usual morning crowd was absent. Soldiers stood like rows of poplar trees at every entrance to the square and lined the dark sides of the temples and public buildings, looking out toward the Rostra. There the court was ready to convene: benches were set out in the dapple of shade of the fig trees; the jurymen, led by Marcus Cato, were waiting patiently, their togas gleaming. Cicero came in and took his place. Behind him, his friends and his servants ranged themselves on the defense benches, but there were fewer of them now. No one sat beside Cicero.

For a moment he looked old there, and Caelius, coming in among his own supporters, was shaken. He has no one with him, he thought. The chorus has left the stage. But Cicero sat like a rock, his handsome head slumped on his chest, his shoulders relaxed. He's all right, Caelius said to himself. This is where he belongs. It is as impossible for him to make a mistake here in the Forum as it would be for a wild animal to misunderstand the forest where he was born. Still, he did not like the way Cicero sat so stilly, and the loneliness of the thick figure bothered him.

Presently there was a noise, and Cicero blinked and sat up. Through the spaces between the vast new Basilica Aemilia and the prison, a small squad of men was marching. At their head came a figure in a white toga—"Milo," Caelius whispered, somehow shocked. Then he remembered that Milo should have been in mourning, for he was an accused man. He should have put on black to show his sorrow at the charges brought against him, and the humility of his hope for justice. Milo wasn't sorrowful, nor was he humble. He marched firmly, almost jauntily, into the court and took his seat beside Cicero. His little troop dispersed itself among Cicero's men and sat down.

"You didn't bring many men."

"No." Milo shrugged. "Just enough to get me to the Forum. Pompey was supposed to take care of the arrangements here. I see he has."

"That's right. I didn't bring many either. Not that I have many. They all seem to have other commitments today." He rubbed his eyes, and his hand shook. "Well, perhaps it's a good thing. The more we bring the more likely there is to be trouble."

"No doubt," said Milo, giving him a curious glance.

Clodius' friends had not felt the same, for they were coming into the Forum all the time, groups of aristocrats chatting among themselves, squads of slaves and gladiators under the supervision of overseers, mobs of freedmen and plebeians hunched together angrily. They all eyed the rows of soldiers and the deserted spaces of the Forum; only when they had gathered behind the prosecution benches was it possible to see how many of them there were. From time to time as they moved, something glinted, and Milo said, "They're armed."

"I'd have expected that." Cicero's voice sounded thin and exhausted. "Why do you think hardly anyone is here to help us?"

"Yes." Milo was looking toward the Temple of Saturn, which was also the Treasury, where two slaves were setting out a chair on the steps. A few moments later Pompey came out and sat down on it, looking very splendid from the distance in his scarlet and bronze, his breastplate winking like gold. He unrolled a book in his lap, but did not read it; he seemed to be looking over the closed and shuttered Forum, blinking sleepily in the sun. When Domitius came in with his lictors and hammered on the tribunal to begin the last day of the trial, he did not even look up.

In accordance with the new law, the accusers' speeches took two hours. The elder Appius Claudius spoke first, making the major points. Young Mark Antony followed with a brief summary of the witness Schola's testimony, followed by a man called Publius Valerius Nepos, who took three quarters of an hour, said little of substance, and made the Clodian gangs, now so much more numerous and spread so thickly that they circled the entire court, weep or groan or shout like the audience in a theater. The gladiators behind them stood impassively, their eyes hard and their mouths shut, but occasionally a ripple seemed to pass over them, like the shudder of an animal shaking off a fly.

Domitius struck his table loudly. "That concludes the case for the prosecution. I call upon Marcus Tullius Cicero, who will speak alone for the defense—" He was interrupted by a shout from Clodius' men, the threatening tramp as they closed ranks. A jangle of angry cries went up. On their benches the jury shifted in panic.

Domitius shouted for silence, but the noise went on. The sunlight glittered on the swords. Cicero got to his feet, his bulk rising awkwardly from the bench. He blinked as if the sunshine were too strong; he seemed to falter and go pale. "Are you all right?" Domitius called to him over the noise.

"What's the matter?" Milo hissed.

"I'm fine," Cicero said to Domitius, and to Milo he added under his breath. "I didn't sleep last night. I was worrying about my speech."

"So was I," said Milo.

Cicero's flexible mouth curved in a smile of pure amusement. He lifted his head and sniffed at the wind, he turned a glance on the prosecution bench, raising his shoulders and setting his toga straight on them. Then, alone, a solid figure in his shining clothes, he strode out into the center of the court. His face was gray with fatigue, his hands shook as he lifted them grasp the edges of his toga. Well, he thought, I've made speeches when I was nervous before.

He stood with his weight balanced on his feet and his powerful shoulders straight, staring at the yelling mob. Presently it grew quiet. On its benches behind the praetor, the jury watched him. He knew it was with confidence and hope. Far away on the steps of the Treasury, he saw Pompey look up from his book and glance at him across the long, sunny, empty space.

"Are you ready, Marcus Cicero?" Domitius asked.

His supporters were gone, melted away like snow on a hillside in the spring sunlight. Cato was on the jury, Marcellus held forth in another court, Faustus Sulla sat at home, young Brutus brooded on Milo's imperfections in angry silence from the safety of his country house. Lucullus had retired to Naples to grow cherries, Quintus was in Gaul. On the defense benches only Hortensius was left, his oldest colleague, and his friend. Milo sat unblinking, Caelius beside him, handsome and cheerful. How much he enjoys this, Cicero thought.

The mob was howling and shouting, a storm of noise that must have been heard miles out into the country. They will know that something is being decided here today, Cicero thought, watching the crowd. As he looked, old Hortensius struggled to his feet. He ran his bent and twisted hands through his white hair, bowed across the benches to Cicero, and went slowly and with dignity out of the Forum. Hortensius. Well, he had made speeches when he was alone before, too.

"Are you ready, Marcus Tullius?" Domitius demanded again. Over the noise of the yelling mob Cicero shouted back, "When you are. When you are." He saw the jury smile. Domitius saw it, too, and took the hint. Leaning back, he spoke to his lictors and one of them sped off. Presently a troop of a hundred infantrymen led by a centurion on horseback marched around the corner of the Treasury and advanced on the court. Over their heads their standard reached into the bright sky, the points of their javelins glittered, the plume on the centurion's helmet tossed like his horse's mane. Far away on the Treasury steps Cicero saw Pompey stand up to receive their straight-armed salute as they went by.

He was not alone. He still had Pompey. His oldest friend. He was still protecting him, in spite of politics, in spite of everything.

The soldiers had reached the back of the crowd and spread themselves out, javelins lowered. Behind them another century marched in, and another. Clodius' supporters eyed them uneasily and fell silent. The rustle of the leaves and the musical clatter of the fountain near the prison were suddenly clearly audible in the quiet.

"Gentlemen," Cicero said, turning to the jury. "It is a shameful thing to begin a speech for the bravest of men in fear, but I must confess to you that I am indeed afraid. It is particularly shameful when Titus Annius Milo is himself more troubled in his mind for the Republic's safety than for his own. I wish I could bring to his trial a greatness of soul equal to his—"

It was odd, but as soon as he said the words his fear fell from him; he felt freer, lighter, warmer in the sun, talking happily to the frightened souls on the benches. He lifted his heavy shoulders, he almost smiled. "Let us admit, however, that there really is something to be alarmed about. This is a new kind of trial, in new circumstances. For we are not surrounded by a circle of interested listeners, as we used to be. A familiar crowd is not packed around our benches. This defense, which has been provided for us, and which we see in front of all the temples and public buildings, is here to prevent the very real possibility of violence."

Now he did smile at them, and weakly they grinned back, cheered perhaps to know that he felt as they did. "Those troops are not here to prevent Milo from doing harm. If I believed they were I would withdraw from this case, gentlemen. In the presence of so much armed force, the law has no place. But Pompey relieves my mind on this score and restores my tranquility. The soundest and most impartial of men, he would not think it right to hand over to the weapons of soldiers a man given to you for judgment, nor would he arm with the state's own authority the reckless passions of a mob."

More soldiers were coming in. There were centurions everywhere now, cantering back and forth across the Forum, flailing their arms and shouting. Clodius' men were fingering the hilts of their swords, their faces clenched with anger. Shouting, they had moved closer, shoving against the men on the benches so that they had to crowd out of the way. Cicero could see their eyes, narrowed with rage as they looked first toward him then toward the shining figure on the Treasury steps.

"Gentlemen, take heart! The rest of this crowd around us, at least all the citizens in it, is with us to the last man!" Cicero shouted. "Every one of all those eyes you see turned on you from all sides of the Forum supports Milo. There is no one who does not realize that a struggle for his country, his children, his future, is being fought to a finish here today."

There was scuffling on the benches; he saw the end fly up as the spectators abandoned it. When it fell, it splinted with a crash that echoed off the buildings nearby.

It might have been a signal. Clodius' men cried out, a huge mindless bellow of baffled rage, and their swords whistled from their scabbards. A man screamed, dust was rising in clouds from the stones. Domitius on his tribunal shouted and hammered on the table; the centurions called; the javelins wavered, then poised. Up on the steps the bright figure of Pompey began to descend.

"Go on," Milo was shouting over the din. "There's a time limit. Go on."

"If you don't," Caelius moaned, "we'll forfeit this case."

"Continue," Domitius shouted, but Cicero was watching Pompey. He had reached the bottom of the steps and was coming across the Forum all alone. Come on, Cicero thought. Put a stop to this. I must finish my speech.

The tumult was louder, but Pompey seemed to come very slowly. Milo's mouth was moving; Cicero could not hear what he said, but his servants on the benches behind were crying and shouting. Surely they must have realized that no one could hear him if he tried to resume his speech? All the same he did try, shouting a few words back into the clamor. "Our opponents and..."

Pompey had reached the last men in the crowd, the few spectators who had not rushed from the Forum, and the first of Clodius' friends. The crowd parted, leaving a path. Cicero could see the great man in his scarlet and gold, his bronze hair lifting with each step, the edge of his tunic curling over his thigh. All right, he thought. Put a stop to this... Already in his mind he was shortening his speech to fit what was left of the time.

But Pompey had not moved; he might have been a statue planted in front of Cicero, thirty feet away. His eyes were as shallow as stones set in marble, and as blank. For the love of heaven, Gnaeus, he cried silently. Don't just stand there. By Hercules, we are old friends.

But that was what they were not. He saw it now. Rivals they had been since their earliest days, and political allies when it suited Pompey, but the friendship had all been on his side. Pompey did not trust him; perhaps he never had. His vast, red face stared back at Cicero across the mob as he drew his sword.

"Gentlemen," Cicero called, trying to collect the attention of the jury. "If I may proceed. Our opponents and—" The crowd let out a howl; a stone hissed past Cicero's ear to clatter on the pavement behind him. For a moment the scene froze like a battle carved in stone on a temple pediment. Clodius' toughs, bristling with clubs and swords, the soldiers, javelins at the ready, were all watching Pompey who stood like the hero in the middle. "Gentlemen," Cicero said again. "Our—"

Keeping his eyes on Cicero, Pompey raised his sword.

Cicero stared, feeling his mouth go dry and his stomach heave. Pompey took a step forward. The mass of men before him let out a scream; they flowed toward Cicero, waving their clubs over their heads. Someone in the crowd was shouting, "Run. Run." A chair crashed over on the stones. Someone sobbed. The soldiers stood at attention, waiting for orders, but Pompey made no move. Hercules, Cicero thought. He hates me. I never realized that.

"Gnaeus, believe me, it isn't true. I didn't try to have you killed," he cried across the noise, but he saw that it did not matter: Pompey had made himself believe it. He was afraid, and where he feared, he hated.

"Gnaeus," Cicero cried again, "since you won't for me, then for the city. Do something."

What was left of the chorus of the defense bench had gathered around Cicero: Milo standing like a boulder, Caelius head back, knife in his hands. Cato had leaped down from among the jurymen and was roaring at the crowd. The rest had left the stage. He was alone. "Go," Cicero said under his breath to Milo. "It's all over. You're not safe here now. Get away while you can."

"No," Milo said.

"Caelius, get him out of town. They'll kill him if you don't."

The boy, nodding, pulled at Milo's arm. Cato cast a look at them and followed.

Cicero hardly saw them go. "Gentlemen—" But the jury was huddled behind the troops and would not listen.

Pompey still stood in silence, his hard blue gaze on Cicero, but he was not unaffected by the scene. No, thought Cicero, not unaffected at all. The great man was waiting. Presently Pompey's pink tongue came out and passed over his lips. What he was tasting was a victory.

Cicero, watching him march away, saw the bright figure as if at the end of a tunnel of darkness. Something seemed to be wrong with his eyes; he shook his head, but the blackness around his vision did not lift.

Far away, Pompey mounted the Treasury steps and sat down in his place high above the marching men. Perhaps it was fear that gave Cicero this unnatural concentration of vision, for he had never seen Pompey so clearly before. As he watched, Pompey raised his arm to receive again the salute of a passing troop; the great hand rose, the studs on his armor flashed. This is what he always wanted, Cicero thought. He is the sole consul; he has all the power in the city. And they have asked him to take it. They, the Senate, the people. It was what he had been waiting for, all those years in the great yellow house in the hills, why he had dismissed his army long ago. He had wanted to be asked. He had destroyed his rivals, humiliated the Senate, forced it to acknowledge his claims.

There was nothing that would save the city now. Sitting there on his chair Pompey looked out over the city he had conquered as surely as if he had laid siege to it. The lock was broken; the wall had failed to hold. Milo was an exile, Caelius a hunted man, he himself had been caught, bound, muzzled, forced to dance to someone else's tune, but Pompey had come home at last.

NOTES

ACKNOWLEDGEMENTS

W hile I was working on this book, my father Dr. Howard L. Kane, who was then Professor Emeritus and Dean of Sciences (Ret.), Edison Community College, Fort Myers, Florida, provided me with a great deal of technical advice and much information, especially about orpiment—the naturally occurring form of arsenic—even showing me a piece of it. I wish it were still possible to thank him, but this note must serve instead.

My special thanks also to Professors Judith Hallett, Martin Winkler, T. P. Wiseman, and especially Allen Ward, who offered me many astute and useful suggestions. They have deepened my knowledge and appreciation for this period, and I am grateful to them all.

HISTORY IN THIS BOOK

The events in this book begin in the year 62 BC when Pompey came back from the war in the East, and end in the year 52 BC, with the trial of Milo, one of the most complex and exciting periods in all of European history. During this time the Roman Republic collapsed, paving the way for the administration of the emperors. Naturally when a complex society like that of ancient Rome is breaking up, the history of the times will be extremely difficult to follow. That is certainly the case here. One famous nineteenth-century historian, Theodor Mommsen, calls this period, in a much quoted phrase, a "political witches' sabbath."

The situation is made even more difficult by the fact that we have an unusually large amount of information about these times, which we owe to the letters Cicero wrote to his family and friends: hundreds of them have survived. In addition, some of the major participants in political life at this time published their own version of its history—notably Julius Caesar in his books on the wars in Gaul and elsewhere, and on the civil war that followed. Historians say that not until the eighteenth century of our own era do we have records of similar detail, a remarkable fact that has the effect of making the events of the first century BC seem as close as those of two hundred years ago, though of course this is an illusion, and there are very large gaps in our knowledge.

For this book I have chosen one path through this labyrinth; there are many others, and depending on which one is taken, the reasons for the collapse of democratic institutions in Rome will appear to be different, or of differing importance. I have tried to suggest what I think some of the most crucial are—in another volume in this trilogy, THE DOOR IN THE WALL, I have discussed some more—but in any case all the major events of this book are vouched for by reliable historians, ancient and modern, and all the people (with one exception—see below) are real. There are a few places where I have departed from strict accuracy for artistic reasons—I hope they are of minor significance. A few examples will suffice: Milo did not return to Rome from Lanuvium until the night following the riots in the Forum and the burning of the Curia, and Caelius, who was a tribune and thus forbidden by law to leave Rome, probably did not go with him to Bovillae, though he was certainly concerned after the fact in Clodius' death. Pompey was not in his house in Rome that night, but in a house he owned in the suburbs. The actor who delivered the lines against Pompey at the games was not Xanthius, whom I have invented for this series (though I based him on two famous actors of the day), but another, and quite real, tragedian. The date of Pompey's birth is less certain than I have implied, as is Caelius'; Metellus may have been somewhat younger than I have made him. I have slightly rearranged the chronology of the events around Cicero's exile, and when Cicero's recall was proposed for popular vote, it was not before the Plebeian Assembly, but before another body, which for various complicated political reasons had been unable to help him before. There are others, but these are the most important.

In one place I have deliberately distorted what we know: neither Caelius nor Cicero has ever been shown to be implicated in Clodius' death before the fact, though they both supported Milo very publicly afterwards. It is no more than conjecture—I think a plausible one—that they may have been involved in the way I have suggested, though, as I pointed out in the text, it would have been illegal for Caelius to have left the city on the night in question.

Aside from all this, there is another difficulty. Any selection is an interpretation; this, even with the most scrupulous attention to detail, is unavoidable. I hope that mine is at least a clear interpretation; further than that I do not believe it is possible to know, and there is no way to tell for sure, of course, what may actually have happened so long ago.

CICERO'S LETTERS

M arcus Tullius Cicero was born January 3, 106 BC and died December 7, 43 BC. By an odd chance we know more about his life and the times in which he lived than about that of any other person or period in ancient times. The odd chance is that Cicero's closest friend, a knight called Titus Pomponius Atticus, lived in Athens instead of Rome. Cicero wrote to him nearly every day, and his servant Tiro, who survived Cicero by forty years, saved and published the letters long after his former master's death. Cicero wrote to Atticus about every facet of life: his political and social fortunes, the progress of his legal and philosophic work, his hopes and fears for the Republic, the education of his children, even the schemes of decoration of his houses. They were so close (Quintus Cicero married Atticus' sister) that when Atticus was in Rome, we have gaps in our knowledge of history. Cicero wrote to other people, of course—to his family and other friends on state occasions, and on personal ones, as with the three authentic letters at the beginning of Part Two (I have abridged these letters, and in the case of the one to Quintus, used material from other letters sent by Cicero to his brother at around the same time; the letter to Diodotus was really written to Atticus). The other letters in this book I have made up to suit my own purposes, but many of the lines, Cicero's as well as those of others, in this book are direct quotations from his letters or from his speeches, many of which also survive. The jokes in particular are his, and a very witty man he was, though he does not have this reputation nowadays. I am not sure why that is, but it is a pity. Perhaps people are too inclined to take at face value the character of the Romans as dour and stern which they liked to give themselves; in reality they were no more glum and humorless than their descendants, and just as fond of laughing at themselves.

A WORD
ABOUT TWO WORDS

T he Roman Republic did not have a written constitution, like the American or French model to which we are so accustomed. Rather, it seems to resemble the collection of ancient documents, statutes, legal precedents and established custom, which is what the British seem to mean by their use of the word. In the case of the Romans, some of the documents would look a little strange to a modern legislature: one of the foundations of the Roman state was a book of oracles purchased by an early king from an itinerant prophetess called the Sibyl. In addition, they had no word for 'constitution', merely using the same term for this institution that applied to the state itself, and to all the business and customs the Roman people had in common. This word is 'respublica' (sometimes written as two words)—it comes down to us as the word 'republic'. I have used it to mean 'state', 'country', 'constitution', 'public affairs', 'Republic' and so on, just as the Romans would have, though where it seemed to me that the meaning was especially close to our sense of 'constitution' I have used that term instead.

In this book, Cicero refers to his sometime allies in the Senate as the 'conservatives'. This was not the word he really used, which was boni; it meant "the good men." They appear to have consisted of a loose coalition, (not a political party, which the Romans had not evolved) of the most substantial men in the state, especially those attached to the traditional power of the Senate and opposed to the growing influence of the other classes. I do not mean to suggest any particular parallel with modern conservative theory by the use of this term, but 'boni' seemed unclear to me, and 'conservative' is a fairly widespread translation of this idea. Another name for this group is 'the Optimates', or the 'best', but that seemed susceptible of even worse misinterpretation than 'conservative'.

THE MEETINGS
OF THE SENATE

Until the year 167 BC it was the practice of senators to bring their sons to hear the debates in the Curia, though in the late Republic meetings of this body were closed to all non—members. For obvious dramatic reasons, I have revived the original custom, and allowed a great number of students and secretaries to attend as well.

A ROMAN POLITICAL CAREER

A Roman was expected to take part in communal life, and if he were a man, and able to afford it, this meant trying for a political career. The process was, in the late Republic, fairly formally organized, with a series of offices of greater and greater responsibility to which a candidate could aspire. It was called the cursus honorum.

The first step was the quaestorship. In the period of this book, the minimum age for this office was thirty. Quaestors served either in Rome as financial officers, or in the provinces under the direction of the governor, and were granted a seat in the Senate. Cicero, whose family was well-to-do, served as a quaestor in the province of Western Sicily; he was elected to this office with a large majority at the earliest legal age and the first time he ran for it. This remained true of all the offices he ran for, in spite of the handicap of his non-Roman and non-patrician birth.

If the citizen's hopes, and his money, held out for further office, the next in the cursus was usually, but not essentially, the aedileship. Aediles regulated the markets and the streets, supervised the water supply and the grain distribution, looked after public order, and put on the games for religious festivals. It was this function that made it a popular office, since an ambitious man might hope to make an impression on the electorate by the lavishness or originality of his games. Cicero appears to have omitted this office.

In 66 Cicero was elected to the praetorship. In the late Republic there were eight praetors, having as their responsibility the administration of justice in Rome, or the leadership of armies in times of danger. After their term in the city was over, they could become responsible for the government of a province abroad. The office carried with the right to six "lictors"—bodyguards carrying the fasces (see below). For a man of Cicero's background, this was usually the highest possible office.

The consuls were the chief civil and military officers of the state in Rome, corresponding in responsibility to our presidents and prime ministers—with the addition that sometimes they might also have to take the field as generals of the army. There were two of them at a time, each elected for one year, as were all the other officers in the cursus honorum; it is thought that this was designed by the earliest leaders of the Republic, immediately after the expulsion of the kings, to prevent the reestablishment of a monarchy or similar dictatorship. To the Romans the consuls were something like replacements for the kings, and had some of their symbols and powers—for instance, the right to twelve lictors, and to carry the fasces—the bundle of rods bound with red bands that were the sign of the power to punish. The fasces became familiar to us in the twentieth century as the symbols of the Italian Fascist movement, which was named after them.

The consuls were elected by the vote of all the people, but had to be senators and proposed by the Senate. Cicero, therefore, could run for this office, since as a former quaestor and praetor he was automatically a member of the Senate. The year in which the consuls served was named after them. Cicero, in a remark in a speech against Catiline, says that he does not fear death, since "a man who has been consul cannot say that his life has been too short." He means that it was the summit of a Roman's ambition, and indeed, it was a very great honor, especially for him, but it was not the highest office in Rome, all the same, nor was it the end of his aspiration.

Undoubtedly the office with the greatest prestige in Rome was the censorship. There were two censors and they represented the last and highest step of the cursus honorum. They were responsible for the control of public morality—which meant that they could remove from the rolls of the patrician or equestrian classes persons whose behavior or income no longer allowed them the right to these dignities. They took the census every five years, and they supervised the leasing of public property and the tax-farming contracts. These were very lucrative, so that it was in the interests of the state that the censors be men of the highest integrity. Given the Roman sense of public service, they often were. The office began as the preserve of the patricians, but in Cicero's time was open to plebeians. At one point, after his return from exile, Cicero considered running for it, but does not appear to have followed through with this plan.

A Roman desiring a political career was obliged by law and custom to proceed in this order, though it appears that in some circumstances some steps might be skipped. It was also possible to start a career outside the regular cursus. At least five people in this book did that: Julius Caesar began his public life as Flamen Dialis, priest of Jupiter. He then served as a quaestor. He next ran for the office of Pontifex Maximus, or chief priest of the state religion. It was a surprising choice for a young and ambitious man, since this office usually went to the elderly and distinguished, as it had influence but no direct political power, but it made Caesar so well known that after it he was able to run for the praetorship. Clodius, Caelius, and Milo all began their careers as tribunes of the plebeians.

The tribuneship had been created to safeguard the rights of the plebeian class; all through the Republic it kept this slightly revolutionary character. There were ten tribunes of the plebeians each year (and a number of military tribunes attached to the armies as well, though that was an entirely different office). Tribunes of the plebeians could veto any act of the magistrates, of the Senate, or of each other (except those of a dictator appointed in wartime). Aside from that their powers were unclear, and changed over the years, causing a great deal of conflict in the later Republic. Tribunes were personally sacrosanct and it was not only a crime but an act of impiety to offer one violence. This was guaranteed not by statute but by an oath taken by the plebeian class, who upheld it all through the Republic.

In this period the tribunes' term of office ran from December 10 to December 10, everyone else's from the following January 1 to January 1.

Pompey's extraordinary and extra-legal career is described in the text: he is the only Roman I know of during the Republic to begin the cursus with the consulship. His prestige as a general was so great that he was able to force the Senate to nominate him for the consulship though he was still under age and had never sat in the Senate. In fact, he was still a knight—a detail which he emphasized on taking office as consul by publicly and ostentatiously turning over his horse to the censors. It must have made the senators grind their teeth.

TIME, DATES,
AND WEATHER

T he Roman day had twenty-four hours, twelve of daylight and twelve of night. This never varied: the first hour of the day was at sunrise, the twelfth at sunset, no matter what the time of the year. Since in Italy, as with us, the period of daylight and of darkness changes with the seasons, it follows that in summer an hour would be longer than in winter during the day, and short-er during the night. Means existed to measure the time of day—by sundials and water-clocks principally—but these were never very accurate.

The Roman year originally had ten lunar months but was a solar year—two methods of measurement so difficult to reconcile that by the end of the Republic the calendar was around three months out of phase. Julius Caesar finally remedied this, some time after the events in this book. I have ignored that problem alto-gether, giving weather, for instance, to the appropriate date without recalculating it. The weather, by the way, is exact where it is mentioned by ancient historians; for instance, the rains and floods of the winter of 54-53 BC that caused such suf-fering in the city are described by Dio. Other meteorological vagaries I have suited myself to imagine, bearing in mind that there is evidence that the climate of Italy has improved in the centuries since ancient times, and winters generally were cold-er then.

DID CICERO DELIVER A SPEECH AT MILO'S TRIAL?

There are several ancient historians who are sources of information on Milo's trial: Plutarch, Asconius and Dio are the most important, but unfortunately, they contradict one another. All of them were born after the deaths of Milo and Cicero, but one of them at least, Asconius, had access to Cicero's own published writings and many of his letters. Asconius was born in 9 AD and wrote his commentary on Cicero around 54. He says that Cicero delivered a speech in spite of the intimidating tactics of Clodius' followers and the behavior of Pompey's men, and though he admits that it was not the speech Cicero would have wished to give, he comments favorably on Cicero's courage in this crisis. Plutarch, who was born in 50 AD, says that Cicero was too frightened to speak at all; Dio, who lived some 150 years later, says that he did not deliver the one he had prepared, but said a few words before fear of Pompey's soldiers forced him to withdraw. A speech of Cicero's does exist, called the Pro Milone (On Behalf of Milo), but all three historians agree that it was written later, and was not the speech that Cicero actually gave, if he gave one at all. There agreement ends.

For a novelist, this is an interesting situation, and I have taken advantage of it. I think it very likely that Asconius' is the correct explanation—he is the nearest in time to the events, he had access to sources that may later have disappeared, his account is very detailed and circumstantial, and seems without obvious bias. In addition, Asconius tells us that both speeches were extant in his day—the one Cicero actually delivered and the one that he published afterwards. (It is possible that he is wrong about this, of course, or, unlikely as it seems, that the text of his essay as it has come down to us is incorrect.) For these reasons, though I have generally followed Asconius in my reconstruction of the trial, but I have conceded something to Plutarch and Dio, and to the general difficulty of getting any news from the past, by making Cicero give the speech he had prepared, but making it incomplete. The passages I have used are from the Pro Milone as we have it now.

ROMAN LEGAL PROCEDURE

O riginally Roman law did not make a distinction between private lawsuits and criminal trials, though in the period of this book it was beginning to. All the same, a complaint in a criminal trial had to be brought by a private citizen—there was no officer of the state corresponding to our District Attorney. Usually a trial had two parts—as with us: first a complaint before a magistrate, which might be answered to that officer's satisfaction and consequently dismissed, or failing that, sent on for a formal trial. In this book I have referred to that proceeding as an indictment, though it was not exactly what we mean by that term, since it was not brought by the state.

If a case went for trial, a jury was chosen, usually very large by our standards—the jury of fifty-six in Clodius' case was smaller than normal—and a date was set for the hearing before the praetor. The parties, both the accusers (whom I have sometimes referred to as the prosecution in this book, though they were not exactly that either) and the defense, usually engaged advocates to speak for them. These men, among whom Cicero was, and is, the most famous, were not lawyers, though they might have studied law, as Cicero did; they were orators who specialized in legal rhetoric. The same man might serve as the lawyer for an accuser on one occasion, for a defendant on another. I have called the advocates lawyers, for the sake of familiarity. They also differed from modern lawyers in that they were forbidden to take any fee for pleading.

Each side made its speeches, and then examined its witnesses (I have allowed the speeches to come last here for dramatic purposes). Roman courts seem to have allowed wide latitude to the advocates in the cases, much wider than would be acceptable to us—some speeches seem little more than hearsay and abuse, and Cicero admits to having carried a baby into court in his arms on one occasion to influence a jury. Speeches were long, and measured by a water-clock. There is an epigram by Martial about one lawyer who asked for seven hours for his speech: the lawyer went on and on, refreshing his dry throat from time to time with stale water from a flask. Why not put us all out of our misery, the poet asks, and drink from the clock instead?

The jury reached its verdict by majority vote, and the judge—a praetor in serious cases—imposed the sentence. There was no appeal, but in capital cases the guilty man, if he were a citizen, was usually allowed to go into exile. Otherwise he might be strangled in the prison, like the Catilinarian conspirators, or, if he were not a citizen, condemned to crucifixion. Infractions of the religious law sometimes had horrible penalties—stoning to death, burial alive, being sown into a sack and thrown into the Tiber, and so on. Less serious crimes might be punished by fines or a term as a gladiator in the arenas.

The end of the Republic was an age of furious litigation, as it became less and less possible to accomplish political ends through the normal political channels. There is some parallel in this with us. It was also, however, an age of corruption in the courts on a scale with which we have fortunately had no experience. Cicero reports that his clients in one case, the people of the province of western Sicily, asked for the discontinuation of the court that heard the cases of foreigners. They could just about afford to pay the bribes their governor demanded, they said, but not those of the lawyers, juries and judges they would encounter if they had to take the governor to court. Another is told about a senator who was tried for corruption and found not to be guilty. When he was asked his opinion of the verdict, he replied that he thought it was a disgrace for a man in his position to be acquitted—for less than three million sesterces.

CAELIUS' PUNNING EPIGRAM

T he little poem Milo quotes to Caelius about Clodia was really written by Caelius, and was quite famous in its day. It is a pun, and impossible to translate literally. In Latin it goes, 'In triclinium Coam, in cubiculum Nolam'. This means, 'In the dining-room [she is] a woman from Cos, in the bedroom a woman from Nola'. 'A woman from Cos' must have implied someone of great sexual appetite or loose morals; Nola is a town near Naples, but the form in which its name appears in the epigram is the same as the present subjunctive of the verb 'nolo' which means, 'I don't want to,' or 'I refuse'.

Another witty comment Caelius made about Clodia was also in circulation at this time. He called her 'quadrantaria Clytemnestra', 'the four-penny Clytemnestra'. A quadrantaria was the price of the cheapest admission to the public baths. Cicero, in the speech quoted in this book, the Pro Caelio (On Behalf of Caelius) calls her 'The Medea of the Palatine'.

ROMAN NAMES

Roman names are indicators primarily of family allegiance and rank. A woman like Clodia or a slave like Tiro had only one name, while a free man like Caelius usually had three. A great aristocrat might have four in this period; later, under the Emperors, we find people with many more. We know of one man who had forty. Caelius' full name is Marcus Caelius Rufus, Cicero's is Marcus Tullius Cicero.

The first element of these names is given at birth just as it is with us, except that these names appear to have been much less important among the Romans. Women didn't have them at all, and for men there were only about a dozen first names in use. Most of the time they are abbreviated, since there are so few of them. The really important name is the second one, for example, Caelius, or Tullius. This identified the owner's family, and was inherited from his father. Many names that we think of as first names are really family names like Gaius Julius Caesar's Julius.

Since families in Rome were usually great clans, and since first names had little significance, some other means of distinguishing one member from another had to be found. This was the third name, a kind of inherited nickname. These seem to have originated in some exploit or physical characteristic of an ancestor. Caelius' name, Rufus, for example, probably indicates that he had a redhaired forebear, though his own hair may have been any color at all. When Marcus Tullius Cicero first took up a political career he was advised to change his last name, which is dialect and means 'chick pea', but he refused, only saying he would make it as famous as some of the greatest names of Rome.

Occasionally these names come from incidents in an ancestor's life, or they may have been awarded, almost like medals, by the Senate. Pompey's name—Gnaeus Pompeius Magnus—is one of these: he was given the name 'Magnus', 'the Great', by the dictator Sulla, at the behest of the Senate, in honor of the victories of his youth.

For women and slaves the situation was different. Women's names were derived from the family name of their fathers. Thus, Gaius Julius Caesar's daughter was called Julia, Marcus Tullius Cicero's Tullia, and so on. Clodia is the daughter of Appius Claudius Pulcher, and should have been called Claudia, but she and her sisters changed the spelling of their name when their brother did to conform to the plebeian rather than the aristocratic use. Women did not change their names when they married, or pass them on to their children. Slaves too had only one name. In the very earliest days it too came from the name of the head of the family, but in later times they were given a name. If they were freed, as was Cicero's famous secretary, Tiro, they combined their names with those of their former owners; thus Tiro became Marcus Tullius Tiro. This reflected a continuing relationship of mutual obligation between a freedman and his former owner.